F BAL
BALL

Ball, John Dudley,
  1911-

The van

$18.95

1/89

DATE			

THE VAN
A TALE OF TERROR

The Virgil Tibbs Series

In the Heat of the Night   *Harper & Row*
The Cool Cottontail   *Harper & Row*
Johnny Get Your Gun   *Little, Brown*
Five Pieces of Jade   *Little, Brown*
The Eyes of Buddha   *Little, Brown*
Then Came Violence   *Doubleday*
Singapore   *Dodd, Mead*

Aviation Adventure

Rescue Mission   *Harper & Row*
Last Plane Out   *Little, Brown*
Phase Three Alert   *Little, Brown*

Mainstream Novels

Miss 1000 Spring Blossoms   *Little, Brown*
The First Team   *Little, Brown*
The Fourteenth Point   *Little, Brown*
Mark One—The Dummy   *Little, Brown*
The Winds of Mitamura   *Little, Brown*

Crime Novels

The Killing in the Market   *Doubleday*
The Murder Children   *Dodd, Mead*

The Police Chief Series

Police Chief   *Doubleday*
Trouble for Tallon   *Doubleday*
Tallon and the S.O.R   *Dodd, Mead*

THE

VAN

A TALE OF
TERROR

JOHN BALL

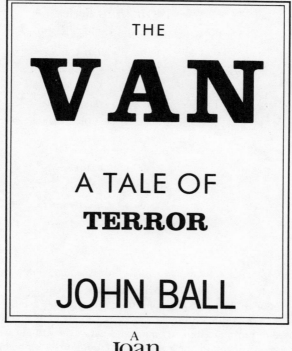

A
Joan
Kahn
BOOK

St. Martin's Press   New York

Design by Debby Jay

Library of Congress Cataloging-in-Publication Data

Ball, John Dudley.
    The van.

    "A Joan Kahn book."
    I. Title.
PS3552.A455V36   1989   813'.54   88-29897
ISBN 0-312-02667-6

First Edition

10 9 8 7 6 5 4 3 2 1

For Sheriff Sherman Block, Los Angeles County, California.
The best there is.

And for two very special friends
in the Los Angeles County Sheriff's Department:

Assistant Sheriff Jerry Harper
and
Commander Roy Brown

Author's Note

The preparation of this book was made possible through the unprecedented cooperation of Captain Robert Grimm and the Los Angeles County Sheriff's Homicide Bureau. The more than one hundred men and women of the Bureau comprise a corps of investigators whose actual exploits and achievements exceed anything that fiction, motion pictures, or TV has to offer.

For the first time this group of skilled professionals has allowed a reservist to share in their activities. Working with these people in the field, at the scenes of many dozens of murders and other violent deaths, at all hours of the day and night, and under widely varying circumstances, has been a profoundly moving and educational experience.

In addition to the Bureau personnel, a great amount of information and help was provided by the investigators and criminalists of the Los Angeles County Coroner's Office and the Sheriff's Crime Laboratory. The willful killer, whether acting in a blaze of passion or in cold-blooded premeditation, has no idea of the degree of expertise and determination that can and will be applied to bring him to justice.

The Los Angeles County Sheriff's Department, including Sheriff Sherman Block himself, the various echelons of command, and the many thousands of uniformed deputies in the field comprise the largest, most versatile, and, in the opinion of a great many informed people, the best such police organization in the world. It has primary jurisdiction over more than three thousand square miles of territory that includes widely varied residential communities, open desert, soaring mountains, wilderness areas and wild animal preserves, miles of popular beaches, offshore islands, extensive recreational areas, national forests, and some of the most crowded, crime-infested urban ghettos anywhere in the nation. In addition, many independent cities within the Los Angeles basin have contracted with the Sheriff for their police services while others regularly call upon him to supply special enforcement teams and other specialists to supplement their own personnel.

The series of bizarre and frightful murders described in the pages that follow is based on an actual case, the complete file of which is shattering reading. The tape recording that formed a vital clue exists. Its content is so terrible that once when it was played for a group of some forty experienced FBI agents only one man was able to remain in the room to hear it through.

This case was solved by a task force made up of detectives from the Homicide Bureau and other involved jurisdictions. The two unspeakable criminals responsible were captured, tried, and convicted. One of them gave a full confession in return for a sentence of life without hope of parole in order to escape the gas chamber. His partner is awaiting execution.

It is the intention of this work to give an accurate accounting of homicide investigation as it is done today by the best professionals in this vital and demanding field of law enforcement.

THE VAN
A TALE OF TERROR

The awful sickness had taken hold of Angelo until the pit of his stomach seemed to be on fire. It had been creeping up on him for the past few hours, draining away his will and taking over his body until he had become impervious to almost everything else. He knew that it was raining: a long, cold, drizzling rain that had soaked through his thin clothing until it clung to his skin like a parasitic creature from some slimy pit. And it was cold—very cold. Even in Los Angeles the icy winds of late winter had swept down from the north bringing 50-degree temperatures in the daytime and hard frosts during the night. In the late evening Angelo was still out, because the awful sickness would not allow him to seek shelter. It demanded that he keep going and somehow find the cure; the wet and the growing cold he would have to ignore.

He had only a few cents in his pockets, not even enough to buy himself a cup of steaming hot coffee. There were

1

places he could go, but if he did his cure would be delayed, perhaps for hours, and his agony would be unbearable. He would have done anything for the money he had to have, but there were few people on the streets, none to whom he could have sold his body. No one would want him in his condition.

He was an experienced thief, but his searching eyes could find nothing he could take, no matter what the risk. It would have to be something valuable, something he could carry in his desperate condition to where he could sell it quickly. He had to have money for his cure; he had tried many times for credit and knew there was no hope. It was cash only, or merchandise worth at least ten times as much.

His sickness had engulfed him, growing worse as the night deepened and the cold grew more intense. He was facing death now and he knew it, but he was powerless— until he had some money. Thirty dollars was all he needed, but he had lost his knife and without it there was no way he could do a mugging.

At last his pain grew to where he knew he would not be able to stay on his feet for very much longer. It was then he acknowledged the soaking rain and the freezing cold that were steadily weakening him even more. He staggered on, his movements automatic and unconscious, until he saw that he was in front of a church.

The church was always open. People came in to pray. It would be warm and dry inside. More important, there was a good chance that there would be no one in the sanctuary. On the altar, there might be valuable things, small enough for him to take.

He could not run in his condition, but if he could grab something of real value, he could hide it under his thin jacket and go as fast as he could to the House. There it would buy him his cure. It would rush through his veins like a wonderful healing elixir, lifting him up, restoring his strength, making him a superman again.

As he stumbled his way up the steps into the church, a prowl car drove slowly past. The deputy who was riding passenger saw him and leaned forward for a moment. But the skinny kid the deputy thought he had recognized was going in to get out of the wretched weather and the church was a good place for that. There was no reason to stop and interview him; it would only prolong his agony. The car continued on.

Angelo came into the back of the church and started up the aisle, his mind frozen on his purpose. But he still looked right and left to be sure he was alone in the sanctuary.

It was very dimly lit, but there was enough light on the altar to pick out the things that stood there. He went up to the railing and, to protect himself, he knelt as though he were in prayer. No one could question him then; he was completely safe. He stayed a full minute, but the only sign of life he saw was in the flames of burning candles.

With the sickness in his body making every movement a fresh stab of agony, he went up to the altar, picked up a gold vase, and turned to make his escape. The center aisle was the shortest and quickest way, but it would be safer to waste a few extra seconds to go down the side in comparative darkness. Hurrying as fast as he could, he was three-quarters of the way out of the church when something soft and round lay across his path. He fell over it and the vase clattered to the ground.

Terror seized him. The vase had rolled under the pews; he searched for it until more lights came on, then he fled as fast as he could back out into the suicidal cold and wet of the night.

The call from the Central Communications Center went automatically to the nearest available patrol unit:

"Baker one twenty-three, Saint Gregory's Church, possible nine twenty-seven David. Handle immediately. Tag one zero six."

Deputy Ed Valdez, who was driving, checked for traffic

3

and then made an immediate U turn on the wet pavement as his partner, Deputy Frank Mullins, picked up the communications mike. "Baker one twenty-three responding. In four." He put the mike back into its clip. "I saw a kid going in there a few minutes ago," he said. "I think I know him—a hype."

"Any MO on him?" Valdez asked.

"Mugger. Uses a knife. In four or five times for theft, possession of stolen property."

Valdez slowed up for a stop sign and checked to his left. Mullins looked right. "Clear," he said and the car sped forward.

In just under four minutes the patrol unit angled up to the curb in front of the church. Valdez and Mullins got out together, fitting their PR-24 batons into their belts as they ran up the church steps. At the top, just out of reach of the rain, Brother Fred was waiting for them. "Thank you for coming so quickly," he said.

"The call we got was a possible dead body," Mullins said. He was not tall, but he was a powerfully built black who radiated professionalism.

"I'm afraid so," Brother Fred confirmed. "But you'd better see for yourselves." He led the way inside, turned left without genuflecting, and started up the side aisle. Then he stopped and pointed. "I tried to help . . ." he began.

Valdez dropped to his knees beside the body of a middle-aged woman, ready to give her immediate CPR if it was indicated. Mullins pulled his extender radio from his belt and held it read for use.

"She's gone," Valdez said. "Stabbed under the heart."

Mullins spoke into his radio. "Baker one twenty-three at Saint Gregory's. Nine twenty-seven David confirmed. Request paramedics and full support."

From the front of the church a priest came hurrying down. Normally the deputies would have warned him off the scene, but both men knew why he was there. The priest put a thin purple strip around his neck, opened a container

4

of anointing oil, and quickly began to administer the last rites. Brother Fred, who was not a priest, clasped his hands in prayer.

Mullins continued to use his radio. "Suspect seen entering the church about ten ago. Male Mex, five eight, one twenty to one thirty pounds, thinly dressed. Tentatively identified as Angelo Gonzalez, known user armed with a knife."

That would get results, and fast: a half-dozen units would be diverted to search the area. The fact that he was out, poorly dressed, on such a night, meant he was looking for a fix. The East Los Angeles deputies would all know that. They would know too that he would not be able to go far in his condition. They would find him.

Valdez gave his careful attention to the dead woman. In addition to the stab wounds, her throat had also been deeply cut; a massive amount of blood had been pumped out onto the floor. He felt again for a pulse and found none. In her condition CPR was hopeless; there was no way he would be able to blow his breath into her lungs.

Mullins turned to Brother Fred. "What happened?" he asked.

"I was sitting reading when I heard a noise from the sanctuary, like someone falling. Then I heard a metallic object hit the floor. I went quickly to the switchboard to turn on more lights. Then I came into the sanctuary. At first I saw nothing, then I found this lady . . ."

"Did you touch her?"

"Yes, I tried to give her assistance, thinking she had just fallen. Then I saw the blood. I ran to the phone and called the Sheriff's Station."

"Did she show any signs of life at all?"

"No, officer. I thought the best I could do for her was to call you at once, then I notified Father Fernando."

"You did fine," Valdez said. "What about the metal object?"

5

Brother Fred pointed. "It's a vase that belongs on the altar. It's there, under the pews. It hasn't been touched."

"Do you recognize this lady? Is she a member here?"

"No, officer. But it would be better to ask Father."

The priest, having finished his office, got to his feet. "I don't know her either," he said. "I doubt if she was Catholic."

The code-three siren of a paramedic ambulance pulled up outside and stopped its electronic howling. Moments later two paramedics came in, heavily laden with equipment. One of them opened a case and went to work without wasting a moment, but in less than half a minute he stopped. "She's gone," he said.

Mullins raised his radio once more. "Baker one twenty-three at Saint Gregory's. Subject pronounced."

Two more deputies who had appeared began to tape off the area.

"Is there any way, Father, that the church can be closed?" Mullins asked.

"Normally not," Father Fernando answered, "but I will arrange something."

"Good."

"Baker one twenty-three, ten nineteen."

Mullins acknowledged and spoke to his partner. "Let's go."

Back in the patrol unit he used the regular radio. "Baker one twenty-three: ten nineteen in six." He didn't know why they had been summoned back to the station, but he could guess. A moment later another car reported in. "Baker one zero four, ten fifteen."

Valdez let his satisfaction show on his face. "They got him," he said, largely to himself.

"I just hope we can keep him," Mullins added. "So far he's been let off every damn time."

There were three patrol units pulled up in front of St. Gregory's when the homicide team arrived from the Hall of

Justice. In command was Sergeant Oliver "Dick" Tracy. Apart from the fact that he never wore a hat unless he was in uniform, it was his misfortune to bear a slight resemblance to the durable cartoon detective, rock-square jaw and all. Since he could do nothing about it, he bore his cross in patience and got on with his job.

Moments later a photographer/print man arrived from the crime lab. He got busy, shooting the body from as many different angles as its position would allow. He was well aware how deceptive some shots could be; a body that appeared to be under a table in one picture could be clearly shown to be at one side in others. Every experienced homicide investigator had run into that.

The victim's purse lay several feet from the body. That allowed Tracy to pick it up and check the contents. She had a California driver's license that gave her name as Mrs. Mabel Irene Lorimer.

The purse contained eleven dollars and seventy-four cents in cash, a comb, a compact and lipstick, and a packet of Kleenex tissues. Tucked in a side pocket there was a small wallet containing a check guarantee card, a silver MasterCard, and two blank checks imprinted with her name and address.

Tracy got to his feet. "The ID looks good," he said to his senior deputy, Frank Levitzky. "Start checking things out, will you?"

Levitzky knew that the painful process would in all likelihood mean a notification of the next of kin, a job that several years in homicide had made steadily more difficult. He was a compassionate man who hated the inevitable moment when too often he had had to break terrible news. He had never found a way to make it any easier.

Tracy lifted blood samples from the floor close to the body and looked for possible traces further removed. Had he found any, he would have sent for a serologist from the lab to check them out. He carefully bagged the vase from the altar while Levitzky searched the area for further

7

evidence. The patrol deputies who were standing by kept all potential sightseers away from that part of the church. Brother Fred remained on hand by unspoken dispensation. The deputies knew him well since he was in the station almost every day on behalf of some Chicano youth who had been taken into custody.

Lieutenant Ralph Mott, who had been on call during the early night homicide watch, came in quietly and conferred with Tracy. Then he went out again and drove his unmarked county car to the East Los Angeles Sheriff's Station to check on the suspect who was in custody. The homicide might be a walk-through, with the killer quickly identified, but that was yet to be established.

He talked with the watch commander and heard a story that was almost painfully familiar. "The suspect is an Angelo Gonzalez, male Mex, age seventeen. He's been in several times before, but nothing stuck. He was in bad condition, soaked to the skin and shaking with the cold. Probably hadn't eaten for some time. He's a known hype and was showing signs of acute withdrawal. I had him wrapped in blankets and sent down to L.C.M.C.* for treatment."

"I'm glad you did," Mott agreed. "Did he make any kind of a statement?"

"Just one, Ralph. Before he left here, he kept insisting that he had gone into the church for shelter and almost fell over the body on his way out. In his condition, I don't believe he was up to doing a mugging."

"He tried to take an altar vase."

The watch commander nodded. "I know. That supports his story that he didn't pull the homicide."

"Maybe he didn't," Mott said. Then he added, "I know a man who fits the MO, but he's inside, doing twenty to life."

"You mean Ivan Dietrich."

*Los Angeles County Medical Center

8

Mott gave him a quick, sharp look. "Did you work that case?" he asked.

"No, but I'm up on it. Brace yourself, Frank. Dietrich's out. He was paroled again about a week ago."

2

$\mathbf{D}$r. Flavia Alvarez de la Torre leaned slightly backward, partially resting herself against the front edge of her desk. Her hands were spread apart, steadying her body, as she surveyed the twenty-odd faces of her students. Once more she wondered how many of them were truly interested in the contemporary sociology course she was offering as part of the university's vast curriculum.

She was very simply dressed in a smooth dark skirt and a white blouse of superior quality; not even the most conservative of regents could find any fault with that. She had been criticized for her viewpoints during the three years she had been on the faculty, but no one had ever been able to fault her appearance, or the way she conducted herself on campus.

Her brown hair was shaped around her face in a style made possible by its natural soft wave. She used very little cosmetics and had no need of any more. Her face and figure

10

commanded full attention despite the presence of thousands of younger coeds with whom she was unavoidably constantly compared.

She was aware of that, just as she knew that many of her students, not all of them male, signed up for her classes because of her appearance and the candor with which she discussed matters of sex in modern society. Yet despite her strong liberality, there was an invisible line that she was careful never to cross. She stayed within the context of her course material and even those who disagreed with her admitted that her lectures were always built on firm ground.

In the second row from the front a tall blond student sat carelessly twisted in his chair, not because it was more comfortable for him, but to demonstrate with body language the independence of his spirit. At the same time he continued his unending, detailed analysis of Flavia's anatomy.

She could not make a movement without his taking note of what it revealed. When she turned toward the blackboard and her blouse was momentarily tightened, he studied the contours of her breasts. If she turned her back, he feasted his eyes on the outlines of her buttocks. What was not inevitably revealed by the fit of her clothing, he supplied mentally. When she faced her class as she was doing at that moment, he carefully calculated the exact location of her pubic hair. Ever since entering puberty he had cultivated an ability to strip females aesthetically naked almost at a glance with the use of a skilled imagination. His regular attendance in the sociology class kept him in sharp practice.

Toward the rear of the room a young woman put up her hand and was acknowledged with a nod.

"Dr. de la Torre, I'd like to ask you about something that was in the paper yesterday, in one of the advice columns."

"What was it?"

"It was a letter written by a mother about her sixteen-

11

year-old daughter. She said that she has raised her . . .
the daughter, I mean . . . 'in the faith.' I presume that
means Catholic."

"Or possibly Jewish."

"Anyhow, she went through her daughter's things and
found some birth-control pills. She threw them away.
When her daughter came back she gave her hell and made
her swear on the family Bible that she'd never do it again."

"You mean, have intercourse."

"Yes. Maybe it was peer pressure or whatever, but now
she's pregnant. Her boyfriend's family called her a tramp
and won't do anything to help her. Are the social mores of
today going to crucify her?"

Flavia raised her head a little. "Not necessarily. The fact
is, a great many girls in her age group are becoming pregnant. Some have their babies, others choose abortions."

"Do you approve of that?"

"I certainly prefer a properly done legal abortion to
kitchen-table butchery. There used to be far too much of
that. And many women did themselves permanent harm
by trying to abort themselves. There have been many
fatalities."

She walked a step or two in front of the desk, acutely
aware of how closely she was being scrutinized. "Taking
this case in point, the mother should have known that once
a young woman has her natural instincts aroused and
becomes sexually active, it's very difficult for her to stop
under normal circumstances. Society's current attitude is
an increasing acceptance of this: an awareness of the fact
that sex is a powerful driving force that's capable of
overriding almost any other. The family's faith isn't
significant; there's no religious order that has historically
succeeded in eliminating all nonmarital sex, although
most of them have tried."

Another voice came from the class. "Dr. de la Torre, do
you think that society will ever condone free sex between
consenting adults?"

12

Flavia glanced at her watch. "The period is over, so I'm going to cop out on that for today."

"Will you answer next class?"

"Of course." She remained where she was as her students filed out. When the last one had gone, she gathered up her papers and went to keep her appointment with the dean.

She was quite comfortable in his presence, because he was always willing to listen to what she had to say. Unlike herself, he ran several miles a day if his schedule permitted, keeping himself in shape like an athlete. He was an even six feet, liked sports jackets, and normally dispensed with a tie. He was an attractive man despite his almost bald head. She knew that many of the females on campus would have been delighted to go to bed with him if he would only ask, which, of course, he never would.

When she came into his office, he greeted her with his accustomed warmth. "Sit down, Flavia, and be comfortable," he said, and gestured.

As she took a chair at the side of his desk, he plunked down behind it and brushed his hand across his bare scalp. "You've gotten the word, haven't you, that the final approval of your grant has come through?"

"Yes, I just heard," Flavia said.

"Good. Good. I'm very glad for you. I lightened up your schedule so you'll have plenty of time for your research. Now I have to ask you a hard question. I know your very liberal opinions and I don't quarrel with them. But do you think you can do a genuinely objective study without them getting in the way?"

"Dr. Cargill, you may remember that I did my thesis on the operation of the parole system in California."

"I remember very well; a good piece of work. Published, wasn't it?"

"Yes, but not importantly."

"Have you talked to the university press people about your new project?"

"No," Flavia answered, "and I don't intend to. I've seen

13

too many academic-style books that read like embalming fluid. You know the kind of thing I mean."

"Indeed I do," the dean agreed. "Lawyers and academics are running a neck-and-neck race to see who can make the most obscure use of the English language. What exactly do you have in mind?"

"I'm going after the parole system again, because I think it's a mess. I can't see that the recent changes in the law have helped a bit—toward genuine rehabilitation, I mean."

"That's pretty broad, Flavia."

"I know that; I covered it in my proposal. There's only one area in California where parole is flexible and that's homicide. I intend to concentrate on that."

"God knows you'll have enough to work with. How do you plan to go about it?"

Flavia straightened up on her chair and drew her shoulders back a little. "I'll work from case histories, of course, if I can get access to them. Then I want to go into the field and experience things for myself. I want to work with the police if they'll allow me. I want to see firsthand how well the parole system is working, as of right now."

"How long do you plan to take?"

"It depends on how things work out. My thesis notes will be out of date now, but at least I do have a background. Dr. Cargill, I'm not motivated by the publish-or-perish syndrome. I see a major social question here and I want to explore it in depth."

"You haven't picked an easy one." The dean got up from his chair without apology, walked to the window, and looked out over the campus for a few moments. "It could possibly be dangerous," he said.

"I'm aware of that."

"You realize that men released on parole have been locked up, often for years, without any women. There's a lot of sodomy and masturbation in prison, and other forms of sexual relief, but none of them adequately substitute for women."

14

She was grateful that he was treating her as a professional, not using euphemisms because she was a female. "I understand that," she said. "I don't know this for a fact, I haven't seen any studies on the subject, but I would assume that men freshly out of prison would find sexual relief with available women fairly quickly. After an initial surge, they would probably settle down into normal sexual patterns."

"Flavia, I have a brother who's well up in the Los Angeles County Sheriff's Department. A chief, in fact. Would you like me to discuss this with him?"

"Yes. I was going to ask you to do that, if you would."

"You understand that present-day crime control is a very rough problem. The recent increases in narcotics trafficking and use has greatly increased the problem—and the risks."

"I'm not living in a vacuum, Dr. Cargill. And I'm fairly used to defending myself in sexual situations, if necessary."

"Do you want me to start some wheels in motion?"

"Yes, please," she answered.

Shortly after eight the following morning Lieutenant Mott met with Tracy and Levitzky, the homicide team that had responded to St. Gregory's Church. No one had had much sleep, but in the Homicide Bureau they were used to that. Much work had already been done during the past night hours and some conclusions were beginning to form.

"From the start," Tracy said, "we've been able to pin this thing down very closely, a minute or two either way. Frank Mullins and his partner drove past St. Gregory's while the rain was still coming down hard. He saw Angelo Gonzalez going inside. Out of habit he noted the time."

"He would," Mott said. "I knew him when I was at East L.A. He doesn't overlook details."

"About six minutes after that Brother Fred called in. He heard a noise from the church, turned on some lights, found the body, and called East L.A. Station. That leaves

15

very little time for Gonzalez to grab the vase from the altar *and* commit a homicide, either before or after the theft."

"Also," Levitzky added, "he was in bad shape. The victim was a well-built woman who weighed at least as much as he does. She would have put up a fight."

"He could have sneaked up on her," Mott said, "but if he'd done that, he'd have grabbed her purse and run. We know he took the vase; his prints are on it."

"What she had on her wouldn't buy him a fix," Tracy added, "but he couldn't know that."

"Why would he kill a woman for the sake of her money and then leave it behind?" Levitzky asked.

"The last I heard, the weapon hadn't been recovered," Mott said.

"Right," Levitzky confirmed. "He had time enough to ditch it, but I'm sure he didn't. His knife is his only way of keeping up his habit."

"What did he have to say for himself?" Mott asked.

"Nothing," Tracy answered. "He's still at U.C.M.C., being held for attempted four five nine. Condition critical."

The phone rang and Mott answered. After a short conversation he hung up. "Angelo's out of it," he said. "The lab says that the condition of the blood found under the body proves that the victim had been dead more than an hour before she was discovered."

"Then where do we go from here?" Tracy asked.

"The full route," Mott answered. "The MO fits Ivan Dietrich, so I want him checked out. But be careful how you go about it: I don't want some defense attorney claiming that we picked on his client solely because he had once committed a similar crime."

"Don't worry," Levitzky said. "We've been around that block before."

"In checking out the victim, see if she may have been a witness at some time, possibly against Dietrich. I doubt it, because he's a professional who wouldn't waste time and take risks just for revenge."

Tracy and Levitzky both knew that, but they let it pass. "I'm going to the crime lab," Tracy said, "to see what if anything they found at the scene. They sent a criminalist out and she was there for some time."

"I'll pick up the coroner's protocol as soon as it's ready," Levitzky volunteered.

"Fine," Mott agreed. "By the time we have all that, we may see which way we want to go."

When his men had left, he ran over the whole thing in his mind and clearly saw the difficulties. Because it had been a miserable, cold, rainy night, the chances of finding any helpful witnesses were minimal. Father Fernando had not recognized the victim as a member of his parish. She had not been wearing any religious jewelry when she was found, nor had her purse contained anything that indicated her beliefs.

It was one of those cases that could break open in a hurry, or it could eventually go into the open file of unsolved homicides waiting for fresh evidence to come to light. The odds on fresh evidence were poor.

When his phone rang again he picked it up automatically. "Homicide, Lieutenant Mott."

He was informed that Chief Cargill would like to see him, when convenient.

That meant Cargill wanted a favor. "I'll be right down," he said and headed for the bank of elevators.

In the Hall of Justice the sheriff himself and the high brass have offices on the second floor. Mott knew Jack Cargill well, but on the job there was a difference in rank that was carefully observed. It had to be that way if the system was to work properly.

It didn't prevent Cargill from giving Mott a man-to-man welcome; they were both members of the same lodge, the Sheriff's Department, and the same fraternity, law enforcement.

As soon as Mott had sat down, Cargill asked, "Are you busy right now?"

17

Mott knew he meant the Homicide Division. "About normal," he answered.

"You know that my brother's a dean at the university."

"Yes."

"He's got a sociology instructor there who did her Ph.D. thesis on the parole system."

"Before or after the law was changed?" Mott asked.

"Before, I think. Now she wants to do a book: the effects of the probation and parole system on the greater community."

"There's a recent Rand study on that," Mott said. "I've read it."

Like his brother, the chief was a big man, six foot two and in condition. Not too long ago he had commanded the Special Enforcement Bureau, commonly known as SWAT, and had kept up with all of the continuing hard physical training that was part of the S.E.B.* assignment.

"I don't know this lady, but Miles told me that she wants out of the ivory tower. She wants access to case histories; that we can give her. In addition to that, in her words, she wants to get her hands dirty."

"How dirty?" Mott asked.

"She's asked to go out in the field with us."

"Jack, there's no way we can let her do that. You're the boss and you know the rules. At homicide scenes only sworn personnel, our own criminalists, and the coroner's people. That's it." Mott knew he was free to speak his mind.

"You're right," the chief agreed, "and the fact that Miles is my brother isn't going to sway my judgment. However, there's another consideration. Miles tells me that she writes very well and has been published before. If her book is successful, it might be of some help to us in a critical area."

"I can see that," Mott said. "But frankly, Jack, I could only go for it if the man himself so ordered. The sheriff is

*Special Enforcement Bureau

18

the best cop I've ever known. I'd trust his judgment on anything."

"That makes it a little easier," the chief said.

It took Mott only a moment. "You mean he's approved it?"

"Yes, personally, through channels."

"Then that's the answer," Mott conceded. "I take it you want to pass her on to me."

"You've got it. She's coming in at two this afternoon to meet you. Look her over. If you think you can keep her busy and out of the way for a while, fine. If not, let me know and I'll make some other arrangement."

The chief relaxed enough to let Mott see that he shared his viewpoint. "Load her up with case histories to study. Give her a desk, you've got plenty. And answer her reasonable questions if you're free."

That gave Mott a clearer view of the picture. "I'll meet with her," he said. "And unless she's impossible, I'll do what I can."

"Good. Captain Grimm knows about it, of course, and he feels much the same as we do. Have her sign a full release and make it clear to her that if and when she goes into the field, if she does, she follows orders, civilian or not."

Mott got up. "I'll do whatever I can," he said.

The chief nodded approval. "Her name is Dr. Flavia de la Torre. That's all I know about her. But I don't think Miles would stick us with a lemon."

"I hope to God not," Mott answered. "Is she F.O.S.*?"

"Not as far as I know. Thanks for the favor."

"No problem," Mott said, and tried his best to mean it.

*Friend of Sheriff, a warning flag to many deputies

3

As Sergeant Oliver Tracy slid his unmarked county car next to the curb on the west side of Los Angeles, he noted that there was a definite neighborhood local pride. The front yards were well kept, most of the houses had recently been painted, and NEIGHBORHOOD WATCH signs were prominently posted. It looked like a largely Japanese sector of the city, and perhaps it was. It could also have been upper-class black, or simply an enclave of ordinary Americans who still took satisfaction in keeping up their homes.

With Frank Levitzky beside him he walked up to the front door of the house where Mabel Lorimer, the homicide victim, had lived. Since it was fairly late in the afternoon, he hoped to God that the notification had already been made. If not, it would be his job, and he hated it with all his heart.

His unspoken question was answered when the door was

swung open and a nine-year-old boy faced him from the inside. The boy's eyes were red from obvious crying, but he had possession of himself.

Frank Levitzky drew breath to ask, "Is your mother at home?" and caught himself just in time. "We're police officers," he said instead. "May we come in?"

"Yeah, sure," the boy answered and stepped aside. Levitzky went in first, maintaining a properly reserved manner. He was on official business, but he was acutely aware that this was a house of sorrow. He passed through the entryway and into a small but tasteful living room where a man and a woman rose to their feet to meet him.

The man spoke first. "I heard what you said, officer. We've been expecting you."

That made things easier. No policeman entering a strange house can be sure of the reception he will get: it can range from sullen silence to violent argument; from a courteous welcome to the front end of a gun with a madman behind it. The boy followed silently behind, watching and listening.

"Thank you," Levitzky said. "You've been given the news?"

"Yes, we have. I'm Ernie Wright; this is my wife, Marie. You've just met our son, Gary."

"Mr. Wright, I'm Detective Frank Levitzky from the Sheriff's Homicide Bureau. This is my partner, Detective Tracy."

The boy looked up quickly. "Mister, are you *Dick* Tracy?" he asked.

"That's what they call me," Tracy answered.

The kid stared at him in wonderment. "Oh golly!" he said.

"Please sit down," Wright invited. "Would you care for some coffee? It'll only take a minute."

"Thank you," Levitzky answered. He didn't really want any coffee, but it would give the wife something to do while they asked some of the preliminary questions.

21

Tracy opened a notebook. "We're very sorry to have to disturb you at a time like this," he began. It was a set speech, but he genuinely meant it.

"I understand," Wright replied. "It's necessary."

"Did Mrs. Lorimer live here with you?"

"Yes, she did. She is . . . was . . . my wife's sister."

Tracy made a note. "How long did she live here, sir?"

"A little less than four years, ever since Mac, her husband, died. We asked her to come and live with us for a while and it worked out well."

"You had enough room, then?"

"Plenty. She had her own bedroom and bath. In return she helped with the running expenses and the mortgage. We got along fine together."

Levitzky took over. "Mr. Wright, was Mrs. Lorimer employed?"

"Yes, she had a very good job."

"In East Los Angeles?"

"No, she works in the Federal Building on Wilshire. I mean, she did work there."

"Did her work ever take her into East Los Angeles?"

"No, I don't think so."

"Did she have any friends there?"

"She never mentioned any. That's a Mexican neighborhood isn't it?"

"Largely, yes."

"I don't think she had any Mexican friends."

"We thought, being Catholic . . ."

Wright shook his head. "None of us are Catholic, or ever were. Mabel especially. She belonged to the Self-Realization Fellowship and went to church there all the time. Sundays and sometimes during the week. She was very serious about it."

His wife came back into the room with a tray. She passed out coffee cups, filled them, and offered cream and sugar. A little uncomfortably, Tracy accepted a cup and took it

22

black. He would have preferred a little cream, but chose not to use it. Levitzky followed his example.

It was Tracy's turn. "Mr. Wright, did Mrs. Lorimer have any enemies? This could include someone who resented her business success, a quarrelsome neighbor, a rejected suitor—anything at all like that."

Wright shook his head. "Mabel was a quiet type of person. Since her husband died, she never showed any interest in anyone else. We're on the best of terms with our neighbors. I don't think anyone disliked her. About her work I can't tell you too much."

"What exactly did she do?" Tracy asked.

Marie Wright answered that. "We don't know. She had a job with the Government. I'm sure it was a good one, she seemed to make a very good salary. But she never said a word about it. All we know is that she had some very high security clearance and that she was in the Federal Building. Gary asked her once and she said she couldn't tell us. She was my own sister, but I've no idea what she did."

"Obviously she was trustworthy," Levitzky said.

"You can say that again," Wright confirmed. "She lived here four years and all I can tell you is that she always went to work on time and sometimes put in a lot of overtime."

Levitzky wrote in his notebook.

"What was her husband's work?" he asked.

"He was a boat broker at the marina. He did very well until he took sick."

Tracy closed his notebook and got to his feet. "Thank you very much," he said. "If we need more, we may have to come back."

"Any time," Wright said.

When they were back in the car, Levitzky stared straight ahead, watching the cross streets, while his partner drove. He was doing some hard thinking. "I don't like it," he said at last.

"In what way?" Tracy asked. He had arrived at his own conclusions, but he wanted his partner's input.

"We've got a woman who apparently had a very sensitive position. She's found dead inside a church that isn't hers in a part of town where she didn't belong."

"Meaning?"

"It was a bad night and she might have gone into the church for shelter, but I doubt it. I think she had an appointment."

"Where she wouldn't be disturbed, or recognized?"

"Exactly. She could have been selling out."

"I had the same idea," Tracy admitted. "I think we should talk to the Feds."

"So do I. Let's go."

Like most professional police officers, Lieutenant Ralph Mott was not enchanted by the idea of having a civilian attached to him or his unit. But if Sheriff Block wanted it done, that settled the matter. His part would be to make the best of it. He had dealt with reporters in the past and understood the need to maintain good relations with the media. The sheriff, after all, was an elected official. This time, however, he was stuck with a college professor.

The fact that she was a female was of less concern: he had a capable female detective on his staff and the Coroner's Office had several criminalists and investigators who were females, many of them young and attractive. He wasn't enthusiastic about the idea of women as street cops, because police work frequently involved some fairly heavy action, but if they could get through the academy, they had to have something on the ball. As far as Dr. de la Torre was concerned, he would wait and see.

The Sheriff's Homicide Bureau occupies an enormous room on the seventh floor of the Hall of Justice. It fills almost the whole end of the building from one side to the other. There is a profusion of desks, but only a few of them are likely to be in use at any given time; the empty ones belong to detectives in the field or off duty. The room is never closed; there are always personnel on hand and

24

investigative teams ready to respond whenever a call comes in. And that, as everyone knew, could happen at any hour of the day or night, on any day of the year.

At five minutes to two Flavia pushed open one of the venerable doors of the Homicide Bureau and looked about her. There was a small cluster of men gathered behind the reception counter near the switchboard; one of them asked, "Can I help you?"

"I have an appointment with Lieutenant Mott," she answered.

"The desk in the far corner, ma'm." He opened a half door to let her in. She sensed almost at once that everyone knew who she was. As she walked down the long room she could almost feel that she was the object of quiet but expert scrutiny. She did not know that the professionals who were evaluating her were deciding that Mott's assignment looked a little more bearable.

He got to his feet to receive her. The closer she came to his desk, the more he was aware of her unusual physical attraction. She wore a simple dark blue suit that set off her very good complexion and the neat shape of her figure. At first glance she looked to be an agreeable person. For that he was grateful.

"I'm Flavia de la Torre," she said. "Thank you for seeing me."

He responded with a policeman's formality toward civilians. "Sit down, Doctor. I hear you're writing a book."

"That's what I hope to do, Lieutenant Mott." Her steady look returned his formality in kind.

"How about some coffee?" he asked.

"If it isn't too much trouble."

At that moment Mott had his first serious twinge of concern. This was a high-class female who was obviously used to the niceties. Homicide investigation was the exact opposite of that.

He led the way into an adjoining small room where a half-full coffeemaker sat with a small assortment of cups, most of them stained from overuse. Mott picked the cleanest looking of the lot, filled it, and then gestured toward an open box of sugar cubes and a jar of dried and caked powder that was a nondairy creamer.

Flavia accepted the coffee, added a little sugar, dug out some of the dry creamer, and stirred it with the one available spoon. "Thank you," she said.

Mott fixed himself a cup and led the way back to his desk. Flavia laid a paper towel she had collected on his desk before she set down her cup. "Tell me about your project," he invited.

She tried her coffee before she replied. "I don't know how much you've been told," she said. "I'm a sociologist. I've been given a grant to do a study on the incidence of serious crimes committed by men on parole, or probation, and the percentages involved."

"Are you excluding women?" Mott asked.

"Women too, of course."

Mott kept his formal tone. "Our job here is homicide. I can give you some facts and figures on that. Then, if you'd like, I can pass you on to our people who handle rape, arson, robbery, ADW, and other heavy offenses."

Flavia laid her hands on top of her purse. "I think, Lieutenant, I can get most of the data I'll need from the library; I won't have to put you to that trouble. So far my work has all been theoretical. What I badly need is some actual field experience. I don't think there's any substitute for it."

"No, there isn't," Mott agreed. "However, sometimes it can be pretty rough, even dangerous." He paused a moment. "Many homicide scenes are downright horrible."

"But you deal with them."

"That's our job."

He had warned her, but she didn't show any signs of backing away. For the time being he was stuck with her. But, he hoped, not for too long.

"If I may, I want to start with homicide," Flavia continued. "I may not have to go any further." She paused and took a fresh tack. "Lieutenant, perhaps the parole system is working well just as it is. Or it may need some revision. What I want to do, if I can, is make a contribution. The way Michener did when he wrote *Sayonara*. And I'm sure you know about *The Silent Spring*. She leaned forward and a fresh intensity took hold of her. "I know from a previous study I did that some of the major crimes committed are done by persons on parole. That's a fact I have to face, and no matter how strongly I may feel about human rights, if I can write a book that will keep just one old couple from being beaten to death, one child from being raped, or one widow from being robbed . . ." She realized that she was overreaching and modulated her voice. "Then I will have accomplished *something*. Isn't that true?"

"Yes, it is," Mott agreed. "Now let me understand clearly. You want to go into the field to actual murder scenes, is that right?"

"Yes," Flavia said, as calmly as she could. "I fully understand that those things are seldom pleasant, and I'm prepared. What should I wear?"

At least, Mott thought, she's being sensible about that. "Something very practical. You may be going into slum areas, or down into wild canyons, almost anywhere at all. Jeans might be a good idea."

Flavia nodded. "I understand."

Mott reached into his desk and produced a document. "This is a full release," he said. "I'll have to ask you to sign it before we can go any further."

Flavia took it, scanned it quickly, and then accepted the pen that Mott held out. Her signature was small, neat, and legible.

Mott then handed her a beeper and showed her how it worked. "When we have a homicide that might be of interest to you, we'll call you. I'll have your number posted at the desk. If you don't answer, we'll beep you. If that

27

happens, please get on the phone as quickly as you can so we'll know whether you'll be coming or not."

"I will," Flavia said.

As soon as she had left, Mott gave some careful thought to what sort of scenes she should be allowed to visit. Obviously, there were many where she would have to be kept away.

When his phone rang he picked it up and said, "Homicide, Lieutenant Mott."

A secretary's voice answered him. "Chief Cargill is calling. Just a moment, please."

The chief came on the line. "Has Dr. de la Torre been in?" he asked.

"She just left."

"Good. I hear she's all right. Ralph, I know you may be hesitating about taking her to many locations, but we might as well find out at the beginning how well she can handle herself."

That answered Mott's question. Also the monkey was now off his back. Still he was cautious. "Do you want us to alert her to whatever we get?" he asked.

"Yes, unless there's a good reason why not. Let me know how she reacts."

"You've got it," Mott said.

4

Jack Ogden, a division chief in the Los Angeles office of the FBI, had a relaxed and easy manner; he preferred to keep things in low key as much as he could. His colleagues were fully aware that behind his calm façade he concealed a penetrating brain that had been honed by a great deal of knowledge and experience. Of average, slightly stocky build, he dressed conservatively in quality clothing that suited his smooth and personable features. He was well liked; the closer he came to his mandatory retirement, the more his colleagues regretted it.

He received Tracy and Levitzky as though they were high-level VIPs. That was part of his technique; in the end it saved him a good deal of time, since people tended to come to the point much sooner.

Tracy was no exception. "We're investigating the murder of a Mrs. Mabel Irene Lorimer, whose body was found last night in East Los Angeles," he began. "She was stabbed in a Catholic church where she may have taken shelter from the rain. When we interviewed her family, we learned that she worked in this building in a classified area. We'd appreciate anything you can give us."

Ogden admired his economy of words; he put Tracy down as a superior performer.

"I want to help, of course," Ogden said, "but anything I might be able to tell you would have to go into your report. So I'm afraid that limits what I can do."

"Suppose," Tracy countered, "that our report will show we called on you, but nothing beyond that."

"That would help. Does either of you have a security clearance?"

Levitzky closed his notebook and slid it into a pocket. "We both do," he said. "We got them when we were assigned to special security work during the Olympics." He placed a card on the desk; Tracy produced one of his own.

Ogden picked up a telephone and spoke briefly. He remained on the line for almost a full minute, then said, "Thank you," and hung up. That done, he gave his attention back to his guests. "This has to be absolutely off the record."

"Understood," Tracy said.

Ogden had no nervous habits; he sat perfectly still as he spoke. "Mrs. Lorimer was with the Government for some time and held a high security clearance. She had access to some very sensitive material. All personnel at that level of security are periodically rechecked, as an added precaution. She always came out Mrs. Clean. Unquestionably, she knew how to keep her mouth shut, which was essential in her job."

"Was she a technical person?" Tracy asked.

"No. She was an administrative assistant."

Frank Levitzky put his fingers together. "We know enough not to ask too many questions," he said. "However, there's one thought that crossed our minds. She was found

30

dead way off her patch in East Los Angeles. Her family told us she had no known friends there she might have gone to visit. We don't think she went into St. Gregory's to avoid the weather. It had been raining since early evening with no letup in sight. Lastly, she wasn't Catholic."

Ogden turned toward Levitzky. "You think she might have gone there to meet someone."

"Yes," Levitzky answered.

"And since it was an unlikely time and place, you guessed that it could have been clandestine."

"That's right." Levitzky was not a big man, but he conveyed a sense of strength by his manner and the way he used his voice.

"I already told you," Ogden said, "that she could keep her mouth shut."

Tracy picked it up. "Which means you know she wasn't selling out."

"No comment," Ogden said.

"Still off the record," Tracy continued, "suppose someone tried to approach her. She reported it and was told to carry on as if she had taken the bait. That would explain why she was in an East Los Angeles church on a wet, raw night. But if that's so she would have been covered, and obviously she wasn't. That part doesn't add up."

Ogden rubbed the side of his jaw with an open palm for a moment. "I won't dispute your logic," he said at last, "but I can't go any further right now. I'd appreciate your keeping me in the picture."

"We'll do that," Levitzky promised.

When they were back outside in their car, Tracy offered a comment. "It looks like we're in pretty deep water."

"No doubt about it," Levitzky agreed, "but I say we don't back off from it. Ogden played ball as much as he could."

"And he didn't warn us off," Tracy added. "As soon as we get out of this high-rent district let's grab a bite before we hit the Coroner's Office."

31

Deputy Roderick Bell and his partner, Stan Moody, were coming toward the end of their patrol shift, having put in most of the hundred miles of driving they would accumulate before rolling back into the Altadena Station to fill out their paperwork. It had been a quiet night. The time had passed more slowly, but there were compensations. One was the knowledge that nothing of consequence had gone down in their neighborhood watch area during the early evening. The few traffic violations they had seen hadn't merited being cited.

Bell had hoped to nail a deuce. He had a long-standing hatred of drunk drivers, so many of whom were repeat offenders. Anyone driving under the influence was a ticking bomb, his vehicle a deadly weapon within the meaning of the law. Bell took that very seriously. Getting one off the road could save someone's life.

The radio traffic that he had been effectively ignoring caught his immediate attention when the call for unit 73 came in. Moody unclipped the radio mike. "Seventy-three by," he acknowledged.

"Possible nine twenty Charlie. One seven eight two four Spring Road. Seventy-three handle, seventy-two assist. Tag ninety-four."

That meant a possible missing person. Bell swung around a corner and headed for the address that was almost at the other end of their assigned area. It would take approximately eight minutes to get there.

When they reached the address, several porch lights were on and three women were waiting for them at the curb. It was a quiet, all-white, upper-middle-class neighborhood where burglary was the most commonly reported complaint. Bell's street instincts, honed by six years on patrol, told him that this could be serious. He fitted his PR-24 baton into its ring on his Sam Browne belt and walked with Moody to where the women were waiting.

Before he could say anything, one of them spoke. "I'm Mrs. Shafer. This is Mrs. Lowell, Marcia's grandmother."

Bell was quick to grasp that. "Is it Marcia who's missing?" he asked. A quick appraisal of the grandmother told him that Marcia would be in her teens at the most.

"Yes, she should have been home long ago."

Moody took out his notebook. "Tell us what happened," he said.

Mrs. Lowell, the grandmother, answered him in a voice she was struggling to keep composed. "I drove her to the youth club church supper a little before six," she said. "That's the First Church of the Redeemer. I offered to call for her, and I should have, but she said I needn't bother because she was sure someone would give her a ride, and it's only a short ways."

Moody was writing industriously.

"She should have been home by eight thirty, nine at the very latest. When she didn't arrive I called the church, but it was closed. Then I called the pastor and he said that the supper was over just a little after eight. So I called some of my neighbors to see if she had stopped in, but no one has seen her."

Another of the women, somewhat younger and more positive in her manner, took up the account. "Since Ms. Lowell was upset, I offered to take my car and look for her. I covered every route she might have taken, but there was no sign of her."

"And your name, ma'm?" Moody asked.

"Ms. Galloway."

"Is that Miss or Missus?"

"It's Ms."

Moody looked at her. "I'm sorry, but that won't do. Please be explicit."

"I don't see what that has to do with it, but if you must know, I'm divorced."

"Are you using your maiden name?"

"Yes."

"Thank you, Miss Galloway. How old is Marcia?"

33

"Sixteen," Mrs. Shafer said. "Her mother is away—in Europe."

"And her father?"

"She doesn't have one."

Moody didn't press that point as he continued to write. "Could you describe her, please."

"She's a very pretty girl with a nice figure for her age. She's about five feet three with long blond hair and blue eyes. She's a cheerleader at her school."

"How was she dressed?" As he spoke another unit rolled up and two additional deputies got out. Bell quickly briefed them. One of them, who was a two-stripe senior, zeroed in on Miss Galloway. "We're going to look for her," he said. "It might help if you would come along."

"Yes, of course." She climbed quickly into the back seat of the patrol unit. It was a cage-back with some added equipment in the trunk.

As soon as the unit had left, Bell put the information he had on the air. The dispatcher notified the watch commander who alerted all units to assist in the search. Since Altadena lay right at the foot of the San Gabriel Mountains, the cars in that sector started a systematic check of the known teenage hangouts. As the handling deputies, Bell and Moody remained on the scene, hopefully to report that the girl had returned on her own.

A civilian car pulled up and a man in his early thirties got out. He spoke quickly to the women, then turned to the deputies. "I'm Reverend Hallman, pastor of the Church of the Redeemer," he said. "I came to help, if I can."

Moody had his notebook at the ready. "Did you see Marcia at the church supper this evening?" he asked.

"Yes, she was there, and in good spirits. She's a popular girl and quite visible."

"Did you speak to her?"

"Only to welcome her when she came in."

"When was the program over?"

"Around eight fifteen. Then two of our volunteer mothers

helped clean up the social hall. I remember looking at my watch when we had finished; it was exactly eight thirty."

"Did you see anyone offer Marcia a ride home?"

"No, I was inside, helping to put things away when the young people left. But I'm sure she wouldn't have accepted a ride from anyone she didn't know."

Moody continued to write in his notebook. "After these affairs, do the young people usually go on somewhere else—like a bowling alley?"

Hallman shook his head. "We discourage that, especially in the middle of the week. Most of the kids still have homework to do, that's why we keep our affairs fairly short."

"You said that Marcia is a popular girl. Does she have any special boyfriends?"

Mrs. Shafer, who had been listening in, answered that. "She has two or three boys that she likes, yes. But we already called their homes. None of them gave her a ride, or saw her after she left the supper."

The loudspeaker atop Bell's unit called, "Seventy-three."

Bell slid into the driver's seat and cut off the outside speaker. "Seventy-three by," he acknowledged.

"Is the subject still missing?"

"Affirmative. No leads so far."

"Stay on the scene. The field sergeant will be there in five."

Throughout the Altadena area the patrol units reported in from their assigned sectors; none of them had spotted the missing girl. Overhead the bright light of an Argus* helicopter split the night as it orbited the church grounds and then searched the foothills in systematic patterns.

Sergeant Nat Aaronson arrived at the scene in a station wagon and set up a command post. By that time it was approaching midnight and any idea that Marcia could have stopped with friends for pizza or a hamburger had to

*Aerial Reconnaissance, Ground Unit Support

be abandoned. All likely places where she might have gone had been checked; no blond attractive teenager in jeans and a pink blouse had been seen in any of them.

As the next shift reported in, all available vehicles were put out on the street. A house-to-house canvass along the way that Marcia should have gone was begun. A sheriff's special frequency was cleared of all other traffic. From the three women who had supplied the first information Sergeant Aaronson obtained the names and addresses of all of Marcia's known boyfriends. Despite the lateness of the hour, detective units called at every home, waking the occupants if necessary. Six youths were interviewed. Four had not been at the church supper but gave satisfactory accounts of how they had spent their early evening time. Three of the four had remained at home, studying or watching TV. The fourth had gone to a show with two other friends who confirmed his story.

The two remaining teenagers both stated that they had seen Marcia at the church supper, but they firmly denied having tried to date her afterward. Neither of them had seen her leave and didn't know if she had been alone or not.

Sergeant Aaronson asked for pictures of the missing girl. Meanwhile he had her run through the computer. She had not as yet gotten a driver's license and had no record of any kind.

He called the station by land line from the Lowell home and spoke directly with the lieutenant. "As of now, nine twenty is confirmed. I see it as a possible two zero seven. Nothing definite from anyone here. I've advised the family to keep this line open."

"I copy," the lieutenant said, and hung up. He lost no time in speaking to his watch sergeant. "The Lowell girl hasn't turned up or called. Aaronson thinks, and I agree, that it may be a possible kidnapping. Pass the word downtown and advise that she has been described as having long hair and being very attractive. And notify the Feds."

"Right now," the sergeant said and got immediately on the phone. He knew that the FBI would not come in immediately, but since kidnapping was a Federal offense, the Bureau should be put into the picture without delay.

For the rest of the night the Altadena Sheriff's Station kept up an intensive search while a temporary extension with a recording device was added to the Lowell telephone. Nat Aaronson carefully coached Mrs. Lowell, the grandmother of the missing girl, on what to say if the phone rang. A deputy was detailed to remain with her and to listen in on any incoming calls.

When the sun at last banished the night and full daylight filled the sky, nothing whatever had been heard from, or about, Marcia Lowell. It was then that Mrs. Shafer, who had refused to go home, burst into almost hysterical crying. In confused words, she blamed herself so violently that Aaronson asked for a paramedic unit. Shortly after it arrived, the two men in it administered a sedative and took her to her home across the street. A neighbor volunteered to stay with her since her husband was out of town and she had no children living with her.

In the Hall of Justice downtown, experienced detectives were already going through the long lists of known sex offenders, sorting them out and checking their MOs. Another team was working on the list of recently released felons who had been granted parole. Deputy Bidwell stopped at one name, studied it, and remembered the case as though it had been only a few days ago. "Bingo!" he said, largely to himself.

The other deputies present looked up.

"Harris," Bidwell said. "Three arrests and one conviction. Two sixty-one A in all cases—attempted rape of teenage females, all picked up off the street and taken into his van. And all innocent kids."

"Don't tell us that asshole's out," a deputy said.

"He's out." Bidwell was bitter. "Paroled about two months ago."

5

Under a sometimes relentless
sun, the road from the north end of the San Fernando
Valley through Big Tujunga Canyon runs eastward for
several miles before it joins with the Angeles Forest
Highway on its way up to the high desert. Closed in much
of the way by brown hills of decomposed granite, it is a dry,
harsh area with sparse, hardy vegetation in the many little
gaps and subcanyons between the hills. At night it is
patrolled by coyotes, out to prey on other wildlife and
whatever else there is to be found.

It was late in the day, with the sun low in the western
sky, when sixteen-year-old Raymond Sikes turned his
bicycle off the paved road up into a cul-de-sac that ended at
a steep rock face. He had to relieve himself and two
hundred feet from possible passing traffic gave him as
much privacy as he felt he needed. He opened his jeans,

looked down at the ground in front of him, and was frozen into immobility.

As soon as the pungent odor reached him he had a sudden urge to be sick. He backed away quickly, urinated at the other side of the gully, and then rode away as fast as he could.

His first impulse was to forget the whole thing and escape any involvement. Then he remembered that his bicycle tire marks were at the scene and since he lived not far away, it wouldn't take long for him to be found. He stopped and carefully dumped the three joints he had in his pocket, turned the pocket inside out, and brushed away the last visible evidence of the marijuana. Then he remounted his bike, rode another half-mile and stopped at a small camp where there was a telephone.

Deputies Cruz and Wallace were given the call. Since there was no need for urgency, they drove at normal speed to the camp and arrived there fourteen minutes later. They conducted a brief interview with Raymond, then asked him to come with them to point out the exact spot.

Getting into the rear of the cage-back patrol unit shook him up a little—he wasted none of his love on cops—until he realized that for the next brief while he would be calling the signals. Making the most of his role, he pointed out where he had turned off and then waited until Deputy Wallace opened the back door and let him out. It could not be operated from the inside.

Wallace had been out of the Custody division for only five months, but his partner and training officer was an experienced senior. Walking in a wide circle to avoid destroying evidence, Cruz led the way to the end of the gully and studied what lay there. Then he glanced quickly into the sky, estimating the amount of daylight that remained.

The body had been only partially buried in a shallow trough; the ground was too hard to admit of much more. Also, it was in view of the road. Cruz saw several other things in the minute or two he took to survey the scene, then he led the way back to the car and used the radio. "Confirm nine twenty-seven David, Big Tujunga Canyon Road, mile marker twenty Adam, three plus fifty-five. Possible Altadena nine twenty."

"Any chance of nine zero two?"

"Negative."

"Ten twenty-three."

Cruz reclipped the mike. Too many people had scanners able to receive the sheriff's frequencies, one of the reasons for the use of codes. In very few words he had confirmed a dead body and that no possibility of life remained. He had also advised that the body might be that of a missing person reported by the Altadena Station. That would bring a full response from the Homicide Bureau, the coroner, and anyone else the watch commander deemed necessary.

While Ted Wallace drove the Sikes boy to the camp where he had left his bicycle, Cruz began to use liberal amounts of yellow tape to mark off the crime scene.

In the Homicide Bureau at the Hall of Justice detective J. D. Smith took the call. As soon as he had the preliminary details he punched a button and relayed them on to Lieutenant Ralph Mott, who had the watch. Mott picked up the phone, listened, and then had a patch put through to Cruz who was on the scene. On a restricted frequency he asked for further details.

"It's a female, fifteen to seventeen years of age," Cruz reported. "Nude with mutilations and burn marks. She was tortured and probably raped. There's blood near her vagina and a wire coat hanger wrapped around her neck imbedded in the flesh. She got it the hard way."

"We'll be right out," Mott said. He knew better than to tell a veteran deputy to protect the scene. "I may have a civilian with me," he added.

"He'd better have a strong stomach," Cruz warned.

Before he went any farther, Mott took the standard precaution of covering his ass. He called Captain Grimm's office and filled him in. "What's your advice about Flavia?" he asked.

"The handling field deputy reported that it's pretty rough."

"Right."

"The word from on high is to let her in. Maybe if she sees this one it'll turn her off for good. I hope so. I'm sorry, Ralph, if you get stuck with a hysterical female on your hands."

"If that happens, I'll get her out of there fast."

"With my blessing," Grimm added and hung up.

Reluctantly Mott checked a number under the glass on his desktop and called Flavia de la Torre. When she came on the line he deliberately made his voice hard and discouraging.

"A body has been found in Big Tujunga Canyon," he said. "Do you know where that is?"

"I can find out."

"I want to warn you that this may be a very rough one. Perhaps it might be better . . ."

"If I may, Lieutenant, I'd like to come."

"Then I'll put you down as responding. Take your time, it's no great rush. Come up the canyon to the three-and-a-half-mile marker; there'll be other cars parked. And Flavia . . ."

"Yes?"

"Wear old clothes. The body was found up one of the small canyons."

At the site a second unit pulled up and the field sergeant got out. Taking careful precautions against destroying evidence, he studied the body and surveyed the surrounding area.

Approximately twelve feet from the body a woman's purse lay on the ground. Since it was disassociated from the corpse and part of the scene, he very carefully opened it and checked for possible ID. There were several

41

photographs in a folder, the usual feminine articles, and a plasticized membership card. Holding it by the edges, he read it and then returned it so that the purse remained, as far as possible, exactly as he had found it.

He waited there until Mott and his two assigned investigators arrived and parked off the highway. Moments later a blue coroner's van that showed only the county seal parked just off the roadway. A third patrol unit, roof lights on, came to help in perimeter control.

Mott checked that the area had been well taped off; a press photographer equipped with a long telephoto lens was already working just outside the restricted area. It was approaching twilight; lights would have to be set up.

Within a short time eight official vehicles were at the scene. Mott was still making a preliminary survey when Flavia got out of her car and after a moment's hesitation stepped across the yellow tape.

She was intercepted by the field sergeant. "Who are you?" he demanded.

"I'm Dr. de la Torre."

"From the crime lab?"

"No."

"The Coroner's Office?"

"No."

"Then what the hell are you doing here?"

"Lieutenant Mott sent for me."

"Stay right where you are, don't move," the sergeant ordered and went to find Mott.

"There's a civilian asking for you," he reported. He showed his strong doubts both in his voice and his manner. "A female, thirty to thirty-five, five feet four or five, brunette. Dr. de la Torre."

The sergeant was owed an explanation. "She's got top-level approval," Mott said. "Temporarily she's assigned to us. Let her in, but keep her well back and watch where she walks."

42

Having done what he should, the sergeant went to carry out his instructions.

Flavia's first impression of the crime scene was surprise that several of those present were women. Then Mott came and led her twenty feet short of the spot where the body lay.

"Let me explain what's going on," he said. "The principal homicide team, Smith and his partner, is working the scene, looking for clues. They're setting up screens to look for anything in the soil. The man with the camera is from the crime lab; he also does fingerprints."

"Is the victim female?"

"Yes."

"Is that why you have a female investigator?"

"No, that has nothing to do with it. The crime scene as such is ours; the body and everything associated with it belongs to the coroner. Of course we work very closely together."

Flavia nodded without interrupting. She was still trying to see the body, but there were too many people around it and a little hillock was in the way. She realized that she was being deliberately kept at a distance and could not help resenting it slightly. She had told Mott that she was prepared for an unpleasant sight, and she had meant it.

"The two men in blue jumpsuits are from the Coroner's Office," Mott continued. "The blond girl is a coroner's investigator; she'll do most of the actual work on the body. The man in a business suit is a pathologist; he may or may not do the autopsy. The woman in the brown outfit is a criminalist from our lab. The other female is also a criminalist attached to the Coroner's Office. Have you got all that?"

Flavia would have preferred that the coroner's detective had been called a woman, not a girl, but it was no time to go into semantic hairsplitting.

"I believe so. Do I have to stay back here?"

Mott pressed his lips together for a moment. "I'll let you see the body if you want to, but I advise against it. It's not a pretty sight." He paused. "The victim's a teenaged girl; she was tortured and then strangled with a wire coat hanger. It's still buried in her flesh."

"I came here to learn all that I can,"Flavia said. "If she endured it, I can look at it."

"All right, come along then."

Six feet from the body Flavia stopped. *"Oh, my God!"* she said.

What had been a pretty girl lay nude on her back. An artist with a large drawing pad was at work sketching the scene. Two men in dark blue jumpsuits with the word CORONER in large yellow letters on the back were moving about. Powerful portable lights being set up emphasized every detail of the inert corpse. On her knees, next to the body, the blond young woman from the Coroner's Office had opened a large kit and was removing various pieces of equipment. It was then that Flavia saw that the nipples were missing from the dead girl's breasts.

The face was also badly distorted. It was unnaturally red, the mouth was open, and the tongue hung out. A wire coat hanger had been twisted around the neck until it had bitten far into the flesh. The upper chest was covered with streaks of blood. Flavia looked toward the dead girl's eyes with reluctance, almost feeling that she was invading her privacy. The eyeballs were fixed out into space, staring without seeing.

A sudden surge of queasiness seized Flavia. Mott took her by the shoulders and led her quickly to the other side of the narrow canyon. "Go ahead and heave if you want to," he said. "You won't be the first."

Flavia fought hard to maintain her composure and speak in a normal tone of voice. "I'm not going to keel over, if that's what you mean. Was she raped?"

"We'll know that shortly. Do you want to go back home now?"

"No," Flavia answered. "I can't learn that way. I just wonder how . . . that young woman working there . . ."

"It's her profession," Mott said. "She's very good at it. And very knowledgeable."

"But working with dead bodies like that . . ."

Mott's voice became firm and hard. "What do you think the Homicide Bureau is?" he asked. "I warned you this was no pink tea, no actor sprawled on the floor in a TV show. This is the kind of thing we're up against all the time. And many cases are much worse."

She looked into his face. "How can you stand it?" she asked.

Mott pressed his lips together and then looked at Flavia in the gathering darkness. "You saw the body. Some inhuman degenerate did that to her: tortured her for his perverted sexual pleasure and then took her life. She was only sixteen years old. Do you want him to go unpunished, to do the same thing to other innocent girls?"

"*No! No!*" Flavia's voice was on the edge of cracking.

Mott softened his voice to make things easier for her. "I talked to your dean before we let you come in with us. I know you believe strongly in rehabilitation. I'll tell you right now that there's no possible rehabilitation for the monster who did that. Our job is to find him and stop him from ever doing such a thing again."

Flavia took some deep breaths and recovered herself. "I see," she said simply. "I'm sorry I was so weak. But I don't want to go home. I want to see this through."

"Can you handle it?"

"Yes. Is that young woman an M.D.?"

"No. The pathologist is, of course. What she's doing is the standard routine for on-site investigation. If you feel up to it, you can learn quite a bit by watching her."

He stopped and changed his tone again. "Remember that the body isn't a person anymore. I don't know what your religion is, and I don't care, but the girl herself isn't here.

45

Her problems are over. The body is what she left behind. Her privacy isn't being invaded; she took that with her."

Flavia looked up at him. "Thank you for saying that. It bothered me terribly, seeing her lying there naked under those lights with no way to protect herself."

"You understand that it isn't her."

"I do now, yes." She took hold of his arm for a moment, reaching for his strength, then started back to where the body lay.

"I think you're a compassionate man, Lieutenant. Are those dark marks on the body cigarette burns?"

"Yes. I told you she'd been tortured."

Flavia stopped speaking and concentrated her attention on the young woman who was at work on the body. With a special pair of scissors she cut a bit of hair from the head and carefully folded it in a prepared slip of paper. She took hair samples from the armpits, from the legs, and from the pubic area, putting each one in a separately marked fold of paper. She took a culture from inside the nose and from the ears. With a special instrument she took a culture from within the vagina.

Then she asked that the lights be turned off. As soon as they were out she began slowly scanning the body with an ultraviolet lamp. She wore a pair of transparent plastic gloves as she tested the flesh and bent as close as possible to see the effects of the light. When she reached the vaginal area, the flesh surrounding it lit up with a faint glow.

Halfway up the abdomen the same glowing appeared. Mott spoke to Flavia without turning. "Semen glows under ultraviolet light," he explained.

Flavia swallowed before she spoke. "She was raped, then." She tried her best to keep the shaking out of her voice.

"Yes. If she had consented to sex, it's most unlikely there would be evidence of semen on her abdomen."

As soon as the lights were turned on again, the sheriff's homicide team continued a minute inspection of the area

46

surrounding the body. When anything at all was spotted, its direction and distance from the body was carefully measured and a photograph taken. The route from the roadway to the site was meticulously studied. The soil was loose and capable of taking a tire track. Several rolls of film were used to record every detail that was in any way unusual.

The coroner's investigator, still wearing transparent gloves, was inspecting the fingers and taking samples from under the nails. The body remained in the position in which it had been found.

Mott spoke to Flavia once more. "A homicide investigation's main objective is to find out who committed the crime, and why. But we also have to gather enough evidence to prove his guilt in court and make it stick. Even with very strong evidence, we can run into legal technicalities that allow the criminal to escape."

"How much longer will all this take?" Flavia asked.

"Another hour at least, probably longer. We'll have to go over the whole area, sifting for evidence, picking up every scrap of material that might be significant, searching for anything that might have been thrown away by the murderer. The victim's clothes, for instance."

"Do you know who she was?"

"We have a preliminary ID, but a formal one still has to be made. They use TV for that at the Coroner's Office. Just the head is shown on a screen and it's made to look as lifelike as possible."

"With her eyes shut."

"Of course. You understand you're not to discuss what you see here with anyone."

"Including general procedures?"

"That's all right. But nothing specific about this particular case."

"I won't," Flavia said.

"Good. You're welcome to stay on here, if you'd like, or if you've seen enough . . ."

"May I stay until they take away the body? I want to understand the whole procedure."

"Be my guest," Mott said. "But there's quite a bit more to come. They haven't even turned her over yet."

"I asked for this," Flavia said, "and unless I'm in the way, I'm going to see it through."

"As you wish. I've got to leave shortly; we have a notification to make. That's always the hardest part. The sergeant knows who you are now."

Almost two hours later a sheet of white plastic was laid out and the physical remains of Marcia Lowell were carefully and neatly wrapped up. Another cover was put over that and fastened, forming a shape that closely resembled a mummy. A gurney was brought up and the two coroner's men lifted the body onto its narrow surface. As they carried it away, Flavia followed. She watched as they loaded it into the back of the van and firmly closed the door.

As the van pulled away, she stood where she was, the slight evening breeze ruffling her hair. Then without shame she lowered her head and spoke a prayer for the girl whose body it had been. After that she got into her own car and tried to collect her thoughts.

There she sat quietly, not ready to drive as yet. Her body still had a tendency to shake, as though by doing so it could erase some of the horror she had just witnessed. She prided herself on her liberalism, but what she had lived through during the past few hours had shaken some of her most deep-seated beliefs.

The murdered girl was pitifully beyond help, there was nothing that could be done for her now. But irresistibly Flavia felt growing within her a consuming desire to see her murderer caught, tried, convicted, and punished. She had long been a determined opponent of capital punishment, but at that moment a blind desire to see justice done overrode everything else. A prison term would not be

48

enough after what she had seen; the killer could only pay for his dreadful crime in the gas chamber.

She started the engine and drove slowly away. She had not had her dinner, but she had no appetite whatever for food. Too many waves of conflicting emotion were crashing on the shores of her mind.

6

Working together as a team, Sergeant Oliver Tracy and Deputy Frank Levitzky were blessed with an abundance of patience and resourcefulness, a fact that had much to do with their outstanding success record. From the first they had sensed that the case of Mrs. Mabel Lorimer would present special problems, but they had encountered that sort of thing many times in the past.

As soon as it came in, they gave very close attention to the coroner's protocol, the official report on the autopsy and cause of death. Beside having her throat cut, the victim had been stabbed with a sharp, narrow instrument that had passed between the third and fourth ribs on the left-hand side of her body. This indicated one of two things: that it had been done by an expert, or that someone in striking the blow had been exceptionally lucky. They all but dismissed the second possibility and concentrated very carefully on the first. Amateur stabbings usually occurred in the abdomen, sometimes even in the limbs. The chances of such an expert thrust being done by an unskilled person were remote.

Early in the morning they returned to St. Gregory's and reinterviewed both Brother Fred and Father Fernando. Their statements were already on file, but with a little time to think things over it was quite possible that one or both of the men might recall some detail they had overlooked the first time or had thought too trivial to mention.

"We have determined that the victim was not Catholic," Levitzky said, "but is there any chance that either of you might have met her somewhere outside the church?"

Father Fernando shook his head. He was a very young man, almost too young, by appearances, to have such an important parish. "Brother Fred and I have gone over this several times," he said. "As far as we know, she was a complete stranger. However, I have said a Mass for the repose of her soul."

"We have no idea why she came to us," Brother Fred said. "To our church, I mean. She could have taken shelter here, since the church is always open, but I doubt it."

"Why?" Tracy asked.

"Because it had been raining for some time. If there had been a sudden shower, she might have done that. But as it was, it's much more likely she would have gone into the all-night convenience store where she could have used a telephone."

"Perhaps she didn't know it was there," Levitzky suggested.

"It's very visible from the church steps, only a short block away," Brother Fred replied. "Father thinks she may have come here to meet someone."

Tracy was writing in his inevitable notebook. "We could use you in our work," he said. "We had the same idea. It's too bad that no one else was in the sanctuary at that time."

"That opportunity was lost, I'm afraid," Father Fernando

said. "Having completed my duties for the day, I was reading a detective story."

"About Father Brown, no doubt," Levitzky said.

"Actually Rabbi Small. The logic is so brilliant. I also enjoy Reverend Randollph, even though he refers to his seminary as East Jesus Tech."

Since that was the end of the road there for the moment, Tracy and Levitzky drove back to the Hall of Justice to begin the dreary job of going through the MO files. By well into the afternoon they had sorted out eighteen possibles. With the help of a computer eleven of them were quickly eliminated. When they had gone through the seven names that remained, Levitzky said, "I don't think the answer's here."

"Neither do I," Tracy agreed.

When the phone rang he picked it up. "Homicide, Tracy," he said.

A well-modulated feminine voice gave him the news. "Chief Cargill would like to see you and Deputy Levitzky. Is he there?"

"Yes, he is. When?"

"Right now, please."

"On the way." He hung up and looked at his partner. "Cargill wants to see us," he said. "As of now."

In less than five minutes they were shown into the large second-floor office where Chief Cargill ran several divisions, including homicide. Cargill was noted for his remarkable grasp; he usually had everything that was going on in his bailiwick at his fingertips.

He wasted no time coming to the point. "You're handling the Lorimer case, I believe," he said.

"Yes, sir," Levitzky answered.

"And you talked to Jack Ogden."

"That's right. When we started working on the victim's background, we found out she worked for the Government in some secret capacity. So we touched base with the FBI. We were routed in to see him."

52

Cargill nodded. "He called me about it. What did you tell him?"

Levitzky answered. "We didn't know what his attitude would be, so we pointed out that this one had happened in our jurisdiction, so it was our baby to rock."

Cargill brushed a hand across his face. "That's just what I told him. Jack's a good friend, so we had no trouble reaching an agreement. He's set up a very good man, a chap named Jack Harvey, to liaison with you. Whatever you need to know about the victim's background or activities, he'll help you as much as he can."

"There's a question that's bothering us right now," Tracy said. "Did the FBI, or any other Government outfit, know *in advance* that the victim was going to East Los Angeles that night?"

Cargill considered that. "I see where you're coming from," he said. "I think Harvey may be able to get you the answer. Are both of your clearances currently in order?"

"Yes, sir," Tracy answered.

Levitzky sensed that the interview was over. "I'm sure we'll get along fine," he said.

Charles Weber leaned back in his chair, toying with a pencil in his restless fingers and staring out the window while he made up his mind. As a leading assistant district attorney he was well up on the requirements of his job, which in his case included a good deal of political infighting. He had a job to do and he did it, much too well to please some people. Now he had had a fresh problem dumped in his lap at a time when he didn't need it. He could handle the media, that never bothered him. He always knew what answers to give. Also, he had protected himself by developing some good relationships with individual reporters. But now he had two major cases coming up on his docket that were consuming most of his time; a college professor ambitious to write a book about

53

the California parole system was, at that particular moment, an unwanted complication.

He would have ducked it without compunction except for a phone call that had forced his hand. Now he would have to see the damned woman, but he was uncertain how much he should say and with what degree of candor. He decided to put out as little as he could and still keep her happy. Politics again, but he couldn't help it.

On the minute of three in the afternoon Flavia de la Torre was shown into his office. As she walked toward his desk and he rose as he was expected to, he was impressed: she was much more attractive than he had expected and she had a notable set of tits. They were not overly large, but ample and fluid in their movement. He offered her a chair.

"I understand you're writing a book, Dr. de la Torre," he opened, giving her plenty of latitude.

"That's my intention, Mr. Weber, providing I can make a good job of it."

"I'm sure you won't have any trouble there," he offered smoothly, knowing the value of a stroking remark. "I understand you've already written about the parole system."

"My thesis was published, but only in a very limited way. I'm starting this project from square one."

He couldn't argue with that. "Then you probably know that the old California Adult Authority controlled the length of prison terms, and that it had considerable latitude in making its decisions."

Flavia had a notebook open on her lap, but she was not writing in it. "I do know that," she said. "I also know it was widely criticized for granting early releases to some very dangerous people."

"Yes, that's true. Of course in saying that we have the advantage of hindsight." He decided to probe a little. "What's your professional feeling on that, Dr. de la Torre?"

Flavia took her time in replying. "You're quite right in pointing out that hindsight is twenty-twenty. The indeterminate sentencing laws, since you ask my opinion, only complicated the problem. What I don't know is how well the new system is working."

Weber decided that the young woman before him was not an ivory-tower academic. "Since you're a college professor . . ." he began when she raised a hand.

"I'm not a professor, Mr. Weber, I'm an instructor. There's a big difference. I don't have tenure, for one thing. And I certainly don't head a department."

"But you could," Weber tempted.

Flavia handled that easily. "Professor Applebaum, who heads our sociology department, has been with the university more than twenty years, and she's an internationally known authority on child abuse."

Weber had ready a standard speech. "The whole business of sentencing a convicted felon here in California is strictly limited by legislation. The judge who sits on the bench isn't free to pass sentence as he or she sees fit. The options are limited, usually to three. There is a light sentence, a medium sentence, and a maximum sentence. Take robbery: the sentences are one, three, and five years. If a robber is caught and convicted, as the law now stands a first offense with mitigating circumstances, such as a man desperate to feed his family, would probably get one year. A repeat offender without mitigation would get the medium sentence, or three years. In a severe case, involving heavy loss, the judge can impose five years. But that's it."

"I do understand that, Mr. Weber," Flavia said. "But it's different in the case of murder, isn't it?"

"Only in the case of murder," Weber replied. "There the Board of Prison Terms has much more discretion. That's why Charles Manson, for instance, and Sirhan Sirhan were repeatedly denied parole. But didn't you cover all this in your paper?"

Flavia shook her head, an action that made her hair swirl a little around her face in an almost enticing manner. "No, because I wrote it several years ago. I expected to be criticized for my findings at the time and I was. I, of all people, was categorized as insensitive to the poor and oppressed."

"As if that had anything to do with it."

"Thank you," Flavia said. "Now, if I can, I want to do something effective. I'm collecting cases about parolees who commit additional crimes after they're released."

Weber tapped a pencil end against his desk. "Don't make the mistake of assuming that all parolees commit additional felonies," he warned. "There are a lot of them who don't. Particularly white-collar criminals. Once they're caught, they normally don't try it again. Of course many of them never get the chance."

"I understand that," she said. "But right now it seems to me that the law is so abominably written justice under it is almost impossible."

Weber looked at her carefully. "I won't contest that," he said.

Jack Harvey had no trouble finding the Sheriff's Homicide Bureau; he had been there many times before. He was almost the idealized portrait of the FBI man: just under six feet, in excellent condition, almost embarrassingly handsome, articulate, and gifted with an admirable sense of humor. For the past several years he had been assigned to counterintelligence. Exactly how he went about that was a matter locked in the secrets of the Bureau, but his long-continuing assignment gave a good clue.

His ID card got him in at once. He put it away and walked down the long room to the desks where Tracy and Levitzky were expecting him. "Jack Harvey," he said, making a minimum fuss about presenting himself.

Frank Levitzky pulled up a vacant chair and opened the session for business.

"I know you want all you can get on Mrs. Lorimer,"

Harvey began. "I also know that you both carry clearances that you got during the Olympics."

"Right on," Tracy said. "And both our clearances are current."

"I know—I checked." Harvey dropped his voice a little. "What I've been authorized to give you now is confidential, is that understood?"

"Yes," Levitzky answered.

"Okay. Mabel Lorimer carried a top secret clearance for many years. She was an executive secretary who typed a lot of highly sensitive material. In all that time she was never the source of any kind of leak. We tested her a number of times and she was a gem: a very capable woman who had the ability to keep her mouth tight shut. Her trust factor was about as high as they go."

"Tough to lose one like that," Tracy said.

"Damn right," Harvey agreed. "Now the part that will probably interest you: several times over the years she was very subtly approached with some tempting offers. A couple of them we set up ourselves. In every case she reported them immediately."

"She was incorruptible," Levitzky confirmed.

"Absolutely. She could have been the President's secretary, and that isn't too far from the job she did have. Now, there's a long-continuing case we've been working on and couldn't get a break. So we decided to make one. We took advantage of Mabel's circumstances, widowed and living with her sister's family, and set up a very slow leak that she was discontented—with her cooperation, of course. It took some time, but at last we got a reaction. A very slight one, but that's all we expected. We fed and watered it very carefully until finally a contact was set up. It was to be a very preliminary meeting where no risk would be involved."

"But you guessed wrong on that," Tracy said.

Harvey lifted a hand. "Wait a minute—you're getting too far ahead."

57

"Sorry."

"Understand that at a meeting of that kind there should be no risk at all. We know a great deal about the KGB and how it operates. They would never endanger a possible new source of information; on the contrary, they'd try to protect it at almost any cost. They've even sacrificed some of their own people to make a source stand up."

"I've heard that," Tracy said.

"It's true. Which is why we let Mabel go to that appointment uncovered. We had to play it very carefully. If we'd planted anyone in that church they would have known it. They're good, don't mistake that. There was just too much risk that we might be spotted, and if we were, the whole operation would have gone up the flue forever."

Tracy's face was a study in momentary confusion. "Wait a minute," he said. "I follow all you've said, and I understand it. But the fact is, she *was* murdered."

Harvey nodded slowly. "Yes, she was. But the point I want to make is this: it's almost certain that the people she went to meet didn't kill her. But don't ask me who did, because I don't know."

7

Northeast of the city of Alhambra a moderately large housing development was not selling as well as its developers had anticipated. Built on gently sloping land, all of the lots had been "engineered," cut out by bulldozers into small, rectangular, level areas. Each one was just large enough to hold a predesigned house with a few feet of land surrounding it to convince a potential buyer that he was really acquiring some property. The lots met the building code, but very little more. It was characteristic that they were advertised as "estates."

A winding paved road ran through the development. At its higher end, where the views were much better, a few homes had been built and were occupied. From there down to the next intersecting north–south street there was a steady parade of empty lots, many of them with their bareness broken by a high, sparse growth of weeds. There was little water to encourage any kind of plant life, or to wash away the steep borders that separated one level from another. With careful foresight the developer had made the less desirable lower lots slightly larger in the hope of making them more salable.

One thing he had not foreseen was the challenge that the stepped lost provided to a whole group of motorcycle riders. Almost as soon as the lost had been completed, bikes began to take advantage of the weekends when no one was about to jump from one to the other. In front the lots met the street in a smooth line, but at the back the sometimes several feet of difference in height between them provided a new thrill and the challenge of a steeple-chase.

Among those who rode was Harvey Zoran. He had not acquired his bike until the lots had been there several weeks, but it did not take him long to get in on the fun, with others or by himself. On Monday afternoon he rode up the paved street, noted that there were no cops or security people about, and gleefully ran his machine across the top open lot to the back. There he gunned his engine a time or two for effect and charged toward the first edge that would jump him some four feet down to the next lot.

He rode the hazardous course down, lot after lot, until he came to what he knew would be the highest jump. He had balked at it the first few times, but he had now done it twice before and felt himself a full-fledged daredevil as he charged his machine toward the edge. In the back of his mind he knew that if he hurt himself there would be no one around to give him any help, but that only increased the thrill of taking a chance. He reached the edge and was airborne; then he quickly looked down to see where he would land. His hands froze on their grips as he saw, in a flashing moment, a naked woman lying there.

He could not control his machine: the jump had been made and the bike would land at the end of a predetermined parabola. Utter terror gripped him; he gulped air and yelled. The wheels landed on something soft, then he managed to regain his balance. He stopped, turned around, and forced himself to go back and see what he had done.

It was a naked woman all right, and a young one. He had landed across her abdomen; his tracks clearly visible. For a long moment he stared at her breasts and her pubic area where a thick triangle of curly red hair emphasized her sex. Then he looked up at her head and shoulders. As soon as he had done that, he leaned to one side of his machine and threw up the contents of his stomach.

When he recovered himself he got off his bike and came closer for a confirming second look. He didn't dare to touch what he had found, but what he saw left no doubt that the girl was dead. His numbed brain told him he would have to report it. Not because he wanted to—he wanted to get away from there and stay away—but his tracks were sharply visible and his machine had just been fitted with a set of custom tires. They could be easy to identify.

Carefully he got back on his motorcycle and rode sedately down the road. He knew where the Sheriff's Station was, but he was in no hurry to get there. At the first stop light he reached, a black-and-white sheriff's patrol unit was waiting out the red. He waved to it frantically, got the driver's attention, rode over beside the open window, and told what he had found. It saved him from going to the station where there would be dozens of cops about and who knew what else.

At the Homicide Bureau Ralph Mott was standing the watch. Tony Toomey was supposed to be on, but he had a dental appointment and Mott was covering for him. When the call came in it was answered at the desk, then piped to him almost immediately. With the aid of a phone patch he talked to the lead deputy in the field, heard his verbal report, and felt a strong sinking in his stomach. A serial killer could be the worst kind of a case and the preliminary signs indicated that he might have one here.

He scanned the room quickly to see if he had a homicide team immediately available. There were a hundred people assigned to the Bureau, but they were spread over three shifts and seven days a week. In addition, five of them were lieutenants like himself whose function was supervision, not the nuts and bolts of detailed investigation. And there were always absences: for medical reasons, vacations, and a variety of other legitimate grounds.

Fortunately one of his top teams, Tracy and Levitzky, was in. They were heavily engaged in paperwork, but that could always wait. "Dick, Frank," he called.

As soon as the investigators reached his desk, he laid it out. "You know about the Lowell case, the teenaged girl that didn't come home from the church meeting. And you know the condition of her body when it was found in Big Tujunga Canyon. This looks like the same killer."

"That's all we need," Levitzky said.

At that moment Mott remembered Flavia de la Torre. He definitely did not want her around on this one, but policy had been set on that. On the way out he spoke to the sergeant on the desk: "Call Dr. de la Torre. You have her number posted."

"Will do."

"If she doesn't answer in three rings, forget it," he added.

"I copy."

In the corridor while waiting for the elevator Mott supplied a few more details to his team. Unexpectedly the door to the Bureau opened and the sergeant looked out. "She answered on the second ring," he reported. "She's coming."

"Oh, well," Mott said.

Whenever there is known to be a homicide, people gather apparently from nowhere and often remain for hours, hoping to get a glimpse of something sensational. If they were allowed to do so, they would probably profoundly regret it within seconds; there is nothing pleasant about a murder scene, even a relatively mild and bloodless one.

This one was outdoors, not in a closely confined room, but even the high expanse of the sky overhead and the feeling of free-flowing air could not dispel the shock and horror of violent death and the stark evidence of uninhibited savagery. The girl had not only been killed; her death had been a fearful one. One look at her and Mott could not have wished her back to life—to face the results of what had been done to her. The only mercy the killer had shown was in letting her die.

Quietly, and without ostentation, the necessary people gathered: from the Coroner's Office, the crime lab, and the nearby Sheriff's Station that supplied the required number of uniforms.

The body lay on an old mattress that had been left half hidden on the vacant lot. Someone had had his fun and hadn't bothered to clean up afterward. Or the killer had brought it himself, but that was unlikely. He had had no desire to make his victim comfortable, and it was improbable that he would leave that much evidence behind him.

The head had been half cut off the body, but that was only part of it. There were horrible burns on the legs and arms and on the abdomen. The tire tracks of the motorcycle were clearly visible, but they did not obscure an obscene symbol that had been carved deep into the flesh exposing some of the intestines just below the girl's navel. By the looks of her she could not have been much over fifteen.

When he saw that bloodstains had been sprinkled over an area at least ten feet from the body, Mott as the supervisor in charge sent for a serologist. The crime lab and the Coroner's Office could supply highly qualified criminalists in a dozen or more different fields; it was up to him to decide which ones were needed. A print-and-photo man was already on hand and at work. The coroner's investigator was there unloading equipment from one of the older brown vans whose purpose was only marked inconspicuously on the passenger door.

Harvey Zoran and his motorcycle were there by request, but were being kept at a distance where he was out of the way. He showed no disposition to leave; since he was not under suspicion, as far as he knew, he was anxious to see as much as he could of what was going on. The other inevitable spectators were being kept at a safe distance, out of the line of sight, by four uniformed deputies. The children who showed up were sent home and told not to return.

When Flavia arrived she parked her car in the street and walked up to the sergeant in charge of the uniformed deputies. "I'm Dr. de la Torre," she said. "Lieutenant Mott sent for me."

The sergeant assumed that she wanted to review the scene before bringing up her equipment. Her use of Mott's name dispelled any doubts he might have had. "Stay to the right of the tapes until you get there, Doctor," he said and pointed the direction she should go.

Mott saw her coming and intercepted her a short distance from the actual scene. "Flavia, this is an awfully rough one," he told her.

"So was the first one, Ralph." It was the first time she had used his Christian name.

"This one is worse."

"Another girl?"

"Yes."

"Also nude?"

"Yes."

"Could it be the same killer?"

"Absolutely off the record, Flavia, it's quite possible."

"A sadist."

Mott's jaw locked for a moment. "A monster," he said.

Flavia knew what he was saying, and what he was very strongly implying between the lines. "Thank you," she said. "I'm fully prepared now."

He knew there was nothing for it; she would not be satisfied until she had seen what might shock her enough to give her nightmares for weeks, or memories that could last a lifetime. Reluctantly he pointed ahead, warning her again silently as he did so. He noticed that she was wearing jeans and flat-heeled shoes. But the jeans were a designer type that had been cut to emphasize her female figure. As he followed her across the almost bare ground toward the place where the body lay he took full note of it. When he had suggested jeans he had not had that type in mind. The less that Flavia did to attract attention at the scene, the better. As it was, no one would mistake her for a homicide investigator.

When she stopped, he stood behind her to catch her if she keeled over. For a moment he thought she was going to, then visibly she gathered herself and began to build that wall that separates the professionals at a murder scene from the inert object under investigation. After half a minute he knew she was going to make it.

She took it all in, staying out of the way of the people who were already at work. This time she was the only woman on the scene, but no one seemed to notice that.

One of the investigators took a moment to acknowledge her. "Dick Tracy," he said.

"Elizabeth Taylor."

"Look, lady, this isn't the time or place for jokes."

She knew at once she had made a bad mistake. He was already turning away, but she took hold of his arm. "I'm sorry," she said. "I misunderstood."

Tracy was reasonable. "It wasn't the first time," he said. "You're the college professor, aren't you?"

Flavia knew better than to correct that. "Flavia de la Torre," she said. "I'm here to learn."

"In that case," Tracy said, "you can see what some so-called human beings can do to others. God knows how this can happen, I don't"

The on-site investigation took almost two hours before the body was removed. Flavia remained for the first hour, gradually trying to condition herself to accept what she saw, reminding herself that this was the clay left behind after the spirit had flown, but it was a near thing with her. When the coroner's examiner reported to Mott that the victim had been sexually abused, and that she had been a virgin, it seemed to complete the absolute horror of the scene.

Mott looked at her. "Let's go," he said. It wasn't an invitation; it was a directive.

Far enough away from the scene to escape from the feeling that it was still close by, she obediently followed his car into the parking lot of a better-class coffee shop. When he asked for a private booth, the hostess led them to the last one at the end of the room. The two others nearest to it were empty.

Mott recommended that she eat. "It's important that you take some food right now," he said.

In response she picked something from the menu, her mind giving it the minimum of attention. When the waitress had left and they were alone, Mott folded his hands on the table and set a firm mood. "I want to know something," he said. "I understand that you're studying the parole system; that's fine with me, I think it needs doing. But why, if that's your purpose, are you coming to murder scenes? I told you I can get you all the statistics you need and you're allowed to read the investigators' reports."

If he thought she would toy with a spoon while she considered that, he was mistaken. She folded her own hands and looked at him directly. "I've been waiting for your to ask that," she answered. "You know as well as anyone how many felonies there are on the books besides murder. There's rape, arson, armed robbery, child abuse, bunko I believe you call it, and many other serious crimes. Crimes that can rob decent people of their life savings, sometimes elderly people who are all alone."

"And treason," Mott added. "There's been a lot of that recently."

"And treason," she agreed. "And by many reports, like the Rand study, a lot of these heavy crimes are done by persons on parole."

"True," Mott agreed.

"Now . . ." She stopped and took a fresh breath. "I can't do a study on them all, the job would be overwhelming. So I decided to concentrate on homicide, because it's the only major crime that's irreversible. Robbery victims sometimes get their property back, or are insured, but homicide is final. So I'm focusing on that."

When she paused for a moment Mott could see tension building within her.

"I'm a sociologist," she went on. "I've studied about murder. I've even written about it. But I didn't know what the hell it really was until I stood in Big Tujunga and looked at the body of that girl. And then—today. Am I coming through to you?"

"Yes, you are."

"Can you understand, then, that I'm not interested only in factual statistics? I want to understand homicide firsthand and, if you'll let me, be in on the actual investigations. And interrogations, too, if possible. Then I want to do a book that will bring it all home: the sharp agony of it, what it does to people. Not just the victims, but to those around them."

Mott checked that the waitress was not on her way to their table. "All that's fine, Flavia; I hear what you're saying. Now, taking it all just as you put it, what's the bottom line?"

67

"The bottom line," she answered, "is that I'm going to bust my gut to do another *Gentleman's Agreement*, another *Sayonara*. So help me God, I'm going to try to make them change the law."

8

In the grip of a demanding urge to escape from the world that surrounded her, Flavia fished her keys out of her purse and found the ones that would open the dead-bolt locks. It still offended her that she needed two locks on her front door, but it had become a necessity. The whole perimeter around the university was a high crime area, the very opposite of what all her sensibilities told her it should have been. The groves of academe were a cruel illusion, at least where she lived and tried her best to teach the meaning of civilization.

Once inside her small apartment she secured both locks and the chain that had been installed for her greater protection. She knew now that the dangers outside were no longer a matter of routine statistics, but of stark reality.

The two minimal rooms with kitchen and bath that were her present home and place of refuge refused to warm to her presence. They offered only a sterile month-to-month tolerance of her so long as her rent checks were fed into a computer by the tenth of each month. The property was owned by some vast corporation and managed by another that periodically adjusted upward the amount she had to pay. As a tenant she was a group of digits and nothing more.

Back in Spain there was a sizable estate that had been in her family for generations. It had withstood the civil war and many other tribulations through the decades without loss of substance or dignity, but its stability and protection were more than an ocean away from where she had chosen to build her career.

Now that she was in what passed *pro tem* as her home, Flavia had a strong desire to get out of her clothes, to let the air freshen her body, and to take a soaking hot bath. The tub that had been provided was part of a one-piece plastic molding that formed almost half of her bathroom; it was much too small for real comfort, but she had learned to make it do.

She got out of the clothing she had worn at the murder site and set it aside to be washed. Then, before the full-length mirror she had bought herself, with no feeling of narcissism she surveyed her body. A sense of strong gratitude filled her, not because of her physical assets, but because unlike the poor, unripened girl she had seen lying with sightless eyes staring up at an unseen sky, *she* was alive, warm, vital, and capable of movement.

She knew that her body was well above the norm; the few men who had seen it had told her so with enthusiasm. She knew how much she was constantly eyed and appraised while she was on campus. But far overriding everything else at that moment was the freshened knowledge that she had been granted the incomparable gift of continuing life with all of the potential that it held for her. It was to remind herself of that fact that she looked in her mirror before she turned away to the small bathroom and began to draw hot water into the featureless tub.

As she lay soaking, letting the muscles of her body relax as much as they could with her knees drawn up so she could fit in, she thought about Ralph Mott. He was a policeman, like so many others, but vividly etched in her mind was what he had told her about the first dead body she had seen. In quiet, even gentle tones he had made it clear to her that the victim herself had long since gone, taking her dignity with her, and that what remained was a residue—nothing more. She had never expected such an attitude, and such understanding, from a homicide detective—or from any man. As a sociologist, she thought it would be interesting to learn more about him.

The bar and grill on the north side of Sunset Boulevard, not far form downtown, was evenly divided between indoor and outdoor areas. A half-hour after noon it was well filled with men standing at the bar, sometimes with heads together in close conversation, or seated at tables in groups of three or four. All of them were young to middle-aged, some wore dark suits with white shirts and tactful ties; the great majority were in sound physical condition. The pungent atmosphere of law enforcement, contributed by many different agencies, filled every corner of the popular establishment.

Off in a corner of the outdoor patio Oliver Tracy and Frank Levitzky were huddled with Jack Harvey. All three of them had chosen their food without much thought from the limited menu; they were much more concerned with the reason for their meeting.

"Tell me something," Tracy said. "I know there are KGB agents in the Russian embassy, but how many other active Soviet spies are there around the country?"

"Several hundred," Harvey answered. "We've identified a lot of them, but there are always more. Some of them are

KGB, others are Americans who spy for them. It's all I've worked on for year."

Tracy wound some spaghetti on his fork. "Then it's a fact that there are many you don't know."

Harvey was a little terse. "Of course there are; we have to assume that. Otherwise we could go home weekends. What's your point?"

Levitzky answered so that his partner could take a moment to eat. "We're trying to put some facts together that don't want to fit. Mabel Lorimer was stabbed. In East Los Angeles that's commonplace, but not in churches."

"I heard that once, during a funeral, some gang members came charging into a church, tipped over the coffin, and dumped the body on the floor," Harvey said.

"That's true," Levitzky agreed. "It was a rival gang member being buried. But that doesn't fit this case at all."

"The point is, the medical examiner told us the stabbing had been done by a pro," Tracy said.

A police helicopter passing low overhead made conversation impossible for a few seconds. When it had gone, he continued. "We agree that the KGB wouldn't have done it, because she was a great potential asset for them—or so they thought."

"Unless," Levitzky added, "there was a leak somewhere and the Soviets knew that she was only playing along to trap them."

"We thought of that," Harvey said. "There wasn't any leak, take my word for it."

"Okay then, who did take her out?"

Harvey started on the second half of his pastrami sandwich. "Murder isn't a Federal offense," he said. "Not under these circumstances. So you tell me."

"I wish to hell we could." Tracy ate the last bit of pickle on his plate. At the bar a beeper went off. A man turned away form this drink and took the telephone that was handed to him across the bar. After a brief conversation he paid and was gone.

"One question," Levitzky said. "And open up on this one if you possibly can. Who else might be interested in Lorimer? What other espionage service?"

Harvey shook his head. "You're both cleared, so I can level with you. The answer is, we don't have a ghost of an idea."

Ralph Mott would not butt in on the work of his field investigators, but he was impatient for them to get back and report. He had some ideas of his own, and what they might be able to tell him would have a lot to do with the direction his thinking would take. He was the supervisor in charge of the Lorimer case and it was his job to call the signals.

He went to lunch at the Sybil Brand Institute for Women with Assistant Sheriff Jerry Harper who wanted to be brought up to date personally on the case. Mott gave him what he had, which was not a lot.

S.B.I. was a jail facility where the inmates prepared much of the food and served it; the salad bar was good and the portions were all that could be asked. "My field team is having lunch this noon with their FBI contact," Mott said. "Principally to ask one question. I want to know if there is any possibility of a leak from their shop that could have tipped the opposition. The Bureau man will deny it, of course, but *how* he denies it can mean a lot."

Harper had chosen a light lunch, largely from the salad bar, which allowed him the indulgence of a dessert. The inmate waitress liked him, despite the fact that he was a bigwig cop, because he still treated her like a lady and took no notice of the fact she was black. The chocolate sundae that she deposited in front of him, therefore, had four generous scoops of ice cream liberally covered with chocolate syrup and from some unknown source a generous portion of whipped cream topping. She knew that he wouldn't eat it all, probably not even half, but he would know that *she* had given it to him.

73

"What if he comes through five square?" Harper asked.

"In that case, I have three alternatives," Mott replied. He looked up at the waitress. "Have you got another of those sundaes?" he asked.

"Yes, sir!" She knew he couldn't get her any reduction of sentence, but there were privileges, such as being a waitress instead of working in the laundry.

"Then please bring it," Harper said as he dug a spoon into the concoction before him.

"First of all, Jerry, I buy Harvey's premise that the KGB would never take out a potentially valuable source of information."

"Unless they were tipped."

"Unless they were tipped," Mott repeated. "That's what we're trying to nail down right now. Personally, I very much doubt a leak form the FBI. They run too good a shop."

"I'll go along with that. Now what are your three possibilities?"

"First, some superpatriotic group could have gotten wind of it, thought she was selling out to the opposition, and took her out before she could presumably pass any information to the Russians. You understand that all I'm looking for here is a motive."

"Yes, go on. Here's your dessert."

The waitress set down a huge sundae. Mott looked at it and said, "What, no nuts?"

"We don't have any nuts, sir. Not in this place."

"No," Mott agreed, "I guess you don't. Thanks a lot."

"Lorimer was expertly stabbed," Mott added. "Some of the hard-right organizations have ex-Army people who are good at that sort of thing."

"A good point," Harper agreed. "What's your second alternative?"

"That a different intelligence organization took her out, not to shut her up, but simply to make the Soviets look bad. To let them take the fall for it, in other words."

"Possible."

"Lastly, and much more likely, someone not in the game at all went after her for a totally different reason. Remember the case a few weeks ago in San Diego when a Mexican illegal thought someone had crowded too close to him in a elevator and stabbed him. It doesn't take much to get a knife in your ribs these days, especially in East L.A."

"What's your best guess?" Harper asked.

"I don't have a guess," Mott answered. "I only know we've got a helluva lot more work to do."

The room in which he sat was not much larger than twelve feet by fourteen, but it was his domain: the almost infinitely tiny corner of the whole world that was dedicated exclusively to him, that served him in dumb obedience to his every wish, insofar as it was able. It held his body, his soul if he had one, and it walled in his secrets. Even in its limited space there were tiny places where certain things could be kept carefully out of sight.

He had no visitors and wanted none. Very occasionally someone came into his room to do essential cleaning. Because the housekeeper's efforts were not appreciated she kept them to a minimum, just as he wished. Any thorough shakedown of his room would reveal far too many things that he wanted forever hidden. Things that probable would mean nothing to an outsider, and a few that would.

Because it was coming close to the end of the day, he carefully hoarded every bit of daylight, making it last until the fragment of sky he could see lost every bit of its color and surrendered to blackness. He sat in a narrow hard chair that suited him perfectly, his hands folded on a little cheap table, and let his mind run free in that wild, kaleidoscopic world where he was the absolute master, controlling destinies, giving life and taking it away, avenging himself with his mighty authority for the times without number when he had been rejected. He did not want it all, he could not accept it all, but he did want his own fair share. And that, he knew, was reasonable and his rightful birthright as a man.

All women had so much given to them: warm comforting bodies with soft inviting breasts. All of them; millions everywhere. The few who had shared their bodies with him had been—he did not try to hide it—old, usually fat, and used up. Infinitely richer were the unspoiled young bodies that were fresh and bursting with new vitality; bodies that were given freely to handsome young studs who were allowed to glory in them, explore their every facet, and then take possession of them for the mighty fire of glorious orgasm.

He thought about them constantly; especially the fresh, new girls who were just coming into their own, but who had already been taught never to give him anything of themselves. Now each one that he took into his custody stood for thousands of others who for all of his lifetime had teased and tantalized him with their bodies, but had not allowed him near them.

He stopped his thinking and listened carefully for any sounds outside his room. When he heard nothing that threatened his total privacy, he went to his most secret hiding place and took out a cassette tape. He put it in his player, a good one he had found left in an unlocked car, and adjusted the headphones around his ears. A deadly stillness engulfed him until he turned on the player and fed in just enough volume to be certain that no sound could be heard outside.

Then he listened to the drama he had recorded. First the casual talk, then the coming of worry, of fear, the onset of demands, then the pleading. After that was over, and he savored every bit of it, the screaming began. Not just ordinary screaming as he had tortured them, but lung-bursting paroxysms of blinding agony worthy of the Inquisition.

An orgasm burst from his groin as he listened once again to what he had achieved, and to the final shrieks as he had

76

twisted the wires around their necks. His mind seemed to have left his body and was spinning in an orbit of unleashed power when there was a sharp knock on his door.

He snapped the off switch on the recorder, whipped off the headset, and slid the machine well under his bed. He opened the door to find a very large black man dressed in a brown business suit almost filling the doorway. He had an open notebook in his hand.

The black man came in without invitation and looked about. He sniffed the air for evidence of marijuana and took in the furnishings with an expert's eye. The room was at least presentably clean. "I'm your new parole officer," the black man said. "I'm trying to take some of the load off Mr. Michaels who was supervising you before. How's your job?"

"I'm working," the tenant answered. "Eight weeks now."

The black man made a quick note in his book. "Any trouble?"

"No trouble, no, sir. I've even got money. Look." He took out a badly worn wallet crammed with paper and displayed a few bills. "I'm going to save some," he added.

"That's good; maybe you're learning something, at last. How's your health?"

"I'm good—real good."

"I'm glad to hear it. You aren't selling your blood anymore, are you?"

"No, sir, I'm making good money now and there's free coffee where I work."

The black man produced a card and handed it over. "Here's where to reach me anytime you need me. You go on keeping your nose clean and you'll come out on top; you hear me?"

"I hear you."

The black man closed his notebook and slid it into a side pocket of his suit. "I'm here to help you, remember that. Do as well as you're doing now and I may be able to get you a better job. It all works out if you play it the right way."

"I will, you can bet on that."

"I am betting. See you next month."

As soon as the parole officer was gone, the man in the room retrieved his tape recorder and put it carefully away where it belonged. The cassette, which could be such damaging evidence against him, he put back in its hiding place where no one would ever find it.

Then he sat still in the growing darkness and hugged his knees in smug satisfaction. He had them all fooled, he knew that, but that wasn't all. He was no longer alone. In the dark nights of prison he had found another like himself. It had taken many cautious months to make sure, months of tentative probing, of gradual mutual admission, until at last he had been sure. It had been hard, working alone, but with a partner the prospects were unlimited. Together they could possess and punish all the women they wanted, and the very thought was enough to send him into a dream world of ecstatic rapture.

9

If Father Fernando was at all put out to have the team of sheriff's homicide investigators back on his doorstep once more, he was careful to conceal it. "It is a pleasure to see you again," he said, which was as close to lying as he was likely to come.

"We don't want to be a nuisance," Tracy explained, "but sometimes we can't help it."

"Whenever someone wishes to come to our church, we are happy to have him do so."

"Well said, Father. We have just a few more questions to ask."

Father Fernando shook his head. "I can't think of anything I haven't told you."

Levitzky put on his most sympathetic face. "Father, we know that. We only want a little more background information."

Father Fernando looked around the spare and sterile

parlor where he was receiving his guests. "I will do my best," he said.

Tracy had developed a gift for asking questions in an easy, conversational tone, one that suggested the occasion was purely social. "Father, the church is open at all times, is that right?"

"We try to keep it that way."

"So in the evening, or late at night, people can come here to meditate and pray."

"Yes. In the Lord's house all are welcome."

"Normally do these people ask for any help from you?"

"Sometimes. Usually they come in quietly, light a candle, and then sit in one of the pews for a little while."

Tracy nodded his understanding of that. "Then if I were to come here, Father, alone sometime during the evening, would anyone be likely to speak to me?"

"It would be very unlikely. Usually when people come to the church at odd times they wish to be undisturbed. We respect that."

Tracy continued. "On an evening when you aren't having any services, how many people are likely to be here, say around ten?"

"It varies, of course. Usually two or three, but it could be more, or the church could be empty."

"And during inclement weather?"

"Fewer I would think." Father Fernando shifted slightly in his stiff, uncompromising chair. "Perhaps I could help more if you were to tell me the purpose of these questions," he said.

"We have a theory, Father," Levitzky said. "We are trying to find out if it will hold water or not."

"I trust it does not reflect on the church."

"In no way, Father."

"I am relieved to hear that. What else do you wish to know?"

"If someone comes to the church at a late hour needing help, how is that handled?"

"Near the front door there is a button to press that rings a bell in here. If that happens, then one of us responds. Usually Brother Fred; that is one of his main duties. If a priest is needed, then I go."

Levitzky was carefully making notes. "This is helping us more than you know, Father," he said.

"It was a terrible thing: that poor woman murdered in our church. Of course I want to help in any way that I can."

Tracy took over. "Talking now about the night of the crime," he said. "There were probably very few people in the church."

"That is true."

"And anyone there would not be likely to notice the victim at all."

"I agree. People who seek the church at that hour usually pay little attention to anyone else."

"I believe I have the picture now, Father," Tracy said and got to his feet.

Father Fernando also stood up. "Are you any nearer to solving this terrible crime?" he asked.

"Possibly," Tracy answered.

Flavia spent most of her free morning in the microfilm newspaper files at the Los Angeles Central Library. She gradually filled several pages of a long yellow legal pad with careful notes written in her neat, legible style. She went systematically through back issues of the *Los Angeles Times* and the *Daily News* that covered the San Fernando Valley in particular. As she did so, she was careful to keep her mind focused on the facts she was noting down, not letting them get to her emotionally.

Several times she looked at her watch to be sure she would meet her one o'clock class on time. After she left the library, she reviewed her lecture notes over a quick sandwich and a glass of milk before she went to her classroom, as always a few minutes early.

She delivered her lecture and then spent the last ten

minutes of the class period fielding questions: a few of them intelligent, the others not worth the time they took. When it was all over, she stopped to refresh herself and then went to keep an appointment at the dean's office.

Miles Cargill welcomed her and then watched carefully as she sat down. He could see at once that she was not quite her normal self. There were no circles under her eyes, but she was more withdrawn than usual and sat more stiffly in her chair. "I want to hear how you are making out with the Sheriff's Department," he said.

Flavia hesitated a moment or two before she answered. "The people I've met so far have been cooperative," she began, "especially a Lieutenant Mott in Homicide. But I still feel very much like a fifth wheel. As though I'm being tolerated because they have no choice."

"I think you may be overreacting a little there," the dean said. "I probably shouldn't tell you this, but I spoke to my brother about it. He told me that they like you and your attitude. They feel that you're very sincere in what you're trying to do."

Flavia relaxed her body, sat back in her chair, and passed a hand across her face. "I've been to the scene of two murders," she began. "Both of them particularly horrible. I was advised against it by Lieutenant Mott, but I went anyway."

"Do you regret it now?"

"No, I don't, but it did take a lot out of me. Please don't tell them that."

"Of course I won't."

She gathered herself together a little. "I asked for this and I can't escape reality by turning my back."

"None of us can. Tell me, Flavia, is this helping you in your work?"

She framed her answer carefully. "Yes, I'm sure that it is. Murders to me have always been accounts in the newspapers and published statistics." She stopped and took a deep breath. "Now I've seen the bodies of two young women; both of them had been tortured and murdered. They suffered horribly."

For a moment she wasn't able to go on, then she did more slowly. "One thing that really got to me was another young woman, from the Coroner's Office. She was about my age. She was down on her hands and knees working on the body, examining it in detail."

There was no need for her to go on. "From what Jack tells me," the dean said, "a lot of the investigators and criminalists who deal with homicide are women. They're professionals and it's their job. They're very good at it."

Flavia gripped the arms of her chair and then relaxed a little once more. "I had a very strong feeling, Dean, that the people at the crime scene, and there were about fifteen of them, were just waiting for me to keel over. Maybe they were expecting to have a hysterical female on their hands." She stopped, reliving the moment in her memory. "But I made up my mind that no matter what, I wouldn't give them that satisfaction. I forced myself to keep my composure. Because if I didn't . . ." There was no need for her to finish that thought.

The dean started to speak, but she stopped him with a gesture. "Then something happened that helped me a great deal. Lieutenant Mott took me aside. I had expected him to be hard-nosed, like most cops, but he was sympathetic. He told me quietly that the body wasn't the murdered girl anymore, and not to think of it in that way. She had gone, free of all pain and suffering. He wasn't religious about it, but he did make me feel a lot better. At first I couldn't wait to get away from there. After he talked to me, I was determined to see it through, so I stayed until they took the body away."

"Good for you," the dean said. "I think you may have learned a lot."

"I did. The second time it wasn't quite so bad. Bad enough, though."

"Flavia, do you want to go on with this?"

"Dean, I have to. I'm not going to give up and become a weak-kneed female. Remember, I'm trying to do whatever I possibly can about all this, because I can't tolerate the idea of such things happening."

"No one would dispute you there, but what has this got to do with your main focus—the parole system?"

She returned to her own professional attitude. "I spent the morning at the library, Dr. Cargill, and I'd like to summarize what I found. These are items from the last few weeks taken from newspaper accounts. I'm not looking for comparative statistics here, only case histories."

"I understand."

Flavia consulted her notes.

"A Los Angeles man convicted of manslaughter was paroled. Within the next month he murdered three more people. He offered to plead guilty to escape the gas chamber. Another man convicted of killing his three children had his death sentence voided by the California Supreme Court. He was released from prison, God knows why. He's now being sought for killing a woman in front of her three-year-old daughter.

"Two men paroled from state prison committed four murders during a single month. They were originally sentenced for attempted murder and assault with a deadly weapon."

The dean interrupted her. "The California parole laws are a mess, we all know that. But go ahead."

Flavia did in an even, factual voice. "Here is a man described by the police as 'extremely dangerous.' He was convicted of a series of crimes against women in the San Fernando Valley; he used ice picks, knives, and guns. After being paroled he invaded the room of a seventeen-year-old blind girl, choked her roommate senseless, then held a knife to the blind girl's throat while he raped her. He told her, 'You're white and I'm going to teach you a lesson.' He said he was on parole for robbery and had nothing to lose."

Flavia looked up, then laid her carefully written notes in front of the dean. "Read for yourself," she invited.

With full understanding the dean picked up the pad and read out loud in his calm, professional voice. "A man on parole for grand theft of guns was rearrested for sexual assaults on thirteen women, including forced oral copulation. A convicted murderer was paroled; within two months he killed his former girl friend's husband and his two sons. He murdered them with a shotgun at point-blank range. God!" he said.

Flavia brushed her hair back as though to clear her mind, then took back her notes. "Listen to this one. A man with a long history of criminal activity was released on parole. He went on a four-month crime rampage that included rape, sodomy, armed robbery, and murder. He's back in prison, but that doesn't help any of his twenty-three victims, including a man he murdered so that he could rob his corpse."

"Can you handle all this?" the dean asked.

"I have to, Dr. Cargill. Believe it or not, there are court decisions here in California that require annual parole hearings for hundreds of convicted murderers."

The dean raised a hand. "Flavia, grim as these case histories are, you haven't taken into account the parolees who stay out of trouble and successfully return to society."

"That's true, Dr. Cargill, but let me quote from the Rand study on probation: 'Most felons who are out on probation use their freedom to commit more crimes.' The study calls them 'a serious threat to the public.' It suggests that the whole system may be breaking down."

The dean remained silent for several moments. When he spoke again, his voice was firm but cautious: "Flavia, you've got hold of something, there's no room to doubt that. It's an intensely hot topic and going to get more so. But if your book is widely read, which it very well may be, have you considered the personal danger this may put you in? These same desperate criminals you've been telling me about must want the parole system to continue as it is. The good people will cheer you, but the others may be after your hide."

"I know," Flavia answered, "but I won't turn back now."

"You're sure of that?"

She clenched her fists, closed her eyes, and saw again the body of the first horribly murdered girl that had so traumatically affected her. "I'm sure," she answered.

"I don't want to press the point," the dean said, "but I've always considered you to be very liberal in your thinking. Now you seem to be changing your viewpoint."

It was silent in the office for several seconds. The atmosphere of the campus that normally filled the room seemed to have been banished by the things that had just been said. There was no way they could be reconciled with a great institution dedicated to providing higher education to thousands of students of every kind and description.

Miles Cargill faced a problem. Flavia was a professional in her field, and that status, he knew, should not be affected by the fact that she was a woman. But hard practical reality forced him to acknowledge that she was unusually attractive and therefore perhaps dangerously unsuited to the task she had set for herself. With the authority of his position he could put a stop to it; for her sake he seriously wondered if he should.

The quiet of his thoughts was interrupted by a sharp beeping sound. Flavia reached for a telephone. "I have to call in," she said.

"Exactly what does that mean?" the dean asked.

Flavia pushed buttons on the phone. "It means there's been another murder," she said.

10

Captain Robert Grimm walked into the main Homicide Bureau room and spoke to the deputy who was manning "the barrel," the desk that took all the incoming calls. "What have we got going?" he asked.

The deputy understood that to mean anything new within the last hour or so. The captain had been in a high-level meeting with Jerry Harper and Assistant Sheriff Bob Edmonds where certain policies were discussed.

"Not very much, Captain," the barrel man told him. "We have a case down in Walnut Park: female victim, black, thirty to thirty-five. Could be suicide."

"Who's handling it?"

"Miriam and Willie." The barrel man hesitated and then added, "I also alerted Flavia; she's responding."

"Oh, shit!" the captain said.

The barrel man pointed to a notice posted prominently

on the board in front of him. "The word I have is to call her whenever we get one," he said.

"Then I'll change that right now," Grimm said. "Otherwise she'll become a damn nuisance in a hurry, granted that she's got great tits. Before she's alerted, check with Ralph Mott or with me."

The barrel man was quick to cover his ass. "As of now," he said, and took down the notice to add the notation.

Grimm was the kind of man who always backed his people, particularly when they were right. "Flavia is a privileged character for the time being, but we can't have her responding every time we have a bar fight and another dead Mexican in the street. She's Ralph's pigeon."

The barrel man nodded that he understood. He had been following orders and the captain knew that.

"Is it his case?"

"No. Lieutenant Gordon."

"I don't think Darrell's ever met her."

"I can beep her and turn her off."

"It's probably too late for that. Nobody will know her when she get's there and she hasn't any ID. She won't get past the tapes."

The barrel man posted the revised notice back on the bulletin board.

As she drove south on the Harbor Freeway, Flavia fervently hoped she would not have to face another scene as bad as the last one had been. She had managed to hold herself under control that time, but she was not sure she could do it again. To keep her mind busy she concentrated on the exit signs as they went past; when she was well down in south central Los Angeles she turned off and began to follow the directions she had been given over the phone.

The whole neighborhood, she noted, was black. As she drove on, block after block, there was not a white face to be seen. The whole atmosphere was different, as though she had crossed the border into a different country. The billboards all featured black models selling cigarettes, trips to Las Vegas, liquor, and cosmetics. There were more people than normal on the streets and around their small houses.

She pulled up in front of the address she had been given and locked her car with extra care. It wasn't that she distrusted blacks, only that she knew the whole surrounding area was heavily crime ridden, so much so that several major supermarkets had had to close and move out. Even with the best security precautions they had been able to install, they had been unable to control the theft and vandalism that had forced them out of business.

She had been told to go to the second house on the lot. Fortunately there was an alleyway toward the rear; as she walked down it she encountered a dense crowd of sightseers close to the orange tapes that marked off the crime scene. The second house was tiny with one more behind it on the same lot; the available land had been used to the maximum. Flavia worked her way through the mass of sightseers and ducked under the tape.

A very young deputy intercepted her almost at once. "You can't come in here," he said. "Back behind the tape."

Flavia sensed his nervousness. "I'm Dr. de la Torre," she said. "Homicide called me to come here a half-hour ago."

The deputy looked at her. "Let's see your sheriff's ID," he said.

She realized abruptly that she had not been given one. Then she remembered her beeper. She took it out of her purse and handed it over, bottom up to show the sheriff's sticker on the back. The deputy looked at it, hesitated, then waved her toward the door.

It opened into a very small living room, hardly eight by ten feet. Another deputy was sitting on a decrepit sofa filling out paperwork. When he looked up she asked, "What have you got?" She had picked up that police expression somewhere and found it useful.

"Lady in there committed suicide," the deputy said. He didn't know her and was clearly being cautious.

Flavia did her best to assume a clinical detachment. She focused her mind on what Mott had told her: that a body was not a person, only the husk that remained after the seed was gone.

She took a few steps into the tiny bedroom and found herself inches from another nude body, this one half leaning against a thin closet wall. The victim was a black female, "well nourished" in police terminology. Her legs were sprawled apart, exposing her vagina and generous pubic hair. There were two detectives in the room who were paying no attention at all to the body; they were carefully gathering evidence from the top of a carelessly made bed and the drawers of a narrow dresser.

There was very little blood this time. Trying to put herself in a detective's place, Flavia studied the body. When alive the victim had been fairly tall and ripe-figured—probably sexy. There was a small black hole in her abdomen, a second in her throat, and a third almost in the middle of her forehead.

On the dresser there were a number of coin sleeves for wrapping up small change. Apart from them, there was a usual amount of cosmetics, some of them expensive brands. Flavia stood quietly for some time, trying to see as much as she could. Every bit of possible space in the little house was crammed full; the narrow closet was jammed to overflowing.

When she had finished looking she went back into the small parlor where the deputy was still carefully printing in block letters.

He looked up, evaluating her. "It's a suicide," he said.

Flavia shook her head. "I don't think so."

"You from the crime lab?"

"The university."

"I'm Tony."

"Flavia."

90

"Nice name. Mexican?"

"No. Spanish."

"Actually, this is the first homicide I've been on. Somebody shot her all right."

Flavia sensed that he could have said more if he had wished. "Who found the body?" she asked.

"Her financial advisor. He's supposed to have come to see her every day for the last five years."

"That's a lot of financial advice. Was the door open?"

"He had a key."

"Oh."

"Yeah, but there's no telling for sure. My partner and I are the responding unit, so we're here to protect the scene."

"Is Lieutenant Mott coming?"

"I don't know him."

"Then I guess I might as well go."

The deputy gave her an agreeable smile. "Thanks for stopping by," he said.

As she left the crime scene, the crowd opened up a little to let her through. The faces were all black, but they were curious, not hostile. She unlocked her car, relocked it after she was inside, and drove away with a strong sense of relief. Part of it was leaving behind her the dead woman in the bedroom, much of it was escaping the environment of packed-in humanity where she could not distinguish between the many decent people and those who would grab her purse in a moment if they had the chance.

Because some unanswered questions were bothering her, she drove up the freeway to the downtown area, got off at Third Street, and wove her way through the traffic to the Hall of Justice. The parking lot had been fairly well cleaned out; when she drove in and displayed her beeper, she was waved on and told to be sure and leave the keys in her car.

She took the elevator to the seventh floor and once more pushed open the ancient doors that let her in to the Homicide Bureau. She didn't remember either of the men at the front desk, but they both obviously knew her. "Is Lieutenant Mott here?" she asked.

"Just came in, Doctor. I'll tell him you're here."

She wished she had been able to stop and at least fix her hair, but she hadn't thought of that in time. It didn't really matter, considering what these men were accustomed to seeing. She wondered a little what their private lives were like.

Ralph Mott appeared in his shirt-sleeves, his tie still carefully knotted in place. She wondered if he had tightened it up for her benefit. "I hope this is convenient," she said.

"Actually, I'm glad you showed. Come on in. Have you been down in the triangle?"

Even though she didn't know what the triangle was, she grasped his meaning. She sat down with a sense of partial security and relief. "I'm beginning to wonder how many homicide victims are nude females," she said.

"A lot of them, Flavia. I don't have to tell you why, that's your field. The man who found the body told us that this was a suicide."

Flavia shook her head. "It isn't possible."

Mott studied her. "Why?"

"The victim was shot three times."

"Was the gun next to her?"

"Yes, it was, but someone else used it." She didn't hesitate to go on. "She was shot in the stomach, the throat, and in the middle of her forehead. All in a row. Even I know that people don't shoot themselves in the stomach, it's too horribly painful. And I don't think that they hold a gun against their throats. That would be fatal, wouldn't it?"

"Very likely, yes. Especially if the bullet went through the spinal column."

"Then she couldn't have done that and then shot herself in the head. Especially right in the center of her forehead, where the third eye is supposed to be. I assume that would have killed her almost instantly."

"Your point is that if she had shot herself in the head first, she wouldn't have survived to shoot herself twice more."

"Of course not. And if she had shot herself in the stomach, which I don't believe, she would have been in terrible pain. To end it she might have shot herself then in the head, but certainly not in the throat."

Mott was clearly interested in what she was saying. "Did you observe anything else?"

"You're a detective, not me, but if that poor woman wanted to shoot herself, I don't think she'd hold a gun in front of her forehead; it would probably take two hands. I've read that suicides usually shoot themselves in the side of the head, or else put the end of the gun in their mouths. To make sure that it will be instantaneous, and that they won't suffer."

"You're right about that," Mott said. "What else?"

Flavia hesitated for a moment. "I don't know anything about powder burns, just that they exist. But the skin around the bullet holes didn't show anything unusual. It was very dark skin, but I think powder burns might have shown anyway."

"Yes, they would," Mott agreed. He took his time, sensing that she needed to relax and giving her the opportunity. "What do you think she did for a living?" he asked.

"I saw something, but I'm not sure how to interpret it. You know the paper sleeves that banks use for wrapping up rolls of coins? She had a lot of them on her dresser."

"Were there any bowls of coins, anything like that?"

"No. And she lived alone, at least there were no men's things around, and no place at all where they could have been hidden."

"She might have been a prostitute," Mott suggested, and watched for her reaction.

"Prostitutes don't do business in small change I would think," Flavia said.

Mott looked at the surface of his desk and smiled, almost

to himself. "You've got the makings of a good detective," he said. "Would you like to become a reservist?"

"No thanks." Flavia shook her head.

"You support law enforcement."

"Of course. It's essential in any democracy. But it's also been abused. Just think of South Africa."

In Mott's mind an idea was forming; he took a few moments to consider it. "Flavia, we have a case going right now that may have some international implications. It's a homicide, but very different from those you've been to see. I have two of my best people working on it right now. How would you like to go into the field with them for a day or two?"

Before she could answer he added a little more. "You can see how a homicide investigation is conducted. It's very different from scene-of-the-crime activity. It's patiently chasing down leads, conducting interviews, doing research, and fitting together pieces of information."

"Wouldn't I be in the way?" Flavia asked.

"No, I don't think so. If we don't want you somewhere, we'll tell you. But it may help you to understand the job we do here: all the careful, tedious digging that's the essence of real detective work."

"It's inviting, but my real interest is in the parole system."

"I know that. We're in constant contact with parole officers; you may get a chance to see how they work, too."

"Will they have me?" Flavia asked.

Mott allowed himself to review her appearance. "I think they might manage," he said. "Frank Levitzky is a very interesting fellow and a top detective. His partner's Dick Tracy."

Flavia didn't bite on that.

"Actually, we've met," she said. "I'll see if I can clear the time."

"With a dean on your side, you ought to be able to work it out."

Flavia let her tensions ease. "I'm looking forward to working with Dick Tracy," she said.

When Ernie Wright answered his door and discovered that the detectives from Sheriff's Homicide were back, he wasn't too surprised.

"Come in," he said to the man in front. "I know your name's Tracy, but I've forgotten your partner's."

"Frank Levitzky," Tracy supplied.

"Of course, sorry. You probably want to talk with Marie. She's here."

Tracy followed his host inside and sat in the same chair he had used before. Frank Levitzky did the same. When Marie Wright came in, both men stood up, a little awkwardly. Her expression was tense and tight. "Have you found anything out?" she asked before anyone else could speak.

"We've been working very hard on the case of your sister," Levitzky answered. "And the FBI is cooperating. We haven't got it wrapped up yet, no ma'm, but we're keeping right after it."

Ernie Wright saw to it that everyone sat down. "I'm sure you'll succeed," he said. "How can we help you now?"

Tracy wished fervently that all the people they had to interview were as understanding and cooperative. "We do have a few more questions," he began. Actually there was only one key question in his mind, but he knew better than to ask it right away. Instead he probed for information about Mabel Lorimer's taste in clothing and food and about the kinds of recreation she had preferred. Levitzky supported him by taking careful notes; also there was the possibility that something might come to light when it was least expected.

When the time seemed right, Tracy put the question he had come to ask, making it one more in a series. "The last time we were here you told us how diligent Mrs. Lorimer was in going to work. Was she usually prompt in keeping her appointments?"

Marie cut in to answer that. "More than prompt," she said. "She was never late for anything." She paused to choose the right words. "Usually she was early. If she went to a reception, say, from five to seven, right at five she'd be there. I tried to tell her that wasn't expected, but she never changed."

"It's possible, then, that she might have been early for her appointment—in East Los Angeles."

"Probably she would be," Ernie added. "Because of the bad weather, and not knowing the area, she would have left early. She had a real horror of ever being late, as Marie said."

Tracy wound things down during the next three or four minutes and cleared the way for them to leave. When they were back in the car and had driven away, Levitzky spoke. "You got the answer we wanted," he said.

Tracy wove past another car in traffic. "Right. Now all we have to do is make it pay off."

When she had finished at the Homicide Bureau, Flavia called at Chief Cargill's office to see if by any chance he was in. He was, and like many busy executives he managed to find the time to be courteous to an unexpected visitor. "How are things going for you?" he asked. The question was general enough to allow her plenty of latitude in answering.

"I'm learning a great deal," she answered. "I've been to three homicides so far. Two of them, I think, are related."

"The strangling of young women."

"Yes. Chief Cargill, I called to ask if I may read some of the recent crime reports involving major felonies, such as rape, attack with a deadly weapon, armed robbery, and the like."

"For what reason, Doctor?"

"Please call me Flavia; everyone else here does. Until

recently, most of what I knew about crime came from statistical reports. I've already changed my mind on a number of things. I want to know more about what crime really is, then maybe I'll be able to write with more authority."

"That's logical," Cargill said. "Are you willing to undergo a background check?"

"Yes, of course."

Cargill reached for a block of paper and made a note. "Flavia, if I give you access to some of our confidential records, you'll have to observe absolute discretion. Particularly concerning any cases that haven't been adjudicated."

Flavia clasped her purse a little more tightly in her hands. "Chief Cargill, I've had extensive training in case histories. In the literature they're always anonymous unless they've become a matter of public record, like the Boston Strangler or the Chessman case."

"True, Flavia, but it goes further than that. For example, what Chessman did to some of his victims has never been made public, and I hope never will. But it's in the reports."

"I see." She had not realized how much she was asking. "Let me put it this way: if I may study these reports, you can depend on my total discretion. Also, I won't publish anything I learn from them until someone on your staff has cleared it first."

Cargill studied her for a brief moment. "On that basis, Flavia, I'm willing to give you some access where you need it. You'll have to be checked out first; that's standard procedure."

"Thank you. May I ask your advice on something?"

"Of course."

"I was sent to a homicide scene in the Walnut Park area. A deputy referred to it as the triangle."

"Yes, what we call the Bermuda Triangle. It's a high crime area that's bounded by three of our stations: Carson, Lynwood, and Firestone."

"When I got there, I didn't know anyone. They asked me for credentials."

"Did you get in?"

"Yes, I mentioned Lieutenant Mott and showed them my beeper. That's all I had."

Cargill made another note. "I'll see about getting some sort of temporary ID issued for you. Before you leave, go to the Identification Bureau. Have them take your prints, and get your picture taken. They'll be expecting you."

"Thank you very much."

Cargill leaned back in his chair. Behind him, on a table against the wall, there was an assortment of pictures. There were several of attractive girls and a larger one of a strikingly beautiful woman. There were also pictures of a forest cabin, a sailboat, and a group of men in scuba gear and wet suits.

"Flavia, I have a question for you. How deep do you want to get into this?"

She looked again at the pictures on display. "I can swim," she said, "but I can't scuba dive." Then she looked very earnestly at the chief who obviously could. "But I can learn," she added.

"All right, Flavia," the chief said. "You asked for it."

11

On the outside the van was a rather drab sand color. A hot custom job, with multi-colored flames streaming back, would have suited the owner's taste much better, but to get something you had to give something and he wanted the van to be as inconspicuous and hard to describe as possible.

Inside the van it was a different story. The plush interior was the flashiest and most luxurious-appearing one the custom shop could provide. It had cost a lot of money, but the van had a very particular purpose that made it necessary. The owner had ordered a special compartment to be three and a half by six and a half feet or thereabouts and deep enough to hold two surfboards. That was a new one, but the designer managed it without too much trouble. If rich kids wanted to spend their money with him he was all for it, although the owner in this case was a little too old for that sort of thing. But you never knew.

As the owner drove the van he kept within acceptable speeds. He also carefully observed the stop signs and waited out the lights until the green was on. Since he was on parole for the second time, he didn't want to run the risk of involvement in any incident that would call attention to himself. Despite what some people thought, cops were everywhere.

Next to the van, his partner, who was riding on the right beside him, was his greatest asset. Finding him had been a miracle, but in the dark of the prison nights they had talked to one another until mutual understanding had been reached. There was no chance that he was an undercover cop; if the driver had had any lingering doubts at all, after the first pickup they were answered. He had learned that his partner was more ruthless than himself, something he had not thought possible.

Nobody would have guessed it because his partner had such clean-cut, handsome looks. Whenever he walked down the beach, the women all stared at him, at his smooth, well-muscled body. Whenever he stopped, they seemed to come out of the ground to be near him.

"I thought of one more thing," the driver said. "Whenever we're out together like this, you're Harry and I'm Joe. Got it?"

His partner looked at him. "Why? There's not gonna be any witnesses."

"I know, but things happen. Like a kid lying in the bushes, hearing us talkin'."

"Okay with me," his partner said. "I'm Harry." He was experienced in using names other than his own, so it was no effort for him.

"And call me Joe all the time. It don't cost nothin' and it's safer."

"Sure, Joe, no problem."

The van cruised on down the street while the driver kept his eyes open. Things had to be done just right, otherwise there could be danger.

After some time his partner said, "I think we got it."

"Where?"

"The pizza place. Pull up."

The driver did. Already the expectation of another capture was creating a tension in his groin, the same sensation he felt when he looked down from high places.

When the van had stopped, his partner got out and opened the side door so the elaborate interior could be seen. "Get a big one with a lot of topping," he said. "The kind the chicks like. I'll look after business while you're inside."

When the driver came out with the pizza, his partner was already talking with a girl. She was a good-looking brunette in shorts and a halter top. He liked the shape of her ass and the promising curves of her hips.

"Here we are," his partner said with enthusiasm. "The best pizza around here anywhere." He took it out of the box and slid it on the table in the back of the van.

"Smells good!" the girl said, and climbed inside.

Ten minutes later they drove away.

When Ralph Mott was summoned to see Chief Cargill, he was more than happy to go. He had something he wanted to ask of the chief and in a face-to-face meeting he could bring it up without having to go through channels.

Cargill knew Mott well and respected his abilities. Since it was not his style to pull rank on anybody unless it was necessary, he made Mott comfortable and put the meeting on a man-to-man basis. After two or three minor matters were covered, the chief brought up the thing that was on his mind. "How is de la Torre doing?" he asked.

Mott had no trouble with that. "Pretty well. You passed the word not to hold back, so the first one we let her in on was the victim in Big Tujunga Canyon. It was on the tough side, but she handled it all right."

"Maybe she had had some previous experience," Cargill suggested.

"I doubt it," Mott said. "At least I got that feeling when we talked at the crime scene. She was shook up all right, but she kept herself under control."

"Is she learning anything?"

"Yes. Whether it'll help her any in her parole project, I don't know."

"Ralph, I called you in to say that if she's in the way, I'll get rid of her for you. She's been to three homicides now; maybe that's enough."

That was a clear open door, but for some reason he didn't himself know, Mott declined to walk through. "She behaves well," he said. "We might as well let her run on a little, get a little more seasoning. She may tire of it soon enough."

"I see." The chief opened a desk drawer where there was a pack of cigarettes and then closed it again. "She's damn good-looking. I don't know too much about her personality."

"She might work out in the technical reserve," Mott suggested.

"Like that, huh? Then she's yours for a while longer. Go ahead: improve the shining hour if you can."

Mott let that pass. "I'm putting her in the field with one of my teams," he said, "so she can see some of the pure sweat we go through."

"Not in any dangerous situations," Cargill warned.

"Of course not. I don't want to get her ass blown off, even though she did sign a waiver. Can we talk about something else?"

"Shoot."

Mott got down to business. "Everything we've got so far on the Tujunga Canyon case and another one that followed it makes them look connected. I think we've got a serial killer, possibly one as bad as the Hillside Strangler or the Night Stalker."

"Go on."

"You know how much effort it took to put those bastards

in high power.* And how many lives were lost before we got them. This time I don't want to wait so long. I suggest we set up a task force A.S.A.P. Both cases so far were in our jurisdiction, but that's no guarantee."

Cargill saw the sense of that immediately. "Okay, I agree with you," he said. "Go ahead and set it up with L.A.P.D. and whoever else you want in. On a standby basis. If we get another one, or they do, then we'll go full bore. Does that do it?"

"That's what I wanted," Mott said.

Sitting at a desk on one side of the huge Homicide Bureau, Flavia stopped her reading to fight down a wave of strong self-doubt that was flooding over her. She was going carefully through a stack of files that had at first annoyed her, then frustrated her, and now angered her. Angered her because of their content, and also because they challenged some of her most strongly held thoughts and beliefs.

She was a professional woman, she told herself. She had earned a doctorate in her chosen field. She was on the faculty of a prestigious university. But the files she had been reading seemed to be telling her, one after another, that she was a neophyte as far as actual crime was concerned.

She looked again at the one that was open before her. The incident had occurred at a small mom-and-pop grocery store in East Los Angeles. A Hispanic man had been in the store, buying a few things, when a seventeen-year-old had come in. Both had reached at the same time for the last package of two marshmallow-filled cupcakes, a small item worth only a few cents. The youth had claimed it, but the man had insisted that it was his. There was a brief argument, according to a witness, then the youth had snapped open a switchblade knife and stabbed the man in the abdomen.

*The jail within a jail, where the most dangerous inmates are segregated under very high security.

103

The victim had been rushed to U.C.M.C., but he had died on the way. The youth had escaped. The soggy, day-old cupcake had remained on the shelf.

Official statistics in various scientific publications reported on homicides; she had read them exhaustively. But the sterile figures had told her nothing about how a man had died for the sake of two cupcakes. Flavia held her head in her hands and wondered a very old question: what was the world coming to?

It hadn't been the cupcakes, she realized, as much as the ego drive: *macho* was the word in use. The youth had killed to assert his importance. If he were caught, his punishment would probably be minimal because of his age.

By law, she knew, he was a juvenile and therefore entitled to special treatment. According to the file his probable identity was known, but he was a hard-core gang member and the owner of the small store was afraid to make a positive identification.

The handling deputy had enclosed a sheet on him. Among other things, he was the known father of at least three children. He had been arrested for rape but had not been convicted. Other charges against him had been mugging, grand theft auto, and assault with a deadly weapon. He would be eighteen in another four months. His street name was Flaco. At the time of the incident, he had been on probation for the third time.

Flavia closed her eyes, trying to banish images she could not face. Then she gathered herself together and opened the next file; she had never believed that by closing her eyes she could make things go away.

Because East Los Angeles is a high crime area where gang activity is intense, the Sheriff's Department keeps almost double the usual number of patrol units on the street. Calls for backup are frequent with response usually only seconds away. In critical situations additional support is available from the Special Enforcement Bureau that is headquartered directly behind the East L.A. Station.

Deputy Ed Valdez had been working East L.A. for more than two years, enough time so that he knew every street and alleyway, every gang hangout, and hundreds of other details to help him in his job. He had spotted a green Chevrolet parked close to St. Gregory's and made a mental note. When he saw it there again the next day, he turned to his partner, Frank Mullins. "Run the plate," he said.

It was unnecessary; Frank already had the microphone in his hand.

The car came back to a Mrs. Mabel Irene Lorimer.

As soon as he heard that name, Frank advised dispatch that the owner had been a recent 187 victim at St. Gregory's.

That started a swift chain of events. Orders were immediately given to hook the car up as evidence and take it to the sheriff's garage. That meant that it would be handled carefully and taped off until the homicide and lab people came to check it out.

Tracy and Levitzky got the word within minutes. As a matter of courtesy, Tracy called Jack Harvey at the FBI and told him that the car had been recovered.

"Shall we go and have a look?" Levitzky asked.

Before Tracy could respond, Ralph Mott came by. "When are you going back in the field?" he asked.

"Right now," Levitzky said. "They've just picked up Mrs. Lorimer's car in East L.A."

"You've both met de la Torre. The chief wants her to have some investigative experience. Would you mind taking her along?"

As soon as the chief was mentioned the verdict was in. "Okay," Tracy said. All three of them knew he had no choice, but Mott had done him the courtesy to ask.

"I'll talk to her," Mott volunteered, "then send her over. Give me five."

"No sweat," Levitzky confirmed.

105

Mott went to the desk where Flavia was working. He didn't bother to tighten up his loose-hanging tie; she was no longer on special-visitor status. "Flavia, you've met Sergeant Tracy and Detective Levitzky. They're two of the best we have. They're going out to look at a car that was just brought in. I think you should go with them. They'll fill you in on the case as you go."

Flavia responded very positively to that. "Just as soon as I put these files away . . ."

"You can leave them there," Mott interrupted. He reached in his pocket. "An ID's been made up for you," he said. "It identifies you as a technical advisor to the Department. It doesn't give you any police powers, you're not trained for that, and no compensation, but it will get you past our perimeters." He handed over a small oblong card sealed in plastic. It had on it a description of Flavia and her photograph. The word *Sheriff* was prominently displayed.

Mott bent over and clipped it on the edge of her jacket. "Don't lose it," he cautioned. "It's an official ID."

Flavia got up quickly. "Thank you," she said. "Am I working for you now?"

"If you want it that way."

"Yes, I do."

"Then let's go."

Feeling very much like the third oar in the water, Flavia rode down in the elevator with the homicide team and followed the two men out onto the parking lot. When Levitzky indicated a plain tan car, she quickly got into the back seat to avoid being in the way. Tracy gave her a good mark for it.

As soon as they were rolling, Levitzky turned around in his seat and laid out for her the known data about the murder of Mrs. Lorimer. The fact that she had been issued an official ID, even though it was a type he had never seen before, eased his mind. He even included the important item that the victim had worked for the Government in a highly confidential capacity.

Flavia listened carefully, storing the facts away in her mind. When Levitzky had finished he asked, "Any questions?"

"Yes. If Mrs. Lorimer parked her car before she went into the church and never came out alive, how can her car tell us anything?" she said "us" without thinking.

"For one thing," Levitzky answered, "she could have had a memo in the car giving the address and time. That would confirm the fact that she went there by appointment. Since she was used to handling classified material, she probably wouldn't leave very much lying around, but you never know."

"I see," Flavia said.

At that moment the radio beeped three times and then put out a call. Tracy, who was driving, unclipped his mike and acknowledged.

Flavia could not understand the radio clearly, but apparently both men did. Much of what was said was in code. Tracy slowed and executed a U turn that slid Flavia well across the seat.

"Sorry about that," Levitzky said, "but we've got another one. It's a female, apparently strangled like the other two. But this time she was thrown over the side of a cliff near Malibu."

12

For several blocks Flavia sat quietly, trying to overcome a growing apprehension she could not dispel. She wished almost desperately that she could take refuge in her small apartment where everything would be peaceful and quiet. On the previous occasions she had had a chance to prepare herself to face a homicide scene; now she was being taken to another one whether she wanted to go or not.

She was unaware that Frank Levitzky had turned in his seat and was looking at her. When he spoke, his voice was surprisingly gentle and understanding. "If you'd like," he said, "we can swing by the Hall of Justice and drop you off at your car. There's no need for you to be in on this one. We may be tied up for hours."

She was surprised at his understanding. He was a sizable man, but so calm in his manner it was hard for her to grasp the fact that he was a policeman, let alone a homicide detective. He was dressed neatly enough, but his brown suit was clearly off the rack and his shirt midrange J.C. Penney. His head was well shaped, but much of his hair was gone: there were only a few strands in the center, which he had carefully combed over the top of his scalp. If there was a woman in his life, she wasn't taking very good care of him.

Flavia understood that he had just given her a golden opportunity, but her pride would not let her accept it. Instead she said, "I'll come along, if you don't mind."

Then a saving thought hit her, a way out that would keep her from betraying her weakness. "But that would put you out. You'd have to come all the way back to get my car."

Tracy, who was driving, had not been following the conversation; he heard only the last part. "That's okay," he said. "We have to come back anyway. This is a county car."

He meant it to be considerate. A small sharp blow on his right leg from his partner's foot woke him up, but it was too late. "Just keep on going," Flavia said. "I'm all right."

She sat still for a short while and then asked the question that was on her mind. "Are there always so many of these . . . killings?"

Frank Levitzky turned once more to answer her. "I'm afraid so. A hundred of us are kept pretty busy in Sheriff's Homicide alone. Then you have to add to that the cases handled by L.A.P.D. and all the other jurisdictions in the county: Burbank, Glendale, Pasadena, Beverly Hills, Santa Monica, and lots more."

"So many murders!"

"Yes, too many altogether."

"One would be too many."

"I can't argue with that."

Tracy decided to redeem himself. He was by no means slow; he had simply been concentrating almost entirely on his driving. "A lot of the cases we handle are what we call walk-throughs. That's where there's no doubt from the beginning who did it and why. We often get a quick confession, although we can't always use it in court."

"Why not?"

"For a variety of reasons, Flavia, the main one being that our legal system is all screwed up. Right now the two biggest disasters in California history are the San Francisco earthquake and our present State Supreme Court." He remembered then that he was talking to a potential author. "Of course that's just one cop's opinion," he quickly added.

When she saw that Levitzky was still waiting for her to speak, she said what was on her mind. "I was thinking about those two young girls that were both killed . . . so horribly."

Levitzky understood. "No, Flavia, that doesn't happen all the time, thank God. What we're afraid of right now is that we may have another serial killer on our hands. The case we're going on may or may not be connected to the other two."

That raised an image in her mind that terrified her, and she could not talk anymore.

At Topanga Canyon Tracy exited the Venture Freeway and turned toward the mountains that form a barrier between the western end of the San Fernando Valley and the ocean. After a few blocks the urban grid ended and the road began a winding climb through the foothills.

The day was bright, sunny, and warm. The sky overhead was clear; the air fresh and clean. Flavia fixed her mind on those supporting elements and let her naturally romantic nature respond to the increasingly rural atmosphere that was beginning to appear. Tracy drove at a very moderate speed, taking the curves so easily she was hardly aware of them. She wished that they could stop the car so that she could get out and walk in the welcoming sunshine.

The car continued on as the mountains became higher and steeper. Then, as they closed in, the road clung halfway up on the side of a deep gorge, two or three hundred feet above the bottom. It called for careful driving as the curves grew sharper and more frequent.

In the middle of a short straight section there was a wide grassy shoulder. Two black-and-white sheriff's cars were pulled up with a four-wheel-drive vehicle and three ordinary-appearing cars. As the traffic automatically slowed while each driver did his best to see what was going on, Tracy carefully signaled and then used a gap in the opposing traffic to cross to the other side where he could park.

"Motherfucker!" someone shouted, and blasted his horn. Not content with that, he jerked a finger in the air.

Ignoring that, Levitzky spoke over his shoulder. "Check your ID."

With uncertain fingers Flavia verified that her newly issued card was securely clipped on her jacket. The beauty of the day lost its hold on her as she realized where she was and why she had come. Levitzky opened the rear door to let her out.

There were several people gathered on the narrow grass strip. Tracy spoke to a man in a business suit and then turned to Flavia. "She's down at the bottom of the ravine," he said. "You'd better stay up here right now."

When she walked to the edge and looked over, Flavia realized that it was at least a 60-degree angle down to the bottom. As she backed away her attention was caught by an energetic female deputy in uniform who was busy tying one end of a rope to the four-wheel-drive vehicle. She was doing it with the sure hands of an expert. Her build, although not heavy, was firmer than many of the other women Flavia knew. Her motions as she continued her work had a decisiveness that proved her competence. She wore a shoulder patch that read MOUNTAIN RESCUE. Around her waist she had a belt of equipment.

When the deputy had finished securing the rope and had

111

given it a quick check, she picked up a brown canvas bag that apparently held the rest of the rope and after a preliminary testing swing she threw it well out over the face of the cliff. Flavia watched as the rope went down, spinning out of the canvas holding bag as it bounced against the steep terrain. Then the deputy asked Flavia, "Are you going down?"

"I don't think so," she answered.

"Not in those shoes, anyway," the deputy said flatly. "I've got an extra jump suit in my truck and I may have some shoes that'll do you, I usually carry an extra pair."

As Flavia tried to think of the right words to say, the deputy interrupted her thought. "Are you checked out on rappeling?"

"No."

"Then don't try it. This is all decomposed granite, the trickiest stuff on earth to deal with if you're not used to it." The deputy had no more time for conversation; she passed the rope under one of her thighs, across her body, and over the opposite shoulder. She slipped on a pair of leather-faced gloves, let the rope slide through her hands as she backed up, and then with total self-confidence launched herself over the edge. Flavia watched, fascinated, as the deputy let herself rapidly down the irregular face of the cliff. Opposite her, a male deputy was descending with even more speed. He was doing it by pushing himself sharply away from the steep face and then dropping thirty feet or more before his body swung back and his feet took the shock of the impact.

Flavia felt a hand on her shoulder. Startled for a moment, she turned to find Ralph Mott standing beside her. "I heard you were shanghaied out here," he said.

"I asked to come."

"Fine, but I don't want you to go down there. You're not dressed for it, and you could be in the way."

"How was she found?" Flavia asked.

"The Malibu Station chopper was checking the canyon for a possible car over the side when the observer spotted her. They went in as close as they could, but they weren't set up the way the S-58's are for air rescue, so a mountain rescue team was called."

Flavia looked over the edge once more and felt the peril it represented. "I was watching that young woman going down there. I don't think I could ever do that."

Ralph Mott sensed her tension. "Sure you could, after proper training. You're perfectly capable and there's no reason why not. It's quite safe if you do it right."

For a moment Flavia visualized herself first in the classroom and then hanging by a thin rope on the side of a mountain. She knew she could do the first thing, but wondered about the second. Then she imagined the emotional charge it would give her to go down a rope that way into an untamed area and possibly help to save someone's life.

With that thought in her mind she turned again to Ralph Mott. "You do so much," she said.

He understood her. "You're damn right about that. In the four thousand square miles of Los Angeles County we've got wilderness areas where you could be lost for days. People disappear from the hiking trails and vehicles go over the side all the time. We cover more than three-quarters of the county, including almost all of the recreational and undeveloped areas. It takes thousands of us to do it.

"But we've got it down to a science now: if someone's hurt anywhere out there, from the moment a deputy reaches him, he'll be in a hospital, receiving medical attention, within fifteen minutes. That's assuming he can be moved. If not, we'll bring a doctor to him."

One of the men holding a hand radio waved an arm for attention. "She's still alive," he shouted.

*　*　*

The electric announcement immediately changed the whole atmosphere; where there previously had been plenty of time, an immediate gripping urgency took over. A deputy ran to his patrol unit and used the radio. The homicide team drew back; it was now a rescue operation and everyone else kept out of the way.

A paramedic went over the side carrying a heavy medical kit; his partner went down the other rappeling rope. When he reached the end of the rope, he scrambled the rest of the way, the loose, fragile rock crumbling under his feet.

As Flavia watched she felt a great load lifted from her. There was a living person at the bottom of the canyon, not another dead body for her to face. She was fervently grateful that she was there to watch the rescue operation.

At the highway a uniformed deputy was keeping the traffic moving past the site. It took vigorous gestures from him to overcome the curiosity of those who were driving past. A few even attempted to turn off and stop. A sports car driver ignored the deputy and did pull over. When he was told to move away he argued. He was promptly cited and a ticket written out. "I'm a lawyer," he shouted as he slowly pulled away. "You're going to hear from me!"

No one paid him the least attention as a body-shaped gurney went over the side to the paramedics below. Less than two minutes later the mounting sound of an approaching helicopter thundered against the walls of the canyon. "That's the one from the Malibu Station," Mott said. "They'll probably lift her out and put her in an ambulance right here."

The helicopter came into view, pulled up in a hover, and then very carefully let down toward the floor of the canyon. When it had gone as far as it could it held its position, a sling hanging from its side. Ignoring the fact that she was standing almost too close to the edge, Flavia watched as the people below carried the gurney, filled with someone wrapped in a blanket, to a spot directly under the heli-

114

copter. The downdraft of its main rotor and the continuous roar of its engine made their job difficult as they fitted the gurney into the sling and made it fast.

As soon as that was done the helicopter began a slow vertical rise with the gurney suspended in the sling well below the fuselage. Two uniformed deputies had already moved patrol units to block off all traffic on the highway. The three civilian-appearing cars were backed up to give more room.

From overhead the helicopter began to lower its hover, guided by the hand signals of a deputy who obviously knew how. Gently the gurney was set down and the sling loosened. As soon as it had been carried to one side, the pilot set his machine down on the cleared space. The engine roar subsided and the main rotor began to slow down. It was still turning when the two paramedics appeared at the edge of the cliff, coming up the ropes as expertly as they had gone down.

One of them called out an order as he ran to his patient. "I need some wire cutters—fast!"

A deputy found a pair in the four-wheel-drive rescue vehicle and brought them on the run. The paramedic took them, pulled back the blanket, and exposed the face of a white teenaged girl. A wire coat hanger had been twisted deeply into the flesh of her neck.

The heavy tool had not been designed for delicate work, but there was no alternative. "I've got to go for it," the paramedic said and dug the points of the cutters into the victim's flesh as far toward the back of her neck as he could manage. The victim's chest lifted up in sudden agony, then the paramedic closed the jaws and the wire snapped open.

Frank Levitzky quickly recovered it and put it in an evidence bag.

"I hope to hell that gives her a better chance," the paramedic said. "She paid for it. Get her to Northridge Trauma Center as fast as you can."

Although the helicopter was basically a two-place

115

machine, the gurney was fitted inside at a sloping angle. As soon as the door was closed the pilot fired up and was airborne within a few seconds. He held in a hover while he turned from south to north, then the nose dipped and the machine climbed rapidly away.

13

As soon as the helicopter had disappeared from view, the gathering at the area began to break up. Backed-up traffic was released with occasional breaks to allow the various parked cars to return eastward toward the Malibu Sheriff's Station. Soon all that remained was the mountain rescue vehicle and two unmarked homicide cars.

Ralph Mott called together his investigative team. "I think you'd better go down there and have a look," he said. "I'll drop off Flavia."

"Her car's at the Hall of Justice," Tracy told him.

"No problem, I'm going in anyway. Call me if you turn up anything." That said he walked over to where Flavia was standing. He sensed that she was feeling thoroughly unnecessary and to a degree embarrassed. "I just won you in the crap game," he said.

She was grateful to him for making light of the situation. "To the lieutenant belong the spoils," she offered.

"You learn fast, lady. Pop in the car and let's get out of here."

Riding in the front seat for a change, she admired the way he maneuvered down the mountain road. He had that extra degree of skill so many drivers thought they possessed, but didn't.

After a mile or two he spoke to her. "Are you okay now? Frank seemed to think you were a little edgy coming out here."

Flavia's first impulse was to admit the truth of that, but she didn't want to denigrate herself as a woman. "I'm fine, thank you. You drive very well," she added, grasping for a conversational straw.

"We have a driving school at the Pomona Fair Grounds," Mott told her. "You'd be surprised at how much you can learn there." Then he changed his tone a little. "Flavia, many homicides are relatively simple to investigate. Do you know what a walk-through is?"

"Yes."

"The exact opposite of that is a serial killer. We've had too many of them lately: the Hillside Strangler, the Norris/Bittaker case, the Night Stalker. You've probably read about them."

He almost stopped to avoid a Porsche that was darting back and forth across the double yellow line, trying to pass where there was no room to do so. He let the car go by, then picked up a microphone and gave the license number. The Highway Patrol would do the rest.

"I'm afraid I'm very much in the way," Flavia said. "My car is down at the Hall of Justice."

"No problem, I'm headed that way. What I was going to say, Flavia, is that this is the third victim to be attacked with the same MO. That's almost certain proof that we have another serial killer on our hands. As it happens, you've been on the scene in all three cases. It must have

118

shaken you up a lot. If you'd like to back off now for a while, all of us will understand."

Flavia had noticed that almost all policemen drove with the window next to them open, fair weather or foul. The wind that was coming in ruffled her hair and made one side of her face much cooler than the other. It seemed also to blow a certain freshness into her mind at the same time; she found she could view things more calmly and objectively. The vista of the San Fernando Valley, when it came into view, gave her a further lift.

"I don't enjoy seeing horrible things," she said, "but the way everyone worked together to save that girl— it was almost a spiritual experience. Please don't think I'm being overemotional."

Mott negotiated a curve at exactly the right speed. "Not at all. One thing I hope you'll put in your book: we're not out here just to chase and capture criminals. Suppose for a moment that all of the law enforcement agencies were taken out of Los Angeles for a month. The Sheriff's Department, L.A.P.D., the FBI, all the adjacent jurisdictions, the Secret Service, and the parole officers, and all the others. At the end of the month, how much of the city do you think would be left?"

It was a challenging thought. Flavia considered it, remembering how looters seem to come out of the ground whenever a disaster strikes. "Not very much," she admitted, although the feeling hung over her that she was somehow betraying her liberal principles. "But I still think that most people are honest," she said.

"So do I, " Mott agreed. "It's our job to deal with the other part."

At that moment the radio came on. It had been doing so intermittently since they had left the rescue scene, but this time the call was for Mott. He unclipped a mike and answered. Flavia could not follow the brief conversation, much of which was in code. As soon as it was over, Mott put it into plain language for her.

119

"They want me at the hospital," he said. "I may be hung up for some time. I can drop you off on Ventura where you can catch a bus downtown or call a cab."

Uncharacteristically she reached out her hand and laid it on his arm. "Please," she said, "let me come with you. I don't care how long it takes."

"If you want to." She knew from his tone that she had made the right decision. The car picked up speed, still within safe limits but getting the maximum distance out of every minute that passed. Although she did not know the valley too well, she was still surprised at how soon they reached the Northridge Medical Center. Mott swung the car into the reserved parking area and slid it smoothly into a slot labeled POLICE ONLY. The emergency entrance was marked NO ENTRY, but that obviously didn't apply to police personnel. A security guard in a tan uniform appeared to intercept them.

"Sheriff's Homicide," Mott said. "I got a call to check in here."

"Right, I know. Follow me." He led the way into the hospital complex, through several corridors, and up in an elevator. Then he entered a small lounge where a middle-aged man in a rumpled business suit was waiting. As Mott came in he got to his feet, a tired man who could have been working for uncounted hours and had no idea when he would finally be free. "You're from the Sheriff's Department?" he asked.

"Yes. Lieutenant Mott, Homicide." He didn't introduce Flavia.

"Sergeant Williams, L.A.P.D. When the girl was brought in, we were automatically called. We took the preliminary steps, then waited for you."

"Outstanding," Mott said, using the familiar police word. "How is she?"

"Very critical. She's in ICU. I've been standing by, in case."

"Can she talk?"

120

The sergeant shook his head. "I only got a quick look at her when they were hooking her up to life support. She was out at the time."

As he spoke, another man came into the room. He wore the usual white coat over a slender, not-too-tall body. His smooth Oriental features suggested that he was in his late twenties, but that could be deceptive. Mott sensed that he had been down a long road that day but was ready to give more if he had to.

"I'm Dr. Wakabayashi," he said and stopped because there was no need to say more.

"Ralph Mott, Sheriff's Homicide. This is Dr. de la Torre."

Wakabayashi reacted to that. "Then she's your patient."

Flavia shook her head, making it a firm gesture. "No, Doctor, I came with Lieutenant Mott."

Mott appreciated that: she could so easily have said that she was with Sheriff's Homicide too, which wasn't strictly true.

"You can look at her briefly, if you'd like," the doctor said, "but be damn careful what you say or do."

"Bet on it," Mott said, and then turned to Flavia. "I think you'd better stay here."

For a moment the rebuff stung her, then she saw the sense of it. If the girl was conscious, too many people around her bedside could be intimidating. She watched as Mott followed the smaller figure of the doctor out of the lounge.

The Intensive Care Unit was immediately through a double door that was placarded AUTHORIZED PERSONNEL ONLY. Inside the unit it was quiet, but there was an atmosphere of hushed alertness. Everywhere there were cathode-ray tubes continuously reading out data; the nurses moved about more than on the regular hospital floors.

Wakabayashi led the way to a bedside where the girl lay. She was hardly visible: part of her face was bandaged and a massive dressing concealed all of her throat. An IV drip was in her left arm, another of a different sort in her right.

Her hands lay at her sides, both bandaged up to the tips of her fingers. Mott was unable to identify the other visible tubes and wires that were connected to her body. He only sensed her complete helplessness—her inability to move if she were able.

He looked at what he could see of her face very carefully. Her eyes were closed, but that could mean she was resting as best she could. He had no way of measuring the amount of pain that was flowing through her body, how much she was silently enduring if she was conscious at all

From her face he looked up at the CRT above her head: it displayed a steady heartbeat, the clearest evidence that she was still alive. He knew that nothing could heal the body better than the body itself, given the necessary time and support. Every few minutes that passed, he fervently hoped, would mark an infinitesimal improvement in her condition.

After two minutes the doctor tapped him on the shoulder and took him aside.

"How much do you have on her?" the doctor asked in a quiet, subdued voice.

"Nothing at all. Take it from square one."

"Her name is Mary Margaret Malone. Age sixteen. Parents divorced, mother apparently deceased. Father works for an electronics firm; he's out of town, but he's being notified."

"Pretty good in such a short time," Mott said.

"She had an ID, so we called her school," Wakabayashi explained. "Despite the divorce, the family's Catholic. At least that's the indication from her personal effects."

"Is there a priest at the hospital?"

"Yes, Father Lum. He saw her and gave her the last rites."

Mott worked his lips for a moment. "She's terminal then." He said it flatly, forcing the reality into his mind.

"Not if I can help it," Wakabayashi replied. "Her age is in her favor."

122

Mott liked the man; he wasn't the kind to take the easy way out.

"This is in confidence, Doctor," he said, and got a quick nod of confirmation. "We've had two other recent cases with the same MO: a wire coat hanger used as a strangling tool. The first two victims were dead when they were found."

"I know about that, Lieutenant."

"Both of the other girls had been tortured and raped. We haven't released that."

Wakabayashi took a careful look at his patient's readout before he responded. "I'm glad you told me. This patient was also tortured," he said. "Enough to severely impede her recovery. I've done all I can risk to lessen her pain, but her life support has to come first. The more she can stay out of it, the better."

"Was she sexually molested?" Mott asked, certain that he already knew the answer.

"No, she wasn't."

That was a surprise. Mott knew better than to question the doctor's statement, but there was another way to put it. "How did you find out so soon?"

"It was simple enough," Wakabayashi answered. "She's a virgin. That's one of the first things we check in cases like this."

Mott knew he could not keep the doctor much longer, but there was one more question he had to ask. "Has she been able to speak—to say anything at all?"

"She tried to when she first came in, before we knocked her out for emergency treatment. Her larynx is damaged, but she wanted to tell us something."

"Please," Mott said, "I need all you've got on that." He put real urgency into his voice.

"She did say a word that sounded like 'man,' she repeated it two or three times."

"I think we knew that already." Mott was grim.

123

"This may help a little more: she made a great effort before she passed out, and gave us two names."

"Thank God! What are they?"

"One was Harry, the other was Joe."

Mott lost no time in getting to a telephone. He swiftly punched out 1-213-974-4341 and had Homicide on the line in seconds. "This is Mott," he said. "Are any of my people in?"

"Miriam and Willie are here."

"Put them on."

As soon as his two investigators were linked in, he gave them the story. "We've got number three in the coat-hanger stranglings," he said.

"We already heard," Willie answered. He was a tall, nearly bald man who missed almost nothing that was going on.

"She's presently still alive in Northridge ICU. The doctor said that her voice box is damaged, but she was able to give him three words. The first sounded like 'man,' that's how he put it, but it could have been 'men.'"

"I copy," Miriam said.

"Here's the best part. She gave him two names: Harry and Joe."

"Pretty damn common," Willie commented, "but we can start digging."

"The point is," Mott continued, "she apparently was attacked by two men. That would be why she said 'men'; she was trying to tell us there was more than one."

"Makes sense," Willie agreed. "The names don't give us much, but the two together could add up."

"Right," Mott agreed. "You know the routes to go."

"We'll start with the sex offenders list," Miriam said, "then recent parolees. After that, we'll go into the general records for any Harry and Joe combinations."

"Good luck," Mott said. He knew how hard it would be, but that was the name of the game in Homicide.

When he had finished, he collected Flavia and went back to his car. "There was no point in your going in to see her," he said. "She's unconscious and hooked up to a mess of equipment."

"Perhaps I could give blood for her."

"That's fine, Flavia, but since this AIDS thing came up, it's gotten a lot more complicated."

They were still driving toward the freeway when Flavia spoke again.

"I know you're a professional, Lieutenant, but I think that this case has got you pretty upset. Am I right?"

Mott kept his eyes on the road. "Yes, Flavia, it has," he admitted. "It's certain now we've got a serial killer, or killers. It happens that all three cases were in our jurisdiction, but the next one could be anywhere. We're going to have to set up a task force of forty or fifty people from different agencies."

"The other agencies will cooperate?"

"You bet they will. We'll provide the facilities, the computers, and all the other stuff that'll be needed."

"Computers?" she asked.

"Hell, yes! Without them we might never have caught the

Night Stalker. Flavia, before this is over, unless we get very lucky we'll have to run down literally hundreds of leads. You've no idea how much work goes into cracking a case of this kind. Or how much it will all cost."

He stopped for a double set of red lights at the entrance to the Ventura Freeway. When they eventually turned green, he took the car-pool side of the entrance ramp and bypassed the metering signal.

As soon as they were established in the stream of traffic, Flavia opened a new topic. "May I call you Ralph?" she asked.

"Sure. Everyone does."

"I heard you're divorced."

"True." As soon as he had an opening he maneuvered his way toward the left-hand lane. "I'm living alone, particularly while I'm in this job. Last month I was close to the peak of orgasm with a lady friend when the damn phone rang."

If the candor of that statement had any effect on Flavia, she was careful not to let it show.

She looked at the digital clock on the dashboard. "By the time we get downtown it'll be after six. Will you be through for the day?"

"Unless they call me again."

"Then how about having dinner with me when you're finished?"

Mott let a momentary traffic complication spare him the need to give an immediate answer. A shield had dropped in place, the one that keeps policemen from getting involved with civilians they encounter on the job. He didn't do it consciously; it was purely automatic.

When he didn't answer immediately, Flavia sensed the reason. "Before you commit yourself," she said, "let me ask a question. Do you like Spanish food?"

"I go to Mexican restaurants every now and then." It was a half acceptance, but the thought of a cool margarita had formed in his mind with three-dimensional clarity.

127

"I didn't say Mexican, I said Spanish," Flavia corrected. "I'm offering to cook for you. I have a little place not too far from the Hall of Justice."

Then she displayed a remarkable bit of feminine intuition. "I make very good margaritas. You can take off your shoes and relax with one while I fix dinner."

That was too good to pass up. "You've got a deal," he said.

It was close to seven when she led the way in her small car to the building where she lived. She showed him where he could park and then took him up to her flat. No one paid them the slightest attention.

Once inside she invited him to sit down, kicked off her shoes, and disappeared briefly into her small kitchen. When she came out again she had two large cocktail glasses filled to the top. Mott tried the one she handed him and felt a fresh revival of life flow down his throat. *"Very* good," he said, and meant it.

"Now just be comfortable, while I get things ready."

The chance to sit still, even in strange surroundings, and the reviving drink did wonders for him. He let his head tip and rest against the back of his chair. Presently Flavia came back with a pitcher and refilled his glass. He didn't make the slightest pretense of refusing.

By the time he had finished his second margarita, a tempting aroma was coming from the kitchen. He felt much better then and was glad he had accepted her invitation. He would be expected to return it, but that prospect had definite advantages of its own. He closed his eyes to relax even more. It was growing dark outside and he was hungry, but he had the prospect of some very good food coming soon.

When he heard a sound he looked up. While he had been resting she had changed into a teal-blue silk pants-and-shirt outfit that set off her complexion and rich dark hair. She offered him a plate of appetizers. "Dinner in about ten minutes," she said. "I hope you can wait."

"Of course."

"Please, take off your jacket and be comfortable."

He was glad to comply. He hung his coat over the back of a chair and put his gun and holster on a table beside it. That left only the beeper on his belt to betray his profession. He took one of the little pieces of food on the plate; it was hot and tasty. "I really appreciate this," he said.

"I'm glad of the company," Flavia responded. "Particularly after a day like today." As soon as she said it she knew it had been a mistake. She was trying hard to help them both forget the things they had so recently seen and done.

"Your dinner smells marvelous," Mott told her, intentionally or not, bailing her out. In return she gave him a smile that ran the whole length of his body. When she turned to go back into the kitchen, her silk pants clung subtly to the shape of her bottom, making him intensely aware of her body.

He wondered what there was about him that could possibly attract a woman of her caliber. She had been under no obligation to invite him. He walked to the window and looked out at the street below and the few trees that relieved the starkness of the scene. He was not handsome in the sense that TV actors are handsome; no girl would ever nudge another if he were to pass by. He knew that he had presentable features, but so did millions of other men. He was not the symbolic six foot or more tall: he was five eleven and weighed one seventy. Not too bad for a man of thirty-seven, but he had to work to keep himself in shape.

He concluded, as he had on some other occasions, that as far as the women were concerned he was about average with the major handicap, to some, that he was a cop. He wanted very much to feel that he was something special, but the evidence to support it wasn't there. The women he had encountered since his divorce had largely been looking

129

for a meal ticket, or the elusive security that was everyone's Promised Land. But there was far too much wandering in the wilderness for most people: too many utility bills, lawyers, and whatever. Camelot was in the far, far past, if it had ever existed at all.

Flavia had come behind him into the room. "Dinner's ready," she said.

She had even lighted candles, which was more than he had expected. He sat down opposite her, content with the fact that for the next hour or so he had hit the winning number. He lifted the glass of wine she had poured for him and clinked it against her own. "Cheers," he said.

"Cheers."

The way she said it added to the aura that surrounded her. She was warm and friendly, she had prepared him his dinner, and visually she was a knockout. It was a helluva lot for a working cop to have come his way, but he was ready to make the most of it while it lasted. That included appreciating the outlines of her breasts as he picked up his silverware. A woman like that . . .

He switched himself off that tack and got down to the business of enjoying his dinner. Much of it was new to his palate, but it was delicious. For conversation they talked about her work at the university, her outside interests, and whatever things they could find in common.

By the time he had finished eating, and had drunk three glasses of excellent wine on top of the margaritas she had made, he was surrounded by a warm glow he had not known for months, perhaps years. It was pure circumstance that had brought Flavia de la Torre into his life, but he was more than grateful for this special evening with her. He accepted the fact that it was a one-time event; there had to be a well-installed boyfriend, perhaps a whole string of them.

Still, he intended to ask her out. She had told him that she occasionally went to the Music Center, which was a good lead. She certainly topped any of the women he knew.

Part of her appeal was her appearance; but even during the short time they had been together he had discovered there was a lot more to her than that.

He waited politely while she cleared the table, reluctant to put his coat back on, but knowing better than to overstay his welcome. When she rejoined him, he thanked her again for the dinner. "I don't remember when I've enjoyed myself so much," he concluded.

"What are you going to do now?" she asked.

"Go home and get some paperwork done. My own personal stuff. I've neglected it too long."

She gave him a quiet, even look.

"If you feel that you must. I was rather hoping that you might stay and make love to me."

That was totally unexpected and for a moment he was stunned. He recovered quickly, but before he could find the right words to say, she pointed to the sofa in her small living room. "Sit down," she invited.

As soon as he was settled, she sat beside him, resting her back against his side. Automatically he put his arm around her and held her next to him.

"I don't want you to think that I'm free and easy," she said. "Normally I'm *very* reserved. Please believe me when I tell you that."

"Absolutely," he answered. It wasn't the word he wanted, but it was the best he could do at that moment.

"You see, Ralph, you're a most unusual man."

That startled him almost as much as her initial statement. "I don't think so," he said.

"Oh yes you are. You just don't know it." She snuggled a little closer under his arm. "Shall I explain it to you?"

"Please."

"To begin with, I'm Spanish, but I could never stand it to go to the bullfights. A spectacle of torture and death isn't my idea of entertainment."

"Or mine," he agreed.

"Professionally I wanted to make a detailed examination

131

of the California parole system, and to publish my findings. You know why?"

"It's a god-awful mess," Mott said.

"Since homicides are treated as a separate category, I decided to focus there. I didn't want to, but it was like going to the dentist."

She stopped for a moment, collecting her own thoughts. "The first time I was called out, I was very apprehensive. On the way to Big Tujunga Canyon I made up my mind that whatever lay ahead of me, I would face it; I used all the resolve I had to fix that thought in my mind."

"You did a good job."

"No, I didn't. I tried my best to look and act composed when I got there, but the truth, Ralph, is that I was almost shaking with fear. That's before I saw the body. Do you remember what happened next?"

"Yes," he answered. "I intercepted you. Even many experienced cops are upset by the sight of violent death. That was an unusually bad one, so I tried to divert you by pointing out who the people were at the scene and what they were doing. I hoped that would satisfy you, but you seemed determined . . ."

Flavia interrupted him. "I had my mind fixed; if I didn't go through with it then, I would doubt myself forever afterward."

The subtle fragrance of her hair and the warmth of her body were quietly exciting his senses.

"When I did see the dead girl, it was terrible, worse than I had ever imagined."

"I was standing right behind you," Mott said, "in case you went over."

She reached up and took the hand that he had laid across her shoulder. "I almost did, Ralph, it was a near thing. Then you took me aside. You told me that the body wasn't a person anymore. I remember your words, 'The girl herself isn't here. Her problems are over. The body is what she left behind. Her privacy isn't being invaded, she took that with her.'"

Her grip tightened on his fingers. "Ralph, I've never met another man who would be capable of saying that. Or who would be willing to. I came back here and thought about it most of the night. And even though we'd hardly met, I wished that you could have been there with me. Just for the sake of your company. I thought then you were an extraordinary man; now I'm sure of it."

"I wish to hell I'd known," he said.

"You do now." She stood up and held out her arms. He took her then, gathering her tightly to him and kissing her warm lips with full intensity. When he had done it twice, she led him toward the bedroom. He helped her with the simple matter of folding back the spread. When that was done, in a few easy movements she took off her shirt, loosened her silk pants, and let them slide down her body.

He looked at her openly: at the whole of her, her beautifully molded breasts and her rich pubic triangle. It was all better than he had thought possible.

He shed his own clothes quickly while she folded back the bed. Then he picked her up in his arms and laid her gently down on one side. He pulled the covers over them both and held her close to him.

Carefully she traced a forefinger down the front of his chest; he responded by burying his head against her neck and gently kissing the very soft flesh of her throat. His hands found her buttocks and pressed her closer to him. Her own fingers massaged the middle of his back.

A new kind of liquid fire began to run through his veins, one that burned hotter and brighter than he had ever known. All of his previous experience was swept aside by the overpowering intensity of his arousal.

Even then he was careful to enter her gently, although she was moist and ready. Soon he plunged in more deeply and felt her respond to him. He rose higher and higher with her until an explosion of orgasm seized his entire being in a paroxysm of rapture.

When it was over he lay very still, continuing to hold her, feeling the warmth of her, and asking no more of God or man. There was nothing else in the world that mattered to him at that moment, not even the beeper that was giving off its staccato sound from the pile of his discarded clothing.

15

A very careful examination of Mrs. Mabel Lorimer's car turned up no useful information whatever. The investigators had hoped for an appointment memo of some kind, but, as discreet in death as she had been in life, Mrs. Lorimer had left nothing in her car that in any way betrayed her professional life. The car *per se* was a dead end.

A thorough check of the neighborhood where it had been left turned up nothing; no one could be found who had seen her with her car, on the street, or entering the church. In view of the weather on the night of her death, that was to be expected, but Tracy and Levitzky tried anyway.

The full protocol from the Coroner's Office confirmed death by stabbing. The examining physician reported that while it appeared to have been an expert hit, it was possible that the attacker had succeeded by chance. Which was no help at all.

When that work had been concluded, it was think time. The two men ate lunch together in near silence, each searching for a possible loose lead—anything at all that had been overlooked. Normally Tracy did not eat dessert with his lunch, but this time he ordered a piece of pie. When it came it was à la mode, although he hadn't asked for ice cream.

As soon as the business of lunch was over, both men returned to the Hall of Justice to hack away at the mounds of paperwork that pile up in any major police investigation.

When Flavia came in, not much attention was paid to her arrival. The barrel man who sat at the desk and took the incoming calls nodded to her, but she had become something of a fixture not directly involved in any ongoing investigations.

In the far corner of the huge room Flavia sat down at the desk that had been loaned to her and looked at the huge pile of folders she had yet to read. Chief Cargill had said she was to have access, so access had been given, en masse.

Because she was well disciplined, she sat quietly to work, taking notes as she went along in her neat small script. Most of the pages she read had been typed, others were uniformly printed in block letters as is standard police style almost everywhere.

Levitzky and Tracy were aware that she had come in, but there was no point in opening a conversation. Ralph Mott was out with another team in the field.

It was ten minutes to four when Flavia picked up the folder of Xavier Portofino, one more in the seemingly endless pile before her. She had already gone through more than enough to give her a clear picture of how many repeat offenders were on parole, but she would not allow herself to short-circuit the job she had set out to do.

Portofino's profile fitted an already too familiar pattern. Born in the East Los Angeles barrio. A fledgling gang member by the time he was twelve. Two arrests before he was fifteen, both dismissed partly because of his age. Involved in a shooting on his sixteenth birthday, but the district attorney had not filed. It had been an election year and he had been anxious to show as high a percentage as possible of convictions. One way was to dismiss as many dubious cases as possible and Portofino, whose innocent-looking baby face might convince a jury that he could not be guilty as charged, was allowed to walk.

Some time in his seventeenth year Portofino had been arrested for 211, armed robbery. He had held a knife at the throat of a shopkeeper's small daughter and drawn a little blood to show his serious intentions. An S.E.B. car had been close by when it happened and one of the deputies had gone into the store to buy a pack of cigarettes.

The case was airtight and the jury convicted. The judge, however, suspended sentence and Portofino had walked out of the court a free man.

A different judge had been on the bench when he reappeared a few weeks later on a fresh charge. This time he drew a sentence at the California Youth Authority and he did not get out until sixteen months later, a hero to his fellow gang members who respected the fact that he had now been fully initiated. He had also learned a number of new techniques in mugging.

During the following three years there had been several more arrests, but in a number of cases the victims had failed to testify and Portofino had walked sneering out of the courtroom. He knew now how to keep the fuzz off his back and himself above the law. One conviction had resulted in a plea bargain. Without conscience he had lied convincingly in the witness chair and earned himself pro-bation.

Flavia had read many other folders that were similar, but one aspect of Portofino's MO caught her attention. To be sure of her ground, she read the entire file, including all of the detailed arrest reports, court decisions, and even the small memos that were part of the whole. When she had done that she forced herself to sit still and think about what she had found. She played her own devil's advocate, but she could not erase the feeling she had. Satisfied that she had done her best, she took the folder and went over to where Levitzky and Tracy sat at adjacent desks. "Can you spare me a few minutes?" she asked.

"Sure," Levitzky said, and pushed a chair out with his foot. Flavia sat down. As she did so Mott came into the room. Tracy lifted a hand and made a beckoning motion. He had no idea what was on Flavia's mind, but something was and Mott would probably want to know. He had a good feeling for such matters.

"You're professional homicide detectives," Flavia began. "I've had a chance to see how good you are."

Levitzky made a dismissive gesture with his hand.

"I'm a sociologist. That's a different discipline, but there are a few areas of overlap. I know something about how people behave."

She opened the folder. "Have you heard of Xavier Portofino?" she asked.

Tracy looked at his partner who looked at Mott. "Not offhand," Levitzky said.

Flavia continued as though she were explaining a point in class. "I've been reading a lot of folders; it's been an education for me."

"It would be," Tracy agreed. Mott stayed silent.

"I know from my own work that when people take up irregular behavior, voyeurism for instance, they tend to follow a certain pattern, their MO. But there's something I didn't know, not until Captain Grimm let me read the manual for homicide investigators."

Levitzky raised an eyebrow; he hadn't heard about that.

"In homicide, and I presume other types of cases, the investigator or investigators always note down the time, the estimated outside temperature, and the condition of the weather."

"That's done first thing," Tracy told her.

Flavia opened the folder. "The subject here is Xavier Portofino, an East Los Angeles gang member. He has quite a record. A gang investigator reported that he's an expert with a knife."

"That's not unusual in the East L.A. barrio," Mott said. "Knifings are pretty common there."

Flavia stood her ground. "I know that, Ralph—or should I call you lieutenant here?"

"Ralph is fine."

"I'm fully aware that knives are all too common in barrio and ghetto situations. But here are two other things. First of all, Portofino tends to stalk his victims, or intended victims, until he can catch them at a place where there are no witnesses."

Mott was tempted to tell her that was standard MO as well, but he kept quiet to let her finish. In a few moments he was fervently glad that he had.

"I presume that isn't too unusual either, pardon the double negative. But in reading Portofino's file I did notice one thing: between the months of November and April, the only months when it normally rains here, Portofino was picked up six different times on mugging charges. What caught my attention was the fact that in all but one of those cases, *it was raining at the time of his arrest.*"

After a few seconds Tracy spelled it out. "A knife-using mugger who picks his victims in places where there are no witnesses is standard. But the rain angle is something new. Maybe not in New York, but it is here."

"I think he has a rain fixation," Flavia said. "When it rains, he goes out to attack someone. At least it looks that way. I don't know if that's important or not."

Mott answered her. "Important enough to look into it right now."

Levitzky reached for the file. "Do you want to come along?" he asked.

"Let me get my purse," Flavia said.

139

It was only a short drive to the East Los Angeles Sheriff's Station. Tracy picked up a county car from the Hall of Justice parking lot and made the trip in less than fifteen minutes. He drove into the official lot and parked at the end of a row of patrol units. At the back door he punched a combination on the lock and motioned Flavia to go inside. "Put on your ID," he said. "They don't like anyone walking around here they can't identify."

A little self-consciously Flavia clipped on her plastic card. Moments later a tall lieutenant came by, glanced quickly at her and her ID, and moved aside to let her pass. For the first time she had a fledgling sense of belonging, of being part of the intricate law-enforcement complex that had taken her at least partway in.

Levitzky stopped at the watch desk. "Is Dictionary in?" he asked.

The desk sergeant nodded and pointed toward the detectives' room. Flavia walked beside the older deputy she was beginning to like very much. "You called him Dictionary," she said. "His name's Webster?"

Levitzky laughed. "Good guess, but no. His name's Al Schumann; he's a sergeant in the gang section. His hobby is the English language; he likes to speak it precisely, often very formally. You'll see."

Schumann was not more than five feet seven and definitely portly. His abdomen bulged far out over his belt; the hardware he wore at his waist threatened to pull his pants down at any moment.

"Do you know a Xavier Portofino?" Tracy asked.

Schumann looked at him. "Your inquiry is most opportune," he answered in a voice that had Shakespearean overtones. "Young Mr. Portofino is currently in residence in our cell block. While committing an infraction he tried to take on Jim Vetrovic, a serious miscalculation on his part."

Levitzky spoke quietly to Flavia. "Deputy Vetrovic is a

140

former national weight-lifting champion," he explained. "He has to have his uniform shirts custom-made." He turned and went out toward the holding area.

"Has he been Mirandized?" Tracy asked.

"Yes: I did it and logged it. But aren't you overlooking the amenities?"

"Sorry. Flavia, this is Sergeant Al Schumann, one of our top gang experts. And a scholar of the classics. Our technical advisor, Dr. de la Torre."

"I'm delighted, Doctor. May I ask your discipline?"

"Sociology."

"Welcome to our Happy Hunting Ground. What was your thesis?"

"The California parole system."

Schumann rested a pair of massive hands on top of his desk. "May God help us all," he said with feeling. "We kick the shit out of the assholes in court and then the Supremes cast flower petals on their path." He looked up. "I trust I'm not being too graphic for your sensibilities."

Tracy took over and led Flavia aside. "We're going to take Portofino into the interrogation room," he said. "I can't let you join us; the courts have held that more than two persons in an interrogation can be intimidating to the suspect."

"Can I have a look at him on the way?" she asked.

"Why not."

Levitzky came back into the room leading a young Hispanic who was making a massive effort to appear indifferent to the whole thing. He was five feet eight with a muscular build, the inevitable mustache, and a pair of black eyes that was clearly missing nothing. A half sneer curled his face as he looked around him at the strictly utilitarian setting. He had beaten the system too many times for it to hold any real fear for him.

Levitzky stopped where Flavia was leaning against the edge of a desk. "I want you to look carefully at this man,"

141

he said. "Is he the one you picked out of the photo lineup I just showed you?"

Tracy held his breath, but Flavia caught on at once. "Yes, he is," she answered. Her voice was cool and distant.

"And is he the man you saw on the night in question?"

Flavia slowly nodded. "Without any doubt. He's the one."

Portofino came to life. "If she's supposed to be a witness, how come she's wearing your ID?"

"We had the place staked out," Tracy said. "Many of our best detectives are women."

Portofino eyed her up and down. "I like them nice loose knockers," he said.

Flavia knew he saw her as naked, but she was used to that.

"You'll get another look at them in court," she answered, causing Tracy to fall in love with her on the spot.

Portofino was led away into the quiet, confined silence of the interrogation room. There was a scraping of chairs as the three men sat down, as if by prearrangement, Levitzky began the process. "Have you been read your rights?" he asked.

Portofino shrugged. "Yeah. Don't bother doin' it again. I know 'em better'n you."

"Do you want to have an attorney present?"

"Naw, I ain't done nothin'." As he slouched in his chair he appeared indifferent, but his eyes kept searching the room. Because he had been through this many times before, he was looking for a hidden microphone or camera lens.

Levitzky opened the folder and pretended to study it. "You got started early," he said. "Bicycle theft at nine."

Portofino shrugged. "I borrowed it."

Levitzky read on. "Two arrests before you were fifteen; you were a busy boy."

Portofino all but sneered. "Cops pickin' on a Mex, that's all. We used to that."

Levitzky didn't even look up. "At sixteen you were busted for armed robbery."

Portofino gave no sign that he had heard.

"Sentenced for the first time when you were seventeen," Levitzky read on. "There's a lot more shit in here: burglary, mugging—especially mugging."

Portofino waved a hand casually through the air. "History," he said.

"Yes, but interesting history." Levitzky shifted in his chair to signify a new phase. "Now we come to Tuesday night, two weeks ago. Where were you then?"

Portofino showed a little more vitality. "Two weeks ago, man—how'm I supposed to remember that?"

Levitzky ignored the open folder; it had done its job. He leaned forward and locked eyes with Portofino. "It was raining," he said with deceptive mildness. "All day long it was raining. You like it in the rain, don't you, Xavier. It does something for you, makes you feel big and strong. It keeps witnesses out of the way. That was the night you stalked that woman, Xavier. You followed her inside where you didn't think there would be any witnesses. Only the lights were very dim and you didn't find out until too late that someone else *was* there. Someone who saw you mug that woman and when she tried to fight, you stabbed her to shut her up. Because you thought someone would come and you'd be caught."

"That's shit, man, all shit," Portofino retorted. "I didn't do nothing to no woman. I was cold man, and wet, so I ducked in to get dry. That's all. I stayed in back."

"In back where?"

Portofino didn't know how a cop could be so stupid. "In the church, man."

"Who said anything about a church?" Tracy asked.

143

16

The interrogation of Xavier Portofino had been going on for only a short while when Deputy Al Schumann hitched up his belt and addressed himself to Flavia. "You came in with Dick Tracy, right?" he asked.

"Yes," she answered.

"I expect that the interrogation of Portofino may take a while. If you'd like, I can arrange a ride for you."

Flavia smiled her gratitude. "Thanks, but unless it gets too late, I'll wait it out."

"Then how about joining me for a cup of coffee?"

"I'd like that," she said.

Deputy Schumann led the way to the day room where a half-dozen plain long tables stood. At five of them little groups of deputies were seated, waiting for their shifts to begin. Flavia's appearance was the signal for some careful, subdued scrutiny. She sat down at the only unoccupied table while Schumann drew two mugs of coffee and brought them over. He laid out some little packets of sugar and dry nondairy creamer and put a stirring stick on a clean paper napkin.

"I'd offer you some pastry," he said, "but what we have comes out of a machine with a malignant disposition. You'd eat it only if you were starving."

"The worst for the finest," Flavia suggested.

"An apt phrase," Schumann said. "I like the good use of language. And I think you can learn a lot if you listen carefully. In my job I spend a good deal of time talking to gang members here in the station. Street language is graphic, no doubt about that, but it's also corrosive. You'd be surprised how much I pick up."

"Have you ever thought of teaching?"

"I do. I give some time teaching English to Asian immigrants. I like it. One of my students from Vietnam recently graduated as valedictorian of her high-school class."

"Do you have an advanced degree?" Flavia asked.

Schumann smiled. "I do, but I usually keep that to myself. Around here some of the more refined niceties give way to the prime necessity of tossing assholes in the can. Now tell me about your work."

A little more than an hour later Tracy reappeared. There was a grim satisfaction in his manner as he drew himself a cup of coffee, dropped a quarter in the kitty, and slid onto a chair at the table. "Portofino copped out," he said to Schumann.

"To the Lorimer murder?"

"Yes." Then he turned to Flavia. "You did quite a job for us, Detective de la Torre." He sampled his coffee and then explained to Schumann. "She dug him out of the files and made him because of his rain MO. None of us had caught that. We hadn't been in there ten minutes before we knew he was good for it. My partner is rebooking him now for one eighty-seven."

145

"I thought she was an eyewitness."

"No, but she was damn quick on the uptake when we planted that idea on Portofino. You've earned your keep today; welcome to the team."

"Thanks," Flavia said. His words were like magic to her and she smiled her gratitude for them.

The work of setting up a room for the task force was moving along rapidly. A large desktop computer had been moved in and made ready for use. A number of desks had been set up, each with a computer station and, most important, a telephone. A small local switching unit had been installed to rotate incoming calls to available open lines. A row of filing cabinets partly filled one wall, and in a corner a table with a hot-water urn, with the makings for instant coffee or tea, was already doing business.

On the blank wall opposite the windows there were photographs of the known victims of the serial killer, three attractive girls smiling at the camera, each hopeful of a happy romantic future. The middle one was in her high-school graduation outfit. Underneath the photographs there was a supply table with pens, stacks of paper pads, clips, and other needed material.

In the captain's office Tracy and Levitzky were summarizing what had happened during the past few hours. "Frank and I had the same idea," Tracy reported. "We put together several known facts. The victim had a reputation for always being on time. She was going to a part of the city—actually the county—where she didn't know her way around. She had an appointment. And it was foul weather. That added up to a near certainty that she would leave early, allowing herself plenty of time to get there before her contact was supposed to show up.

"However, there was little traffic that night and she reached the church well before her contact expected her. We know the time because she had reported it to her superiors."

"So she was in the church early and that's when the mugger hit her. But why did he kill her?" the captain asked.

"We got that," Levitzky supplied. "Portofino spilled his guts. He thought the church was empty when he decided to hit her. At the last moment he saw that there was someone up front kneeling in one of the pews. So he knifed her to keep her still. That's all of it."

"Damn," the captain said. "This time you've got him cold, but if he'd been handled properly when he was busted for two eleven, this never would have happened."

"If he had been, he'd already be out on parole by now," Tracy said. He could not keep the bitterness out of his voice.

"Now tell me about de la Torre."

"As far as we're concerned, Flavia has earned herself a place on the team," Tracy began, then he told how she had spotted Portofino's proclivity for rainy nights in his folder. "Also," he added, "she was damn quick when we faced the suspect with her. When we asked if that was the man she had picked out of the photo lineup, she confirmed it immediately without knowing at the time what a photo lineup was. And when we asked if the suspect was the man she had seen in the church, she identified him without hesitation."

"We owe her one," the captain said. "I'll let Chief Cargill know. He'll be pleased."

Lieutenant Ralph Mott slid the county car he was driving into one of the POLICE ONLY parking slots at Northridge Medical Center, got out, and carefully locked the vehicle before he went in through the emergency entrance to the hospital. Once again a security man stopped him. Mott produced his badge. The security man looked at it carefully and checked the photo ID before letting him through. "Where to?" he asked.

"ICU."

147

"Do you know the way?"

"Yes, thanks."

When he arrived at the Intensive Care Unit, Mott was stopped again at the double doors and once more he identified himself. "Is Dr. Wakabayashi in?" he asked.

"He left about an hour ago. Dr. Finegold may be able to help you. Which patient are you interested in?"

"Mary Malone."

The supervisor's face tightened. "I should have known. If you'll wait in the lounge just behind you, I'll ask the doctor to come out. It may be a few minutes."

Mott went into the small lounge. A pay telephone on the wall had several numbers scribbled beside it. The furniture was reasonably new, but it was already scarred by cigarette burns and worn with hard use. There was a NO SMOKING sign on the wall. The few magazines, although current, were torn and limp from constant handling. It was past visiting hours and the room was otherwise unoccupied. Mott sat down and prepared to wait, an art in which all policemen become adept.

Within five minutes Dr. Finegold appeared. He was over six feet without an extra ounce on his body. His white coat hung loosely from his shoulders as though it was embarrassed to be there. Although he was still a young man, he had lost much of his hair. He had quick black eyes; together with his lean body and the slight forward thrust of his head they gave him the look of a domesticated vulture.

Mott got to his feet and held out a card. "Lieutenant Mott, Sheriff's Homicide," he said.

Finegold waved toward an already worn settee. "Yes, of course," he said in a surprisingly gentle voice. "How may I help you?"

"Doctor, I'd like to know as much as you can tell me about the condition of Mary Malone."

Finegold blinked his eyes before he answered. "At present she's still very critical. She was that way when she was brought in. We've been able to stabilize her, but her

148

condition hasn't shown any real improvement. She's drifting in and out of a coma. Occasionally she opens her eyes and looks if she wants to speak, but she hasn't made a sound for at least twenty-four hours."

"But she did say something when she was first brought in."

"Yes, that's on her chart. She's probably suffered some brain damage; it would be a miracle if she hasn't. She was brutally strangled. She has severe abrasions over much of her body, other cuts and lacerations, and three broken ribs. Plus some internal injuries. She either fell or was thrown over a cliff, I hear."

Mott nodded. "On Malibu Canyon Road. She fell or rolled down two or three hundred feet, as a guess."

"She may have been unconscious at the time," the doctor said, "from the severe strangulation. If so, by being perfectly limp her body probably absorbed less traumatic injury than if she had been conscious and struggling. But it very nearly finished her off anyway."

For a moment Mott shut his eyes and held them hard closed. With a conscious effort he tried to free his mind of the picture of a sixteen-year-old girl undergoing such terrible abuse, falling down the hillside with a wire coat hanger cutting into her throat, and found that he could not. "We understand, Doctor, that she hadn't been sexually molested."

The doctor shook his head.

"That's not correct, Lieutenant. She was molested—orally. There were traces of saliva on her genital area. But she wasn't raped. She's a virgin."

Mott's eyebrows came closer together. "I don't get it," he said, almost talking to himself. "There've been two other victims with the same MO; in both cases the victims were raped before being murdered. Yet this girl escaped that and is still living. It doesn't add up."

When Finegold had nothing to say about that, Mott

gathered himself and asked the question he wished he could avoid. "What's the prognosis?"

The doctor's voice was clinical. "As far as survival goes, she's on the very edge. As of now, I can't give her more than a twenty percent chance."

"But she does have a chance," Mott said.

"Yes," Finegold said, "in the physical sense. But there's almost no chance that she'll recover enough, physically and mentally, to be able to lead any kind of a normal life. We're doing everything we possibly can to save her, but if she doesn't make it, it might be the kinder thing for her."

17

Harry was worried. The girl he and his partner had dumped off the cliff had somehow managed to cling to life. He knew that she was in the Northridge Medical Center, that had been in the paper, but he knew almost nothing about her condition. As far as he knew she had recovered enough to sit up and shoot her mouth off to the sky.

The only names she would know were Harry and Joe; again he was thankful for his partner's foresight in never using their real names.

But she could describe them—and the van that was registered to his partner with his right address. They had talked about getting rid of it, but it was set up just right and they had decided there was no way the girl could give the number to the cops. She had climbed right in and there was almost no chance at all that she had seen a license plate, let alone remembered even part of it. A lot of people didn't even know the plate numbers of their own cars.

All the same, Harry was still worried. He had to be sure. Suddenly he jumped up and set off for a busy shopping center where the crowds would give him the security of anonymity.

He checked the number of the hospital, then took his time for a few seconds practicing a tone of voice he thought would do the job. He hadn't forgotten the cross the girl had been wearing around her neck. When he was ready, he went into a phone booth and punched in the number.

When an operator answered, he spoke in his rehearsed voice. "This is Father Williamson," he said. "I'm inquiring about Miss Mary Malone."

"One moment, Father."

The internal ring was quickly answered. "Intensive Care, Quigley." The voice was female.

"This is Father Williamson. I'm very concerned about Mary Malone. Is she still in your care?"

"Yes, she's here."

"Is it possible for me to visit her?"

"Father, I don't believe a visit would help her right now. She's still in a coma."

"Oh, poor child! I take it that her condition is grave."

"That's right, Father. Father Lum, who serves us here, has given her final absolution."

"Then she's dying?"

"It doesn't look good, Father. Which parish are you from?"

The caller gave a very convincing sob over the phone before he hung up.

To meet her class Flavia had chosen a casual designer suit with a loose-fitting jacket. She was acutely aware that her physical attributes were the subject of close attention, so she usually dressed to minimize them. Once or twice she allowed herself to speculate on the probable results if she

152

were to wear a snug-fitting sweater to class without a brassiere. It would probably blow her diligent observer right out of the water.

After her lecture, the usual questions were slow in coming. She sensed what was in the wind. Finally a hand did go up.

"Dr. de la Torre," a girl asked, "is it true that you've been going out with the Sheriff's Homicide Bureau?"

"Not all at once."

There was a round of laughter.

"I mean, you've been seeing dead bodies and things like that?"

"Yes, I have," Flavia answered.

"How do you stand it?"

Flavia walked along the front of her desk before she turned to answer the question. "It's not a pleasant experience," she said, "but homicides do take place and have to be dealt with. I've been observing how professionally that's being done. It's not at all like TV where a detective walks once around a body, tries flexing one arm, and then says, 'Okay, take him away.'

"Last week the body of a young woman who had been strangled was dumped in an undeveloped park area. Someone put in an anonymous call to the police. The homicide team and the coroner's investigators arrived at about the same time. It was more than an hour later before the body was even turned over."

"What were they doing all that time?"

Flavia drew herself up. "I know you're interested, but this isn't the subject we're here to discuss. Our concern is the reasons why such things take place. What are the pressures that bring them about? What percentage of homicides are committed because of outside social pressures and what percentage are triggered by the basic viciousness that is part of some people's character? Most murder victims are killed by someone they know. The police

153

investigate crimes; it's the job of the sociologist to help to prevent them."

A young man raised his hand. "Is there any evidence that sociology has had any material effect on the existing crime rate?"

"Yes, definitely," Flavia answered. "We are constantly learning more about crime: what causes it and how it can be forestalled. Also the definition of crime has changed. It used to be that fornication was a punishable offense; now it's generally recognized that what consenting adults do in private is their own affair and not police business."

For the first time that she could recall, Flavia saw the man who usually spent his class periods diligently studying her body raise his hand. "Mr. Hellman," she said.

"We're accustomed to discussing things frankly here," he said. "I want to go back to your work with the homicide squad."

"It's the Sheriff's Homicide *Bureau*," she corrected. "What's your question?"

"The people who handle murders, day in and out, must become hardened."

"I haven't observed that."

"According to the newspapers, many of the victims are mutilated. And a lot of them are nude."

"Yes, that's true."

"Since you're a sensitive young woman, and not married, how do you keep sights like that from driving you out of your mind?"

Flavia took her time in shaping her answer. "By looking at them academically. No problems can be solved by ignoring them. Murder goes back to Genesis. I doubt if it can ever be totally eliminated, but a better understanding of human behavior and motives can be discovered."

"The papers have been talking about a new serial killer. Have you been exposed to any of that?"

"I prefer not to discuss that," Flavia said.

"Well, what kind of a person would he be?"

"Someone who is killing for the thrill of it, or someone who hates women."

"Hates them, Doctor?"

"Yes. Hate, Mr. Hellman, can take many forms. I'm not implying a homosexual here, rather someone who feels frustrated—who has been rejected by women sexually or in some other particular way and who in his sick and distorted mind is trying to get even."

"You're talking about a nut case, then."

"It's arguable that any murderer is unbalanced, but in this case I'd say no. According to the papers, the victims were apparently chosen at random. All of them were sexually violated in one way or another; all of them were tortured and then strangled. If these reports are true, then an unbalanced mind is not an adequate explanation for viciousness of this kind. This is deliberate, premeditated murder."

"With special circumstances."

"By the legal definition, yes."

"Then when the person is caught, would you favor giving him the death penalty?"

It was a direct challenge to her known position and it made her hesitate. Then she took refuge in the truth. "If anyone ever deserved the death penalty, the person committing these crimes does."

Hellman left the classroom and crossed a section of the campus to where a row of machines held a variety of food and beverages. There was a cafeteria, but the noise and crowding were more than he could stand. He settled for a chicken-salad sandwich and a Coke. He took them to one of the few open tables in the outdoor eating area and sat down, hoping that a girl would come and join him. He had long since learned that his good looks and muscular figure drew them like flies. If he got lucky, his one afternoon session would be an easy one to cut.

The girl who did choose to join him was another member

155

of his sociology class. She was bright, cheerful, and intelligent, but she was also vastly overweight. He endured her company for a few minutes before he excused himself and set off for a group of public telephones. Some of them were in use, but he had no trouble finding one that was not in use.

He dropped a coin and punched out a number. When the call was answered, he spoke with casual confidence. "Hello, Joe," he said. "This is Harry."

18

The first meeting of the new task force convened a little after eight in the morning on the first Friday of the month. The only jurisdictions represented were the Sheriff's Department and L.A.P.D. Later, other departments might be invited to join in.

The fact that he had been named commander of the operation had no outwardly visible effect on Mott; he drew his coffee like everyone else and was about to sit down when Willie and Miriam came in. "Sorry we're late," Willie said. "We've been on a hot one all night."

"Anything good?" he asked.

"Yes, we've got a suspect. He's in the can in Blythe now on an unrelated charge. They're holding him on three thousand dollars bail. If he makes it, they'll rebook him on suspicion of homicide until we collect him. A team's on the way."

That didn't require any immediate follow-up, for which

Mott was grateful. He was about to start things when four more men came in, two of them in L.A.P.D. uniform. Mott pointed toward the coffee urn, then helped to move a group of chairs into an informal circle.

"Sergeant Berkowitz," one of the plainclothesmen introduced himself. He wore the blue-and-white ID of the L.A.P.D. on his jacket lapel. "My partner, Larry Owens. Officers Reimschneider and Logge. They responded to a homicide this morning that may or may not fit the pattern."

"Glad to have you. I'm Lieutenant Mott, Homicide." He introduced the others and then asked a question. "Does anyone know about a body found in Glendale about an hour ago? I got a flash on it, but that's all."

"I just called them," Berkowitz said. " The victim is male and it looks like a another homosexual killing."

"A lovers' quarrel," Willie suggested.

"Probably," Berkowitz agreed.

Since that clearly didn't fit, Mott dropped it and began laying out the groundwork. "The phone lines are already open with a special number. There's also a direct line in from Homicide. I've laid on an eight-hundred number so that anyone in California can call us toll-free. I don't want to lose a good tip because someone in Burbank or Woodland Hills doesn't want to drop forty or fifty cents.

"You all know the drill: all incoming calls, including the wacko ones, go into the computer. Don't turn anything down that's even coherent."

"Including the psychics," Miriam noted.

"They've been known to be right," Mott said. "Anything that looks good at all, flag it and pass it on. We'll have more manpower in here as soon as it's needed. We're setting up files here with all the data we've got on known sex offenders, parolees that fit the time frame, and releases from the Laughing Academy."

He turned to the two uniformed L.A.P.D. patrolmen. "Tell us what you've got," he invited.

158

Reimschneider, who was obviously the senior man, had his notebook out.

"At four fifty hours this morning my partner and I responded to a possible one eighty-seven in the Watts area. We reached the scene at four fifty-three and found the victim with a ligature wound tightly around her neck. She was a female black, medium build, nude, age thirty to thirty-five. I got the ligature off while Jim called the paramedics. I gave the victim CPR with an AIDS mask for about five minutes until the paramedics got there and took over. They worked on the victim, but she was gone. They pronounced her at five eleven. Then I called Homicide."

"Good," Mott said. "Any questions?"

"Any background on the victim yet?" Levitzky asked.

"A little," Reimschneider answered. "We have a tentative ID. According to a neighbor, she was divorced. Her ex-husband was in the slammer for two eleven: he almost beat a stop-and-rob clerk to death because there wasn't enough money in the register to please him. He's a male black, six two, two hundred and thirty pounds, in for the third time. Paroled twice before, once for two eleven, once for rape."

"Still inside?" Miriam asked.

"Paroled four days ago," Logge answered.

"Then he's probably good for it," Mott said.

"The only common elements are strangulation and a female victim," Tracy pointed out. "In the three cases we're working on, wire coat hangers were used and the victims were all white teenagers."

"Another thing," Willie added. "The ex-husband was inside when the two homicides and the one attempted we've got went down."

"Still, I want it in the computer until L.A.P.D. wraps it up," Mott said. "Anything that even smells like what we're working on I want reported in full."

Deputy J. D. Smith from the Homicide Bureau came into the room. "On the Glendale thing," he reported. "It's a male victim, stabbed. He was still alive when G.P.D. got there. He lived long enough to name his live-in male lover as the perp."

"Pass on that one," Mott said. "The Com Center's notified all jurisdictions in the area that the task force is set up. We've asked that all patrol units be alerted and that all personnel have this number. That's for openers."

When Mott returned to his desk, there was a message for him to call Nurse Quigley at the Northridge Medical Center ICU. He read it twice as though by doing that he could dilute what it had to mean. Once more he told himself that the Malone girl had probably been brain damaged and that it was better this way, but it still was hard for him to accept. She had looked so pathetic lying motionless on her back, tubes and wires attached to her body, her eyes closed in a merciful coma. He pressed his lips together and punched out the number.

Nurse Quigley came on the line almost immediately. "I thought I'd better call you," she said.

"Thank you," Mott said. "I'm glad that Mary's out of her misery."

The nurse's voice rose a bit. "No, it isn't that, Lieutenant. She's still hanging in there. Dr. Wakabayashi feels that she may recover consciousness before long, although she won't be able to speak. I called you about something else."

For a moment Mott felt almost lightheaded with relief. "What is it?" he asked.

"Yesterday afternoon I took a call from a Father Williamson. He asked after Mary. He wanted to come and visit her. I told him that there would be no point in a visit, that she was still in a coma and that Father Lum, our Catholic chaplain, had already given her final absolution. Then when I asked him what parish he was from, he hung up on me."

Mott's mind was quickly weighing possibilities. "I take it you didn't feel right about this call," he said.

160

"No, Lieutenant, I didn't. So on my own I called the diocese this morning. They have no Father Williamson in this area. As soon as I learned that, I thought it best to call you."

"I'm glad you did," Mott said. "Look, I want you to notify hospital security immediately and also Sergeant Williams of L.A.P.D. He's familiar with the case."

"I've already alerted our security, Lieutenant, and the officer assigned to Mary. She still has a twenty-four-hour police guard. I'll call Sergeant Williams immediately."

Mott thanked the nurse before he hung up. Then, remembering that the Catholic Church was not the only one that used the title "Father," he checked a number and picked up the phone again. It took him less than a minute to reach the Episcopalian bishop in Los Angeles, who responded to his question at once from memory.

"I know Father Williamson very well," he said. "A splendid man. At present he's in Phoenix. How may we help you?"

Mott outlined the situation and added that it was important to keep everything confidential.

"It's quite possible that Father Williamson is a friend of the Malone family," the bishop said. "May I have your number?"

Mott gave him his direct, unlisted line, then leaned back to think. In less than five minutes the bishop called back. "I've spoken with Father Williamson," he reported. "He had read about the attack on Miss Malone in the paper, but he doesn't know her or any of her family to the best of his knowledge. Definitely he didn't call the hospital. He offered to help you in any way possible; I have his number if you need it. Oh, yes. To the best of my knowledge, and his, there's no other Father Williamson of any denomination anywhere in this area."

"I'm most grateful to know that," Mott said. "Please thank Father Williamson for me."

161

"I already took the liberty of doing that. Am I right in assuming that Miss Malone is Catholic?"

"Yes."

"Then her own people will be caring for her. However, if we can assist in any way, please call me directly."

When Mott hung up he was fairly certain that "Father Williamson" was the man who had attacked Mary Malone. His motive for the call was obvious: he wanted to know if she was still living and if she was likely to be able to talk very soon. Clearly, then, the attacker was frightened, which meant that he might attempt some desperate action.

Despite the fact that there are almost seven thousand sworn members of the Sheriff's Department, the internal-communications grapevine is a marvel of invisible efficiency. It's particularly potent in the Hall of Justice, where the sheriff himself and all of his higher level executives have their offices.

Well before ten in the morning Chief Jack Cargill knew that the Lorimer case had been cracked and that Flavia de la Torre had contributed to solving it. It gave him a moment of satisfaction. He had gone against procedure in allowing her as much rope as he had, but it had certainly paid off. If he had not stuck his neck out a little in letting her see some of the departmental files, she would never have spotted the clue that had led to Xavier Portofino.

He picked up a phone. "Get me Dean Cargill," he said.

The call took less than a minute to complete. "Morning," the chief said. "I've got a little story that might interest you."

"About Flavia?" the dean asked.

"Yes." In a few concise sentences he passed on the facts. "So what I called to say, Miles, was if you have any more over there like her, send them in. I can use them."

"Flavia is a bright gal," the dean agreed. "I'm very glad to hear that this is all working out. How's she doing at the crime scenes?"

"The first two she drew were pretty rugged, but, for a civilian with no previous experience, she held up well. Four seasoned investigators were impressed."

"You don't mind having her a while longer, then?"

"Not at all. By the way, while I have you on the line, has she done any field work up to now?"

"Partially," the dean said, "but she doesn't know that."

"Fill me in."

"Not long ago Cal State Northridge was asked to waive their normal entrance requirements and take in five hundred inner-city blacks who otherwise would have no opportunity for a college education."

"How did it work out?"

"Inside a month increased vandalism became a major problem. Wash basins were torn off the wall, toilet bowls were smashed, graffiti messed up the walls, and corridors stank of urine. The good part is that a few of the group showed some potential and were encouraged to continue. One of them is a candidate for Phi Beta Kappa. The rest were terminated."

"Too bad," the chief said. "What about Flavia?"

"Right now we're running a confidential state test program: a limited number of selected parolees have been admitted as undergraduate students. Frankly, I'm not happy about it, although a few of them seem to be shaping up and may eventually graduate. Flavia has one or two of them in her classes. She doesn't know it, nor do any of the other instructors. The campus police have a list, but it's in a restricted file."

"Flavia is single, isn't she?"

"Yes, she lives alone in a small apartment near the campus. She doesn't have any family in this country as far as I know."

"It isn't my problem, but I don't like it. Flavia is an exceptionally attractive woman, and with what's been going on lately, I can't help being concerned."

163

"I agree with you, Jack," the dean said. "Now add to that the fact that there are fifteen thousand other females here on campus and you'll understand why I don't always sleep too well at night."

19

On Sunday the *Daily News* ran an extended feature story on Mary Margaret Malone. The savagely injured girl who lay mute and unconscious in the Northridge Intensive Care Unit had already aroused wide public sympathy. The story summarized how she had been rescued from the bottom of a canyon by helicopter and rushed to the Trauma Center where highly skilled medical care had managed to stabilize her and give her a chance for life.

The story detailed some of the complex medical steps that had been taken to save her life. The reporter was careful not to say so outright, but he made it clear that there was little chance she would ever be able to speak again. The prognosis was uncertain: she might be able to survive for some time, but no great improvement was expected. The story concluded with a withering condemnation of the man responsible for the unspeakable things that had been done to her.

"Harry" read the story with great interest. When he had been through it twice and digested all of the details, he made a phone call. A little less than an hour later "Joe" picked him up in the van.

"We're okay now," Harry said. "The girl is out of it; it's all in the paper. Her brains are cooked and she can't talk—never will."

Joe was cautious. "Maybe she could write."

"Okay, say that she could. What's she going to put down?"

Joe thought for a moment. "Nothing," he concluded. "It's been more than a month. She won't remember nothin' except may be two guys in a van. She never saw the plate, I know that."

"So let's go have some fun. Did you bring the tape?"

"Yeah. It's in the place we fixed."

Harry smiled. "This damn van'll rust apart before they ever find it."

He was in an unusually good mood; the story in the paper had cleared his last fears away. He didn't know that before filing his piece the man who wrote it had checked with the Public Information Section of the Sheriff's Department. He was quickly put through to Captain Hinkle, the commander, who asked if one or two minor changes could be made in the story. As a result the published prognosis did not report that there had been a recent small improvement in the patient's condition, or that she was on the verge of coming out of her coma.

Also omitted from the story was any mention of the twenty-four-hour police guard that was still being kept over her.

Sylvia Estes, age fourteen, did not normally go out alone. Even though it was bright sunshine, and there was safety in numbers at the beach she loved, she was only allowed to

166

visit it with a group of other girls who went to the same church school and were approved of by her mother. She had been told repeatedly that she was too young to date although she was already five feet three and her breasts were developing very nicely. She knew that she would never be sensational, but she would not be flat-chested either. And who knew, she wasn't through growing as yet.

Because her mother wasn't feeling well, Sylvia had been sent to bring a few things from one of the last remaining small grocery stores in the Santa Monica area. She didn't mind; she could go on her skateboard and it was a way of getting out of the house. Every time she planned a small excuse, such as going to the library, her mother would find something for her to do. She understood beyond her years why her father had left his family. She loved her mother, but she could not wait for the day when she could get a job and gain some element of freedom. Because the girl in the TV ads looked so cute, she hoped that she too could sell Kentucky Fried Chicken.

She spent six dollars and forty cents for the items her mother wanted and started home. She was speeding along the sidewalk, enjoying the mobility of her skateboard, when the bottom of the paper sack suddenly gave way. It had been improperly glued and when she had shifted it in her arms, it had simply let go.

She jumped off her board, stopped it with one foot, and bent down to retrieve her purchases. Fortunately nothing was broken. It was then that a van pulled up to the curb and a nice-looking man got out to help her.

"Your bag's broken," he said. "Let me give you a lift home."

"No, thanks," Sylvia said, "I can make it okay." When she smiled her gratitude for the help she had been given, she looked quite pretty, almost as pretty as the girl in the TV ads.

Then the man clapped one hand across her mouth to keep her quiet, picked her up, groceries and all, and carried

167

her bodily into the van. With his right foot he kicked the sliding side door shut. Joe pulled away from the curb and seconds later swung around the next available corner. As far as he could see, there had been no witnesses.

Nevertheless, he took no chances. With the girl in the van there was no way they could talk their way out of a jam if they were caught. In six short blocks he reached a freeway entrance. He waited a few seconds for the light to change, then turned east on the Santa Monica Freeway. Not much more than five minutes later he took the transfer ramp north on the San Diego Freeway and in so doing verified that there was no police car or anything like that behind him. He was headed now across the Santa Monica Mountains into the San Fernando Valley. Five lanes of northbound traffic formed a steady stream of protection.

In half an hour he was clear of the valley and climbing up into the foothills of the San Gabriels. When he at last turned off the freeway, he was once more reassured to see that no other vehicle took the same turning directly behind him. He took a deep breath, and being careful not to attract any attention with his driving, he turned into a smaller road, then finally onto an unpaved fire trail that led up into an isolated area of the mountains.

Despite the fact that she was very young, and completely inexperienced in many ways, Sylvia Estes made some surprisingly adult decisions. She quickly sensed that the more she struggled and tried to scream, the harder she would make it for herself. She knew that she was in trouble, terrible trouble, and that the only way out would be to pretend complete cooperation, to make her abductors believe that she was enjoying the adventure.

She had had no sex experience of any kind. Once she had come close, but someone in the party had made a strong reference to San Quentin Quail. Besides, she had been having her period. As she lay in the van, on her back on the floor, she used every available minute to plan her strategy as best she could.

She had no hope they would just let her go: she had been kidnapped and she knew that was a very serious offense. If they wanted sex—and she was terribly afraid of that—no matter how much it might hurt, she would have to let them do it to her. But if she could take the initiative, pretend that she liked it and wanted more, they might take her back if she promised them another date real soon.

When the van at last came to a stop, on a completely secluded little plateau, Harry loosened the gag he had stuffed in her mouth. "You didn't have to do all that," she said. "I wasn't going to scream or anything."

She carried it off well and quickly saw she had scored a point; the handsome man had expected her to protest and plead. "We just picked you up to have some fun," he said.

"I like fun too," Sylvia answered. "Why spoil it by tying me up like this?"

"If we let you loose, what will you do for us?" Joe asked.

"What do you want me to do?"

Harry answered. "Well, you're a pretty cute kid. We like good-looking girls. We like to look at their bodies."

Sylvia's heart jumped; so far her plan *was* working. "Gosh, you can do that all over town," she said. "There's lots of nude bars."

"Yeah, but those babes aren't fresh and new like you. A lot of them are married and have kids. We like the ones like you, the kind everybody hasn't seen. So take off your clothes."

"You mean everything?"

"Yes, and don't tell us that you're on the rag."

She knew she had to appear daring, it was the best card she had to play. If it worked out, God willing, no one would ever know.

She shook her head. "I'm not. Make you a deal. What if I take off my clothes and . . . dance for you. Right here in the van; it's high enough. Have you got a tape deck?"

Harry looked at her oddly. "You don't mind?"

"I've done it before," she lied. "Some of my friends and I do it for kicks. Only it's more fun when there's a roomful of guys."

"What's the deal?" Joe asked.

"After I dance, take me back and don't let on what I did for you. On Saturday I'll take you to the beach house where we go for fun. I can't do it yet, I'm too young, but the other girls like to be with new guys. You know what I mean."

It was her one mistake. Up to that moment there was a chance they might have believed her. But when she brought up her age, it was a fatal error.

"Okay," Harry said, "it's a deal. What'll you tell your mama?"

"She never knows whether I'm in or out. Or cares."

Joe pushed a tape into the stereo player and turned the ignition key backward. Heavy-metal rock abruptly filled the van.

Sylvia tried to hold down her terror, knowing that now she would have to go through with it. She had no idea how, but she would have to try.

The first step had to be to take off her clothes. Holding herself in a tight grip and trying not to realize what she was doing, she went to the rear of the van, turned her back, and slowly took off her sneakers and socks. She tried to pay attention to the music and make it work for her. She had never let anyone see her body, but now she had no choice. That wasn't all: she would have to convince them that she liked to do it, that it was her kind of fun.

Concentrating on the music, she took off her blouse and then her slim little bra. She dropped them in the corner. Keeping going because she didn't dare to stop, she unzipped her shorts and added them to the rest. That left only her panties. She blinked hard and then pulled them off.

With her back still turned, she looked down at the little

170

pieces of cloth she had discarded. They were her only defenses, and she was desperate without them.

She had no idea how to dance nude, she had never seen it done. But they didn't really care about her dancing, she knew that. They wanted to see her boobs, her ass, and what pubic hair she had. All right, she'd do her best to try and show them. If they liked her enough, they might let her go.

She stood up, her back still turned, and moved her hips back and forth, letting them look all they wanted at her slim buttocks. She was acutely aware that she was naked, but at least she was not too bad-looking, and that would help. Blinking back quick tears that had appeared unwanted in her eyes, she pivoted around and tried to sway her body as though she was on a dance floor with a boy partner. She turned a little each way to make the most of her breasts, the best thing she had to offer. Then, remembering some cigarette ads she had seen in magazines, she curved her hands around her hips, showing herself off the only way she knew. She was so frightened she almost ignored the crashing beat of the music.

Turned around in the front seat, Joe was watching. Harry snickered.

She had never been a good dancer; if her mother had only let her go out on a few dates, she would have been able to do better. She was desperately trying to be convincing. Everything now depended, she believed, on making them lust for more. On Saturday. With more girls to show their bodies.

"Pretty classy stuff," Joe said. "Shall we take her back?"

Harry slowly shook his head. "Can't take the chance," he said. "She's too far under age. We better do like we planned."

Joe, his blood already pounding in his veins, did not argue. He took the tape out of its hiding place and put it into the recorder. When he had done that he looked at Harry and let a slow, knowing smile form on his face. They had another one and where they were it was dead safe to do whatever they wanted with her.

Despite the little plateau they were on, from a quarter-mile away the van could not be seen at all. The night was closing in fast. At first Sylvia pleaded as best she could, then the van was filled with the deep sobbing cries of a girl just verging onto womanhood.

She submitted, as she had to, to heartless rape until both men had exhausted themselves sexually. Then she was forced to perform acts that made her glassy-eyed with horror. She tried her best to lock her mind out of the frightful realities she could not escape: her pitiful attempt to win her release with her clumsy little dance, and her brave lies that she had so desperately hoped would save her.

When she could do no more, and lay on the floor of the van bleeding from her vagina and her rectum, Harry opened a compartment and took out a coat hanger. As he began to twist it around her neck, he did it slowly so that her screams would reach a maximum of intensity. They would sound better on the tape that way.

When they knew that she was at last dead, Joe drove the van away. He knew they shouldn't dump her there; the spot was too good a place for the next time. Harry rolled her body into the compartment that had been built supposedly to hold surfboards. Back on the freeway they drove many miles before turning up into the mountains once more to find a dump site.

20

After her daughter had been gone for more than two hours, Mrs. Thelma Estes made some frantic calls to the grocery store and to the homes of Sylvia's friends where she might have gone. Then she phoned the police.

The Santa Monica sergeant who answered the call began by following the policy of not taking reports on missing teenagers until they had been gone for twenty-four hours. There were far too many cases of valuable and needed manpower wasted on chasing down kids who had just taken it into their heads to go to the movies, or to visit friends, or to join in impromptu slumber parties. Also, many children stayed away from home because they were fearful of reprimands or punishment awaiting them for being late in the first place.

Nevertheless, the sergeant asked some preliminary questions. How old was the girl? How long had she been expected to be away? How tall was she and how much did she weigh? What was the color of her hair and eyes? Had there been any kind of a misunderstanding or quarrel before she went out?

The sergeant took the call-back number and then rang the watch commander. "I've just had a report call on a missing juvenile," he said. "Female white, age fourteen, five three, a hundred and five to a hundred and ten pounds, blond and blue. Left to go to a nearby market to buy groceries a little more than two hours ago."

The watch commander knew immediately why he had been called: it could fit. "Was the market checked?" he asked.

"Yes, by the mother. It's a neighborhood mom-and-pop. They remember her coming in. She was on a skateboard."

"When?"

"About two hours ago. It's only five minutes, according to the mother, from the home to the store. She's already called all of the girl's nearby friends. All replies negative."

"Is she attractive?"

"The mother says she's very pretty. When I heard that, I called you."

"Send a detective unit," the watch commander ordered. "Also notify the L.A.P.D. task force that we have a possible." The lieutenant knew he might be overreacting, but in a case of this kind he wasn't going to take any chances.

Sixteen minutes later a dark blue Chevy with plain black tires drew up a few steps from the home of the missing girl and two men in business suits got out. When the very upset woman inside answered the door, they held up their police ID cards.

"Come in," the woman said and led the way into a ten-by-fourteen living room. It was neat and plainly decorated with inexpensive framed prints. A small spinet piano was against the wall in one corner. "I'm Sergeant Blaylock," one of the men said. "This is my partner, Detective Swenson."

174

The woman sat on the front edge of a chair, weaving her fingers together in shapeless patterns. When the two men remained standing she said, "Oh, sit down. I'm sorry, I don't know what I'm doing."

Despite the fact that he appeared to be a gruff, middle-aged man in a somewhat hard-boiled mold, Sergeant Blaylock was unexpectedly sympathetic. As he spoke, he listened for the sound of footsteps that could come at any moment. "You're the missing girl's mother?" he asked. Beside him his partner already had his notebook open on his knee.

"Yes. I'm Thelma Estes. I'm . . . separated from my husband."

"Tell us about your daughter," Blaylock invited.

Carefully the miserable woman did her best. She left to get a box of Kleenex and began to wipe her eyes. She answered all the routine questions carefully, adding more details as she remembered them.

"What kind of skateboard did she have?" Blaylock asked.

"The usual kind, I guess. It's oval-shaped with wheels underneath. I think it's dangerous and I don't like her to use it, but so many of her friends have them . . ."

Swenson got up and asked to use the telephone. He was a slender young man who did not let his sharp intelligence show on the outside. He was number one on the promotion list to make sergeant.

"You've called all of her known friends," Blaylock confirmed.

"Yes. No one's seen her. They all promised to call me back the moment she shows up . . . if she does."

The fact that it was already late twilight underlined the uncertainty.

"Could she have gone to a show?"

"No, she'd never do that. And she had groceries to bring home for our supper."

"Would you like us to call her father? She might have gone there."

"I've no idea where he is."

"Mrs. Estes, all of our patrol units have been notified. One of them is checking every step of the way from the market back to here."

The woman broke down in tears. When Swenson came back in the room he drew a female shape in the air and lifted his eyebrows.

"Would you feel better, Mrs. Estes," Blaylock asked, "if we have a policewoman come to be with you?"

"I don't know that that would do any good." More tears followed. Blaylock stopped and let her get it out of her system. He glanced at his watch; the girl had now been missing for more than two and a half hours.

The silence was split by the sound of the doorbell. The woman looked up in sudden expectation, but before she could get to her feet, Swenson had already gone to answer it.

Because there was no entryway, a uniformed patrol officer could be seen in the doorway. He was holding a skateboard by the edges in his hands. "We looked for footprints," he said quietly, "but there's no chance. It's all paved or hardstand."

Swenson took the skateboard and came back into the room. He squatted down and showed it to the mother. "Is this your daughter's property?" he asked.

"Yes, I think so." The woman shook her head. "But I can't be sure. I never really looked at it. I didn't like it and . . ."

The doorbell rang once more and again Swenson was quick to respond. A man in a business suit was outside. "J. D. Smith," he said. "Sheriff's task force."

"Homicide?" Swenson asked under his breath.

"Yes."

"Come in."

Swenson introduced the newcomer to Mrs. Estes who looked up in questioning concern. "This is Deputy Smith from the Sheriff's Department. He's with a special task force that looks for missing persons."

"Thank you for coming," the woman said. "I've just given these men all the information I have."

Blaylock supplied a quick and concise summary, suitably edited so as not to alarm Mrs. Estes any further. He knew all about the task force and why it had been organized.

Blaylock made a decision. "Mrs. Estes, I'm going to assign an officer to stay with you until your daughter returns. If the phone rings, let him answer it; he'll know what to say. If Sylvia calls, we'll have her picked up and brought right home."

The woman lifted reddened eyes to Smith. "Are you a detective?" she asked.

"Yes, ma'm, I am. We look for missing persons all over the county."

"Do you . . . find them?"

Smith gave her a confident smile. "We have a very high success rate." He stole a quick glance at a clock mounted on the wall, then without asking went to the telephone. He dialed the number for Homicide. When the barrel man answered, he spoke quietly and clearly. "I'm at the home of Sylvia Estes who was reported missing by her mother about three hours ago. She left to run a short errand to the local grocery. She got there and bought some things, but she hasn't come back as yet."

The barrel man knew that Smith was speaking that way because others could hear. "Any significant similarities?" he asked.

"Some, yes, as of this moment."

"Do you want backup?"

"Not right now. But notify Mott and the task force."

"Will do, immediately. He's off, but Lieutenant Gordon is available."

"Good. I'll supply details as soon as I touch base with the Santa Monica Station."

Smith gave the call-back number and hung up. When he turned from the phone, Mrs. Estes was on her feet weaving

177

her fingers together again. "Are you going to find my daughter for me?" she asked.

"Believe me, we're going to do our best. So are these gentlemen. And you have no idea how good we can be."

Blaylock went to the door and signaled to the patrol unit that was still parked outside, near to, but not directly in front of the house. When the patrolman who had recovered the skateboard responded, he intercepted him outside. "I want you to stay with this lady," he said. "Handle all phone calls. Have you had the course on that?"

"Yes, sir."

"Outstanding. Call in any developments immediately."

"I'll do that." He paused a moment. "The other fellow?"

"Sheriff's Homicide; he's assigned to the coat-hanger killer task force."

The young officer received that news with real concern. "How about the girl, sir— what do you think?"

Blaylock hesitated before answering. "I don't like the way it looks at all," he said.

Deputy Don Stotts, who worked out of the San Dimas Station, drove a mountain patrol unit. It was a high-off-the-ground four-wheel-drive vehicle that was built for hard work over rugged terrain. It was painted the standard sheriff's black and white and had code-three capability: roof lights and a concealed siren that could clear the way in an emergency. In the back, behind the rear seat, there was a considerable stock of equipment that was likely to be useful in the wilderness areas of the San Gabriel Mountains.

Deputy Stotts had an expert's knowledge of the mountains and the roads through them: the few that were paved and the many that led off into dead-end canyons or served as fire breaks up to the top of many of the peaks. He also knew the people who lived in the mountains and often why they were there. He knew which of the isolated houses held an elderly lady who was a Cordon Bleu chef and famed for her unmatched onion soup that he had been invited to

178

sample many times. He knew the isolated sites where devil worship had taken place and could point out the 6's painted on posts and poles to show the way there.

It would surprise most people to learn that within a few minutes' drive of the foothills there was a 63,000-acre wilderness area set aside for protected bighorn sheep. The animals were seldom glimpsed by those who drove the narrow, winding paved road that led deeper into the designated recreation areas. Farther still in the range there was another, even larger haven for the sheep that looked as though no human being had ever invaded the area. It was almost impossible to believe that only a few miles away, as the helicopter flies, was the vast, congested sprawl of Los Angeles with its lush estates, its ghettos, its rich and its poor whose bits of land, if any, were measured off in square feet or even inches.

In the mountains all this was invisible; much of the vast area seemed as virgin as creation. Miles to the north lay the desert, adding to the feeling that here time had elected to stand still.

However, there were some facilities thinly scattered along the few paved roads: a general store with a lunch counter, a mobile home park tucked away on a small bit of level ground, and a Federally operated campsite for those who wanted to bring their campers, tents, or motor homes up where trees grew unmolested and the air was fresh and pure. These people, too, needed police protection; Don Stotts helped to provide it. He was skilled in rescue techniques and in CPR and other forms of first aid, and he carried radio equipment that could summon any help that might be needed.

Halfway through a cool, bright morning, Deputy Stotts rolled his unit into the parking area of a combination campground, store, and restaurant. It was the only such facility for miles around. He bought himself a soft drink and went outside where three forest rangers, two male and

179

one female, were seated at an impromptu picnic table. One of them pushed over a bag of potato chips to be shared.

All four knew the mountains intimately. Whenever an occasion rose, they worked together with smooth cooperation, never drawing sharp lines of distinction between whose job was what. Safety and security in the mountains, and the protection of the environment, were their common objectives. Whenever the rangers felt the need for backup, Don represented The Law, as did the K-9 patrol car assigned to the area and the second patrol unit that was on hand weekends. On call where mountain rescue teams, paramedics, fire fighters, and other resources, but the whole huge area was handled by just a handful of sworn personnel, each of whom had a greater area to cover than almost anyone else in the 4,000-square-mile county.

When he had finished his drink and exchanged all of the fresh information of the day, Don visited the washroom and then got back in his car to resume patrol. The stop had been close to an almost dry riverbed; now the road began to climb, winding through wild and desolate country that had changed little in a hundred years. There were occasional short spur roads that led off to the side, sometimes no more than rutted tracks in gravel. Deputy Stotts knew every one of them and he checked them all out regularly. Experience had taught him that it paid to do so.

He also knew every place where a car or other vehicle had gone off the road, often to lie rusting at the bottom of an almost inaccessible canyon. He could read the marks along the roadway in a manner that Daniel Boone would have admired. Whenever anything was significantly different from his last patrol, he automatically checked it out.

Which is how he found the body of Sylvia Estes. It had been dumped underneath a clump of high bushes fifty feet off the roadway.

As soon as he saw what he had, he backed his unit to block off the access and called in. "Eighty-one Adam King."

As soon as that was acknowledged, he said, "I've got a nine twenty-seven David, confirmed. Subject is a white female, age fourteen to seventeen. Request full one eighty-seven response. Also request notification to special task force unit." He added an accurate description of the location.

That done he took out a thousand-foot roll of yellow crime-scene tape and began to close off the area. He was careful to string the tape around everything that might be affected or contain any clues. Before he finished the K-9 unit rolled up and the driver helped him with the task. In the back of the car, a big German shepherd waited, ready for his call to duty.

A forest ranger car was the next to arrive. The girl in it took over traffic control, keeping the few drivers who came by from stopping to gawk.

The radio on Don's unit came over the outside speaker he had turned on. "Eighty-one Adam King."

"Eighty-one Adam by," Don responded.

"Have you pronounced?"

"Yes."

That meant that no emergency medical assistance was needed; the coroner would be notified instead.

"Eighty-one Adam, advise if MO matches previous task force cases."

"Affirmative."

Normally a deputy in the field would not pronounce a person dead; to do that usually took a sergeant or better, a paramedic, or another medically qualified person. The few mountain patrol deputies, with their exceptionally heavy responsibilities, did not hesitate to expand their own authority when the circumstances required it, an arrangement that worked out well.

The response was heavy. A homicide team rolled, the coroner's team with a criminalist following behind it, a staff artist, a photographer and print deputy, two specialists from the crime lab, and Mott, who had just

181

returned, as field commander. As the handling deputy, Don Stotts stood by at the scene with the K-9 unit backing him up. Two more forest rangers came to supply further backup. Normally the crime-lab personnel would not respond unless summoned by the field commander, but this was a special case where time might be of the essence.

When Mott got there he walked carefully around any possible footprints or tire tracks until he stood beside the body. He looked down at the slender, naked form of what had been an attractive teenager. Her budding breasts had been ripe with the promise of womanhood, her pubic triangle small but developing. Around her throat, much of it invisible where it cut deeply into the flesh, there was another coat hanger, twisted and fastened in the same manner he had seen before.

Despite his experience, and the discipline of his profession, a gradually mounting anger built within him until his body began to shake. The evidence of unspeakable cruelty was clear and stark on the arms and abdomen of the body. The kind of monster that could inflict such wounds outraged him beyond his ability to control himself. He was still fighting to recover his composure when J. D. Smith appeared beside him. Smith had a picture in his hands. Without comment he knelt down and carefully compared the picture to the body, back and forth several times. "Can you ID her?" Mott asked.

"Yes."

"Where from?"

"Santa Monica."

It remained silent for several seconds before Mott trusted himself to speak again. "I'm going to get him," he said with an abrupt hardness in his voice. I'm going to get him. *And make him pay.*"

"We will," J.D. confirmed.

"And if the Supremes let this one off, I'll kill him myself with my bare hands."

His voice was shaking with emotion. J.D. knew that no

field commander should ever say such a thing, but he felt exactly the same way himself.

He did not dare to tell Mott that the California Supreme Court had just handed down a new decision. The Court had ruled that although the defendant had fired a gun at his victim from a proven distance of nineteen and a half inches away, that still didn't constitute proof of intent to kill. The defendant's death sentence had been reversed on that basis.

If Mott had known about that at that particular moment, he might not have been able to contain himself at all.

21

It had been a long and unre-
warding task, but Tracy and Levitzky had interviewed
almost everyone who had attended the church meeting
where Marcia Lowell had last been seen alive. Carefully
and tactfully they had extracted bits of information that
the young people they talked with had not known they
possessed. As a pattern began to emerge, they agreed to
save Jenson Murdock for the last. When they sat down with
him, they wanted to have everything they could possibly
get first.

At seventeen Jenson had an overabundance of self-
confidence. He knew about a lot of things that were going
on and how to play dumb if he were asked any questions.
He was certain that he was not only smart, but also sharp
and fully mature. Any suggestion to him that his intellect
and his body were not yet fully developed would have met
with disdain. If any homicide detectives came to see him,

he was confident they would leave no wiser than when they had come. It would be a good chance to play cops and robbers with real cops.

When Jenson's mother answered the door and they introduced themselves, she was not surprised. She had already heard that the attendees at the church meeting were all being interviewed. "Jenson's here," she said. "He's up in his room—studying. I'll call him for you."

Levitzky picked that up very smoothly. "Please don't," he said. "We have only a few things to ask him and it would be much simpler if we could go up."

"Yes, if you'd like. I'll go and tell him . . ."

Tracy offered a generous smile. "Don't bother," he said. "We do this all the time." Quietly he started up the stairs.

Which is how it happened that when Jenson answered the soft knock on his door he found himself facing two homicide investigators whose combined experience was longer than his lifetime. As soon as they identified themselves, he made a good show of cordiality. "Oh, sure, come on in," he said. He cleared a stack of books off one chair, a pile of clothes off another, and invited his guests to sit down.

"You want to talk about Marcia Lowell, is that right?" he asked. When he got an answering nod, he continued. "She was a swell girl. Everybody liked her. None of us have gotten over what happened to her yet. I keep thinking about her; I can't help it."

"I don't blame you," Tracy said in his most sympathetic voice. "I never met her, of course, but I've seen pictures. She was lovely." She had not looked very nice on the autopsy table, but he was not about to mention that.

"You got that right, man."

"How well did you know her?"

Jenson perched himself on the edge of his bed, trying with his body language to express complete cooperation. "As well as any of the guys, I guess. We spent some time together."

185

"What do your friends call you, Jenson?" Levitzky asked.

"Jack. I hate Jenson; it was my mother's maiden name. And I sure as hell don't like Jenny."

"Of course, Jack. Anybody would understand that."

Tracy took out his notebook and opened it conspicuously on his knee.

"Now, you were at the church meeting when Marcia was there—right?"

"Yeah, I was there. I'm not so big on the church thing, but as long as I keep going, they let me use the car."

Tracy made a note. "How many guys would you say Marcia dated?"

"Not many; her family was tough about it, you know."

As Tracy wrote, Levitzky spoke. "I can understand that, since she was so attractive and, as you said, well developed for her age."

"Yeah, I guess so."

"Do you know many of the men she went out with?"

At the word *men* Jack swelled up a little like a young bullfrog learning the art. "Sure, I know most of the guys. We're kinda by ourselves up here, like a closed society."

"What kind of things did she like? Bowling, for example?"

"No, she didn't go for that. She liked disco if she ever got a chance to go. The movies sometimes."

Tracy took up the conversation and asked a number of other questions, making a note after each one. By then he had a very clear impression of young Mr. Murdock.

When he was ready to start a new tack, he made a careful show of putting his notebook away in his pocket. "Now," he said, "I'd like to put this interview on an off-the-record, man-to-man basis."

"Sure," Murdock said.

"First of all, Jack, I'll tell you straight out that we don't think that you had anything to do with Marcia's death."

"Hell no, man; no way!"

186

Levitzky nodded sagely. "Also you've got a solid alibi. We checked on everyone, you understand."

Jack shifted to a new position on the bed.

"Let me explain just who we are," Tracy said. "We're Homicide. Our job is to find out who killed her, and that's what we're going to do. That's all that concerns us. We're not narcs or anything like that. That kind of stuff is chicken shit to us."

Jack nodded that he understood.

"Now the word we get," Tracy continued, "is that several guys took her out when they had the chance, but you were number one in her book. You were seen with her more than anyone else."

"I guess that's right." He tried to make it sound like an admission, but his pride showed through.

"Now," Tracy continued, "do you know if anyone offered her a ride home from the church party?"

The response came quickly to that. "I saw a couple of guys ask her; I could tell that's what it was."

"But they didn't make out."

"No."

Tracy leaned forward. "Remember, Jack, this is strictly off the record—you know what that means."

"It's like you didn't hear it."

"You've got it. Did you have her lined up?"

Jack hesitated and moved again on the bed. "Yeah, in a way," he answered.

"She was waiting for you."

"That's right."

Tracy crossed his legs, smiled, and relaxed more comfortably in his chair. Levitzky already appeared to be fully at ease.

"Okay, Jack, now between men. We know she was under age, but that doesn't concern us. In some states a girl can get married at fifteen."

"I know a girl who did," Levitzky contributed to build up

the atmosphere. "And she'd been behind the barn a lot before then."

"So don't worry about that," Tracy continued. "How much did Marcia enjoy being female?"

"She liked it a lot."

"Did she like being around men?"

"Sure. Of course."

"We hear that she sent an application to a model agency," Levitzky said.

"Yeah, but her mother didn't know about it. How did you guys find out?"

"It doesn't matter," Tracy answered. "Now the way we figure it, when you drove her home, the two of you found a few minutes to neck a little."

"That's a gone word," Jack said, "but I know what you mean. Sure, we liked to get close. We knew a place. But we could only stay five minutes or so."

"Five minutes with her could still be a lot of fun," Tracy said.

"That's right," Jack conceded.

The atmosphere of understanding between the men appeared to be growing, as Tracy intended. Jack seemed completely at his ease. "Young as she was, I hear she was pretty well stacked," he said.

Jack decided to try his own gambit. "This is still off the record?"

"Absolutely."

"She had everything a girl could want," he said. "Not a mark on her. And her tits were the nice light kind. They stood right out and didn't hang down." Then he waited for the reaction.

"There's nothing wrong with admiring a pair of tits. There's no law against it." Tracy passed it off as inconsequential.

The moment being as good as he could expect, he asked the key question. "If everything was okay, Jack, would she put out?"

It was just a little too much. Jack hesitated and the moment was lost. "I didn't have her," he said without conviction. "Too much risk. She could get knocked up or if a cop caught us . . ."

Levitzky picked it up and tried for the rebound. "Still, she could have been worth it. Especially if you were careful."

Jack came halfway. "Like I said, I didn't screw her. But I'll tell you this: she wasn't any virgin."

Tracy dismissed it with a gesture. "We already knew that," he said. "Where did you drop her off?"

"Around the corner from her home. Her family, you know."

Tracy stood up. "Thanks a lot, Jack," he said. "You've really helped us. One more question. When you dropped her off, did you see anyone else around?"

Jack shook his head.

"Was there any other traffic?" Levitzky asked.

Jack started to shake his head again and then stopped. "I think a van went past," he said.

"What kind of a van?"

"Not much of a one. The paint was real plain, not classed up at all."

"What color was it?" Tracy almost held his breath.

"I don't know. Gray, maybe. It was night and I was thinkin' about other things."

Joe could not go very long without driving his van; he was too proud of it. Its drab exterior was by his choice and for a purpose, but nobody could put down the interior. It was pure luxury and built to look that way. Once the chicks saw the inside they were half hooked. And it was dead safe, because there was no law against having the best-looking job of its kind on the beach or the strip.

He liked to park it and then sit with the side door open so that everyone could see what a classy job he had. Sometimes he would sit in the doorway and just talk to people who came past, building up the idea that he was a nice open guy who would never do anything wrong to anybody.

He was still on parole, but there was no way anyone could tell that. If any cops came snooping around, he was looking good. And he was careful never to hang around the same place too long.

When Harry was with him, that was different. Sometimes they would just go for a ride, enjoying themselves and talking about what they had already done. A few times they picked up a couple of girls and had sex with them in the back of the van. It was an in thing. As long as the girls weren't clearly juveniles, the cops wouldn't do anything about it. Probably they didn't want to, because they liked to get laid themselves. There was no point in spoiling a good thing.

Each time he picked up Harry, he did so in a different place. It was a simple precaution. They had also agreed to let at least a week go by before they went for another female, just to be sure that all their tracks were covered behind them. There was always the possibility that someone might have seen them somewhere and remembered. But after a week had passed, their minds would have already been filled with too many other things.

He picked up Harry at the place they had agreed right on the minute. It wouldn't pay to be seen hanging around.

It was only eight days since they had had the incredible excitement of torturing and slowly strangling the dumb little bitch who thought she could dance her way out of trouble. It had been Joe's first killing, the only one where Harry had not had to help. Joe still remembered his humiliation the first time, when he'd had to stop before he was through and Harry had had to take over and finish the job. Now he had redeemed himself and he knew that Harry was pleased. They had become a full-fledged team with confidence in each other's abilities.

Because it was too soon to take another one, they drove

up into the mountains, away from everyone, and played the tape. Once again they listened to and savored the requests to be let out, then the demands, then the desperate pleadings for mercy. After that came the terrible screams that almost burst their eardrums. They were so loud, Harry turned down the volume a little to be sure that the sound wasn't carrying too far.

Joe's eyes were shining. "Great, great!" he said. "I almost forgot how good that first one was!"

"You still got the Polaroid pictures safe?" Harry was always careful.

"Nobody's ever goin' to find them," Joe answered. "It's impossible."

"Not if they take your room apart, piece by piece?"

"They're not in my room. I got 'em put where if the house burns down, they go too. But they can't be found."

"I'm thinking about the tape," Harry said. "If they ever get this van, they'll find the tape."

"I'm not so sure," Joe said.

"Then be sure: the pigs ain't stupid. So I got an idea."

Harry's ideas were always good, so Joe listened carefully. "It's why I've brought my ghetto blaster," he said. "I boosted it from a pawnshop when the old kike went in the back to get something. It's top of the line and can make copies."

"You want to make another one?" Joe asked.

Harry looked at him with near contempt. "Hell no! The tape and the pictures are evidence, so we've got to be damn careful. If we get stopped sometime and they search the van for dope, they might find the tape. It's possible. So I'm going to take one of our regular tapes and let the music run on for fifteen minutes. Then I'll copy onto the rest of it what we've got."

Joe saw it. "Then we'll put that tape with all the others."

Harry sat perfectly still; he liked to do that. "If they find one tape stashed away, they've got to be suspicious of it. But if they see sixty, it won't mean a thing. Even if they

191

happen to pick up the right one and play it, they'll get hard rock for a long time. It'll be safer that way."

Joe knew then how smart he had been when he had picked his partner. He watched as Harry deftly fitted tapes into his machine, let the prerecorded one run a third of the way through on high speed, and then set up the copying circuit. As the screams sounded through the van once more, he felt a powerful tightening in his groin. He would not give up what they were doing for anything on earth!

When Harry had finished he took the original cassette and with two pieces of tissue wiped it clean. "It isn't safe just to copy over something," he explained. "One of the guys in the joint got caught that way."

He got out of the van and walked to one side until he stood at the edge of a wild, almost impassable canyon. There he ground the cassette under his heel until it was completely shattered. He gathered up the pieces and with a powerful throw flung them far down into oblivion.

"I got another thing to tell you," he said when he was back in the van. "You know I'm going to the university on that parolee program."

"You told me," Joe said.

"I figured it would be a very good way to meet chicks who like to fuck."

"Are you making out?" Joe asked.

Harry didn't answer. He sat still once more; not even his hands moved. He took his time before he spoke. "I've got this one class in sociology. The teacher is the sexiest goddamned bitch I've ever seen. I don't care how she dresses, her body would drive anybody mad. She's older, maybe thirty, but she's so stacked I don't give a damn."

Joe had a partial flash of insight. "We're going to fix her, right?" he asked.

Harry's face seemed to burn with a massive inner passion. "We're gonna fix her, all right! Somehow I'll work it so we can. And when we do, it's going to be better than anything we've ever done before. She'll get down on her knees and do me, and you, and we'll take her any way we like as often as we want to. And after that . . ."

"You got something special in mind?"

"You bet I have," Harry said. "And don't ask me what it is. You don't even want to know, not yet."

"Whatever it is, I'm game," Joe told him.

"I'm counting on that," Harry answered. "Because I guarantee it's going to make a man out of you."

22

Despite the sunlight that burned a bright pattern through the windows and onto the floor, the atmosphere in the room was thick, heavy, and grim. The men and women who were gathering there moved almost mechanically as they helped themselves to cups of coffee. Some took one of the doughnuts that Winchell's had thoughtfully provided. When Ralph Mott came in, a few of those present were surprised to see that he had Flavia in tow.

Without his asking, the task force room quieted down. Most times when cops gather together, even under grim conditions, there is some banter, perhaps because it makes the job easier. This time there was not even mention of the fact that the California Angels had moved up to a solid three-game lead in the division. It was a different and in some ways a dangerous mood, because no one could predict with certainty what the all-too-human members of the team might do if the killer they were all after fell into their hands.

It did not take long for everyone to settle down. As soon as it was quiet, Mott began a short briefing. He kept his voice well modulated and under control, something that required a conscious effort on his part, at least on this occasion.

"To begin," he started off, "I'd like to introduce two new members of the task force: Sergeant Tim Blaylock and Detective Arvid Swenson of the Santa Monica P.D."

There was a slight vocal stir, but that was all.

"We all know the fact we have to face," Mott continued. "We've got another one. The idea of a copycat killing has been looked at and dismissed; this latest homicide is the same MO, and with certain details that we haven't let out to anyone. The victim is Sylvia Estes, female white, age fourteen, blond, said to have been very attractive. She disappeared from the street within a maximum of three blocks from her home in broad daylight. No witnesses. She went to get some groceries, bought them, and started home on a skateboard. After that—nothing."

His listeners were familiar with those facts, but he laid them out for the sake of good procedure.

"Blaylock and Swenson are the detective team who responded to the Estes home a little more than two hours after the girl was missing. They started an immediate investigation, but they had almost nothing to work with. J. D. Smith responded on behalf of the task force and had no better luck." He raised his voice just a little. "I've been over what was done by these people and I can only tell you that they lost no time at all and made an exhaustive search for witnesses. They got nothing. The area from which the girl disappeared is all either paved or hard soil that won't take any kind of a print."

Mott stopped and took a very deliberate deep breath. He let it out slowly while he prepared himself for what had to come next.

"I have to tell you, and this is not for publication, that the Estes girl was horribly tortured; she suffered the most of any of the four victims we have—so far. I hope to God there won't be any more. The pathologist who did the autopsy said that it is the worst thing he has seen in more than twenty years on the job."

Most of the people in the room were taking notes, printing in block letters as procedure demanded.

When everyone had caught up, Mott went on. "Now on the plus side. One of my best teams, Tracy and Levitzky, has been working on the Marcia Lowell case." He nodded toward the portrait blowup mounted on the wall. "They're satisfied that no one in the immediate neighborhood of the dead girl is responsible for her murder. They learned two things that may be of help. First, the girl herself was already sexually active, at least to some degree. Second, they found a witness who saw a van cruising in the area just before she disappeared."

"Description?" someone asked.

"Yes," Mott answered. "The witness reported that it had a dull paint job. He believes it's gray, but it was night and he isn't sure. You know that van owners usually keep their machines looking good, and that a lot of them have custom paint jobs to set them off. A dull gray van without any lettering could be what we're looking for. It's thin, I admit, but I've got something else."

He stopped to be sure that everyone was listening. They were; even the man refilling his coffee cup was paying more attention to Mott than he was to the job he was doing.

"Mary Malone, the third known victim of the killer we're after, has been reported in the press as still in a coma and with very little hope of recovery. That story was a plant; we had media cooperation. The good news is that her prognosis is much better. She's coming out of a coma and has rational moments. She has had surgery on her throat and her larynx has been virtually restored to normal. As of this morning, her recovery is expected."

That *was* good news, but everyone present knew that it had to be kept a tight secret. The atmosphere in the room loosened and several of those present shifted their postures. Miriam, the homicide detective, got up and helped herself to a doughnut.

A living witness was desperately needed and it looked as if they were going to have one.

"I don't want you to be too optimistic about this," Mott told them. "Physically she's making a comeback, at least she's off the critical list. Mentally, it's a different story. When she's conscious, and she is quite a bit now, she just lies there and stares ahead. Remember, she was tortured and then thrown down a steep, two- to three-hundred-foot cliff. Some of her bones were broken. She had very bad abrasions and other injuries. Then she lay there, with a coat hanger strangling the breath out of her lungs, until the paramedics got to her. Do you wonder that her mind won't function, that it's trying to block it all out?"

He stopped and reminded himself that the people he was talking to were professionals. This case was just a lot worse than most—that was all. "Now," he said, "despite everything, she did manage to speak a few words when she was first brought in. I was told she said something that sounded like *man*, or *men*. It wasn't *man*, though, it was *van*. I'm sorry it took so long for me to see that. Then she gave us two names: Joe and Harry. We've run that combination in every way we can think. We did turn up several makes of the Harry and Joe combination, but none of them checked out. Any comments so far?"

Detective Swenson from Santa Monica had one. "We don't have all the data as yet, but so far it seems to us as if the victims are being chosen at random, based on the opportunity to pick them up. All four of them, as we understand it, were taken off the street."

"Good point," Mott agreed. "At least two of the victims disappeared very close to their homes. By the way, none of them had anything to do with prostitution; we're sure of that.

"Now as to motive. We have our own department shrink and a good one, but he's in St. Louis at a convention. I've asked one of the advisors to the Sheriff's Department, Dr. de la Torre, to tell us what she can. She's a sociologist and has been out on several recent homicides."

Flavia stood up, because she was accustomed to talking to a group on her feet. "As Lieutenant Mott told you, I'm a sociologist, not a psychologist, but the two disciplines overlap to a degree. Given the fact that these four known victims have all been teenage white girls, and all were attractive, there's one motive that fits very accurately. It's turned up many times in the past.

"The man who is doing these terrible killings has a common delusion: he sees attractive women on the street, in gatherings of various kind, on buses, on the beach, at ball games, wherever he encounters any reasonable number of people. In his distorted mind, he believes that all of this female flesh, to put it his way, is going to waste. That nobody else is making use of it and therefore it should be his for the taking.

"This can become a violent obsession, and I believe it has here. The killer you are after sees an attractive girl, young enough to be unattached, but old enough to be used sexually. That stimulates him beyond the danger point. I admit this is theory, but the literature is full of cases of this same kind."

To Mott's surprise, and partial gratification, Flavia had to field several questions. She did so with a candor that surprised even some of her listeners. Clearly they accepted the fact that she knew her subject and wasn't afraid to talk about it. Up to that time she had been a privileged spectator at homicide scenes and little more—officially. Now, in her own field, she was clearly showing that she too had something on the ball.

"One more point," Mott added after Flavia had finished.

"The coroner's protocol on the Estes girl isn't in yet, but one finding has been confirmed. From the semen found inside her body, it's been definitely determined that she was assaulted by at least two different men. Presumably Harry and Joe. We aren't looking for one killer anymore—we're looking for two. That would also help to explain how these girls have been snatched so successfully off the street."

"One man to grab the victim, another to drive," Tracy suggested.

"I think that's right," Mott said.

When the meeting was over, Mott stopped at the homicide desk. "I'm going to the Aero Bureau," he said.

The barrel man lifted a hand in acknowledgment as Mott turned away. He rode down in one of the few elevators in the city still operated by hand and picked up a car from the parking area in front of the main doors. Minutes later he was on the Harbor Freeway headed south.

Less than a half-hour later he drove into the sheriff's area on the east side of the Long Beach airport. A number of helicopters were precision parked on marked spaces. There were Hughes 300's and four-passenger 500's and older but highly capable Sikorsky S-58's, one of which had been fitted with a turbine engine. Parked on the south side of the area were several fixed-wing aircraft that were used frequently to transport especially dangerous prisoners, along with various other chores.

Inside the Bureau office Mott clipped on his ID in case it was necessary and was shown in to see the captain. The office was a fairly large one. In addition to the commander there were two lieutenants and four two-man flight crews. "We got the word you were on the way," the captain said. "Nancy will bring your coffee right in."

"Thanks," Mott said, "I like it . . ."

"She knows."

Faced with that kind of efficiency, Mott got down to

199

business. "This is a strictly confidential briefing," he said. "Need-to-know only, and under no circumstances outside the Aero Bureau. That doesn't apply to the brass, of course, but for the time being, don't give the media a thing; 'no comment' to everything."

"You heard the man," the captain said, which made it a firm order.

A uniformed female deputy came in with Mott's coffee and a doughnut on the side. It was just the way he wanted it.

"The sheriff has given his okay to use anything and everything to assist the task force. We need you."

He stopped to take some coffee.

It hit the spot exactly; he needed something to relax the tension in his mind.

"So far we have four known victims of two killers who also are guilty of kidnapping, rape, sodomy, forced oral copulation, mayhem, and severe torture. They're almost certainly driving a van that may be a dull gray in color—at least no flashy paint job of the usual kind. We have two names, Harry and Joe, but nothing beyond that."

On the wall there was an aerial chart of the whole county; as Mott walked over to it the captain handed him a ruler to use as a pointer.

"Victim one was snatched off the street around nine thirty P.M. in Altadena; a dark-colored van was seen in the vicinity at that time. Her body was found later in Big Tujunga Canyon, which is some distance away. There was an attempt at a half burial. We did the scene completely and came up empty; we got nothing whatever and no witnesses."

The captain and several of his listeners were making notes.

"Victim number two was found dumped at one of a series of empty lots near Alhambra that are part of a housing development. This time there was no attempt to conceal the body. Almost certainly it was dropped at night. The same MO, only—if anything—worse. The victim, age seventeen, had come to this area hoping to break into films or TV. Where she was picked up we don't as yet know. Again, the recovery scene came up dry; we didn't get a damn thing."

"Was she attractive?" one of the lieutenants asked.

"Very. We have pictures from her family. Five five, blond and blue, a knockout. She might have made it."

"Again, near the San Gabriels," the captain noted.

Mott gave an affirmative nod. "Victim three is still living; she's in the Northridge Medical Center, probably brain-damaged in addition to everything else. She was dumped over the side in Malibu Canyon and rolled down approximately three hundred feet. It's a miracle she survived. Again, the scene gave us nothing and the girl is unable to communicate."

"Where was she picked up?" the other lieutenant asked.

"Apparently she got in the van close to the beach. We have a team out there now looking for witnesses. So far, nothing."

Mott gathered himself together. "Now number four, and this is where you come in. She was picked off the street in Santa Monica and found dead by the San Dimas Station mountain patrol. That's a helluva long ways to transport a body.

"Out of all of this, we've put a few things together. The most obvious one is that in three of the four cases the San Gabriel Mountains are in some way involved. The victims were chosen haphazardly; they were targets of opportunity who were at the wrong place at the wrong time. None of them had any known enemies, rejected boyfriends, or whatever. None of them knew one another, as far as we can determine. But one thing is certain: when they were tortured, and take it from me it was severe, they screamed."

"I see what you're driving at," the captain said.

"Right. There's hardly any place at all that the killers

could have taken their victims in an urban area where screams like that wouldn't be heard. We thought of deep underground garages, but they are regularly patrolled. We even considered a boat well out from shore, but I can't visualize two men dragging a struggling, or even inert, girl through a marina to put on a boat. And sound carries well over water."

"It has to be the San Gabriels," the captain said. "The Santa Monicas are too well built-up all the way from the Hollywood hills. The only really wild or desolate areas are in the San Gabriels."

"What we need," Mott summarized, "is a detailed air search of the whole range all the way to Mount Baldy. We need to find every possible place where a van could go in the mountains and be isolated enough so that what must have been terrible screams wouldn't be heard."

"How long were the victims tortured?" the captain asked.

"There's no way to say exactly," Mott answered, "but I asked the pathologist that at the last autopsy I attended. He guessed between forty-five minutes and an hour. And it was damn rough, horrible."

One of the pilot deputies spoke for the group. "We'll find it," he said.

"Depend on that," the captain added.

202

23

Before setting out on his search mission, Sergeant Otto Ferguson gathered some extra equipment that he put in the back seat of his Hughes 500 helicopter. There was seating for two people in the rear of the machine, but it was a close fit and they would have little room to move. The passengers would have to be strapped in by seat and shoulder belts to confine them further. For a helicopter, the visibility from the rear seats was very limited, but comfort had not been a major factor in the design. Speed, range, and maneuverability had been the principal considerations.

There was plenty of room, however, for the extra gear that Sergeant Ferguson thought might come in useful. He even added a few cans of soft drinks, just in case. The San Gabriel Mountains were much wilder and more extensive than even the people who lived near them usually realized.

When he was through, and had made sure that the fuel

had been topped off, he went back inside to confer with Lieutenant Snodgrass, who was heading up the search operation, and his own observer, Deputy Eggleston.

Over a spread-out chart he outlined his plan. "I'm going to concentrate on the Estes girl," he said. "She was the most recent victim and therefore we'll have the best chance to find any traces."

With the dull end of a pen he pointed on the chart. "She was picked up about here in Santa Monica. From this point, it's only a short distance to the Santa Monica Freeway. I think it's ninety percent certain that her abductors took it east to the junction with the San Diego Freeway, which isn't far, and went north toward the mountains from there."

"I see it the same way," the lieutenant said.

"Okay. Then they went through the pass to the San Fernando Valley, up Highway Five and into the San Gabriels. Total time in normal traffic, forty-five minutes to an hour."

"How do you think they kept the girl quiet that long?" the lieutenant asked.

"Probably bound and gagged, since there were two of them," Eggleston suggested. "One tied her up while the other was driving. Assuming he knew how, it would be quick and easy. The driver's job was to see that he didn't risk a traffic stop; that would have been the end of it."

The lieutenant laid out another chart, this one of the San Gabriels as far as the county line. It had already been overlaid with squares defining the individual sectors that were to be flown. "Which search area do you want to cover?" he asked.

Ferguson pointed to sector eleven on the chart. "That one for openers," he said.

"Good enough. We'll notify air traffic control. If you see any other aircraft, advise immediately."

"Will do."

Ferguson took three or four minutes to secure the

additional gear he had put in back. He had two long lengths of nylon rope, evidence bags, two cameras, and a canvas carryall loaded with a full supply of minor items.

When he had finished, he strapped himself in the pilot's seat and ran through the checklist. Meanwhile Eggleston had filled the observer's seat, stowed his charts, and made a radio check.

Sergeant Ferguson started the engine and watched as the compact main rotor gathered speed. Almost within seconds he split the needles with the collective and lifted off the ground. Just south of the sheriff's area he hovered a few feet off the ground while he cleared the Long Beach tower. When permission to depart was given, he revved up, dipped the nose, and pulled the 500 across the field and up into the sky.

Twenty-three minutes later he reached the base of the San Gabriels at the point where Highway 5 begins to climb over the ridge route. Maintaining an altitude of seven hundred feet above the terrain, he followed the highway north until he had passed the Magic Mountain amusement park. Then he flew almost directly east until he entered a corner of the search quadrant he had picked for that day. Thirty miles east of his position another 500 was already flying a precision search pattern.

The area Ferguson had chosen was in a section of national forest where the terrain was almost useless for recreational purposes. It was dry and in many places steep. The sparse, tough vegetation did nothing to make it more appealing. Nevertheless there were vehicle tracks and self-made trails to be found, most of which did not appear on any map.

When he was well clear of the freeway, Ferguson dropped down lower, occasionally going into hover to inspect a possibly suggestive spot. Eggleston had a pair of binoculars that he used at frequent intervals. Because of the turbine howl in the cockpit, communication had to be by intercom. Both men wore helmets, which helped a little in cutting down on the noise.

At the end of two and a half hours they had found nothing. They had maintained a moving line search, with frequent departures from it to check out possible-looking sites.

Once more Ferguson reported by radio that their search had been, so far, unproductive.

But both he and Eggleston kept up their careful inspection of every visible bit of terrain. Although tedium was wearing away the sharp edge of their concentration, their strong belief that there was a site to be found kept them both alert.

Eggleston tapped his partner on the knee to get his attention. Rather than use the intercom, he pointed ahead at a two o'clock angle.

Ferguson swung the helicopter around 60 degrees and looked for himself. Because of the turbulence that had been building up, he had been flying at a somewhat higher altitude. He dropped the collective down and let the machine settle rapidly toward a thin set of car tracks that were barely visible on the harsh, hard surface. Fifty feet off the ground he hovered, then flew sideways a short distance.

It was the most promising thing they had found since their search had begun. The faint set of tracks apparently ended on a small level area. A steep canyon was only a few feet away.

Ferguson used the intercom. "I'm going to land," he said. "It's worth a closer look."

He flew once around the small area, then picked a spot to one side. He didn't want to let the powerful rotor blast blow away any evidence that might lie in the center of the little plateau. As he set the machine down, the landing was almost feather light.

The first thing Ferguson did after he got out was reach in for one of the soft drinks and pop the tab. He took a deep draft and shook his head. The place where he stood was pure wilderness. Because of the lack of summer rain, there was very little growth to mask the baked hard surface of the soil. It was part of a national forest, but there was not a tree worthy of the name to be seen anywhere within range. It was not yet desert, but it was high scrub, desolate and uninviting. In that forbidding area, the helicopter looked like a mechanical creature from another age.

Eggleston popped a drink for himself and then wiped his mouth. "Those are definite car tracks," he said. "Who the hell would ever want to drive up here? There are a lot of places closer to the freeway to knock off a bit of nookie."

Together the two men walked carefully toward the marks they had spotted from the air. They were present, but very faint. The wind had wiped out any visible characteristics; only very careful sighting from a squatting position made them visible at all. "I don't think pictures will help very much," Eggleston offered, "but I'll take some anyway." He went back to get a camera.

As he did so Ferguson walked a circle around the little plateau, searching for anything else that might be evidence—even a cigarette stub. The crime lab could do wonders with even the most unpromising material. When he came to the edge of the fall-off, he stopped and looked carefully for anything unnatural that might be visible. In the bottom of the defile, where some of the scant supply of water might have gathered before it evaporated, the brush was a little thicker, although hardly any green at all was showing. Brown predominated everywhere.

Basically a modest man, he kept his back to his partner as he unzipped his pants to relieve himself. He watched as his urine arced down into the canyon where the thirsty earth would absorb it in seconds.

As he finished, he thought he saw something that was man-made far down, halfway to the bottom. "Bring the binocks, will you," he called to his partner.

Eggleston, who had just finished emptying his own

bladder, brought over the set of ten-power binoculars that were standard equipment on all of the Argus helicopters. "What have you got?" he asked.

"I don't know yet."

Standing as close to the edge as was prudent, Ferguson adjusted the focus and studied the point that had first attracted his attention. "Something's down there," he said. "A long ribbon. No . . . wait . . . it looks like recording tape." As Ferguson continued to study the gully through the binoculars, Eggleston waited patiently for him to finish.

"It's tape all right, or something close to it," Ferguson said.

"Hell of a note," his partner added. "You can't go anywhere now without finding litter. Even in a place like this. What's planet earth going to be like in another twenty or twenty-five years." It was a statement, not a question. Eggleston was a member of the Sierra Club and had strong feelings about promiscuous littering, particularly of non-biodegradable material.

Ferguson shook his head. "It's getting worse all the time," he agreed. "Anything else here?"

"Let's go," Eggleston said. "I've got plenty of pictures, but I doubt they're any good."

Within a minute the Hughes 500 howled off the ground and the two men in it continued their meticulous search. They covered the entire area they had picked. They discovered a wrecked car that wasn't marked on the chart, but its condition indicated that it had been there for some time. Watching his fuel supply, Ferguson turned back toward Long Beach content that, although the results had been entirely negative, they could turn in a thorough search report.

By the time they were back at the Aero Bureau, three other helicopters and a fixed-wing Cessna were already in. The results of the day's careful work, the fuel consumed, the time on the aircraft, and the manpower expended added up to zero results, other than eliminating certain areas from further close scrutiny.

No one complained, however. They were, after all, policemen and accustomed to that kind of frustration. The lieutenant called the task force and reported on the day's activity. On a duplicate chart that was being maintained at the Hall of Justice, the searched areas were ticked off as completed.

24

Deputy Wilson Fields was driving a casual patrol in the area of the county that lies south of the city of Whittier. His partner, Doris Leesing, had been with him only two days; he was her training officer. After close to ten years on the job, he could not keep himself from wondering how effective she might be as a street cop if she were called upon to face a drunken and enraged two hundred twenty-pounder with an eight-inch switchblade knife in his hand.

He didn't know exactly, but he estimated her to be five feet two, and a hundred and thirty pounds max, and uncomfortable loaded down with all the hardware she had to carry on her slender frame.

Still, she had gotten through the academy and that had been no picnic, not even for the young fit men who pumped iron every day and turned down football scholarships to become cops. The PT program was tough and there was no letup for females. If a five-mile run came up on the worst day of their period, they still ran five miles. Or else.

A vagrant thought came into Fields's mind. "How did you make out with the six-foot wall at the academy?" he asked, keeping his voice friendly.

"I climbed over it," Doris answered.

"You're pretty agile, then."

"I've had several years of dance lessons," she said. By way of illustration she lifted one foot and laid it across her lap. Then she put the other one on top of it to form the full lotus posture.

Fields couldn't have done that if his life depended on it. "How about the range?" he inquired. After all, he had a right to know how well she could shoot.

"I practiced until I qualified expert."

"I'm glad to know you're that good," he said. "You understand why I asked?"

"Of course. If we get a four fifteen bar, you have to know if I can hold up my end."

Ahead of the patrol unit a man stepped out in the street and flagged it down. Obligingly Fields pulled up with the man on Doris's side. "What can we do for you?" she asked, using the exact words the academy had drilled into her.

The man bent down and rested one arm on the window sill of the car. "You might want to check out that house right there," he said. "It belongs to a young fellow who owns a restaurant. He's always gone by this time; that's his car in the driveway."

The informant nodded toward an expensive black Porsche. "A while ago I heard some loud noises from the house, then it was all quiet—too quiet."

"Do you have anything more?" Doris asked.

"Just my feeling about it," the man said. "I was a sergeant in L.A.P.D."

211

That put things in a very different light. Experienced cops could smell trouble that civilians seldom foresaw.

"We'll check it out," Fields said. "Doris, you take the back."

He slid the car up to the curb, reported in code six, and fitted his PR-24 baton in its holder on his belt. As soon as Doris was well toward the back of the house, he went to the front door and knocked.

There was no response. "Deputy sheriff," he called out in case someone was afraid to open the door. Then, knowing that many people still didn't understand the nature of the Sheriff's Department, he added "Police officer!"

When he got no answer to that he tried the front door. It was locked. He went to the side of the house and looked through a partially uncovered window. What he saw seized his entire attention.

Remembering that his partner was a rookie, and a female at that, he went to the back where she was obediently covering the rear entrance. "Did you try the back door?" he asked.

"It's unlocked, but we do have enough PC* to go inside?"

Fields maintained a calm tone. "We have a possible homicide here. Go back to the car, give this address, and ask for paramedics."

Doris ran to do her assigned duty. She reported in clearly and gave the dispatcher what information she had.

"Stand by," she was told. "Paramedics, backup, and field sergeant will be there shortly."

That done, she quickly rejoined her partner at the back door and reported.

"I'll check inside," Fields said. The back door opened into an added-on covered porch. He walked through the porch into the kitchen. There he immediately saw multiple small

*Probable cause

bloodstains on the counter and on some of the drawer fronts. He walked on toward the living room and found a scene he would not soon forget.

The wall to his right was heavily smeared with bloodstains. Crumpled at the front door was the body of a young man who had obviously been trying to get outside. One hand was stretched up to grasp a doorknob, but there were several locks he had been unable to reach. He had obviously died there, trying to get outside and find help.

Since it was impossible for Fields to reach the body without stepping in at least some of the mass of blood that was all over the floor, he made a prudent decision to wait until the paramedics arrived. He had no doubt that the victim was dead. Knowing exactly what to do, he got a long roll of crime-scene tape, printed in both English and Spanish, and with Doris's help he began quickly to protect the scene. He taped off the whole front of the house from the sidewalk in and each side halfway between the house and the adjacent property.

The paramedics, running code three as always, arrived quickly. Fields sent Doris to intercept them and lead them to the rear door. By this time a considerable crowd had gathered and one woman of obviously Hispanic origin was weeping profusely.

Carrying their equipment, the paramedics went inside. In less than a minute they pronounced the victim dead. The moment he heard that, Fields went back to his unit and was patched through to Homicide.

Sergeant Bob Perry, who was working the barrel, notified the standby team of Sergeant John Laurie and Deputy Jack Fueglein. Then he called Lieutenant Ken Chausse who had the watch. "Do you want me to alert Flavia?" he asked.

Chausse hesitated a moment. "Go ahead," he said. "Ask her if she wants to respond."

Flavia answered on the second ring. "We have a

213

homicide down near Whittier," Perry told her. "Male victim, twenty-five to thirty, in a private house. Do you want to go?"

Flavia was learning the police language. "I'll respond in five," she said, and took the address.

Within a half-hour the area inside the tapes was the scene of intense activity. The coroner's van had arrived with an investigator and a criminalist. A fingerprint and photo man from the crime lab was accompanied by a female serologist; three more black-and-white units had responded to block off the area and aid in crowd control.

The former policeman came out of his house carrying a large coffee maker; his wife followed him with a stack of Styrofoam cups, cream, and sugar. "I called Winchell's for some doughnuts," he said. "They'll have them ready for a unit to pick up."

Hospitality like that was unusual, but welcome. It was early evening and some of the people responding would not have had their dinner.

Sergeant Laurie and Deputy Fueglein, both highly experienced homicide detectives, were meticulously at work. Lieutenant Ken Chausse had arrived as field commander. One more black-and-white rolled up with four cartons of doughnuts from Winchell's.

The refreshments that had been set out on the porch of the adjacent house were liberally used by the sworn personnel. Several young people from the surrounding crowd tried to help themselves, but were quickly discouraged.

Sergeant Laurie didn't know the attractive young woman in civilian clothes who appeared just outside the tapes, but she had a sheriff's ID clipped over her left breast. "May I come in?" she asked.

Lieutenant Chausse looked over. "She's okay," he said.

Laurie lifted the tape to let Flavia through. "It's a damned bloody mess," he said.

214

In his usual quiet manner, Chausse briefed her. "The victim is a male Hispanic, twenty-five to thirty. He was found near the front door trying to get out. Probably bled to death. You can stand just inside the door, if you like, but don't touch anything."

Carefully keeping out of the way, Flavia looked around the house, seeing how much she could learn. The place was small, but the kitchen equipment was expensive; the food processor was state-of-the-art.

She looked into the bedroom and found no evidence of a woman's touch anywhere. The male victim had apparently lived alone, but he slept on a water bed.

Outside, a stocky middle-aged man in clericals appeared and asked for the officer in charge. Chausse met him and took him aside. "I'm Father Gregoravitch," the man said. "I came as soon as I heard. Is the victim dead?"

Chausse nodded. "Yes, Father."

"Then I would like to administer the last rites."

Chausse was noted for his tact. "Since the victim has been dead for several hours, Father, I'm afraid the soul has already left the body."

"Then may I pray over the remains?"

"It's a very grim scene, Father."

"I'm quite prepared."

"Then come with me."

The only exception to the ban on outside civilians at homicide scenes was for members of the clergy. As they went in the rear door of the small house, Chausse nodded significantly to Deputy Fields, the senior member of the handling unit. Fields understood at once and fell in behind the priest to catch him if he went over.

The priest came in and stood in the very small area where he would not disturb any of the evidence; he looked quickly at the body and then took refuge in his prayer book. The serologist, who was down on her hands and knees lifting blood samples, the coroner's people, and the sheriff's personnel all stopped work and waited respectfully while the priest read a brief prayer and made the sign of the Cross over the deceased. The professionals present would have done exactly the same thing if the clergyman had been a Protestant, a rabbi, or a Buddhist monk.

As soon as the brief service was over, Chausse guided the priest outside. "There's a woman crying copiously in the crowd," he said. "Perhaps you can comfort her." As the priest turned to his new assignment, Chausse drew himself a cup of coffee and chose a doughnut from the assortment that remained.

Presently the coroner's people wheeled out the body, well wrapped, on a gurney. At the sight, fresh lamentations burst from the unhappy woman in the crowd; the rest of the watchers began to disperse.

Coffee and doughnut in hand, Chausse went back into the house where Flavia was standing in the middle of the add-on porch at the back. "Have you found out anything?" he asked.

"I'd like to be useful in some way," she answered. "I don't want to just stand around."

"Why don't you take over the telephone," Chausse suggested. "It's already been printed. Don't give out any information, just say that Mr. Cruz, he's the victim, isn't available. But get a call-back number if you can."

"Gladly," Flavia said. For the first time she felt as if she was at least of some use and not just in the way. At the same time, she was suddenly grateful that she was not at a scene where another young woman had been tortured and then strangled to death. She didn't know how many more of those she could take. She was sorry for this victim, but his abrupt death did not cut quite so close to home.

As she sat waiting for the phone to ring, she watched the meticulous way in which the two homicide investigators were going through the house. They checked in every possible place. Eventually they poked aside a small loose plywood panel that gave access to the crawl space between the interior ceilings and the roof. It was hardly four feet high and filled with the dust of years. Still Fueglein climbed up and wormed his way along the exposed rafters.

The serologist began to pack up her kit, her job at the scene completed. The print man was also finishing his work; he had taken multiple photographs and had lifted some forty prints, all carefully marked for analysis.

Flavia handled four incoming phone calls, her first active participation in a homicide investigation. In each case she reported that Raul couldn't come to the phone at that moment. When asked who she was, she put warmth into her voice and said, "Just a friend."

Two of the callers refused to identify themselves. A third said, "Tell him Max called."

"Has he got your number, Max?" she asked.

"You must be new. I'm his partner."

"Sorry, Max. You sound nice. I'm looking forward to meeting you."

Ken Chausse, who was standing by listening, gave her his silent approval.

She did get one call-back number and carefully noted it down. It was not an important job, but at least she was being useful.

"Bingo!"

The call came from the crawl space just underneath the roof. Presently Jack Fueglein passed down a pair of pan scales and then a medium-sized case. Everyone watched as it was opened on the kitchen table; inside it held equipment used to prepare and package cocaine.

Flavia studied it with interest; she had never seen anything like it before. "He was a dealer?" she asked, to make sure.

"No doubt," Laurie answered. "And there's your probable motive. A lot of homicides are the result of dope

217

deals going sour. It also accounts for the expensive sports car outside. We're going to have a look at it next."

With the spectators gone, the search of the car began. It had been locked, but the keys had been recovered from the body. After some twenty minutes of expert probing, a hidden compartment was found. In it was a large amount of cash.

On the kitchen table the money was carefully counted; it came to exactly forty-two thousand dollars. The cash was carefully put into an evidence bag, logged in, and the bag sealed.

When that had been done, the on-site investigation was completed. The tapes were taken down and the property left for the next of kin.

The woman who had been weeping so much asked, "Can I drive the car? He was my brother."

"As far as I'm concerned, you can," Chausse told her.

The official vehicles pulled away. As the handling deputies, Fields and Leesing were the last to go. As they pulled away, almost no visible outside evidence remained to testify to the brutal death that had taken place on the quiet, residential street.

When she got into her own car, Flavia took care to see that both doors were securely locked. She was by then acutely crime-conscious and more than a little disturbed in her own mind. The streets she drove were relatively quiet, but a strong sense of anxiety invaded her and she was unable to banish it.

This time the homicide victim had been a man, but the evidence of a brutal crime would remain in that little house for a long time to come. She wondered who would be willing to go inside to clean it up, and how it would be done.

She brushed that thought aside and allowed the one that had been struggling for recognition at last to take command of her mind. She was, herself, a potential victim. It didn't help that that was true of almost everyone; the

218

danger still lurked there and could become a reality at any time, without warning.

Before she reached the Harbor Freeway, where she knew she would feel a little safer, she stopped for a red light. In the lane next to her a nondescript van pulled up and waited.

She grabbed hold of her steering wheel as tightly as she could and wondered what she could possibly do if someone were to jump out of the van and attack her. Even though the car was locked, he could smash a window and then . . .

When the light changed she breathed a silent prayer of thanks that nothing like that had happened. She drove home still in the grip of her fear. When she parked in her accustomed place, she was almost afraid to get out and expose herself once more. She hurried inside the building where she lived, ran up the stairs, and fumbled with the double lock on her front door.

Once inside she made completely sure that the door was firmly locked. Then she turned on some lights and walked quickly through the small apartment to make sure no one was hidden inside.

As safe then as she could be, she poured herself a drink and forced herself to take it. She didn't want to resort to that, but she was badly shaken.

Gradually she managed to focus on the thought that most women went through life without ever being the victim of a criminal attack. But so many thousands of others were not as fortunate. She remembered the cases she had seen, especially the innocent young girl who had been lifted out of the Malibu Canyon after suffering such fearful agonies.

Except in desolate areas, there were always spectators where there was a homicide: they seemed to come out of the ground. The terrible possibility lingered before her that whoever was doing these unspeakable killings might well have been among the watchers.

She had been warned that what she had undertaken could be dangerous. She had never realized how much. The dreadful killers could have seen her, and if they had, she could possibly be their next chosen victim.

25

For the next three days the men and women of the Aero Bureau flew many hours of careful search patterns over the San Gabriel Mountains without making any significant discoveries. It was a considerable expenditure of equipment, time, and man-power, but the job had to be done.

On the morning of the fourth day Deputy Ross Eggleston allowed a thin idea that had been germinating in his mind to come to the fore. During the usual coffee break after briefing he laid it out for his partner.

"Do you remember the place where we found the tracks and landed, the first day we were out on this?"

Sergeant Ferguson nodded. "Yes, of course. What about it?"

"I've been thinking," Eggleston continued. "After we looked over the area, I went to the side to take a leak."

"So did I."

"And we saw something, remember?"

Otto Ferguson considered that for a moment. "There was some litter down there. Tape, as I recall."

"I've been thinking about that tape. That was about as isolated a spot as you could find. So who would go there to throw away a tape? Some beer cans, maybe, I could understand, but recording tape? And I think that's what it was."

"Most tape now comes in cassettes."

"Exactly. But this one was spread out, I remember that."

Ferguson took a moment or two. "It is a little odd," he admitted. "Although I didn't think much of it at the time."

"Neither did I, but the thought keeps coming back to me. It's the circumstances. A thrown-away cassette we probably would never have seen. But why would anyone deliberately break up a cassette and then spread the tape out like that?"

"I'll speak to Snodgrass," he said.

The lieutenant listened with care. "It's awfully damn thin," he said, "but if you'd feel better about it, go on back and recover the tape if you can. You can fly your regular sector after that."

"Thanks," Eggleston said.

They had no trouble at all finding the same little plateau; Eggleston had marked it very carefully on their detailed search chart of the area. This time Ferguson set the helicopter down closer to the edge of the canyon near the spot where the tape had been spotted.

Ferguson got out with the binoculars and checked the area where the tape had first been spotted. "It's still there," he said. "It's very narrow, so it's hardly visible, but it's there."

By that time Ferguson's interest had quickened a little. "If it is from a cassette, a little thing like that would be easy to throw away; a good arm could send it far enough to fall in the bottom of the cut."

"But this tape is spread over twenty or thirty feet. What does that tell you?"

"That the cassette was split open. That's why it was thrown away."

"Not good enough. To get rid of a tape in a place like this, what would most people do?"

"Just toss it away," Ferguson conceded.

"Right. But this cassette, if that's what it was, had to be broken first and then thrown over the edge. Otherwise the tape wouldn't be as spread out. The car tracks are a good twenty feet away, so someone walked over here to pitch it."

"You've got to be right about that. Even if it were accidentally dropped, or even run over, that doesn't tell us why anyone would take the trouble to pitch it into the canyon. Ecology isn't the answer. It looks like deliberate destruction."

Ferguson checked the gear he was carrying in back and came up with a long rapeling rope. "I'll go down and get it," he said.

"No way," Eggleston argued. "You weigh two ten, I'm one seventy-four. I go. If something goes wrong, you can fly us out of here. I can't."

"All right. But take the biggest evidence bag we've got. Be careful not to crimp the tape. And if you can find any pieces of the casing . . ." He stopped there, remembering that his partner had come to the Aero Bureau from Detectives, where he had earned a good reputation.

Eggleston was considerate enough to overlook the unnecessary advice. He talked too much himself sometimes. He got the bag and two or three other things including a pair of surgical gloves from the general kit bag. He rapeled easily down the steep face, unavoidably kicking loose some of the decomposed granite on the way, and went to work.

A half-hour later he came back up. The large evidence bag held a mass of carefully looped tape and eight fragments of a standard-sized cassette. "I couldn't find all the parts," he said. "But it looks to me as if the case was deliberately broken."

He reported in by radio that the find was indeed a cassette recording tape and that it had been recovered.

Lieutenant Snodgrass passed the word they were to bring it right in.

Two minutes later the high whistle of the turbine split the sleeping air and the 500 lifted off. It was back over a densely inhabited area in a matter of minutes, speeding on its way to Long Beach.

At the crime lab the tape was rewound with meticulous care while the cartridge parts were being subjected to detailed microscopic examination. Unfortunately, black heel marks and subsequent weathering had virtually destroyed any print evidence. The faint traces that could be detected were not enough to be fed into the computer that could do near miracles in matching up latent and fragmentary prints. Nevertheless, the pieces of the cassette casing were carefully stored in an evidence locker. Once a suspect was in custody, they could be contributory evidence that would help to place him at the scene.

When the tape had been respooled and set up, the technician handling it ran a sound test. At first there were only two males speaking, then a voice, young and female, began sobbing.

The technician listened carefully with growing antipathy to the most horrifying piece of evidence he had ever handled. He tried not to believe what he was hearing, but there was no escaping the terrible sounds that the tape was yielding. When the awful screams began, he cut the sound off. With a trembling hand he reached for a phone.

224

26

Ralph Mott was within five minutes of leaving for home when his phone rang. Years of police work had taught him not to anticipate what it might be. "Homicide, Lieutenant Mott," he answered.

The technician at the crime lab told him briefly about the recovery of the tape, that he had it in playing condition, and what was on it.

As he listened, Mott felt a mounting sense of urgency running down his spine. "I'll be right over," he said.

He picked up a car from the lot in front of the Hall of Justice and headed west toward the crime lab, one of the best in the country. As he drove, his mind gyrated with the possibilities that this new piece of evidence might unlock. His hands were tight on the steering wheel and he was not tolerant of other drivers who tried to cut in front of his path.

At the lab he parked in one of the several vacant spaces

and went to the back door where he held up his badge before the scanning camera. The latch clicked and he went inside.

The recording technician intercepted him before he had gone very far. "I know how much you want to hear this," the lab man said, "but I want to talk to you first."

Mott was not in a mood to be reasonable, but he kept himself under control. "All right, where?" he asked.

The technician took him into an empty office. "Look," he said, "I know that homicide can be a rough deal. You worked on the Night Stalker case, didn't you?"

"Yes, but why . . ." Mott began, then stopped when the technician held up a hand.

"I've seen the evidence photographs, so I know what kind of scenes you had to deal with. What you're going to hear is a damn sight worse."

"That bad?" Mott asked.

The lab man looked at him. "If you've got the stomach to listen to it all the way through, go ahead," he said. "I haven't." Leaving it at that, he led the way to the sound room, put Mott in a chair, and started the tape.

Mott listened intently to the beginning conversation and to the first pleadings of the victim with firmly controlled emotion. When the sounds of torture being inflicted began to mount, he tried to keep his objectivity, but the engulfing horror of the screams totally shattered his professionalism. He became only a human being listening to the unbelievable, as it took over his whole consciousness. The small room reverberated with the hideous sounds of frightful agony.

With a fierce determination to do what he had to do, he listened until a sudden wild burst of horrifying sound torn from a human throat ripped his remaining composure to pieces. "Turn it off!" he cried and pressed his hands over his ears.

The technician stilled the awful sound. "You haven't heard the worst of it," he said. "I took all I could, then I spot-checked the rest at low volume. There are four different victims, as near as I can tell without doing a full analysis. I've made a copy for you if you want it."

Mott stood up, fighting to regain his normal composure. "You were right to warn me," he said. "I'm sorry if I was short about it."

"No sweat, Lieutenant. I'll make one more copy and then log the original into the evidence register."

"Be sure to include a statement that the tape was not cut or edited in any way," he warned.

"Of course."

Mott realized that he had just told a competent professional how to do his job, something he himself always resented. "Sorry," he said.

The technician nodded, the best way to express his understanding. "Here's your copy," he said, and he handed over a small brown envelope.

In the midafternoon of a fine day the strip of parkway that separates Ocean Avenue in Santa Monica from the steep cliffs that front the vast Pacific is one of the most pleasant places to be in the whole Los Angeles basin. There are inviting palm trees, scattered beaches, various recreational facilities, and plenty of green grass for the enjoyment of the public. There is even a *camera obscura* to provide a few moments of unusual entertainment.

The park is populated in some areas by senior citizens enjoying the relaxing sunshine, in other places by young people who gather for the same reasons that draw them together everywhere. Portable radios pound out rock, but usually, by some unexpressed agreement, at reasonable volume. Many pedestrians walk up and down, a few joggers puff their way at not much greater speed. Even the consistently heavy traffic on Ocean Avenue does not break the restful mood of the attractive parkway.

Mrs. Agnes Schoenfeld, whose penetrating eye had been constantly on the alert since the age of six, walked slowly along beside her daughter Mildred. It was always her hope that in some miraculous way they might be taken for sisters or, more probably, as a girl out with her surprisingly youthful aunt. Mrs. Schoenfeld had had two previous disastrous bouts with matrimony, but she was not yet ready to give up the ship. Like Katesha, she felt that she had her finer points and that if they were properly displayed, they would be duly noted to her advantage.

In her more rational moments she knew in her own heart that she was living a delusion. She was corseted until she could barely draw breath, but her too ample figure still refused to be denied the full splendor of its proportions. However, some men liked them well rounded and who could tell?

Her immediate concern, however, was Mildred. At twenty-three Mildred was more than marriageable, but the woeful lack of candidates—who would have to be rich, of course—caused Mrs. Schoenfeld some acute distress. She knew all too well from her own experience that youthful appealing lines do not linger too long unless strict measures are taken to preserve them. That opportunity *she* had let slip by until it was much too late, particularly because of her fondness for rich, heavy food. She had an impressive collection of diet books, most of them by medical men of reputation, but unlike herself the books had preserved their virginity.

If Mildred had been a striking beauty she certainly would have attracted men, some of whom might even find themselves interested in her mother. But that had not been natures's gift. Mildred was not plain; she was simply ordinary. Her features were acceptable enough, but unimpressive. Her figure was conventional, but nothing more. Her mother had seriously considered advising her not to wear a brassiere, but when the experiment was tried, the visible change was too slight to be noticed. Acutely aware of these conditions. Mrs. Schoenfeld had almost reached the point where she would be willing to settle for an attractive suitor who was *not* rich, so long as he would be inheriting money later on.

All of these things Mildred knew, for she was an intelligent girl. If left alone to seek her own life she might have done surprisingly well, but her mother would never trust such a thing to chance; she would consider it a betrayal of her parental duty. It never occurred to her that her constant presence was throttling almost every hope the poor girl had for a social life of her own.

Oddly enough, it was Mildred who first spotted the two young men sitting together on one of the benches. With sure instinct she knew that they were friends, not lovers. At that moment her mother was sizing up a white-haired but vigorous man who was leading a handsome dog. Mildred gave the two young men her casual attention.

One of them was definitely attractive. He wore a pair of well-cut slacks and an open-necked shirt that had cost at least twenty dollars. The loafers that he wore were quite new and of designer quality. His hair was a trifle too long in back, but his pleasant, open face was definitely engaging.

His companion was not as visibly muscular or as well dressed, but he had about him the air of someone who would be the first to volunteer his help if a friend were in need. If only her damned mother weren't making a complete nuisance of herself as usual, she would have wandered by and struck up a conversation. There were a lot of things she didn't have, and she knew it, but she was still a female and that always counted for something.

Joe was enjoying himself enormously. It was a warm day, the chicks were out in force, and practically all of them were wearing minimal clothing. With very little effort he was able to see them all naked, one by one. His imagination was aided by his collection of the raunchiest of the men's magazines to be found in the porno shops. Sometimes just looking at the pictures gratified him, because these were girls who were willing to let him see all they had. Quite obviously they got a kick out of it, which helped to satisfy his emotional needs.

What drove him up the wall was the huge quantity of material that was going to waste; girls who had so much to give and who held it back from him. Although they were hiding some parts of their bodies from everyone, at least in the park, he chose to take it personally. They were holding out on him. But now he and Harry could have any one of them by tracking her down and getting her in the van. After that she would be their personal property. It gave him great delight to pick out candidates and then to imagine how he and Harry would "do" them.

Harry looked at things differently. For years he had had sex with a great many different girls because he was good-looking. He blow-dried his hair, chose his clothes carefully, and practiced the casual, sophisticated manner that knocked them all out. He had once met a girl and had had her in bed with him in sixteen minutes. It was his best record. He did not feel deprived as Joe did, but he had a driving, blinding ambition for power. Not just to have women give themselves to him, but to control them absolutely, like a Turkish sultan. The power of life and death, that was it. The sultans had exercised it; they had had dozens of women tied up in a sitting position and then lowered into the Bosporus where their loose hair would float around their unseeing faces—all because they had found a moment of disfavor. Sure, they weren't around anymore to give the sultan his pleasures, but there was an unlimited supply of new ones all the time and he could have his pick, no matter who or what they were. Or who they belonged to.

That was the kind of power Harry wanted.

"That one wants to talk to us," Joe said. He had spotted Mildred looking at them and their eyes had met.

"A dog," Harry said. "And the old bag is her mother."

"The best screw I ever had was a girl who didn't look too good," Joe countered. "Anyhow, they're coming over."

230

They were, because Agnes Schoenfeld had spoken to her daughter in a half whisper. "The good-looking one, see how he's dressed? Expensive; he has money."

Mildred detested her mother's constant references to money: it seemed to be the nucleus around which her world revolved. She had enough, God knew, after two husbands, both of whom had left her generous endowments. "I like the other one better," she said.

"Look, they're nice young men, you can see that. And not pansies either. I'm a good judge of character. Let's meet them."

Harry wished they had left him alone; nothing about the younger one attracted him in the least, and as for her mother . . . !

Joe looked at Mildred as she approached and decided that while she didn't look too good, she might have a nice cunt. It was hard to tell.

"Isn't it a lovely day," Mrs. Schoenfeld offered in what she hoped was an inviting voice.

Just for his own amusement, Harry decided to play the game. "Yes, ma'm, it certainly is. Care to sit down?"

"Well, just for a moment. We were just enjoying the park. I never get tired of looking at the ocean. How about you?"

Harry coined one of his winning smiles. "We were just talking about it, about the far places it could take us."

"How romantic! I'm Agnes and this is"—she hesitated and then made the sacrifice—"my daughter, Mildred."

"Hi," Mildred said with subdued emphasis.

"And what do you do?" Agnes asked.

Harry loved to improvise, because he knew he was good at it. "I'm in the talent department at M-G-M. I help look for new people we can use in films. Joe here is a computer specialist at the Rand Corporation. Don't ask him about his work, because he can't tell you."

Agnes was all but overcome: such a lucky meeting! Two such exciting men, and right out of nowhere!

231

"I'm retired on my investments," she volunteered. "Mildred is taking an advanced degree at UCLA."

That was good bait and much of it was true. She kept the conversation going for several more minutes while Harry amused himself by turning on the charm. Agnes was very flattered and wished that Mildred would show more interest. Finally she opened her purse and took out a small card.

"I know you gentlemen can be trusted," she said. "I could tell that right away. This is our phone number, unlisted of course." She handed it over.

Harry took it with a smile of gratitude. "It would be nice to get together," he said in his most pleasant voice.

Agnes rose, sure that her seeds had been planted in fertile soil. It was worth the whole day to meet such desirable men, and neither one had mentioned a wife.

After they had been gone for a half-minute Joe asked, "You want to do Mildred?"

"Why her?"

"She's not cute, but she's got a nice ass. Remember that skinny little wimp who tried to dance for us? Her ass was nothing. I like nice round ones."

"We aren't going to do Mildred," Harry said. "First, she's a dog, I told you that. And her mama had a real good look at us. Soon as Mildred goes missing, mama screams for the cops. How long before she tells them about the nice young men she met in the park, and gave her address to?"

Joe was suddenly silent. He had thought of himself as being able to cover all the angles, but he had just made a very bad slip.

He looked behind him, saw that the Schoenfelds were far enough away, and tossed the card they had given him on the grass.

Harry pointed to it. "Tear it up," he said, "and put it in the trash can. If someone else uses it, we could get blamed."

Joe did as he was told. Harry was hard to get along with

sometimes, but he was as sharp as hell. It was carelessness that put people in the slammer. With Harry as a partner, he was doubly safe. "You want to do a girl tonight?" he asked.

"Maybe," Harry answered. "It depends on how I feel."

27

Despite the efficient air-conditioning system in his apartment, Ralph Mott spent a long, hot, and restless night. When too vivid images forced themselves into his mind he turned over on his other side, pounded his pillows into submission, and tried to fix his mind on something else. Normally he could do it, but this time he found it impossible.

Finally he got up, went into the bathroom, and looked for the vial of Valium tablets that had been prescribed for him some time ago. He made it a point not to allow himself to need them, but tonight was different. He turned on the water, swallowed a pill, and making a cup of his hands washed it down.

He went back to his rumpled bed, threw off the covers, and left a single sheet on top of his naked body. Still the waking nightmare persisted until his exhausted mind yielded to the tranquilizer and sleep came at last.

When his alarm radio buzzed, he got up, shaved, showered, and dressed, but he had no stomach for breakfast. He told himself he would catch a cup of coffee at the office; not the right way to do things, but it would suffice. The task force was meeting at eight and he would have to listen again to at least part of that unbearable tape. He was in command and it was his responsibility.

When he reached the seventh floor of the Hall of Justice and went into the task force room, he found that most of the troops were already there. For the first time since he had met her, he was not pleased to see Flavia on hand. She had a right to be there, that had been cleared, and she was wearing her ID exactly as she should, but this was one time he would have to ask her to leave.

He touched her on the shoulder and motioned toward the hallway. When they were far enough away, he turned to her. "Flavia, if you don't mind, I'm going to ask you to skip this session."

"Ralph, you know you can trust me . . ."

"That isn't it." He was brusquer than he had meant to be and softened his tone a little. "We've got a new piece of evidence I don't think you can handle. I had a very tough time of it myself. I'm trying to spare you a very bad experience. Afterward, if you want to wait, I'll tell you about it."

"What kind of evidence, Ralph?"

He glanced again at her ID. "We've recovered a tape recording. The men we're after recorded the screams of their victims as they tortured them. It's horrible, take my word for it. I couldn't listen to it all the way through; it made me ill. You see why I'm trying to spare you."

"Up to now, how well have I been doing?" Flavia asked.

"Very well; you know that."

"Ralph, you have the best reason in the world to know that I'm a woman, but I'm also a professional— just as you are. I want to hear the tape. I'll promise this: if it gets to be

235

too much for me, I'll leave the room. Don't worry that I'll keel over first; I don't do that."

Mott debated. "All right," he said, "but don't expect to sleep tonight."

"In that case, perhaps you'll keep me company."

He looked at her intently, wondering if she really meant it. She quirked a little smile at him and suddenly the day took on a whole new aspect.

Mott opened the meeting with an announcement. "We've got a very important piece of new evidence," he said. "Also, thanks to the Aero Bureau, we've located at least one of the places where the suspects have been murdering their victims. But first, what have any of you got?"

Miriam answered. "Willie and I have run the Harry and Joe combination into the ground with no positive result. We turned up eighteen possibles, but when we checked them out, one way or another they were out of it. Unless you have some new ideas on where to look, we've reached the end of that road."

"L.A.P.D.?" Mott asked.

Sergeant Berkowitz answered. "We've had three more homicides since our last meeting, but none of them fit the pattern. Every patrol officer we have is watching for plain-colored vans. We've stopped many of them on various probable causes, but they were all clean."

"Anyone else?"

Detective Arvin Swenson of the Santa Monica P.D. responded. "Because we have a lot of the beach area, and streets near it, we're making an intensive search of any and all plain vans. We've logged twenty-seven of them that checked out okay. All of our patrol units have the cleared list. If they spot a van that isn't on it, one way or another we'll check it out."

"We haven't had any new cases, thank God," Mott said. He walked toward the large map of the county that was posted on one wall. "After checking on the places where the

236

victims were picked up, and where they were subsequently found, we were satisfied that the San Gabriels are the area where the homicides were committed. Everything fits into that except for the girl we recovered in Topanga Canyon. She's doing a little better, by the way."

"Outstanding," someone said.

"So we brought the Aero Bureau into the act," Mott continued. He explained how the most probable areas had been chosen and how all the available aircraft had been put to work searching them from low altitude. He told how one of the helicopter teams had detected faint traces of car tracks leading to a small, very isolated plateau, had landed, and recovered the tape.

He held up a cassette. "I have a copy of it here," he said. "When I heard it I damn near lost my cookies. You can't imagine how bad it is. While those guys— Harry and Joe, as far as we know—were killing their victims, they recorded their dying screams. I'm going to play a little of it for you; the beginning isn't so bad, after that it's unendurable. I won't ask you to listen to more than a small part of it, but it will tell you what kind of animals we're after. If anyone wants to leave the room at any time, don't hesitate. I had to."

He fitted the cassette into a player he had ready and started the machine. With a quick nod to Willie he indicated that the door should be closed. "I'll keep the volume down when it gets loud," he said. "I don't want to shake up the whole place."

He stole another look at Flavia. She was sitting quietly with the others. For a moment their eyes met, then the sounds began. At first it was just conversation: two men and an obviously already frightened girl. "So that's how it is, honey," a male voice said. "All we want to do is to be happy together. We'll give you some fun, you give us some fun, and that's it. We'll take you back wherever you want to go."

"No, I can't," the girl's voice cut in, totally frightened now. "I'm having my per . . ."

The sound of a hard slap hit the walls of the room.

Another male voice took over. "Oh yes you can. We don't care whether you're on the rag or not. You're going to do it for us, three different ways, and you know exactly what I mean."

"Stop it!" Flavia called out.

Mott hit the stop button and turned to her. "You haven't heard anything yet," he said. There was irritation in his voice.

"Please, play that part again!"

Mott backed up the tape for a second or two, then replayed the tape at a slightly higher volume. Flavia was listening intently; everyone else was watching her.

"I'm sorry," she said, "but that voice. I think I've heard it somewhere."

The reaction in the room was electric.

"Go on," she said, "let me hear some more."

Mott pushed the play button again.

"You can't get away, you're miles from nowhere," the first voice said. "So take your clothes off," the second one cut in. "Nice and easy. Otherwise we'll have to tear them off. Then you won't be able to put them back on again, will you?"

Flavia held up her hand. "I'm almost sure," she said.

Mott looked quickly at Sergeant Dick Rogers. "Take over," he said, "while we check this out." He motioned Flavia toward the door and followed her into the hallway.

He opened the door for her at the Homicide Bureau, then led the way to his desk. When they were both seated, he said, "Tell me about it."

She sensed at once that he was willing to listen; that he didn't think she was the victim of an overactive imagination.

Just as calmly, she laid it out. "I know this may sound like an impossible coincidence, but I'm almost certain the voice I heard on that tape is familiar. I can't place it, but I'm sure I've heard it before. Please don't think I'm crazy."

"I'll never do that," Mott said, "but you know how many millions of people there are in the greater Los Angeles area. A lot of them are bound to sound alike."

Flavia brushed a hand across her forehead. "You're right of course, it was stupid of me to speak up like that."

"No, it wasn't stupid, you did the right thing. If you can put a name to the voice, we'll check him out, of course."

Flavia shook her head. "Somehow, somewhere . . ." she said. "Later on, after the meeting, will you play that bit for me again?"

"Of course."

She waited as long as she could, but then she had to go to meet a class. As it was, she barely arrived in time. Tormented in her mind by a memory she could not bring to the fore, she delivered her morning lecture as she had prepared it, but she knew she was doing badly. At the end there were few questions and she was aware that, on this occasion at least, she had lost her audience.

She had no appetite for lunch, but she drank a small carton of milk and nibbled at a cheese sandwich. Time after time she told herself that the odds against her knowing that voice were astronomical, but things like that *did* happen. She had met someone she knew, once, on the streets of New York, and she had only been there overnight.

She made a firm resolution that she would not let her afternoon class be the disaster that her morning session had been. She was better than that—she was a professional. She would address herself to her topic and put all other thoughts out of her mind.

When her students gathered, she held to her intention. She did a good lecture, she knew that, and endured as always the continuous scrutiny of Franklin Hellman. She had become enough accustomed to him to ignore it.

When she had finished, a female hand shot up. It belonged to a young woman who enjoyed calling attention to herself. "Dr. de la Torre, do you think that the AIDS epidemic is the biggest sociological problem at present?"

"It's really a medical problem," Flavia answered, "but there is no question it has great sociological importance. A generation ago homosexuality was almost a forbidden topic. Now the word 'gay' has been appropriated to describe that particular group, and all the restraints about discussing their situation have been lifted. As you know, they are the particular victims of this disease."

"But not exclusively," someone said.

"No," Flavia agreed. "Drug abusers are a target group, and also many heterosexuals have been infected, by being intimate with bisexuals, or in other ways. The only sure preventative that's known, as of now, is to avoid nonmarital sex completely."

A male hand went up in the second row.

"Mr. Hellman."

"Do you think that will ever happen? It never has in the past."

Flavia abruptly froze in sudden shock: for a few seconds she could not move or speak.

She knew!

Finally she managed to shape an answer. "I doubt it," she said.

When the bell rang, it saved her from a near panic. She waited, her body tight and tense, until the room had cleared. Then she left, forcing herself to act as normally as she could. She unlocked her car with shaking fingers, and without even thinking about it, she drove to the Hall of Justice. When she got there, she gave thanks to God that Mott was in.

She got him aside, but she was still so shaken she could hardly speak. He took her to his desk, sat her down, and then asked, "What's happened?"

As calmly as she was able, she laid it out. "I know this sounds impossible, but I'm almost certain the voice on that tape belongs to a student of mine."

Mott reached for a pen. "I agree about the odds against it, but let's find out. What's his name?"

"Hellman, Franklin Hellman. He's taking my course in Sociology One."

"What can you tell me about him?"

Flavia folded her hands in her lap. "I think I told you once that I had a student who scrutinizes me to distraction. He sits in the second row and watches every movement of my body."

"You did mention that," Mott said. "Now let me ask you something: is it possible that the annoyance this man is causing you suggested him to you when you heard the tape?"

Flavia didn't take offense. "No," she answered. "Definitely not."

"All right; go on."

"I've been looked over before; I'm quite used to it. But Hellman has a fixation. I know he strips me naked the moment I stand up to lecture; I can even feel his eyes on me when I turn my back."

That last bit Mott discounted, but he could understand the feeling.

"I've even been careful to dress to frustrate his analysis of my body. I couldn't help wondering what would happen if, toward the end of the term, I were to wear a tight sweater and no bra. It would probably drive him crazy. But I'm not about to take that chance, even though undergraduates do it all the time."

Mott understood that too. "Would your dean be in by now?" he asked.

"Oh, yes."

Mott pushed his phone toward her.

Flavia took the instrument. "Dial nine first?"

"Yes."

She punched out a number from memory and waited for a ring. As soon as she had it, she passed the phone to Mott.

"Dean Cargill's office."

241

"May I speak to him, please."

"I'm sorry, sir, but the dean is in a meeting and can't be disturbed."

"This is Lieutenant Mott of the Sheriff's Homicide Bureau. It's very urgent that I speak with the dean."

"Just a moment, please."

A half-minute later a mature masculine voice was on the line. "This is Miles Cargill."

"Dean, this is Lieutenant Mott of the Sheriff's Department. Dr. de la Torre is here with me."

"I know your name, Lieutenant; she's spoken to me about you several times."

"For purposes of identification, Dean, would you speak with her now?"

"Certainly."

Mott handed over the phone.

"Dean, this is Flavia. What would you like me to say?"

"I've heard enough already. How is it going?"

"Don't ask me right now. Here's Lieutenant Mott." She handed the phone back.

"I appreciate your taking this call," Mott said. "Are you where you can speak privately?"

"Yes. When you said it was urgent, I assumed it would have to be private."

"Dean, I need to know immediately anything you can tell me about a Franklin Hellman who's taking one of Flavia's classes. In confidence, of course."

"I understand. Wait a moment, please."

Mott endured almost a whole minute of silence before the dean came back on the line. "I'm sorry to have been so long, but I had to clear something with another office. This is privileged information, Lieutenant. We have an ongoing program here aimed at the rehabilitation of selected parolees. Quite candidly, it wasn't our idea and I'm not entirely comfortable with it."

When Mott heard that, Flavia's credibility took a sudden surge upward.

"We've accepted a limited number of parolees as students," the dean continued, "to find out whether an academic atmosphere with the opportunity to learn is a sufficiently therapeutic environment. If I sound skeptical, this same idea has been tried out before without much success."

Mott knew it was his turn.

"Let me level with you, Dean. We've got a recording that implicates the people who made it in a series of homicides. I don't like to say this on an open telephone line, but Flavia recognized one of the voices on the tape as Franklin Hellman. At first that seemed an impossible coincidence; now I'm not so sure."

"Hellman is one of our parolees. We've not told any of our faculty members their identities, so Flavia didn't know."

"I understand. Thank you again, Dean."

As soon as Mott hung up he called the Records Bureau. While he waited, he took Flavia into the coffee room and poured two cups. By the time he had done that, a return call was in from Records. Hellman was on file; his folder was being sent up.

Flavia sat tensely on the edge of her chair, only sipping her coffee, waiting for the record to arrive. Meanwhile Mott called Captain Grimm and filled him in.

The folder held a lot on Franklin Hellman. He had had three arrests as a juvenile, two on sex charges. One of the files was sealed. As an adult he had been arrested four times. One case had been dismissed for lack of evidence; a second had been quashed when a female witness had refused to testify.

He had been convicted twice: once for armed robbery with violence. While on parole he was rearrested and subsequently convicted of rape, including charges of forced oral copulation and sodomy. He was currently on parole again and undergoing a special rehabilitation program.

That was enough for Mott. He handed Flavia the folder to

read, then he put in an immediate call to the campus police and asked to have Hellman picked up for questioning. As soon as Flavia had read the folder, he took her with him to the task force room. As he came in, there was a sudden quiet; obviously everyone knew he had something to say.

"This morning Flavia told me she thought she recognized a voice on that tape, but she couldn't place it," he said. "We both knew it was a pretty wild chance, but it looks now as if she may have been right." He filled them in on the information he had and on the contents of Hellman's folder.

Sergeant Berkowitz grabbed for a telephone. "We may have a break," he reported to his superior. "A big one. The university campus police are picking up a Franklin Hellman for questioning. I recommend we give them immediate backup."

That would probably call for Metropolitan units that would be on fast-response standby. Also, if Hellman wasn't on campus, it would alert the whole L.A.P.D. network in the area that he was wanted. All necessary steps would be taken to see that Hellman was taken into custody as quickly as possible.

The atmosphere in the room, which had been shocked into near inertia, was suddenly optimistic. The routine work was begun again, but this time there was a fresh new hope.

Mott went back to where he had left Flavia. "What are you doing the rest of the day?" he asked.

"I'm going home. And I'll stay there."

Mott was still thinking hard. "Flavia, what worries me is that your name might leak out. Too many people know about your involvement here."

"What do you suggest?" she asked.

"First of all, I'll arrange to have an undercover L.A.P.D. officer in each of your classes from now on. Females if possible; they'll be less suspect. Then I may set up a surveillance over you. Do you know Deputy J. D. Smith?"

"Yes, we've met."

"I'll ask him to take you over. I can't do it; I've got an appointment. He'll cover you until you're safely at home and we have Hellman in custody."

"You're taking awfully good care of me," Flavia said.

"I intend to," Mott told her. "It's part of my job. You're a vital witness now." He paused for a moment. "Also, you might be a little hard to replace."

28

By noon the following day, Franklin Hellman had not been located. He had had an eleven o'clock class, but he had not put in an appearance. The instructor had previously reported that he cut it frequently and had recommended that he be dropped. For a reason the instructor had not been told, his suggestion had not been accepted.

The place where Hellman lived was rechecked; he had not been there overnight, but that happened quite frequently. The resident landlady assumed he had been sleeping with a lady friend. She identified his car as an old Chevrolet Camaro; as far as she knew, he didn't own a van. She was cooperative and allowed two plainclothesmen to look in his room.

Hellman's personal effects appeared to be all in place. An electric razor was plugged in in the bathroom. A quick check of the premises, carefully done to avoid possible future legal complications, turned up nothing unusual. There was no indication whatever that Hellman would not be back fairly soon. The landlady promised to call in as soon as he returned.

Flavia had met her first class without incident. An attractive brunette, new to the class, but who looked very capable, sat in the back and took notes. No one paid her any attention. When the session was over, she left with the rest.

In the faculty lounge, where Flavia took refuge between classes, a man she had not met exchanged a pleasant word with her. When no one was within earshot, he told her quietly that Hellman was still at large. As of that moment, all he was wanted for was questioning; there was insufficient evidence to hold him on any other charge. Her next class, which he was scheduled to attend, would also be covered by an armed L.A.P.D. officer sitting in as a new student.

When the bell rang and it was time for her to return to her classroom, she did so with some trepidation. There was no visible way that Hellman could know she had identified him, but news of that kind had a hard time staying within strict boundaries. She walked down the corridor conscious of the sound of her heels on the hard floor. She drew her breath in, lifted her head a little more, and resolved that if Hellman did show up, she would not betray anything by her face or manner.

The class gathered as usual. The dark-haired girl she had not met was there once more, this time a little farther forward in the room. Hellman's usual seat was empty and when it was time for the class to begin, it remained that way.

Resting her hands on her desk, as she normally did, Flavia delivered her lecture. Her notes were open beside her; when she turned to consult them, she was subtly aware that she was not under the usual close inspection. Otherwise everything was as usual; Hellman's absence did not seem to be noticed. The question-and-answer period was lively and stimulating. Not until the bell rang once more and the students filed out was she aware of the tension that had been with her all the time.

Obedient to the instructions she had been given, she reclaimed her car from the faculty lot she used and drove to the Hall of Justice. Because she was a little on edge still, she paid extra attention to her driving and did not spot the plain car that stayed discreetly behind her. She pulled into the Hall of Justice parking lot, where space was usually at a premium, and was assigned a slot.

When she came into the task force room, Mott met her and steered her into a vacant office across the hall. He had an impulse to take hold of her, at least her hands, to offer a little comfort, but the Hall of Justice was not the environment for that. "I know that Hellman's didn't show up," he said. "And so far we haven't got him. L.A.P.D. is covering all the bases in their jurisdiction, but as of now, we have no idea where he is."

"Could he have found out, somehow . . ." Flavia began when Mott cut her off.

"It's quite possible. There wouldn't be any leak from here, but too many others know we want him."

"I'm a little scared," Flavia admitted.

"I don't blame you. Hellman probably knows something. What I don't know is how much."

"What happens next?" Flavia asked.

"Hopefully, Hellman will be nabbed; that could happen any moment. Meanwhile, I want you to stay here. Can you find something to do?"

"I have a lot of files to read."

"Do that, then. Don't go anywhere without seeing me first. I mean out of the building."

"Of course."

By six thirty there had been no new developments. Flavia had patiently read files until she was sick of them, but kept

248

at it, almost afraid to do anything else. The shift had changed and there were new barrel men up front as well as at some of the many desks in the room. All of them obviously knew who she was, but they left her strictly alone.

When Mott reappeared he had a slightly harassed air about him. He sat down beside her and for a moment said nothing. She assumed she was an embarrassment to him, but he had told her to stay there and she had followed his instructions. "May I go home now?" she asked.

Mott let go of whatever was troubling him and smiled at her. "How about having dinner with me instead?"

She knew at once she would like that, but she didn't want it to be a duty thing with him. "If that's what you want," she answered.

"Of course it is."

She remembered their being in bed together and the memory flooded her with warmth. "Where would you like to go?"

"There's a nice place up the coastline from Malibu."

"Ralph, I'm not dressed for anything elegant," she protested.

"You're just fine. It isn't the kind of place you go to see and be seen. But it's right on the ocean and the food is great."

"I can be ready in ten," she said.

He drove her out of the center of the city via the westbound Santa Monica Freeway. The traffic was still heavy, but after they crossed the San Diego Freeway it lightened. Minutes later they went down the incline and onto the Pacific Coast Highway where they headed north. Flavia rolled her window down and let the breeze come in. When Mott did the same, on the ocean side, it was strong enough to whip the hair around her face. The fresh, tangy salt air blew more than the city's stuffiness out of the car, it forced out unwelcome thoughts of grim realities.

Presently they began to pass the exclusive beach clubs and the small but very expensive homes that had been built between the highway and the beach. Some of them were up on concrete piling; all of them defied the danger of the storms that sometimes came off the Pacific with the force of near hurricanes. Each time that happened sandbags were piled up by the thousands, often against the inevitable. Homes were washed away, possessions were lost, but eager buyers waited to acquire any of the properties that came on the market. To them owning a home right on the ocean was too dazzling a prospect to allow any other considerations to intervene.

They drove past Malibu and on up the coast toward Santa Barbara until a fresh strip of oceanside land appeared. There was a restaurant perched almost over the water; Mott turned into the parking lot and waved off the red-coated valet waiting to take the car. He slid it into a vacant slot, locked up, and guided Flavia toward the front entrance.

He offered the parking valet a bill. "Police unit," he said. "Keep it clear if you can."

The valet waved the money aside. "The people from Malibu Station come here a lot. Parking is on the house."

In the lobby Mott excused himself long enough to make a brief call. "I told them where I am," he said when he came back. "My beeper may not reach this far."

Flavia wished he hadn't done that: it spoiled the illusion that they were out together for the evening, just to enjoy themselves for a little while.

The head waiter came, glanced at the two of them, and obviously approved.

"I have a reservation: Mr. Mott," Ralph said.

Flavia wondered how long it had been since he had been plain "Mr. Mott."

"Right, sir, I've saved a good spot for you." He led them across the room. Their table, which normally seated four, was next to a window with a commanding view of the ocean. Twilight was already beginning to fall, turning the sky ablaze with the passionate colors of a superb sunset. They both fell silent, content to look. At that moment Flavia was filled with an enormous wanderlust. She had never been to the Orient, that strange and mysterious part of the world that lay several thousand miles to the west— the direction of adventure. She wished passionately that she could throw her whole lifestyle aside and answer the call of the sea, of distant islands, of new and different people far down into Oceania, even to New Zealand and Australia.

She awoke to the realization that a waiter was standing by to take their drink order. "Piña Colada," she said, because it fitted her mood.

She had a sudden, unexplained desire to be running naked down an unspoiled and deserted beach with the wind caressing every part of her body. With her breasts free of their inhibiting binding, her whole being utterly free, with the sea beside her and the virgin sky overhead.

Ralph would be there behind her, as free as herself, running after her, and gaining. Then in a magic moment he would catch her and together they would fall onto the soft sand, their arms around each other and with nothing, nothing at all, to spoil their togetherness.

Ralph sensed her mood and didn't break in on it until after the drinks had been served. Then they clinked glasses. "To us," she said in a moment of abandon.

"To us," he echoed.

After that the dinner was everything she could desire. The service was splendid and the food the best she had had in weeks. Perhaps most of all, she detected an occasional admiring glance from a stranger directed her way. It was a time when she needed that kind of reassurance very much.

When they were outside once more and it was dark, the freshness of the ocean air still worked its magic. If only life could be like this all the time!

She got into the car almost reluctantly. She rolled the

window down to let in the ocean air while Mott took his place beside her.

Then he spoke quietly to her. "Flavia, I don't want to bring this up, but I asked to have them call me if Hellman was apprehended."

"He hasn't been," she said.

He took his time driving off the lot and joining the southbound flow of traffic.

"No, he hasn't, but that's only part of it."

"What's the other part?"

Mott didn't answer her directly. "You told me how Hellman scrutinized you, studied every part of your body he could through your clothing. I'm sure he'd give almost anything to get his hands on you."

"That's probably true," she had to agree. The thought did not make her any happier.

Mott laid an arm across her shoulders. As she felt it there, she knew that it wasn't an official gesture, that it came from him as a man: a person who liked her.

"Flavia, I don't want to take advantage of you, I'd never do that, but I think it would be a good idea for you to move in with me for the time being—until I know you're safe."

For a moment the vision of them in the sand together flashed back into her mind. "Ralph, I understand, and I'm very grateful. But just for a night or two I can go to a hotel, register under a different name. I'm sure that's done all the time."

His voice became a bit firmer.

"Yes, you could, but it isn't all that safe. You'd be too easy to follow, for one thing. The other part of it is that there's two of them. We know about Hellman, but we don't know anything at all about his partner. It's almost a sure thing that Hellman will have told him about you." He stopped for a moment before he went on. "I hate to remind you, but you know what they've done to other young women, victims who never hurt them in any way. Can you imagine . . ."

252

He hesitated and reshaped his thoughts as he drove automatically. "If they ever got their hands on you, I don't think I could endure it," he said. "And if our theories are right, they *do* know about you. You could be a prime target for them."

"Do you really think so?" she asked.

"Yes, and it has me scared stiff. I want to look after you myself; I'm pretty good at that. If you can put up with my company, we can work out any sleeping arrangements you'd like."

Flavia put her hand in the one he had across her shoulders. "Of course we'll sleep together, nothing else makes any sense. Let's go to my place now. It won't take me long to pack."

29

State Senator Estelle McWilliams sat in her office chair fuming over the morning edition of one of the local Los Angeles papers. It had published two letters from readers that were sharply critical of her political activities. She was not a woman who took kindly to any kind of negative publicity. There had also been letters commending her, but they did nothing to lessen her anger. She expected praise as her rightful due, particularly from her own people.

The leather-bound calendar on her desk reminded her that she had an upcoming appointment with a Lieutenant Mott from the Sheriff's Homicide Bureau. She did not want to meet with Mott and knew in advance everything he was likely to say, but it was an election year and she could not afford to alienate the law enforcement establishment any more than she had. She didn't give a damn about Mott, but if she didn't see him he might kick up a stink that could hurt her.

As a member of the State Senate her frequently expressed views carried weight; but all that would be gone if she were not reelected. Her seat, based in almost entirely ethnic areas of Los Angeles, had once been considered entirely safe, but now she faced opposition from an intensely popular Olympic athlete who was Phi Beta Kappa, a brilliant speaker, and, to add to her discomfort, disgustingly handsome as well. Of late the polls had not been in her favor.

She was also acutely aware that beauty was not one of her assets.

Mott arrived on time. When he was shown into her office, she saw a six-foot man who was well built, attractive if not handsome, and better dressed than she would have expected. His dark hair was well cut and still full; his brown eyes were pleasant but gave nothing away.

In ten seconds she knew he had good manners and was able to handle himself. She would have preferred a traditional plodder waiting out the time to his pension; men of that type were easier to dominate. Unfortunately, they were getting less and less common.

It did not take her long to discover that Mott was also very intelligent. He accepted the secretary's introduction comfortably and seated himself without giving anything away. "I appreciate your seeing me, Senator," he said.

She tried to find a patronizing tone in his words and failed.

"What can I do for you?" She made it calm, but unyielding.

"I'm sure you're aware of the series of recent torture murders involving young women," he began.

"Of course."

"I'm in charge of the task force working on that problem."

"So far the victims, I understand, have all been white."

255

"That's correct."

"So there's prejudice even in the choice of murder victims."

Mott was unruffled; he had been well briefed on Senator McWilliams. "It's more likely," he said, "that the men responsible for these crimes have not been operating in any black areas."

"There are black young women everywhere; the fair employment statutes have seen to that. Perhaps they are not considered to be equally attractive."

Her attitude annoyed Mott immensely, but not for the first time in his career he put his personal feelings aside to get the information he needed.

"Senator, I would not attempt to say what goes through the minds of these men. I can only tell you that they are subhuman monsters. The full extent of their crimes has not been made public."

"How can I help you?"

Mott came to the point. "Senator, I understand that you sponsored a program to give selected parolees the opportunity to get a college education."

"I not only sponsored it, I created it. You must know, Lieutenant, what the poor and underprivileged have had to do just to live and care for their families. Affirmative action is now their only hope. That means not only jobs, but equal opportunities for higher education. Men and women on parole have very limited opportunities. They can wash cars or work in junkyards. What I have done is to force our colleges to give them the equal opportunities they deserve."

"And have they lived up to your expectations, Senator?"

The senator shifted in her chair. For some reason she was freshly reminded that she was putting on unwanted weight and spreading a great deal in her hips. She knew the answers: diet and exercise, but for the present she had no time for either one.

"I think you know, Lieutenant, that in any experimental

program, there will be some disappointments. Quite frankly, I expected them. No matter how hard we try to protect the identity of our parolee scholars, the word soon gets out and once more they have to face hostility and discrimination. It's not surprising that they react. I'm sure you would too if you were in their position."

Mott quietly ignored that. "I have in mind one particular case, Senator, where you may be of considerable help in clearing up this series of attacks on women. And the next one, God forbid, could easily be black."

"What case do you have in mind?"

"A man named Franklin Hellman. In strictest confidence, Senator, we have a partial identification of him as a possible suspect. I would appreciate knowing as much as you can tell me about him, and in particular how he was şelected for this program."

Senator McWilliams picked up her phone. "Ellyse, see if you can find anything on Mr. Franklin Hellman, who is one of our parolee scholars."

There was no conversation at all while the file was being located. The senator gave her attention to papers that were on her desk. She saw no need to excuse herself for doing so. She did not hold a very high opinion of policemen.

When Ellyse came back in, she contrived to give Mott a quick smile as she walked behind the senator's desk to deliver the file.

The senator picked it up and read it through at her own pace. If Mott was in the least annoyed, he concealed it admirably.

"You say this man is a suspect?" the senator asked.

"I'd prefer to say that we'd like to talk to him."

"What if he's innocent?"

"Then he has nothing whatever to fear."

"I'm not so sure of that."

Mott remained silent.

"Very well," the senator said. "In the case of Mr. Hellman, our investigation revealed that he had a very deprived childhood. Later he was arrested four times. Twice he was exonerated, on two other occasions he was convicted. There is some doubt that all of his rights were fully respected, but nevertheless he went to prison. Are you aware of his record?"

"Yes."

"Then you know that he is a very virile young man who allowed his natural sex drives to overcome his better judgment. He has certainly paid for those mistakes. He was chosen for the parolee higher education program because my case worker reported that he has a superior intelligence, an agreeable personality, and fortunately makes a very good appearance." The senator paused here. "She further reports that he is very sympathetic to the plight of the underprivileged and wants to make a career of helping them. He also gave a very solemn promise to conduct himself properly if he were given this opportunity."

The senator stopped and thought openly for a moment. "Equal opportunity works both ways, Lieutenant. It's true that most of our parolee scholars are black, but we wanted to be sure to give everyone the same chance. Mr. Hellman is white; that was a partial factor in choosing him."

"And I take it that the nature of his previous convictions did not disturb you."

"I believe I've already answered that."

Mott thanked her and left.

Cautious as he was in his movements, Frank Hellman had not yet picked up the fact that the campus police were looking for him. In the midst of the noon-hour crush he walked into the cafeteria's seating section, with his tray in his hands, looking for some acceptable female company. He saw the girl he wanted almost immediately. She was seated by herself at a table that was littered with the residue of her recent companions, but that didn't deter him in the least. One glance at her blond good looks and slightly

258

pursed lips made up his mind for him. He stopped beside her and asked, "Mind if I sit here?"

Without waiting for an answer he made a place for his tray, then piled the debris on the next table. He was completely confident because he knew he was good-looking. That asset had been clearing the way for him since he was twelve. In his teens he had had thirty different girls in bed before some of his less fortunate classmates had had even one.

"I'm Frank," he said and gave her one of his winning smiles.

"Mary Ellen."

"I like that; it fits you." He sat out the food from his tray, looked at it distastefully for a moment to show his sophistication before he began to eat. "I think I'm lucky to find you alone."

"It happens sometimes." Not for the world would she tell him she had spotted him coming in and had deliberately lingered knowing she could reel him in. She too was attractive, cute rather than beautiful, but she could play a symphony with her facial features. She loved to do it so she could watch the impact on men. They fell all over their feet when she wanted them to, as they had ever since she had been a little girl.

"I can't imagine why I haven't seen you before," Frank said.

She gave him a half smile. "I'm not often here. Sometimes I have other things to do."

At that moment he knew he had it made. There were two classes on his schedule for the afternoon, but that meant nothing at all. He looked openly at her breasts; they were rich and full. Anticipation filled him to the point where he could hardly eat, but he knew better than to jump through the hoop for her. "What are you taking?" he asked.

"Public relations."

"You won't have any trouble finding a job."

"I've got one already."

That could mean she was married: hell, that kind of merchandise didn't lie around very long. But even if she was, she was available. Not to everyone, but to him for the same reason as always—his good looks. They could get him by anyplace: they had twice in the courtroom.

"You live at home?" He was sounding out the ground, aware that she would know that.

"Yes."

Too bad. But there were plenty of warm-bed motels he knew around Lankershim Boulevard in the valley.

She was in no mood to waste any more time. She had spotted him earlier in the week and knew she could handle him any way she liked. "Right now my family's in Las Vegas. They go every month," she said.

In his car she rolled the window down and let the air play with her hair. It made her look utterly desirable: a half-wild, half-tame creature that a man would give his soul to possess. When they got to her house she showed him where to park and then used her key on the side door. It was quite a place: half a million at least, Frank estimated as he stepped inside. If only no one else was home . . . !

No one was. As soon as the door was shut he reached for her. As their lips came together, she opened her mouth.

Before he had his clothes off he was ready to explode, but she kept him at bay. "I want you to pay some attention to me first," she directed.

He was very good at that. He doubted if she needed any arousing, but in five minutes or so he gave her the works. Then when she was thoroughly wet he entered her and had an orgasm in seconds. A huge one that seemed to drain him dry.

When he had done that she got off the bed and walked with easy calm into the bathroom. He looked at her bottom and had a jolt of unexpected joy; she had a gorgeous behind. At that moment he couldn't help remembering the

260

thin little twerp who had tried to get off the hook by pretending she could dance naked. She hadn't had enough meat on her ass to feed a starving dog.

When Mary Ellen came back she moved her shoulders slightly as she walked toward him so that her breasts would swing from side to side. She had picked up that trick by watching a professional stripper perform. That girl too had had good full boobs that stuck out nicely from the rest of her body. As she had walked downstage, showing how well they could move, the men in the audience had all been excited, at least Mary Ellen had assumed so. She had a flat-chested friend who was desperately unhappy about it.

Deliberately displaying herself, she walked about the room, letting him look all he wanted. She knew he was thoroughly experienced, but few girls had bodies like hers. When she was ready she came back to him and began systematically to stimulate him once more. To her delight he was ready very quickly and this time he gave her a much better orgasm of her own. She loved to have sex with handsome men, not just ordinary handsome, but the kind that would make every girl turn her head. Other girls might crave them, even lust after them, but she got them: all of them she wanted.

For the rest of the afternoon they reveled in each other, totally without inhibition and each delighting in the fact that the other was so compellingly attractive. While he was momentarily resting, Frank knew that he and Joe would never do this girl; she was far too valuable just as she was. He intended to keep her indefinitely. There was sure to be competition, but whatever came up, he would handle it. She was going to be his woman.

Between six and seven they raided the refrigerator together, enjoying their nakedness. They found enough to make up a good meal. After that they went back to bed once more. For the first time in his life Frank was unsure of his ability to perform anymore, but when his partner began to give him head with a skill even he had not known existed, he yielded himself to overwhelming bliss.

Assured that no one was coming, he spent the night, exhausted, but sailing on a euphoric cloud. In the morning they coupled once more; then they dressed and Frank headed back toward his apartment.

All that he had been through during the past several hours had not taken away his careful sense of alertness; it was a cultivated thing that had become a conditioned reflex with him.

He listened to the news and heard nothing of interest. If three hundred-odd people had died in a ferry sinking in Bangladesh, it meant nothing whatever to him. There was no mention of the search for the killers of young women.

As soon as he was half a block from his room, he spotted the police car in front of the house. It was unmarked, but the plain black tires and characteristic color betrayed it at once.

He did not waste a second; he drove on past without changing his speed or doing anything to attract attention. He turned at the first available corner and got out of sight. Free of immediate danger, he headed westward on Adams Boulevard, turning off two or three times to be sure that he wasn't being followed before he continued on.

Within a few minutes he reached a nondescript lot where an assortment of cars of various ages were parked under a sign that read AL'S SAV-MOR RENTALS. He turned in and parked his vehicle as far back and out of sight as he could.

Keys in hand he walked to a shack with a needless sign that said OFFICE. What paint was left on the sides of the building was in the last stages of defeat; relentless weather and bright sunlight had faded it into dull decrepitude. Inside, the office was equipped with a small counter covered with worn-through linoleum that was curling at the edges. Seated in a derelict chair that groaned under his weight was a very fat man who looked up with casual unconcern.

"Remember me?" Frank asked.

"I know you." Flat and unemotional.

"I need to get my car off the street."

The fat man swiveled sideways enough to glance out of a grimy window. "You can leave it where it is. It's out of sight."

"Can you put some different plates on it?"

The fat man lifted his shoulders an inch and let them fall. "How hot are you?"

"I don't know. I caught them casing my pad."

The fat man showed little interest. "You want different wheels?"

"Yeah. Usual arrangement. My car for security."

"Were you inside?"

Frank nodded.

The fat man reached up to a board where a variety of keys were hung. He took down a set and tossed them on the counter. "Dark blue Nova. You brotherhood?"

"Yeah. Check me if you want to."

The fat man stirred in his chair. "If you're bullshitting me, you won't last the day out."

"I know that," Frank said.

"You in on that bank job in Whittier?"

Frank shook his head. "Not me: I got a different problem."

The fat man showed no further interest. "A hundred a day," he said. "That's with full protection."

Frank nodded, counted out some bills on the counter, and went out the door. The protection was worth a lot more than the car. He drove back to where he lived, and cruised around the block; if the place was under surveillance he couldn't spot it. He parked the Nova in the driveway and slipped inside.

His landlady met him. Before she could open her mouth

he said, "I know. I'm going to take some things with me, leave the rest. I'll be back as soon as I can."

Her eyes widened a little. "Frank, are you in trouble?"

The dumb fool! He dropped his voice a little. "Come in while I pack," he said. She followed obediently while he quickly took out the things he wanted and put them in a suitcase he had stored under the bed. Then he turned to her. "Look, there's some things I can't tell you. Do you know what undercover means?"

"Of course, Frank. Don't tell me you're CIA or something like . . ."

He cut her off. "I said, I can't tell you. But if anybody asks, you haven't seen me."

She wasn't all that stupid. "They looked through your room. If they come back, they might notice that a lot is missing."

He had a ready answer for that. "All right, if they do and ask you about anything, tell them that a man came to get some of my things. He had a note from me. A tall guy, more than six feet, thin, white shirt, dark pants, glasses. Got it?"

She nodded. "You'll be all right, won't you?"

"Come here." He stood behind her, holding her body against his, and fingering the nipples on her breasts through her clothing. He had banged her a few times just for the hell of it; she had all but asked for it outright. No husband, but still at an age when she could get a kick out of getting laid, especially by a man as handsome as he knew he was.

When she reacted, and held one of his arms across her breasts, he reached down and rubbed her where her legs joined her body. "I'll be back," he whispered, as though she were actually near and dear to him.

He left, knowing that she would cover for him with her last breath. He was her dream man who once in a while took her into his bed. He knew how she had magnified those moments into major events in her life.

The blue Nova successfully eluded the APB that was out on him. He deliberately drove past the university and saw the added number of cop cars that were in the area. That told him all he needed to know. He had to have a place to hole up where he was sure he would be safe.

30

When he thought about it
objectively, Mott realized that the evidence against Franklin Hellman was at best both thin and circumstantial. He lined it up carefully in his mind and went over it step by step, evaluating each item.

Flavia was sure she had recognized his voice on the tape. Possible, but at first the odds against it were enormous.

Hellman was on parole after two convictions for major felonies. That cut the odds way down, in Flavia's favor. Or rather, in favor of Flavia's having been right.

Hellman was a convicted sex offender. Another point in favor of Flavia's identification, but far from conclusive.

He had been admitted to the university as a special parolee student. Interesting, but it added nothing new.

Flavia had complained that Hellman was obsessive in scrutinizing her body. Annoying, but that was all. No legal significance; inadmissible as evidence.

Hellman had apparently disappeared just at the time he was wanted for questioning. Unless in so doing he had broken his parole, again no violation. Suggestive, but no basis yet for an arrest.

And that was it.

Mott had put four of the best people he had in the task force on Hellman's background and recent movements. All of his known associates and instructors on campus were being interviewed. Insofar as possible, all of his movements were being traced.

Armed with a warrant, a team had searched his room without finding anything of interest. His landlady had reported that a man had come with a note from Hellman to get some of his things. She had watched as the man had taken them away. All the items were either clothing, textbooks, or personal gear. The man had been quite tall, over six feet, and very thin. He had been wearing a white shirt and dark trousers. She hadn't noticed his shoes. When she was asked if she remembered anything else at all, she recalled that he had been wearing glasses. He had not given her his name. No, she had not kept the note.

Mott decided against putting surveillance on the house. It would be too expensive in manpower. Instead he asked that the regular patrol units in the area check it out frequently. That was much easier and L.A.P.D. was happy to cooperate.

Santa Monica P.D. had checked almost forty more vans. In two cases the drivers had been arrested. One had tried to elude the police by high-speed tactics; in doing so he ran several red lights. The seventeen-year-old driver had a suspended license, no insurance, and there was open beer in the car.

The other was a middle-aged homosexual who, with his male lover, was under the influence of cocaine.

Mott brushed those items aside as he concentrated on his main objective. He was busy jotting down pros and cons on a yellow legal pad when Miriam came in and dropped a photograph in front of him. It was an eight-by-ten black-and-white print of portrait quality.

The face that looked out from the picture was of a strikingly handsome young man who looked in his early twenties. There was an easy confidence about it, and also a sense of openness—of offered friendship.

"Damn good-looking, isn't he," Mott commented.

"The women fall over in rows," Miriam said. "Even his landlady; I got that out of her. To her he's Prince Charming."

"I hope you kept her confidence."

"I was careful about that. She likes me. Incidentally, she's convinced that he's some kind of undercover agent of the Government: the kind of a man who's trusted with important secrets."

"Poor woman," Mott said, "I hope she doesn't come down too hard when she learns the truth. How about getting some comps?"

"Right here," Miriam answered. She opened the large envelope she was carrying and took out five more prints. Each of the pictures was of a young man in the same age bracket: all ranging from good-looking to handsome. "An actor and four deputies," Miriam said.

Mott took the pictures. "I'll be out for a while," he said. "I want to do this one myself—alone."

He turned the task force room over to Sergeant Rogers, picked up an unmarked county car on the lot, and headed up the Hollywood Freeway toward the San Fernando Valley.

When he reached the Northridge Medical Center he parked in one of the specially reserved police slots and went inside. The lobby was moderately full as he took the elevator up to the Intensive Care Unit. He had deliberately not phoned ahead; if there was any problem, it would be harder to put him off if he was here in person.

Nurse Quigley remembered him immediately. "Dr.

Wakabayashi is here," she said. "I'll see if I can find him for you."

That meant, of course, that she would ask if Mott was to be admitted. In less than half a minute she was back with the Nikkei resident, who was probably older and more experienced than he looked.

"I know I haven't called you with a report," he said, "but I've been terribly busy. We've got three cases of attempted teen suicide here right now. That's getting to be a serious problem. No real reason for any of them."

"There never is."

"About Mary Malone . . ." Before he could go on a nurse hurried up with a sheet of paper. He read it with a frown on his face. "Ask Dr. Dempsey to look at him, will you?" he said. "He's on the floor; I saw him a few minutes ago."

As soon as the nurse had left he started again. "About Mary: she's been making very slow but fairly steady progress. She can't speak because of the damage to her throat, but she's conscious most of the time now. Sometimes she lies by the hour staring at the ceiling. She's probably relived what happened to her fifty times over."

"I'd like to see her if possible," Mott said. "It's quite important."

"All right."

Out of conscience Mott hesitated: the wretched girl had been through hell and back. "Doctor, this is highly confidential, but we have a possible suspect we're checking out. I have his picture here along with some others. I want to see if she can pick it out, but I don't want to do anything that might set her back."

Wakabayashi approved. "Mary is a gutsy girl. She's only just sixteen, but she's got what they call the right stuff. I think she can handle it."

"Then let's try it."

The doctor led the way across the ICU and out a door on the other side. It opened onto a short corridor with a row of private rooms. "This is still an intensive care section," he said. "For patients that are past the critical stage." He reached the right door and pushed it open.

Mary Malone was not pretty to look at. Her head was completely bandaged except for her eyes, which were barely visible, and her mouth. Her throat was encased in some kind of cast that came straight down from the sides of her head.

The upper half of her bed had been raised 40 degrees so that she was half sitting. The top sheet that covered her was partly folded down revealing another mass of bandages. "We stopped counting the stitches," Wakabayashi said quietly, then he walked up to the head of the bed. "How goes it?" he asked.

The girl, who looked more like a newly wrapped mummy than a human being, blinked her eyes twice.

Mott tried to read her expression, but he could only see the pupils of her eyes and they told him little.

"Your chart is much better. Enough so that I'm going to let you have a visitor."

With visible strain the girl moved her head a very little until Mott was within her range of vision. He immediately blamed himself for making her do that; he should have had sense enough to stand beside the doctor where he would have been in easy view for her.

"Mary, this is Lieutenant Mott of the Sheriff's Department. He's in charge of the task force that's tracking down your attackers."

Once more the girl blinked her eyes twice.

Mott tried to be as gentle as he possibly could. "Mary, I saw you when they first brought you in. You may not think so, but you look a helluva lot better now. Thank God you're on the mend."

The girl blinked twice.

"That means either 'yes' or that she understands," Wakabayashi explained. Then he looked at her. "Lieutenant Mott was in command of the rescue party that saved you," he added.

Two more blinks.

Mott came closer where she could see him more easily. "Mary, we have more than forty men and women working around the clock in the task force. We don't care how long it takes, or how much it costs, we're going to find the men who did this to you. Now I want to ask your help."

She looked at him steadily.

Mott held up the envelope. "I have some pictures here. I'd like to show them to you one at a time. Is that all right?"

Two blinks.

"Will it upset you too much?"

One blink.

Carefully Mott opened the large brown envelope and took out the first picture. On the back it was identified as Deputy Ross Perez of the Firestone Station. He held it up so that Mary could see it. Her eyes fixed on it and then she blinked—once.

The second picture was of a young actor who was a reservist attached to the motion picture section. In exactly the same manner the girl looked at it and then blinked once again.

The third picture was of another deputy who doubled as a stunt driver on his time off. One blink.

With no change whatever in his manner, and with his face as impassive as he could make it, Mott held up the fourth picture.

A strange, unnatural sound came from the girl. An inhuman thing without shape or form; a sound shrouded in agony. When Mott looked at her eyes once more, she was blinking as rapidly as she could without stopping.

To avoid giving any possible opening to a defense attorney, he showed her the remaining two pictures, one at a time. She shut her eyes for a moment or two, then blinked once for each one.

"I'd say that was positive," Wakabayashi offered.

Mott spoke to the girl again, as gently as he could. "Is

271

this one of the men who attacked you?" he asked and showed her the picture once more.

In reply she blinked twice, several times in succession.

"Are you sure?"

Two very firm blinks.

"When you get rid of all those bandages and are fully recovered, I'd like to take you to dinner," Mott said. He knew it was an improper thing for him to say, but he meant it.

"You're at the end of the line," Wakabayashi said. "I'm first." he looked at Mary. "Isn't that so?"

Two blinks.

31

At three thirty in the afternoon on the high desert the sun was still shining with grim ferocity in a cloudless sky. It was a high sky, scarred only by a few scattered vapor trails that hung suspended over Edwards Air Force Base and Muroc Dry Lake. The wind was blowing gently and hot, stirring the hardy plants that were able to survive the harsh arid conditions in which they had taken root.

South of Edwards and east of Palmdale the community of Littlerock was sparsely populated. It was laid out in a complex grid of streets that gave birth to such addresses as R-14 and U-12 avenues. Many of the named streets did not yet exist; only even-numbered ones appeared to have been actually cut through in accordance with some master plan that at least its creators understood.

The comparatively few houses in Littlerock were for the most part well separated. Plenty of vacant land was available, but despite the urban crowding of Los Angeles, only a limited number of people chose to live on the high desert north of the San Gabriels. It was just too far away and the amenities were limited.

Robert and Jesse Lanier were walking home from school. Both of the brothers had been born on the desert and had lived there all of their lives: to them it was an entirely normal environment. The intense heat of summer and the sometimes biting cold of winter they endured without complaint because that was how things were; at five and nine years of age the ideas of other places and climes had not entered to any degree into their consciousness. The desert was home and that was fine with them.

They lived in a nice house; they were very much aware of that. There was no lawn, only a rectangle of soil and rock where one might someday be, but grass on the desert was not expected and the lack of it no disgrace. The house itself was small so that the brothers had to share a room and sleep in bunk beds, one above the other, but they did not mind. Even as young as they were, they knew that their home was much cleaner and better maintained than those of any of their friends. Their mother was an immaculate housekeeper, and even the blowing winds across the open terrain, and the dust and dirt they carried, could not deter her from keeping the kitchen counters shining bright, the furniture spotlessly clean, and the stored linens in their closet carefully piled in neat stacks for future use.

Their father, who worked at Lockheed, would be home before too long. Later the whole family would sit down to a dinner that was sure to be well prepared and made up of things they liked. It was a very good life; they would not have exchanged it for any other kind they could have imagined.

Jesse, who was the older, went into the house first, followed by his brother, who ducked quickly into the bathroom.

"Hello, Mom," Jesse called out. When he did not receive

an immediate answer he peeked into her bedroom to see if she was resting. What he saw caused his breath to lock in his throat.

His mother lay face down on the floor, her hands lashed behind her back with some of his father's neckties. Her feet were also tied. With still more neckties her hands and feet and been pulled together, forcing her body into a back-bowed position.

What had been her head was a shapeless mass of blood.

Jesse wanted to scream, but the sound would not come. When he heard the toilet flush he backed away to intercept his younger brother. He took Robert's hand and led him into the kitchen where the telephone stood on the counter. Above the phone there was a little bulletin board that held a shopping list and a panel of frequently called numbers. Thumbtacked at the top was a card printed in red:

EMERGENCY

FIRE–POLICE

DIAL 911

Still holding his brother firmly by the hand, Jesse punched out the number with a quivering finger.

In the Antelope Valley Sheriff's Station a small screen lit up, displaying the calling number and the address. It was a vital help in setting up a fast response, particularly if the calling party was unable to give enough essential information.

The call was answered immediately: "Sheriff's Station, Deputy Morton."

Jesse was just beginning to feel the impact of the awful thing he had seen. "My mother," he said, stumbling over the words. "She'll all tied up."

The dispatcher was trained to be sure the call was valid, not someone's mistake or idea of a sick joke. "What did she say to you?" the female deputy asked.

275

"She couldn't say anything. Her head is all bloody." That was all that Jesse could do; the phone fell from his hand and clattered onto the counter.

The dispatcher heard that too; she sent the nearest available patrol unit to the scene code three, then quickly called the paramedics.

Within a minute and a half the helicopter stationed at Antelope Valley took off with two more deputies. It was a substantial response, but there was a strong possibility that life was at stake.

The deputy doing the flying knew that section of the desert intimately. In hardly more than five minutes he set his machine down within a hundred feet of the house from which the emergency call had come. Before he had shut down his engine and jumped onto the ground, the flashing red lights of an oncoming patrol unit could be seen, the howling of its siren clearing the way although there was no other visible traffic.

The four men met in front of the house. The lead deputy from the patrol car, who wore two stripes on his sleeve, went quickly inside. He already knew that a child had put in the call, so when he spotted the two brothers in the small kitchen that was visible from the front door, he went directly to them. He looked at the older one, Jesse, and asked, "Where is she, son?"

Numbly Jesse pointed toward the bedroom.

By that time the two deputies who had come by air had taken up station in front of the house and the lead deputy's partner was covering the back.

The very tall lead deputy walked down the short corridor leading to the master bedroom without touching the walls: they might hold evidence. He looked carefully at the body of the woman on the floor. He saw no signs of life; the condition of her head made it virtually impossible.

As he walked back out, the siren of the paramedic ambulance cut out in front of the house. The deputy signaled with his hand that there was no need to hurry.

Nevertheless the paramedics carried their equipment inside; they were there and they never gave up when there was the least hope. One of the two deputies who had come in the helicopter went inside to be with the boys. He was a mature man with a natural gift of warmth and understanding.

The paramedics came out again after a minute or two and met the lead deputy outside. "Did you pronounce?" the deputy asked.

"Yes. For God's sake keep the kids out of there."

"Thanks for coming."

"No sweat."

The paramedics stored their gear in their vehicle and drove away. The lead deputy went to his patrol unit and used the radio.

"Confirm nine twenty-seven David," he reported. "Requesting full one eight seven response and additional backup. Be advised two juveniles present."

As soon as he had done that he opened the trunk of his unit and took out a long roll of two-inch-wide yellow tape to mark off the crime scene. His partner lent a hand. Meanwhile the helicopter pilot had taken the two boys out of the house and was showing them over his machine.

It was Lieutenant Darrell Gordon's turn to go out, but his team was already overloaded with an excessive number of cases. Lieutenant Gary Vance had just been reassigned to the Sheriff's Office. Fortunately Ralph Mott was somewhere in the San Fernando Valley, twenty or twenty-five miles closer to the scene. The first report was that a female had been attacked, tied up, and killed. That might be one for the task force, in which case Mott was the right man to respond.

The barrel man raised him in his car. "We have a female one eighty-seven victim just reported in Littlerock," he said. "Apparently tied up before she was killed. Can you respond?"

"Yes," Mott answered, "On the way. ETA an hour plus fifteen. What's the address?"

When he had that information he added, "Send full response team, a criminalist from the lab, and advise the coroner to lay on the works."

"Got it. Want anyone from your task force?"

"Yes, two investigators and Sergeant Perry. Also someone from the public information section. This could be another one."

"I know. I'll get 'em rolling."

"Feed me anything more as it comes in."

"Ten four."

Mott drove as fast as the traffic conditions would allow. Halfway across the valley on the San Diego Freeway he caught the flash of red lights in his rearview mirror. He pulled over as quickly as he could, got out, and went back to the Highway Patrol unit that had stopped him.

He produced his badge. "Lieutenant Mott, Sheriff's Homicide," he said. "I'm responding to a one eighty-seven in Littlerock."

"Can we help?" the patrolman asked.

"I've been advised to get there A.S.A.P."

"Go ahead. I'll put out the word. You won't be stopped again."

"Thanks much."

Even with that dispensation it took Mott more than an hour to cover fifty-plus miles and climb up the more than three thousand feet on the Antelope Freeway to the Pearblossom turnoff. There he asked for and got detailed directions to the crime scene.

On a tactical frequency he talked directly with the field sergeant who was at the location.

"We've got two suspects in custody," the sergeant told him. "But it's pretty thick here. The husband is expected home at any time."

"Has he been told?"

"No. I've got a unit stationed to intercept him before he gets here. How soon can you make it?"

"In twelve to fifteen, best guess. My people are coming, also the coroner's team."

"We've got that. The scene is secured and with enough uniformed backup."

"Good. If the husband arrives before I get there, don't let him inside the tape."

Without requesting authorization, Mott hit the siren. With a husband due to arrive shortly, two kids to handle, and two suspects in custody possibly in the vicinity, things could come to a boil in a hurry. And as the ranking officer in the field, it was his responsibility to handle everything.

He didn't have to search for the crime scene: Antelope Valley had several units on hand, there was the usual accumulation of spectators outside the taped-off area, and a press vehicle was just arriving.

As he pulled up, a deputy waved him empathically on. Before he could get out, the man was at the window of his car.

"Mister, please don't stop your car here. Keep it moving."

"Lieutenant Mott."

The deputy opened the car door for him. "Sorry, Lieutenant. I'm afraid we're all a little jumpy at the moment."

Mott got out. "Is the husband here yet?"

"No, but he's expected any time. He's driving a brown Toyota; a unit is set to intercept him."

"Who's in charge?"

"Sergeant Matthews."

"Jim Matthews?"

"Yes."

"Good, I know him."

There was a hasty conference held outside the house where the walkway met the unpaved road. It included

279

Mott, Matthews, the senior handling deputy, and the two deputies who had come by air.

Matthews laid it out. "We have a one eighty-seven victim, white female, thirty to thirty-five, but it's hard to tell, the condition she's in. Her head is beaten in. The homicide team is estimating ten to fifteen. The same for the coroner."

"What about suspects?" Mott asked.

"Two brothers; they're black. They live in a camper shell about a quarter of a mile from the house. Apparently their mother owns it and has permission to park it there."

Down the road a brown car was approaching at normal speed. A black-and-white unit stopped it a block from the crime scene.

Matthews anticipated the next question. "I called the duty chaplain and got him here about ten minutes ago."

"Where are the suspects?"

"Out of sight, around the corner in a cage-back unit."

"Are they good for it?"

"That's my bet. We followed tracks from the house to the camper. When I interviewed them there, they didn't have the right answers."

"So you hooked them up."

"Right. I had plenty of probable cause."

"Then this one may not take too long."

"Maybe not, but no matter how you look at it, it's a bad can of worms."

Mott went inside the house. He observed carefully where he put his feet, and avoided touching the walls. When he entered the bedroom he did what was often his habit: he looked for the small things before he gave his attention to the body.

On the carpeting, plainly left there, was a good-sized claw hammer. The metal end was blood-covered with a number of long dark hairs clearly visible. Also on the carpeting was a tiny triangle of blackened metal. Mott looked at it intently, but until it had been photographed *in situ* he knew better than to touch it.

He looked at the king-sized bed and the tasteful spread that covered it, then at the pictures on the wall. They were all prints of nature scenes: none of them expensive, but chosen and hung with care. There was no dust on the tops of the frames and the glasses were all spotless.

It was the kind of room that would be a credit to almost any home he had ever been in. None of the furnishings was expensive, but every dollar had been spent wisely to create a comfortable, relaxing bedroom.

When he had finished his inspection, he began to study the body. He observed the way the victim had been trussed up, and the condition of what had been her head. He glanced at a picture on the dresser in a simple silver frame. It was of a man and a woman standing together, each completely happy in the other's company. The woman, he noted, was attractive; the man was obviously taking pride in her.

The lead deputy appeared in the doorway. "We need you, Lieutenant," he said.

Mott followed him out and down the short cement walk to the unpaved road. A man in a pair of dark slacks, a light shirt, and a casual sports coat with no tie stood there with a deputy flanking him on each side. His arms were shaking; he seemed on the verge of completely losing control of himself.

"My wife!" he cried. "I've got to see my wife!" His voice rose into an anguished cry. *"You've got to let me in there!"*

Mott walked up until he could rest his right hand on the man's shoulder. "I understand," he said. "I know what this means to you. But you don't want to see her right now, take my word for it."

"I don't care, goddamn it, I don't care!"

"What have they told you?" Mott asked.

"She's been killed. They strangled her."

Mott caught the "they."

"She is dead, that's true. But please believe me, you don't want to see her now. In a few minutes I'll try to arrange it."

Four vehicles in a small procession came down the road. Mott spotted a brown coroner's van third in line.

The two lead cars had brought his homicide team and the investigators he had asked for from the task force. The last person out of the second car was Flavia.

Before he did anything else Mott motioned her to join him. Then he stepped aside where he wouldn't be overheard. "Flavia," he told her, "I know you're authorized to come on these call-outs, but we've got a very sensitive situation here. I've got to ask you to stay out of the way, across the street, until I tell you."

Without a word Flavia turned from him and did what she had been told.

During the brief interval the distraught father had crossed the street himself and was talking to a neighbor. As he listened, his face darkened and a violent rage visibly burst within him. He was a man almost out of his mind when he literally ran back to Mott. "You've got 'em," he shouted. "You've got 'em, haven't you?"

Mott cursed himself for letting his attention be diverted even for a moment. "We have two suspects in custody," he said. "But that's all they are: suspects." Since the neighbor had obviously talked, there was no way he could withhold that.

The man put out his hand and tried to force his way past Mott. Two deputies grabbed and held him, one on each side. "Let me in there," he shouted. "I want my gun. I'm going to kill every goddamned nigger I can find!"

Mott nodded to the field sergeant, who took over the situation. Jim Matthews, who had earned his stripes the hard way, knew what to do.

Sergeant Lou Danoff of the Homicide Bureau and his partner had been examining the rear of the house. As soon as Mott was free, Danoff claimed his attention. "There are some very good footprints out back," he said. "A tap was leaking and the ground is moist."

Mott glanced at the sky, which was beginning to darken. Twilight would not linger very long over the desert.

"In your opinion, were they made since the husband left for work this morning?"

"No doubt at all."

"Then as soon as he can do it, have the criminalists cast the best ones."

Danoff was not finished. "It's a very distinctive pattern. The whole sole is covered with short studs. It's some sort of a special athletic shoe, but I don't know what kind."

"Lou, before it gets too dark, check if this shoe pattern made the prints that lead to the camper shell where the suspects live."

"My partner's doing that right now."

Mott went himself to look at the tracks. They were clear and distinct, the best he had seen in his experience. His blood quickened a little: this was prime evidence that even an unsophisticated jury would be able to understand.

When he came back out front, the coroner's team had just gone inside. With the two prime homicide investigators and the print and photo man added to the party, the inside of the small house would be crowded.

He went over to speak to Flavia. "I didn't mean to be short with you," he said, "but a whole lot of things were hitting the fan at the same time. I couldn't spare a moment."

"I understood that," Flavia told him. "May I come with you now?"

"If you can find a place to stand."

"Is it a bad one?"

"Very. If you're feeling the least bit squeamish . . ."

"No, I just wanted to be prepared."

As Mott had anticipated, the bedroom, although moderately large, was crowded with technical personnel.

When she saw the body Flavia gasped, otherwise she had the good sense to remain quiet.

The print and photo man was steadily shooting pictures while Deputy John Paillot was making a sketch of the scene in his notebook.

Mott called attention to the tiny bit of dark metal on the carpet. "I've already got it," the photo specialist said and straightened up. "That's it for the first go-round."

In response the coroner's investigator, a tall French-Canadian, cut through the ties that held the body in its bent-back position. The feet dropped, the arms more slowly since rigor had begun in that part of the victim. He cut the other ties away as Sergeant Matthews came in to speak to Mott.

"Her husband is frantic and in tears. He's explosive one moment, overcome the next. He keeps pleading to see his wife. What do you think?"

By now the body was lying in an almost natural position, face down on the carpet. "Put something over her head," Mott said, "and hold up for a moment. Keep those neckties out of sight."

The deputy coroner produced a small cloth from his gear and carefully covered the head and neck.

"All right," Mott said. "I'm going to bring him in for a moment. Keep it low key while he's inside."

Mott went out himself to talk to the man. He knew that he would wait indefinitely until the body was wheeled out on the coroner's gurney. That would precipitate a fresh burst of grief: he had seen that too often.

"Mr. Lanier," Mott said, "I understand why you want to see your wife. Do you clearly understand that she's dead?"

Lanier took a fresh hold on himself. "Yes, I know that. I just want to see her." He paused a moment. "She is clothed, isn't she?"

"Yes, she's fully clothed."

"Thank God for that. All right, I'm ready now."

Walking fairly slowly, as if out of respect for the dead,

Mott led the man inside. He was careful to stay ahead as they went down the short hallway. There were eight people already in the bedroom, but they had stepped aside to let the bereaved husband in. Mott stood beside Lanier and let him look at the body, lying as if in sleep.

Lanier's hands tightened. "Her clothes," he said.

"What about them?"

"That isn't what she had on this morning. She almost never changes during the day. Even if she had, she wouldn't wear those. They're her party clothes, and we weren't going anywhere."

32

John Lanier continued to look down at the body of his wife for a long minute as though by his willing it with all his being she would be able to move and possibly speak to him. When the impossibility of that had at last penetrated his consciousness, he turned and in a surprisingly mild voice said to Mott, "Thank you."

All those in the room understood: he was speaking in the presence of his dead wife and he would not violate the peace in which she now lay. Almost calmly he turned and walked out, his eyes straight ahead, refusing to look at the home she had made for him and their sons.

When he emerged into the darkening night, Sergeant Matthews joined him to keep him company.

"Was it quick?" Lanier asked.

"She never knew or felt a thing," Matthews lied with a completely clear conscience. The bereaved man was bound to learn differently later on, but for the time being he needed every shred of comfort he could get.

The duty chaplain came up to them. "Robert and Jesse are at the Webbers'," he said, indicating a house across the road. "I suggest we join them there."

For the moment emotionally exhausted, Lanier allowed himself to be escorted to his neighbors' home. Herbert Webber stood in the doorway, waiting to invite him in. His wife had wanted to do that, but Webber thought it better if she didn't.

"Come in, Jack," he said, and held the door open. The chaplain took his cue and did not follow.

A few moments later Mott emerged from the house where the woman had been killed. Flavia came to him and asked, "Isn't there something I can do?"

"Mainly, Flavia, don't get in the way of the investigators and be sure that you don't destroy any evidence. If you go inside, don't put your hands on the walls or the door-jambs."

"May I sit on a stool in the kitchen?"

"I think that will be all right."

Sensitive to the fact that this particular crime scene was an unusually volatile one, Flavia perched on one of the three kitchen stools, took out the notebook she had learned to carry, and began to write with careful precision.

In the bedroom the coroner's chief criminalist was on her knees next to the body. Her evidence kit was beside her while the French-Canadian investigator worked with her. Both wore the thin white surgeon's gloves that are always used to avoid contaminating evidence.

After three-quarters of an hour of careful work, they turned the body over so that it was lying on its back. With no attitude other than that of scientific investigation they pulled up the skirt above the hips, exposing the triangle of pubic hair. With a pair of surgeon's scissors the criminalist cut off a tiny sample and folded it into a carefully prepared

287

paper packet. She took a similar sample of hair from the abdomen and looked for any at all on the legs, which were clean shaven.

Then she picked up her ultraviolet lamp. Without being asked, someone turned off the overhead light. Beginning at the feet the criminalist studied the body with minute care under the ultraviolet. When it was just above the right knee, the French-Canadian said, "There."

The criminalist nodded and continued her detailed examination. When she reached the victim's pubic area, the body glowed almost brightly under the light. Meticulously she noted the pattern and how far it extended up onto the victim's abdomen. One of the homicide investigators drew a diagram of the area. The French-Canadian held the lamp while the criminalist made some exact measurements with a small steel tape. When she nodded that she was through, the lights were turned on again.

Mott knew what she had to tell before she spoke. "The victim had sexual intercourse, probably with at least two men, shortly before her death. It was definitely rape. At this point I'd guess that each man violated her twice; the quantity and distribution of semen indicate that."

"How about the party dress?" an investigator asked.

The criminalist shook her head. "She's not wearing underwear, so obviously she didn't put it on with any idea of going out. I thought at first that it might be a wedding anniversary or something like that and she planned to surprise her husband when he came home. But she put the dress on because she was forced to."

"Before or after she was raped?" Mott asked.

"I can only guess at that until we do the lab work. I'd say they stripped her, raped her, then made her put on her prettiest dress before they raped her again." The criminalist was being completely professional but she was also a woman, which, in this case, was an advantage.

Because there was nothing more for him to do at that

moment in the bedroom, Mott went back to where Flavia was sitting patiently. He took a stool next to hers so that they were facing one another. Before he could speak Sergeant Matthews came in. "Brace yourself," he said.

"Let's have it."

"I examined the shoes on both of the suspects."

"And they don't fit the prints," Mott supplied.

"You've got it. Something more: there's a car outside with blacks in it."

"Any trouble?"

"No, they seem like good people just waiting and watching. One of them is the mother of the suspects. She's also the owner of the camper shell where they live. We've confirmed that she had permission to leave it there."

"Detach two of your best people and send them for a warrant; we'll need it A.S.A.P. Meantime see what you can do to get mama to sign a consent form." He turned the sheets on his clipboard and extracted two of the needed forms that were exactly where they should be. Silently he handed them over.

When that was done, he turned back to Flavia. "You know that under the Bill of Rights the police or any other authority can't enter a private dwelling without the owner's consent. The idea being that a man's home is his castle. The only other ways are either to obtain a warrant signed by a judge or in 'exigent circumstances.' If a police officer hears a woman screaming inside a house, he can reasonably assume that she needs help and go inside.

"Now, there's what's called the homicide exception. If murder has been done, or there is good reason to suspect it, the police may enter the premises. There are certain other exceptions that very from state to state."

"That's only rational," Flavia said.

"Unfortunately rationality has little to do with the law. And there's another consideration, Flavia, and that's the massive number of lawsuits that are filed. Some of them are decided in ways that are hard to understand. For

289

instance: here in California a burglar broke into a home, tripped over a loose rug, and hurt himself. After he was captured, he sued the home owner, and won."

"That's hard to believe," Flavia said.

Mott took a moment to settle himself down. "I want you to understand why we're having to tread so carefully here. There's a U.S. Supreme Court decision that all police agencies have to follow, Mincey versus Arizona.* In essence it says that police officers at a murder scene may make a cursory search of the premises to look for more victims or possible suspects. They can look in a closet, for instance, but they can't open drawers. They can only collect evidence that is in plain sight or within arm's length of the suspect, if there is one. Once they leave the scene the Mincey decision takes hold and they may not return without the owner's permission or a warrant."

"So if we leave here, it will take a warrant to get us back in."

"That's right. Which is why we can't go back into that camper shell. We were there once when the suspects were arrested."

Mott went out to check on the progress in getting the mother's permission to search the camper shell. Flavia followed him, then stopped to watch the criminalist from the lab casting a footprint with his yellowish-green plaster solution. She wondered what was going on in the bedroom, but thought it best to keep out of the way.

It is just as well that she did, as the coroner's criminalist was using her sex offenses kit and that involved taking samples from the vagina and many other parts of the body. The coroner's investigator had made the necessary puncture and was taking the temperature of the liver. A large heavy plastic sheet had been laid out to receive the body.

Sergeant Lou Danoff, who was never seen without a hat

*437 U.S. 385, 57L, Ed. 2d, 290 (1978)

on, was intently studying the tiny bit of metal that still lay on the carpet. Finally he picked it up using surgeon's gloves and looked at it from all sides. When he detected evidence of blood, and a fleck of possible brain tissue, he did some careful thinking.

Quietly he went to the living room and checked the small set of tools beside the fireplace. The end of the hook on the poker had been broken off.

At almost the same moment Sergeant Matthews handed Mott two copies of a search consent form, duly signed and dated by the mother of the suspects. "Is there going to be any static about how you got this?" Mott asked.

"None whatever. I told her truthfully that we would get a warrant anyway and that the sooner we made the search, the sooner we would be able to transport her sons from the scene. She's obviously afraid they're going to be attacked."

Mott looked up and saw that the crowd around the scene had been growing in size and restlessness.

While the two regular homicide investigators went to search the camper shell, Mott released his task force people from the scene. They were overdue to be off duty and he wanted them to rest up.

The phone rang and he took the call. It was Records with the background of the two suspects. Both of the brothers had rap sheets with heavy felony convictions, including armed robbery and rape. Both, he noted grimly, were on parole.

In a way the public was to blame for that, because every time the state wanted to build a new prison, wherever it was to be located, the local residents did their utmost to block it. With every existing facility overloaded to the bursting point, it was either build new ones or give the inmates already in custody early release. There had been no real choice. The money for the prisons had already been voted, but everyone wanted them built somewhere else.

Sergeant Bob Perry appeared with a pair of athletic shoes in his hand. They were canvas and had been freshly

291

washed; they were still wet. Silently Matthews turned them over and displayed the closely set studs on the bottom. "Do they fit the prints?" Mott asked.

"Exactly."

"Where were they?"

"In the camper shell."

"Take the suspects to the station and book them."

The case, as far as he was concerned, was solved, although far from over. Presently the coroner's gurney with the body wrapped in plastic and then a concealing blanket was wheeled out and slid into the van.

Sergeant Danoff came to speak to him. "I think we're through here. We've got all we need." He told Mott about the poker.

When the scene had been secured and the tapes taken down, and all the evidence that had been gathered had been loaded into the appropriate vehicles, Mott took a last check. Then, finally, he turned to Flavia. "Let's go home," he said, weary with fatigue.

"Shall I drive?" she offered.

"No, I'd rather."

She understood that he wasn't reflecting on her driving skill; he wanted to do something with his hands and feet, something to keep him occupied.

Under an almost full moon they drove across the desert to the Palmdale Freeway. Then they started down the seventy-odd miles they still had to go.

"I have a question," Flavia said.

"Go ahead."

"Why do they call the reception desk, if that's the name for it, the barrel?"

Mott drove on in silence for a brief bit. "It goes back to an old lumberjack joke," he said. " A rude one, I'm afraid."

"I expect it would be."

"There was a greenhorn lumberjack who went out to work in one of the isolated camps. He'd been there a week or so when he stopped and asked his foreman, 'What do we do for women around here?'

"The foreman told him that there weren't any women, that everyone used the barrel. He pointed out a barrel that had a number of inch-and-a-half holes drilled in the side. 'When you need it,' the foreman told him, 'find a hole that isn't in use and stick you cock in it.'

"The greenhorn tried it and discovered that within a short time he had a wonderfully satisfying orgasm. He tried it twice more the next day and each time it was a great release. So he looked up the foreman and told him how good it was.

"'That's fine,' the foreman told him. 'Just remember that come Thursday, it'll be your turn in the barrel.'"

Flavia leaned her head back and laughed, letting all the tension of the last few hours flow out of her. "So that young woman who told me that she worked the barrel for several months knew the story."

"Of course—everyone does. It's in our official literature."

"What would policemen do if they didn't have a sense of humor?" Flavia asked.

"Suffocate. The job does that to you. That's why you'll hear so many jokes around a murder scene. The investigators aren't heartless, they're just letting off the tension we all feel."

By mutual consent they didn't talk anymore until they reached Mott's apartment. He put the car away, looked at the pile of work that he had loaded in it, locked the door, and went inside unfettered.

Flavia handed him a drink. He took it gratefully. "Now if it were only served by a topless waitress," he said.

"That can be arranged."

He dropped onto the sofa. "I'd rather have you here beside me."

She took her own drink and fitted herself under the curve of his left arm. There was a masculine odor about him that she liked. She had never noticed it before, but then, she had never been out on the hot desert with him long enough to notice it.

"You've got quite a job," she said.

"True," he answered. "But I wanted to be in law enforcement, and I am. You wanted to teach."

They sat together quietly, assimilating each other by a process of spiritual osmosis, until the phone rang.

She wanted him to ignore it, to go to bed and make love to her at a time when she needed it very much.

"Mott," he said, and listened.

He turned and kissed her, sharpening her desire even more. "Sorry, love," he said. "I've got another one."

"Another homicide? Can't someone else take it?"

"No," Mott said as he got up. "I'm the task force commander."

She made a fist and fitted it against the front of her mouth. "You mean . . ."

"A girl seventeen or eighteen, nude, evidence of severe torture . . ." He paused to let the bitterness sink in. "And with a wire coat hanger twisted into her neck."

33

Flavia felt as though some-
one had smashed a hard blow squarely on her stomach.
She had not realized how involved she had become with
the victims; hearing the same dreadful story one more
time, when she had been particularly vulnerable, almost
took the breath out of her body.

Mott went into their bedroom to get his hardware: his
gun, handcuffs, beeper, two fine-point brush pens, and a
fresh notebook. He used a separate one for each case
because if he produced it in court, then anything else that
might be written in it would be open to the defense,
whether it pertained or not.

On the back there were two large stamps. One provided
spaces for Date Assigned, File #, Coroner #, Crime, Date
and Time, Victim, and Suspect.

The second stamp had spaces for Location, Station
Reporting, Headquarters, and Detective. Not included, but

always written down, were the outside air temperature, weather conditions, and all other pertinent data concerning the nature of the crime scene, indoors or out.

Mott picked up his heavy black flashlight and then turned to speak to Flavia, but before he could do so, the phone rang again.

The barrel man was on the line. "When we got the call on the coat-hanger killing, we notified the captain immediately. Those were his orders. He knew you'd already had a full day, so Chuck Bradley is taking it. Have a nice night."

A wave of welcome relief surged over Mott. Bradley was a good friend and highly capable. Whatever there was to get, he and his people would get it.

He turned to Flavia. "You've met Lieutenant Bradley, haven't you?"

"Yes. I like him."

"He's going to handle the case for me."

She flashed him a worried look. "You aren't in any trouble, are you?"

"No way: captain's orders." He began to unload his equipment. His gun and holster were the last: he took them into the bedroom and put them carefully out of sight, but where he could reach them quickly in case of sudden need. Emergencies were a large part of his life.

He took off his coat and hung it up. Then he stripped off his tie and set his neatly shined shoes in the corner of his side of the closet. When he went back into the living room, he was almost a different person. "May I talk to you?" he asked.

"Of course." She waited until he was seated, then curled herself against him, using her body language to tell him how grateful she was that he didn't have to go out again.

He put his arm across her shoulders and drew her to him. For a few moments he was more than content to just sit there, drinking in her presence, like some splendidly vintaged Spanish wine. He watched her breasts rise and fall as she breathed and was grateful that she was able to do so, steadily and evenly.

"You wanted to talk," she prompted.

"Yes, and now is a good time."

He paused to get his thoughts in just the right order, because any mistake could be critical.

"You know that when you first identified one of the voices on that tape as your student, I found it very hard to believe."

"Of course," Flavia said. "The odds against it were enormous."

"I'm glad you understand. Then when I found out he was a parolee with a heavy record, I suddenly became very worried about you."

"You told me that. I was grateful."

Mott seemed not to hear her interruption. "I knew you lived alone in a low-security building. And that you had no relatives anywhere in the country. Because you'd told me how he scrutinized you in class, I knew he had ideas about you. And I know that his kind of person never lets go of an obsession."

She folded her hands in her lap and looked at him. "Ralph, we've been over this before. You forget sometimes that I'm a sociologist, a professional like yourself in a related field. I know about obsessions."

He waited until he was sure she had finished. "There's something I want to add," he said. "That's why I brought it up again."

"I'm sorry," she said. "I should have realized."

He thought how remarkable she was: so few women would be willing to accept the blame like that.

"It's just this, Flavia: I brought you here for your safety, at least that was my honest excuse. But because I did, and you accepted, doesn't mean . . ." He stopped, because the words he wanted stubbornly refused to come.

In an unexpectedly soft and warm voice Flavia finished the thought for him. "You mean, Ralph, that because I

297

accepted your offer of shelter and protection, you don't want me to feel that I'm obligated to sleep with you."

"That's it—exactly," he said.

"Look, Ralph, if I hadn't been willing, I wouldn't have come. I knew you wouldn't assume too much, even though we'd already made love together. So clear that concern out of your mind. Any time that I want to sleep separately, I'll let you know."

He looked at her, knowing she was the most desirable woman he could ever imagine. For a short while she was his, to live with and to hold. He thrust aside the bitter knowledge that it would soon have to end: there were just too many reasons why he couldn't hope to make it permanent.

Flavia got to her feet. "Would you like something—a cup of coffee, perhaps?"

"How about some cocoa?" he asked.

"A good idea; I'll join you."

After the cocoa had been finished, he settled down with the current issue of the *FBI Journal* so that she could have the full use of the bathroom for as long as she liked. When he heard her turn off the light and go into the bedroom, he forestalled his impatience for a few more minutes so she wouldn't think he had been waiting for her to be through.

Then he made his own preparations for bed and climbed in beside her. It didn't matter so much if they made love or not, just as long as she was there, warm and affectionate, beside him.

When Mott arrived at the Homicide Bureau a little after eight the next morning, Chuck Bradley had not yet gone home. "Let's get some coffee," he said.

When they had filled two mugs and returned to Bradley's desk, Chuck laid it out. "It was a female victim all right, but not as we first expected. The informant had been reading too many newspaper accounts."

He took a sip of his hot coffee.

"The victim was black, twenty-five to thirty, and with stretch marks that the coroner's criminalist said indicated the birth of several children. It was a dump-off job: the body was alongside a roadway about as far east as we go. The victim was nude: no ID of any kind. Teeth badly neglected, with no significant dental work. We're running her prints, but until we get something back on that, or a match-up with a missing-person report, she's Jane Doe."

Mott took some of his own coffee. "It doesn't sound like another one for us," he said. "But until we know better, we'll take it on. What else have you got?"

"There was a coat hanger wound around her neck, but the coroner's first opinion was that she was already dead when it was used."

"Any evidence of torture?"

Bradley shook his head. "I had everyone look particularly for that, but there was nothing visible. They're going to do her at eleven; I'll give you all I can when I get back from the autopsy."

Mott finished his coffee, spoke his thanks, and went in to meet with his task force. He laid out what facts he had on the new murder. "For the time being, it's Bradley's case," he said. "I'll know by this afternoon if we're going to take it on."

He spent the next three-quarters of an hour going over everything the task force had been doing. He listened intently and was careful not to interrupt any of his people while they were having their say. At the same time he was acutely aware of an element of discouragement that had been growing for the past several days. So much hard, tedious work had been done, all of it with no visible results. Hours and hours had been wasted on trying to put together the Harry and Joe combination. Hundreds of files of known offenders had been read and reread without uncovering a single tangible clue. Cases in other jurisdictions had been studied without success.

The members of the task force were all skilled professionals, but they were also human, so the general atmosphere of failure was thick in the air. Everyone was waiting for a break, but not, God willing, another similar case, another victim.

When everyone was finished, Mott did his best to pick things up. "We've had a positive identification of Hellman," he said, and then added the unavoidable qualification, "but we probably can't use it." Carefully he explained his visit to Mary Malone and her reaction to Hellman's picture.

"Both the doctor and I felt that her identification was without question, but the poor girl can't possibly appear in court, or even sign a deposition, if the judge would allow it. She's hooked up to a dozen different pieces of equipment that are keeping her alive, but any idea of moving her is out of the question. And I'm not going to put that girl at the mercy of a defense attorney who would want to cross-question her. I know, and now you know, that Hellman is one of our prime suspects, so getting some sort of a line on him is our present best bet.

"Now I want a concerted effort to interview any and all of his known associates, as far back as we can go. Particularly any special friends he had when he was inside. Be very careful that you don't give out any information other than the fact that we are looking into his background. Under no circumstances say why. Don't call him a suspect. Have you got all that?"

There was a stir of agreement.

"If you run across him, and I stress the *if*, call for backup if you can and take him into custody. Don't Mirandize him in the field. Stress that he's only wanted for questioning. If you get him, transport him to the nearest holding facility regardless of jurisdiction and let me know immediately."

The field members of the task force left to carry out their assignments. Those who stayed behind to answer the phones and use the computer were positioning themselves to carry on as before.

300

Sergeant Blaylock talked at length with a psychic who claimed that if she had some of the killer's personal effects, she could determine from them where he was. Blaylock listened carefully, because he knew of several cases where psychics had been called upon and where they had supplied useful information. Absolutely no bets were being overlooked; the call that sounded like nothing at all could conceivably be the one that would supply a desperately needed break. But the sense of frustration still hung heavily over the whole room and over those who were working so hard within it.

When his phone rang, Joe picked it up and said. "Yeah?"

He was relieved when he heard Harry's voice on the line. "Let's talk," Harry said.

"You wanna come here?"

"No. Come in the Honda."

"Where?"

"Same as last time." The line went dead.

Joe understood that they weren't going to do anyone this time out; it was to be strictly a conference. He locked his room, went down to where he kept his old Honda Civic parked and got in. He had been able to buy it cheaply and had fixed the engine up himself. His precious van was in the securely locked garage at the back of the property. No one had ever tried to get in.

It took him forty minutes to reach the place in West Hollywood where they had met last time. As soon as he had drawn his car up to the curb, Harry opened the right-hand side door and climbed in. No one would pay any attention to that; it was an avowed homosexual city where many of the members of the city council were admittedly either male homosexuals or lesbians. Meeting here was an additional safeguard, and Harry never took any unnecessary chances.

"Drive around a little," Harry said, "but don't attract any cops."

301

Obediently Joe pulled into the flow of traffic, heading generally toward the beach.

"I've got to ask you," Harry said, a sudden deadly hardness in his voice. "Have you told, or hinted to anyone, what we've been doing?"

The question shocked Joe, but he was able to answer it with conviction. "Not on your life! I don't know anybody. But if I did, it's none of their goddamned business."

"I thought that maybe you'd dropped a word or two to some of the brothers."

Joe shook his head almost violently. "You think I'm crazy?"

That satisfied Harry, at least for the moment. "Right now I'm laying low," he said. "I don't know why, but they're looking for me."

That sent a cold chill down Joe's back and his knuckles whitened on the steering wheel. "What happened?" he asked.

"I found out the campus rent-a-cops were looking for me. You know what dumb shits they are. They asked one of the brothers if he'd seen me and he tipped me off. My landlady let them in to search my place."

"Did they find anything?" Joe tried hard to keep the panic out of his voice.

Harry laughed at him. "Nothing for them to find. You've got the tape and the pictures. You told me they'd never be found."

"Never," Joe confirmed. "You don't know how well they're hid."

"I want you to think hard," Harry continued. "About any witnesses. Anyone who might have seen us making a pickup."

"There aren't any." Joe spoke with a hard emphasis. "You know how we checked that out. Even if we did miss something, and we didn't, what can they tell? A van, that's all. There's no chance at all that anyone was close enough to see the license plate."

302

"The girl in the hospital can't talk," Harry told him. "She's still in a coma and she isn't coming out of it."

"How'd you find that out?"

"I did a little checking. She's on life-support tubes—a vegetable. Sooner or later they'll pull the plug. She's never going to be any better: that's for sure."

"Still, I'll feel better when it's over with."

Harry became all business once more. Joe had high trust in him when he was like that, because he always thought of everything. "I want you to have the van painted," he said. "You know a place that can do it on the Q.T.?"

Joe was delighted that he had the answer. "I sure do. It's a chop shop; they can do a class paint job overnight on anything. You wouldn't know your own car after they've worked on it."

"Good. Take the van there and have them do a hot-shot job: custom but not too much so. How much will they want?"

"About a grand. As far as they'll know, it's one we lifted."

"Get it done right away. I'll give you the money."

"Why're we doing this?"

Harry looked straight ahead, through the windshield. "I know they're looking for me, but I don't know why. The only thing I've done is what we've done together. So maybe they got a tip somewhere; some pair of eyes might have seen the van. So we change it. A classy one like you've got doesn't go with a dull paint job. So get it fixed and make it like all the others with a custom interior. It could be too suspicious otherwise."

"I'll take it in tonight," Joe said. "I used to hot-wire Caddies for them: I got five hundred apiece for every one I delivered. Maybe they'll need some more cars."

"Where do they sell them?"

"To a broker in Mexico who ships them to South America. I've made some deliveries; that's how I got the van."

"Then listen: here's the word. Until I find out what they want from me, get the van fixed and then keep right in line.

Go to your job. Don't boost cars for the chop shop; live on what you make. It won't be for long. If anyone comes around to talk to you, you've been keeping your nose clean. You've learned your lesson: got it?"

"Easy," Joe said.

"If they ask about me, you know me and you heard I was in school. That's the last word you have."

"How about the van?"

"Get the shop to hold it for you. Don't keep it in your garage anymore. You remember how to reach me?"

"Same number?"

"Yes; leave a message. But not too soon after you've been interviewed—if you are. I'll call you back with a meet."

Joe was mildly curious. "What're we goin' to do after this blows over?"

"You just wait," Harry answered. "You're going to see the best-looking woman you ever dreamed of, bare-ass naked. You're going to screw her, front and back, as much as you want. Then we'll do her a whole new way. And take it from me, you're going to love every moment of it."

34

During most of the long night that followed, while Mott slept quietly beside her, Flavia lay wide awake on her back with her mind filled by an all-consuming idea. While sleep kept its distance from her, she relived the idea time and again, seeking out any flaws that might make it invalid. There were some minor technicalities, but there were several ways she thought they could be overcome.

As the minutes, and the hours, moved silently by, she worked out every detail she could from the data she had been given. She needed some more specific points of information, but that was no problem because she knew where they were to be found and that she would have access to them.

Because her mind was a disciplined one, she systematically examined every objection that might be raised and dealt with each one of them. When daylight finally came, she knew what she was going to do. Then, and only then, she turned on her side and let her restless mind try to find its own peace.

At a little after seven Mott got up as silently as he could and checked the lecture schedule that Flavia had laid out on the corner of the dresser. As soon as he had determined that she had no commitment for that morning, he slipped into the bathroom where he shaved, washed, and prepared himself for the day with as little noise as possible.

Realizing what he was trying to do for her, Flavia lay still with her eyes closed, pretending to be sound asleep until after she had heard the front door close softly behind him.

Five minutes later she got up and began her morning routine. She did not concern herself anymore about the plan she had made; she had resolved it to her entire satisfaction during the dark hours of the night just past. It only remained now for her to put it into operation.

When she had had her breakfast and it was past eight o'clock, she consulted Mott's list of Sheriff's Department numbers and found the one she wanted. She dialed it and noted how promptly the secretary answered.

"This is Flavia de la Torre," she said. "Is Captain Grimm in?"

"One moment, please."

Very shortly the captain was on the line. "Good morning, Flavia. What's on your mind?"

"I'd very much like to see you this morning if that's possible," she answered. "Privately."

"Any trouble?"

"No—none. None at all."

"Then come right over. I'll arrange parking for you."

"Thank you very much, Captain." She replaced the phone with the feeling that the signs and portents so far were all good.

As she rode up the elevator in the Hall of Justice, her only concern was that she might accidently bump into someone she knew, or who would know her, from the Homicide

Bureau. When she got off on the seventh floor the double doors to the Bureau remained mercifully closed for the few seconds it took her to walk past them on the way to the captain's office. Once inside his private suite she dismissed that worry from her mind.

The captain's secretary smiled a greeting and picked up a phone. "Dr. de la Torre is here." After a second or so she looked up and said, "You can go right in."

Captain Grimm paid her the tribute of getting to his feet to welcome her. Then he walked over and closed the door after her before settling down once more behind his desk. With his hands folded in front of him, he waited for her to speak.

"Ever since I first came in here I've been in a privileged position," she began. "I'd have to be an imbecile not to realize that. I don't know whether to thank the fact that there's real interest in my work, that my dean is Chief Cargill's brother, or that you've given your own personal blessing, but somewhere I owe a considerable debt of gratitude."

"The man you most have to thank, Flavia, sits in the corner office on the second floor."

"You mean the sheriff himself."

"Definitely. Sheriff Block runs this department and nothing goes on without his knowledge and approval. He personally okayed you based on the reports he's seen. I don't have to tell you that they've been favorable, otherwise you wouldn't still be here."

With her first hurdle crossed, Flavia went directly on to the next. "At this point, Captain, I want to reassure you that I know I'm not a policewoman, or qualified to be one."

The captain leaned back a little. "If that's what you have in mind, Flavia, I'd better warn you that you have to get appointed first. That can probably be handled. Then there's the physical exam, and I see no problem there. But after that there's four months of intensive work in the academy, with virtually no time off at all until you

307

graduate. After that you'd have to put in at least several months at Sybil Brand or some other detention facility. That's the curse of this department: the sheriff has the responsibility for running the jails and we need hundreds of sworn officers to do that."

"I understand all that, Captain."

"One thing more, Flavia: with your doctorate and academic experience, you might well be regarded as over-qualified. You'd have to talk your way around that."

She was careful not to embarrass him. "I'm glad to have that information, even though I'm not at present a candidate."

He was just as quick to support her. "If you change your mind, be sure and let me know. Now how can I help you?"

Flavia looked at him steadily without blinking. "I'd like to ask you, Captain, to take what I'm about to tell you as a serious proposal. Please don't dismiss it until you've heard me out."

"I won't, Flavia. It's no secret that you've earned our respect around here. I've had reports on how you've conducted yourself in the field. You've been to some pretty bloody messes and handled them well."

"I'm certainly not a homicide detective," she said, "although I'm currently doing my best to learn the business. But I'd like to point out that within my own discipline I'm a professional. I studied for a good many years to become one."

"No one here doubts that."

Flavia took hold of the advantage she had been given. "Then as one pro to another, I'd like to ask some questions, if I may."

"Of course. I'll answer them if I can."

"I'd like to start with Franklin Hellman. I identified his voice on the tape, but there had to be a wide margin for doubt in that."

Grimm, who was not given to nervous habits, sat quietly still. "That's true, of course. The coincidence was too

308

strong, plus the fact that there are millions of people here in Los Angeles and a lot of them sound alike."

"But you did take the trouble to check him out."

"At this stage of the game, Flavia, we're checking out everyone and everything. If someone had called in anonymously and said that Hellman was the man, we'd have looked at him thoroughly on that alone. In fact, we're doing exactly that right now on dozens of other tips from all kinds of sources."

"No stone unturned," Flavia said.

"Exactly."

"Now, Captain, *after* I'd identified Hellman as one of the speakers on the tape, I reported to Ralph how intensely he'd scrutinized me in class. I even made it a point to dress to defeat him as much as I could."

"But didn't you tell Ralph that toward the end of the semester you intended to show up in a tight sweater, without a bra, and blow him right out of the water?"

Flavia was unfazed. "I did tell him that, although I didn't really mean it. But I'd like it understood that it wasn't Hellman's incessant study of my body that suggested his name to me when I heard the tape. He was totally out of my mind at the time—until I heard his voice and realized that I had heard it many times before."

"I'll accept that," the captain said. "You know, of course, that when we looked into Hellman and found that he was a convicted sex offender out on parole, our interest in him picked up a lot."

"Of course. But despite my identification of him, and his known record, and the fact that he's disappeared, there still isn't enough of a case against Hellman to make an arrest. Or to file with the D.A. Isn't that right?"

Grimm nodded. "That's right. I can have him brought in for questioning, but that's all. And he can only be held for a limited time. As far as filing against him, that's out of the question without a lot more solid evidence."

Flavia folded her hands in front of her. "Captain, when a

policewoman goes into the field to carry out an assignment, particularly one where there might be an element of
danger, how well is she usually protected?"

Grimm had no trouble answering that. "We cover her
like the sky. As many as thirty officers, including specialists
from S.E.B., will be backing her up. Out of sight, of course,
but right there if needed. If anyone walks up to her on the
street, he'll be in a marksman's cross hairs. If he reaches for
a weapon, the moment it comes in sight, he's taken. If she
signals that she needs help, and she'll have several ways of
doing that, the response will be almost instantaneous."

"Indoors as well?"

"Anywhere."

Flavia straightened up and put on her professional
academic demeanor. "All right, Captain, we've covered
some valuable ground. We've established that within the
limits of my own field I'm accepted as a professional. And
that work is often closely related to law enforcement and
the causes of crime."

She stopped to let that much sink in. "To establish
beyond question that Franklin Hellman is one of the men
who is raping, torturing, and killing these young women,
additional, firm evidence is needed. Proof positive if
possible, of his guilt."

She turned on an added intensity that Grimm had not
seen before and for a moment it startled him.

"I'm not only a woman," Flavia continued. "I'm a
particular woman to whom he's paid detailed, almost
fanatic attention. And not just because he's been bored in
class. Without flattering myself, I can tell you as a fellow
professional that he wants to get at me, to explore my body,
to have sex with me, and then—knowing his behavior
patterns—to climax his triumph by killing me, more than
any other female alive."

"I can see why you're concerned," the captain said.

"No!" Flavia blazed at him. "You misunderstand me

310

entirely. What I'm telling you is that I'm the one person who can go into the field, entice him out of hiding, and get the evidence that you need to convict him. And his partner. And what's more, Captain Grimm, I know how to do it."

35

For a period of several quiet moments the captain considered that remark. He had more than a hundred homicide specialists under his command. While many of them knew and liked Flavia, he didn't know how far they would welcome her intruding into their work. Then he reminded himself that they were always ready to listen to anyone who might come up with some right answers.

"Have you discussed this with Ralph?" he asked.

Flavia shook her head. "No, because he'd try to talk me out of it and I don't want him to."

"Incidentally, how are you two getting along?"

She wasn't surprised by his question. "Very well. I feel safe living with him and I'm enjoying it."

"He's a good man," the captain said. He contemplated adding, "and a lucky one too," but decided to withhold that comment. Instead he picked up a phone.

Ralph Mott was surprised to find Flavia in the captain's office, but he was careful not to show it. He sat down and moments later accepted a cup of coffee, made the way he liked it, from the captain's secretary.

"Flavia has an angle we might look into," the captain said with characteristic understatement.

"I'd like to hear it." That made it clear that this was news to Mott also.

"A university campus isn't just the groves of academe," Flavia said. "It's also an active center of politics, grapevine communications, and quite a lot of other things, including sex. I think we can make all this work for us."

She put her fingertips together under her chin and looked up as she spoke. "Suppose we create an arsonist," she said. "He's twenty-two years old and was in trouble several times as a juvenile. He's very slender, uses cocaine when he can afford it, and smokes marijuana. And he loves to start fires."

"Has he got a name?" the captain asked.

"Call him Henry Smith. He's a transient who hangs out on skid row, working a little now and then so he can buy himself food and drugs."

She paused and looked at her two listeners to see if she was coming across. They were paying attention; beyond that she couldn't tell.

"Next we put out a routine news release about him, one the won't attract much attention."

"You lost me there," Grimm said.

"It would be a fictitious release," Flavia explained. "The heading would read something like 'Arson Suspect Arrested.' Then it would go on more or less this way, 'Yesterday afternoon sheriff's detectives arrested Henry Smith, twenty-two, a transient, as a suspect in a series of recent arson fires. The arrest climaxed several weeks of undercover work by the arson squad.'

"Then a new paragraph. 'According to a Sheriff's Department spokesman, "We know we have the right

313

man." Smith is being held in the county jail in lieu of bail.'"

"All of which is fiction," Mott confirmed.

"Yes. Now the important part, the last paragraph: 'Prior to Smith's capture, several anonymous phone calls to the Sheriff's Department claimed that the arsonist was a university student. Sheriff's investigators have been working closely with the campus police in looking for any students who could be legitimate suspects.'

"If we need it," she continued, "I'm sure the dean will give us a statement to the effect that the university is much relieved to know that no one in the student body was responsible for such a series of antisocial action."

"I don't buy that last bit," the captain said. "The dean might say something to the effect that he is relieved and glad that a suspect not from the university is in custody. No more than that."

"That's better," Flavia agreed.

"After which Henry Smith is never heard from again," Mott concluded. "And no one is particularly concerned."

"Exactly."

"You might smoke out Hellman that way," the captain said. "By making him think that the campus police have been looking for an arsonist rather than a murderer. But how will he hear about it?"

"The campus paper will play it up without being asked," Flavia answered. "Once he's convinced that he's not under suspicion for anything, he'll have to show up to avoid violating his parole."

"Then what?" Mott asked.

"I'll be very careful about it, but I may entice him a little," Flavia said. "I've got a designer knit outfit that I've never worn on campus. It was actually quite expensive, and this if the appropriate season."

"That makes good sense," the captain said. "It'll make you even more the desirable woman he sees all the time but can't have."

"You're a very good psychologist," Flavia said. "You ought to take your degree."

The captain pointed to the inconspicuous 187 pin in his lapel. "That's my degree," he said. "Are you planning to move back into your apartment?"

"I'd rather stay where I am," Flavia said. "With Ralph I'll be safe nights. During the day I'll meet my classes, go shopping, and do the usual things. I can give Hellman plenty of chances to intercept me when he thinks that I'm alone."

The captain swung his chair a little the other way. "Ralph?" he asked.

"Personally, I'd rather she didn't. Professionally, if she's willing to take a chance like that, she's the best possible bait to nail him."

The captain rang for his secretary. "Ask Captain Hinkle if he can join us for a few minutes," he said. "You might tell him it's urgent."

The commander, who was next in line above Grimm, disapproved from the first moments onward. "I understand the situation," he said, "and I fully appreciate Dr. de la Torre's offer, but the fact remains she's a civilian."

"She's already signed a waiver," Grimm said.

"Fine, but that doesn't cover all the bases. There are some rights you can't sign away. Furthermore, the defense would have a field day if they ever found out that we nailed their client by means of a false news item. Entrapment. Also, Bob, we simply can't afford to be caught lying in a press release; it would take Billy Hinkle months to get out from under it."

"Then what's your suggestion?"

"The liability of putting a civilian at risk that way is too much of a gamble. No matter how willing she is, she isn't trained. We can have a female deputy impersonate her. She'll be armed and wired. If Hellman jumps her, he'll get a helluva lot more than he bargained for."

"Let's play out that scenario," Grimm suggested. "It goes down just as you laid it out. Hellman jumps her; she nails him. Now what've we got?"

The commander considered that and saw Grimm's point. "Not what we're after," he conceded. "But I still can't see using a civilian in that kind of an assignment."

"Would you mind if I asked Chief Cargill about it? He knows Flavia and might have some thoughts."

"With my blessing. Obviously I'll go along with whatever he decides."

As he drove his unmarked homicide car, Sergeant Frank Salerno was in a reflective mood. It was brought on by an eight-minute delay at the scene of a traffic accident where three L.A.P.D. units were much in evidence, roof lights revolving.

"That's it," he said. "About all the public sees or knows about police work. Unless someone gets busted himself."

His partner, Detective Gil Carrillo, refined that. "Or *her*self," he added.

"Or herself," Salerno agreed. "They never see the hours we put in, sweating our balls off doing paperwork. Arrest reports, field interviews, booking forms . . ."

"And the endless field work running down hopeless leads, always trying to find that one break . . ."

"You ought to write for television."

"God spare me that. Do you want to take code seven, or shall we go on to the next one?"

"I'm not really hungry, Gil. Let's do one more and then eat."

"All right, here's the poop on him." Carrillo consulted his clipboard. "Stan Witkowski, male Caucasian, twenty-six, on parole, a graduate of the Soledad heist and dramatic school. One major juvenile offense, when he was fifteen. The record sealed by the court. Two adult misdemeanor convictions, no time given for either one. A suspect in a child molestation case but the D.A. didn't file—insuffi-

316

cient evidence. He finally got his ticket for attempted two eleven; he was caught gun in hand by the Pasadena P.D. While inside he was in contact with Hellman; a guard remembers seeing them working together."

"He turned the page over on his clipboard. "Seen by his new parole officer about two weeks ago. At the time he had held a job for four months, claimed that he was saving a little money. He was sober and seemed to have his act together."

"Maybe he does—until the next time," Salerno said. "But we'll see what he says."

The house had once been an upper-class residence, but it had been cut up into small apartments and single rooms for some time. There was a good-sized backyard. At the very rear there was a tangle of neglected shrubbery that all but engulfed a wooden single-car garage. It was unpainted, the only recent improvement was a reasonably new hasp and padlock.

The woman who answered the doorbell was much younger than they usually encountered, but she could be a stand-in for the landlady. "Is Mr. Witkowski in?" Salerno asked.

"Is he in some kind of trouble?"

The fact that she had IDed them at once didn't faze Carrillo. "No, ma'm, not as far as we know. We just hope he can help us with some information."

She didn't buy it. "If you're going to bust him, let me get him down here first. I don't want any more fuss than necessary."

"My partner meant just what he said," Salerno told her. "We're not here to arrest Mr. Witkowski, only to ask if he can help us with a case we're on."

Still dubious, the young landlady stepped aside. As she continued to hold the door open, she drew a deep breath and brought her shoulder blades closer together. It could have been an intentional display, she did have fairly good breasts, but it was more likely a reluctant acceptance of the situation.

"Upstairs to the right," she said.

The two men went up, Carrillo first and Salerno behind him, found the door, and knocked.

The man who answered was in jeans and an undershirt that displayed his thin chest and near-minimum development. His hair was vertical for a scant inch and then fell away toward the back and over his ears. He was not likely to attract much attention at the beach.

"We're police officers," Salerno said. "We'd like to talk to you for a few minutes if you don't mind."

"What about? I'm clean now; you ought to know that."

"That's what we heard. We just want some information. Can we come in?"

Witkowski shrugged his slender shoulders and half gestured with his left hand.

The room was in better order than either of the deputies had expected. The single bed had been made with the corners tucked in. A plain wood cabinet that was not much more than a box held a neat row of LP records. There was a covered turntable and two small speakers set in the corners of one wall. There was also a student's desk, a narrow shelf of books, and some pinups mounted on the walls with a modicum of taste. There were nudes, but of the less overt kind. It was clear why the parole officer had been favorably impressed.

Frank Salerno stretched a point. "Nice place you've got here," he said.

"I like it. Sit down."

The room only had two chairs, neither of them very inviting. Witkowski perched on the corner of the bed, leaving the chairs for his guests. As casually as they could, the two deputies accepted the hospitality and settled themselves.

Gil Carrillo began in low key. "Stan, you're not in any

318

trouble. In fact, we've heard some good reports on you since you got out. We hear you've been keeping a job and have started a bank account."

"I don't want to go back," Witkowski said. "Never."

"We don't blame you. But you're all square now and we think you're smart enough to stay that way."

Witkowski shifted his position. There was nothing unusual about it, but both officers noticed it automatically—though sitting on the bed could not be too comfortable and his back was unsupported.

"Stan," Frank Salerno said, "we'd like to ask you some questions about a man you might know, Frank Hellman."

On Witkowski's brow a very thin film of perspiration appeared. Presently he raised a hand and wiped it away. In the second or two that it took he remembered the story that Harry had been smart enough to think of in advance. Harry always thought of everything.

"I know him," he said. "We were inside together. I remember because he was such a good-looking guy."

That made it clear that they hadn't been close friends. Harry had never come to the place where he lived; there was no way the landlady could recognize his pictures.

"Is he still there?"

"I don't think so; he got paroled about the same time I did. I heard someplace he was going to school. He used to talk about learning to do welding. It's supposed to pay big money and you can be your own boss. That's important when you've got a record."

"What kind of guy was he, Stan?" Salerno asked.

"He knew he was good-looking. It hurt him to be away from women, because he could score anytime. He got jumpy now and then."

"With other inmates?"

"Not me; I never punked for anybody. You know how it is inside. Nobody's normal."

"Would you call him a friend of yours?"

319

Witkowski didn't seem to know how to answer that. "I guess," he said finally.

"Have you seen him since you got out?"

"Once. I don't remember now where it was."

Gil Carrillo rubbed his right ear to get rid of an itch. Frank Salerno noted the signal and shifted in his chair. That masked the movement as he activated his hidden tape recorder.

"I really appreciate the cooperation you're giving us," he said. "I'll mention it to your parole officer."

"Thanks. Glad to help."

That was a lie, of course, but called for under the circumstances.

"Stan," Carrillo went on, "Frank Hellman has been in school, that's right. There's a special program for parolees at the university. He had a high-school diploma, so he got his chance. By the way, do you have one?"

"No."

"That's too bad, we might have been able to put in a good word for you. Anyhow, Frank's disappeared."

Witkowski pretended to be surprised. "Disappeared?" he repeated.

"Yes. It's hard to figure, because he'd been doing real well. But if he stays away too long, it'll be a violation of his parole. You know what that means."

Witkowski's brow was wet again and his hands were unconsciously grasping handfuls of the bedding. "Why tell *me* about it?" he asked.

Frank Salerno surprised his partner with his answer. "Because, Stan, we're trying to save his ass. We don't get too many who can hack it in college, but he's been doing it. We're hoping to find him, because he's only got a few days left. If he goes back to Soledad, the whole program will be hurt."

That took a big load off Stan's mind. As soon as he was alone once more, he'd call Harry and tell him about this new development. He didn't trust the cops for a moment, but he was sure they didn't have anything on them. Harry was just too damn smart to get caught. He'd just been playing it safe, because he didn't know what the heat on the campus had been for.

Gil Carrillo picked up his cue with no trouble at all. "Sometimes when a man ducks out of sight he calls his friends to find out what's going on. If Frank calls you, please tell him that time's running out on him. They want to keep the program going, that's why we're trying to get the word to him. If he fouls up, the whole program may go down the drain and we'll look like assholes. We can't afford that."

As well as he knew his partner, Salerno had to admire that performance. There was a flaw in it, but he was sure Witkowski wouldn't catch it.

"If he calls I'll tell him," Witkowski promised.

Salerno stood up. "That's good," he said. "Remember, you may be able to keep him from having to go back inside. And you know what it's like in there."

"Hell yes, man. I just hope he calls."

When they were safely back in their car, Carrillo spoke. "He's a possible," he said.

"I know it," his partner answered. "When he said,'I just hope he calls,' it was a little too much. Just to look at him, you wouldn't think he had the balls for it."

Both men knew that the Lombroso Theory of Criminal Man, based on appearances, had been long discredited, but the comment had some meaning: Witkowski was not an impressive figure, not for the crimes of extreme violence they were investigating. And his MO didn't fit.

But they had a recording of his voice to compare with the tape that was the most valuable piece of evidence yet recovered.

Later that night an L.A.P.D. patrol unit went slowly down the alley beside the house, side lights on, checking on the backyards. The local residents who saw it were glad to know the cops were on the job, protecting their property.

321

At the overgrown, locked garage, the car paused a moment while the officer who wasn't driving got out and for a moment or two shone his five-cell flashlight through a small encrusted window set in the side. One quick look was enough; the garage was empty.

36

It was only a few minutes past six when Ralph Mott woke up. He had not been able to sleep well all night. Chief Cargill had listened carefully to both sides of the case and then had provisionally authorized Flavia to act as an undercover deputy by special appointment. She was duly sworn in as a reservist and issued a badge and a new ID. She made no attempt to conceal the pride she felt in this new status, but she took it all very seriously. "Now I've got to earn it," she had said very quietly to Captain Grimm, who she suspected understood better than anyone else exactly how she felt.

Next to Mott, Flavia lay on her side facing him. Like him she always slept nude. In the early-morning light her face was smooth and peaceful, but even as he looked at her one eye came open and she asked, "Are you awake?"

"Yes," he answered.

"Then hold me, please."

323

He was anxious to oblige. She moved over toward him until their bodies were together as they faced each other. He felt her warmth and was eternally grateful that God had created woman. He put his upper arm around her and held her close, but gently.

He hadn't set out to get her; it had just worked out that way. Like the rest of the men in the Homicide Bureau he had fully appreciated her exceptional beauty, the way she moved, even the way she wore her hair. Not long after those things were noted, her intelligence became a subject of admiration. Unstated, but accepted, was the fact that women like that went only to men who were young, strikingly handsome, and outrageously wealthy: men who could quite literally give them everything. Life in that fast lane was not the predestined fate of homicide detectives. Or lieutenants. Or even captains.

Yet here she lay in his arms, despite the fact that he would never be a candidate, under any circumstances, to play James Bond.

He was tormented by the realization that it couldn't last. All he could do was to make every moment count and to that he was giving his very best effort.

She reached out a finger and drew it, gently and slowly, down the center of his chest. That was enough to trigger his response. He kissed her gently, then her wide-open eyes looking into his told him she wanted it too. He crushed her to him, put his hand on her bottom and pressed her hard against the epicenter of his physical being.

He made love to her with all his heart and being, because this was the best that it could ever be, in this life or any other.

When it was over he fell back exhausted, his mind whirling with the impact of what his karma had done to him. He was not a particular believer in Oriental philosophy, but the theory of karma was a great convenience in explaining so many things. When Flavia leaned over and gently kissed the side of his face, he wished to heaven that he didn't have to get up and go to work.

While he showered and shaved, she got their breakfast. Her first class was not until eleven, so she had put on a simple robe that tied at her waist. They sat down together to eat four-minute eggs, toast, and slices of breaded tomatoes. Normally Mott got himself some instant coffee and usually a bowl of cereal. He kept a half-dozen kinds on hand to give himself a modicum of choice. Flavia, he knew, was spoiling him rotten.

"When you finally catch these people, what are you going to do?" she asked.

"We're going to walk on eggshells to be sure that we do everything according to the book. You know the recent record of the California Supreme Court: if there's any way to let off a mass murderer, they'll find it. The victims, of course, have virtually no rights at all."

"You sound bitter."

"No, just experienced." He ate some egg and followed it with a good-sized bite of toast. "Not long ago, Flavia, we had a genuinely vicious child molester down cold. In fact he gave us a full confession to get it off his chest. At the preliminary hearing the D. A. put a six-year-old boy on the stand. Normally they wouldn't do that, but the kid was remarkably mature for his age and his parents wanted him to tell what had happened."

Mott drank some coffee. "The boy told a very clear and accurate story. After he'd done that, the defense attorney started in on him. He asked him how old he was. When the boy answered that he was six, the attorney said, 'Six what? Six months? Six weeks? How do you know what six it is?' He went on like that until he broke the kid down completely. I don't think the judge should have allowed it, but she did. When he had the kid completely confused, the defense lawyer spread his hands in front of the judge and said, 'I move for dismissal, because this witness is incapable of telling a straight story.'"

"That's immoral," Flavia said.

Mott nodded as he ate more egg. "It is, but the judge agreed with the defense and let the guy loose. That's why we're so damn careful to dot every I, cross every T, so that there won't be anything that the defense can attack."

He became suddenly very serious. "When you leave today, you're going to be covered every moment. You won't see it, but it'll be there."

"How many people does it usually take to do that?"

"Up to eighteen at one time. And that means eighteen pros who know exactly what they're doing. Part of your cover will be by us, part by L.A.P.D. We're going to put a wire on you. If anyone speaks to you, we'll hear it. If you see possible trouble coming, tell us immediately; don't wait to see what happens. Just say 'red' and we'll understand."

"If I have to do that, how long will it take . . ."

"Seconds, and not many of them."

Despite her determination, nervousness was creeping up on her. "I'll do my best," she promised. "I just hope he doesn't shoot me from a distance. In that case, Ralph, look after things for me. Will you?"

"He won't do that," Mott said. "He's fired by a blind ambition to have you, alive and kicking. That's what he wants. Dead you'd be no use to him. He wants to use you first. But it won't get that far, I can promise you that."

"Will you know about it?"

Mott was suddenly very grim. "I'm commanding the operation," he said.

After Mott had left, Flavia began considering the position she was now in. She had volunteered and her offer had been accepted. Therefore she could blame her growing concern on no one but herself. No one had talked her into it; in fact, Ralph had tried very hard to discourage her from taking unnecessary chances.

She had made her decision as she knew so many people do: by considering only one side of a question and never allowing opposing thoughts to intrude in the process. She had said she would do it without ever stopping to consider how little qualified she was for the role she had asked to play. But it was too late now to allow herself to get cold feet.

Nevertheless, doubts began to assail her. If the people assigned to protect her kept far enough away to be out of sight, how much help would they be able to give her in the event she needed it very quickly? She did not like to ask herself rhetorical questions, but that one was as persistent as a cork floating on water.

She dressed carefully, as she usually did, in a conservative outfit suitable for faculty campus wear. If Hellman were to reappear, it would be very unlikely that he would do so that same day. She smoothed her skirt and was giving herself a final inspection in the mirror when the doorbell rang.

She hesitated; it was Ralph's doorbell, not hers. But logic told her that whoever was there probably wanted her, unless it was a call from Jehovah's Witnesses or some other door-to-door campaign. She looked through the peephole and saw a trim young woman holding up a badge.

It could be a fake, but perhaps her guardians were already in position. Whatever, knowing she could not live in a cocoon all her life, she opened the door.

"Deputy de la Torre? I'm Sergeant Pinelli." The young woman held out a sheriff's photo ID card. "May I come in?"

Although Ralph had cautioned her not to trust *anyone* until this matter had been settled, Flavia accepted the ID as genuine, knowing that at that point she had little choice.

A few moments later she knew she had done the right thing. The sergeant sat on the front edge of a chair and got right down to business.

"I'm here to put a wire on you," she said. "Have you ever worked with one before?"

"No," Flavia answered.

"Some of the old Fargos were a little clumsy, but we have

327

much better equipment now." She opened her purse and took out an interesting medallion on a chain. "This one is quite effective over a half-mile-plus range. Because it's out in plain sight, no one suspects what it is. I've been searched in the field when I was working undercover, and I always got by with this on."

She passed the device to Flavia, who put it around her neck. "Do I have to turn it off and on?" she asked.

"No, it's on all the time when it's in use. Lieutenant Mott can put in a fresh battery when it's needed. Here's another one."

This time the device was disguised as a jade pendant. "That's real jade," the sergeant said. "What appears to be the mounting has the transmitter inside. It's principally for use in dress-up situations, but in your case it should work well on campus. You're a rather exotic lady and the idea of wearing jade fits in well."

"Do they both work the same way?"

"Yes, as far as wavelength goes. The jade piece has a little longer range, so wear it whenever you can."

"If anyone asks, I can say that Ralph gave it to me," Flavia suggested. "That would account for my wearing it a lot."

Sergeant Pinelli nodded briskly. "That's a good idea. Now, some instructions. Don't finger the piece; you'll make it send out signals like mad. Don't wear wired bras when you're using it. Never look down at it, that's a giveaway. It'll hear you, even if you speak softly. Try to keep away from areas where there's a lot of background noise. If you're riding in a car, roll up the window, unless there's a good reason not to. Always talk normally; you'll be picked up. All clear on that?"

"All clear," Flavia repeated.

"Now, watch your language when you have it on. I don't mean by that you can't cuss—say whatever you like, have sex if you want to—but don't use the word *red* unless you want help, and fast."

"I'll be careful."

"That goes too if you use it in a sentence. If you say, 'Look at that gorgeous red sunset,' that's a help signal."

This time Flavia nodded.

"One more thing: wear your wire every time you go out, and it won't hurt to have it on in the house if you're here alone. Ralph knows how to turn it off when he's here with you. We're not interested in listening in on your private conversations, but if anyone talks to you, in the street or wherever you are, we'll copy. It's a sensitive piece of electronics, so try not to drop it or get it wet. Any questions?"

"I guess not," Flavia answered.

The sergeant suddenly became human. "Scared?"

"Yes," Flavia admitted.

"This may help: you can talk to us at any time. Just say something like, 'I don't like the man who's coming toward me.' Or if you get lucky, 'I think I see the suspect.' In that case, give us a clock direction."

"You'll have to explain that."

"It's very simple. Just say, 'I think I see him at ten o'clock.' Remember you'll be under observation."

"And if I go to the ladies' room?" Flavia asked, with a half smile.

"We'll know all about it," the sergeant said.

A half-hour later Flavia carefully locked the door behind her and went down to where she had parked her car. She looked about, as she did every day, evaluating the weather and the circumstances around her. She saw no evidence whatever that she was being watched. She drove to work as she always did and parked in her assigned space. While she locked her car, she told herself not to look around again; she would have to get over the habit of doing that.

It was a five-minute walk to the building where she taught. As she made her way, she was unexpectedly conscious of the sounds around her, of the click of her heels on the sidewalk. She felt as though she might be carrying a small vial of nitroglycerine somewhere on her person.

"Good morning, Dr. de la Torre."

She turned quickly toward the female voice and saw that it was one of her students. The girl came over to join her. "Are we going to talk about group sex today?" she asked.

Flavia nodded. "Actually today's topic is plural marriage."

"But that really isn't marriage, is it?"

"Why not?" Flavia asked as she walked. "It exists in society, it's on the increase, so it falls within our area of interest."

"Did you hear about the arsonist?"

Flavia felt a slight internal twitch at that, but kept it from showing. "What arsonist?" she asked.

The girl was delighted to have a piece of gossip to pass on. "They've been looking for an arsonist on campus, strictly on the Q.T. A lot of people have been questioned."

That last was fresh invention, but it hyped the story. "Anyhow, they caught him; it's in the paper this morning. Some nerd off Main Street."

Flavia walked up to the door of the building where she held her classes. She opened it for herself and went inside, her face giving nothing away.

The girl followed her inside. "I wondered why Frank Hellman hasn't been around lately. Has he been excused from class?"

"No," Flavia answered, "but if he doesn't come back soon he'll lose his grade."

"I bet he'll be here tomorrow," the girl said.

37

It was only a little after eight in the morning when Officers Arthur Deming and Raymond "Lew" Archer of the Glendale Police Department observed a plain-colored van run directly through a stop sign at Norton and Glen Oaks Boulevard. As Deming, who was driving, turned in behind the vehicle his partner picked up the mike and advised the dispatcher of the traffic stop. The Glendale police cars were equipped with transmitting computers, but there were many times when voices communications were to be preferred.

Deming followed the van for a block and a half with his overhead lights on; when the vehicle he was behind showed no sign of stopping, he touched the siren. In response dirt spurted from behind the rear tires and the van took off.

Archer was on the ball. "We are in pursuit eastbound on

Glen Oaks," he reported. "Subject is a gray, unmarked van. Speed now approaching seventy, running code three."

The words "gray unmarked van" caught the dispatcher's attention. She put out an immediate broadcast to all units advising of the pursuit. "Subject vehicle fits description of one wanted for multiple one eighty-sevens. Suspects should be regarded as armed and extremely dangerous." She put out the broadcast on frequencies that would be copied by L.A.P.D. Burbank, Pasadena, the Sheriff's Department, and the Highway Patrol.

The response was immediate and heavy. Two nearby units rolled backup from Burbank, the Highway Patrol closed off the Ventura Freeway, three L.A.P.D. units responded from the Eagle Rock area, and four more cars from the Glendale P.D. closed in on the suspects, forcing the fleeing unit toward the Verdugo Road area. There five units from three different jurisdictions made a classic felony stop, forcing the suspects out of their van at gunpoint and spreading them face down in the middle of the roadway.

Captain Leonard of the Glendale P.D. had just been arriving for work when the call was put out. He had responded personally and was the senior officer present. Under his direction the suspects were given legal pat-downs for concealed weapons and then cuffed. While this was going on, Deming and Archer, guns drawn, kept a steady watch over the van; they had no idea who else might be inside.

Once the two known suspects were secured, Captain Leonard had the side door of the van opened in the approved manner. Inside there was a young woman, tied up and gagged. When she appeared unable to control herself when released, the captain ordered paramedics. Overhead an Argus helicopter circled in a steady orbit.

There being no question of probable cause, the van was searched. More than five pounds of marijuana were recovered and a glassine bag of white powder suspected of being morphine was found in the glove compartment. Also, there were three loose wire coat hangers in the back of the van.

While all this was going on, Mott had been at his desk for about ten minutes. The newly typed report from Salerno and Carrillo was already awaiting him. He shuffled through several sets of papers the task force had brought in, but the Salerno report held the best promise. He began to read it with his usual meticulous care.

It was not his fault that halfway through his phone rang. He picked it up. "Homicide, Lieutenant Mott," he said.

Sergeant Berkowitz was on the line. "A hot one, chief. Just in from Glendale P.D. They stopped a van, plain paint job, no outside markings."

"Probable cause?" Mott asked quickly.

"Ran a red light wide open. Van had two male occupants, twenty to thirty, several ounces of morphine, *and* a girl frightened out of her wits tied up in back."

"Wow!" Mott exploded. "Have they got backup?"

"Damn right, with a captain on hand and several other units. Two of our own people are on the way there now."

"Who?"

"Blaylock and Swenson from Santa Monica P.D. You know how sharp they are."

Mott could not hold down the sense of triumph that was beginning to take over his body. "This sounds like it," he said. "Keep me up to date, minute by minute."

"Done." Berkowitz hung up.

Mott tried to turn back to the Salerno report, but his mind refused to focus. He kept looking at the telephone, willing it to ring. Which is probably the reason he missed something he would ordinarily have caught automatically.

The phone did ring and he scooped it up. "Mott," he almost barked.

It was Berkowitz again. "I got a patch through to Cap-

333

tain Leonard of Glendale P.D.," he said. "He wants to talk to you. He's on the scene."

"Hello, Lieutenant Mott," a businesslike voice came through.

"Mott here. Apparently your people have just done a terrific job for us."

"We've got a damn good bust, no doubt of that. Legally it's airtight, thank God. We have two male suspects in custody, a stolen van, narcotics in quantity for sale, and a kidnapped female. Not too sure of this last, she's a very young hooker, high on something, and quite possibly retarded. The paramedics are transporting her now."

"You sound like you've made the bust of the year."

"Maybe, maybe not. There are bloodstains in the van and three loose wire coat hangers. Now the bad news."

Mott could hardly contain himself. "Yes?" he asked.

"Both male suspects and the girl are black. We understood your suspects were Caucs."

Mott felt as though someone had just thrust a pin in his favorite Fourth of July balloon. "Black?" he repeated.

"Definitely. Also gang members, with tattoos."

"If they're that dirty, how come they ran a red light where they could be seen?"

"They're stoned also. At the moment we've got them hooked up. They're sitting on the curb muttering incantations."

Mott took that literally. "Witch doctor stuff?"

"Could be. You're welcome here if you're interested."

"I've sent two of my best people. Blaylock and Swenson from the Santa Monica P.D. are on their way. They'll be under your command, of course."

"We'd like to play the suspects our way, if you'll go along. They think right now that we have them for the serial killings. They're frightened out of their wits. To beat that rap they may be willing to tell us what they've really been doing."

334

"Outstanding," Mott said. "When my people get there, tell them they're to treat the suspects as if we're sure they're good for several torture murders. We have a living witness, but she can't testify."

"Not at all?"

"Strictly in confidence, she's given us a positive ID on our number one suspect, but so far we have nothing at all on his partner. We're working on that now. Blaylock and Swenson are both very sharp; they'll give your suspects a good going-over. You've covered the legal bases."

"Damn right; a public defender is standing by now to represent them if necessary."

"Rap sheets?"

"We'll have to print them first. All they'll give is Muslim names. No driver's licenses, vehicle registration, or other ID. Hold on a minute."

After a brief period of silence Leonard was back on the line. "One of our detective units just rolled up. Both suspects are known to them. At least three major felony convictions each, for openers. On parole for the past two weeks."

"It's good to know that such valuable citizens have been returned to society," Mott said. "Are they from your area?"

"No, south central L.A. Now they're saying that the fruit of Allah will rule the world. We'll book 'em into C J* on the narcotics charge, you might like to take over from there."

"With pleasure," Mott said. "We have L.A.P.D. people with us right here. We'd like to impound the van."

"Be my guest. I'll have a unit stand by until your hook gets here. Just keep me in the picture, will you?"

"Bank on it," Mott said and hung up to call the impound yard. Then he ran a patch through and briefed Blaylock and Swenson.

"One thing, Lieutenant," Swenson said. "Can you tell us

*Central Jail

335

that as of now you have no line at all on the second suspect in the serial killings?"

"That's right," Mott said. "I have no reason to believe, for example, that he couldn't be black."

"That's what we wanted to hear, officially. We don't want to be accused of harassing known innocent suspects."

"You're in the clear on that."

"Good. You'll hear from us later."

Because his mind was so full at the moment, Mott pushed aside Salerno's report and instead went into the task force room to be sure that everyone there was up to the minute on the Glendale bust. Even though everyone knew that the black suspects were not the right ones for the coat-hanger killings, there was no telling what might be learned from them. And a unit from San Dimas Station had a fresh lead on a possible partner for Frank Hellman. He owned a van that he was having repainted and when questioned he was evasive. There was a warrant out on him that earned him a trip to Central Jail where a routine blood test was given over his vigorous objections. He was afraid of needles.

He came up AIDS positive which, as far as the handling deputies were concerned, punched his ticket for good. Still they both took careful showers before they went home.

Meanwhile, unknown to the task force, L.A.P.D. had been setting up a small sting operation on boosted cars. Too many Cadillacs were disappearing from Beverly Hills and too many late-model Acuras were being picked up from all over the city. Beverly Hills cooperated and set out several bait cars in likely places. Huntington Beach arranged for six Acuras to be parked outside class restaurants and other places where a thief might be tempted. Each bait car was equipped with a well-hidden signaling device that the patrol helicopters in the air were equipped to read.

Three cars were taken the first night of the operation, but

as luck would have it, none of the bait cars was touched. No one was too distressed about that; sooner or later that would change.

Mott was still so heavily engaged he completely lost track of Flavia and what she was doing.

38

The eleven o'clock class went well. The same dark-haired girl who had sat in before was there again, industriously taking notes. At one point she asked a pertinent question and took down the answer. When the period was over and the students had filed out, Flavia took stock of herself and realized that she was much relieved in her mind. Not because the girl from L.A.P.D. had been there, but because she knew she had given a good lecture and that it had been well received.

She ate her lunch in the cafeteria. The food was provided under contract by a large service corporation and tasted like it. The "barbecued ribs" that had been on the menu had been fabricated, bone and all, from some kind of ground meat pressed into a mold with a dab of sauce added. The so-called mashed potatoes were of the rehydrated variety. Portion control was vividly in evidence.

Free of the clearly misnamed dining hall, Flavia went to

her desk and reviewed papers until it was time to meet her two o'clock class. She lectured on social customs during the Industrial Revolution in England. Possibly in rebuttal to the miserable meal she had eaten, she made it so interesting that just before the bell rang, her students were still paying close attention.

It was a morale uplift she could use; she was still basking in its afterglow when the beeper in her purse went off.

She hastened to a phone and called in.

"Sheriff's Homicide, Finnegan."

"This is Flavia de la Torre."

"We have a murder in El Monte, Doctor, that may be in your field. Lieutenant Chausse suggested we call you. Can you respond?"

"Yes, I just finished my class."

"I know; we have your schedule here. Do you have a Thomas Guide handy?"

"No."

"Then I'll give you directions." The city of El Monte was on the east side of the Los Angeles complex, some distance away. For a moment she wondered about her cover people, then as she hurried toward her car, she used her head. If they hadn't wanted her to go that far afield, she wouldn't have been called in the first place. It was even possible that they wanted her there.

She got into her car, clipped on her sheriff's ID, and started out toward El Monte.

As she neared the address she saw that she was probably in the worst part of the city. Even though it was bright daylight, she would not have trusted herself on the street she was driving. It was nothing she could define, only an inward awareness that this was not a comfortable place to be.

Two parked police units marked her destination. The address she had been given was for a motel. Superficially the property was laid out that way, but it was so dismal it had no possible pretensions of attracting any transient guests. There was a long, narrow, one-story building faced by two others that were shorter with a break between them. They were a flat, weathered gray, innocent of any effort to make them even slightly attractive. Halfway back the familiar yellow tape had been stretched across the driveway.

Because she did not want to leave her car on the street if she could avoid it, Flavia drove in and parked to one side of the coroner's van. There were also two other cars she recognized as unmarked units.

A large man strolled up to intercept her. He wore a full red beard, a checkered shirt, an oversized pair of jeans, and tennis shoes. "You can't park there, lady," he said. Then he bent down and saw her sheriff's ID. "Sorry, didn't recognize you. Bert Larson, El Monte Police: Vice Narcotics."

"Can I leave my car here?"

"Sure. It'll be safe enough with all of us around. You from Homicide?"

"They sent me here."

"It's up ahead in unit three."

Flavia got out of her car, locked it, and trusted that the undercover man would keep it safe. There were several people gathered about, including a heavyset woman in a shapeless dress who had a cluster of half-naked small children surrounding her. Flavia ducked under the tape, went past the unmarked units, and paused. In front of her there were four uniformed El Monte patrolmen and several men in ordinary business suits. She was the only woman present.

Lieutenant Ken Chausse came to meet her. "Hello, Flavia. Since sociology is your field, we thought this one would interest you."

"Thank you."

"Here's what we've got." The lieutenant led her a half-dozen steps to the open door of one of the motel units and invited her to look inside. The room was a stark, featureless

340

gray like an animal pen. It was essentially bare: uncarpeted, unpainted, and unfurnished except for a small wrecked counter and a mattress that had been shoved in one corner. Set in the wall next to the door was an air conditioner so derelict its whole front plate was missing; its visible working parts were caked with rust. A narrow doorway led to a presumed bathroom; the only thing visible was a toilet with the seat missing.

Half on the mattress and half on the bare floor was the nude body of a young woman. It lay in a semifetal position with a wrapping of soft cloth around the neck. Outside the cloth was an electrical cord wound around three times and pulled tight.

As Flavia studied the scene she noted that the victim had been small, probably not more than five feet one, slender-waisted and with trim smooth legs. Her pubic hair was peculiar: the top had been left intact, but the lower half had been shaved from a horizontal straight line downward. Her rectum was discolored by a dark bruise an inch or more in diameter.

"Not a very nice place to die, is it," the lieutenant remarked.

"Was she a prostitute?" Flavia asked.

"Oh, yes. Why don't you talk to Sergeant O'Farrell; he can fill you in on the whole picture. Do you know him?"

"I'm not sure," she answered. "I've met so many people . . ."

"I don't blame you." He turned and gestured to one of the senior detectives. When the man came up Chausse said, "Frank, this is Dr. de la Torre. I don't know if you two have met or not."

"Just in passing," the sergeant said, relieving her embarrassment.

"You know she's a professor of sociology. If you have time, you might fill her in on all this."

With the easy manner of long experience O'Farrell took her in tow. "May I call you Flavia?" he asked.

"Please do."

"All right, let's have a look at the body. You understand we're not allowed to touch it. A coroner's criminalist just rolled in: he'll make the examination, but we can watch. Will that bother you?"

"I'm getting used to it now."

"Good. Come on in."

He led the way into the little room, stepping around the body as he did so. "Since I know you're here to learn the business," O'Farrell said, "accept the idea that this isn't a body, but a piece of evidence. It very well may be the best one we'll get. Now what do you see?"

His words had a supportive effect on Flavia. By a conscious effort she summoned up her training as a scientist and put that in front of everything else. Almost at once she experienced a definite change of mood.

"Take it right from the beginning," O'Farrell invited.

"Well, obviously she's nude."

"Then it might be a good first step to look for her clothes."

Of course! Flavia told herself. Even in this neighborhood the girl couldn't have come in here with nothing on. That focused her attention on the mattress. She saw a half-used pack of cigarettes, an open matchbook folder lying so that she could not see what was printed on the outside, a man's wristwatch, a small group of keys, a cheap pair of sunglasses, and two bits of clothing: a halter and a brief pair of shorts. She looked around a little more and saw a small pair of thong sandals behind the counter.

"She didn't have any underwear," Flavia said. "And her clothing was minimal."

"It's quite possible that's all she owned. I know most of these girls. They're out day after day in the same outfits. What else do you see?"

Flavia bent over the body, intent on discovering any information she could just by observation. She looked at the inner arms and found them smooth and free of needle tracks. "I can't judge her muscle tone very well," she said, "but there's no excess fat on her body at all. Her waist is slender and trim. She looks in good condition, but it could be that she only ate sparsely. I don't think she was the sort of person to be taking a physical fitness course."

"Definitely not," the sergeant agreed. "Keep on, you're doing fine."

When Flavia's careful inspection reached the victim's abdomen, she felt a little emotional reaction, a tiny thrill of discovery. "She has stretch marks," she said. "She had a child." When O'Farrell didn't comment she looked again and saw two faint lines across the abdomen. "I think those are scars," she added, "but I'm not sure what kind."

O'Farrell squatted on his heels. "She had a Cesarean delivery," he said. "Quite well done, I'd say, with minimum scarring. They're careful with that now, because so many women don't want to have disfiguring marks on their bodies to distract their husbands."

"Or whoever," Flavia added. "She could have worn a bikini easily without those marks being noticed."

"I'd say so. Good point. Now look carefully at her ankles."

Flavia shifted her position and paid very close attention to the ankles and feet. At first she saw nothing unusual at all, then, after going over the same area visually a second time, she discovered what appeared to be faint scratches on one ankle. At that point she wished she had Sherlock Holmes's magnifying glass and knew why that immortal had always carried one. To her naked eye it could have been caused by an accidental brush against a briar. Not content to settle for that, she continued to study the marks until an indistinct pattern emerged.

"What is it?" she asked.

"You know the symbol for a female: a circle with a vertical line down and a shorter one intersecting it."

"Yes."

"Now look again."

Flavia did so and made out the symbol. Except there appeared to be two of them, one partially on top of the other.

Frank helped her out. "It's a tattoo," he said. "Two female symbols that way, one above the other, signifies lesbianism. From the looks of it, I'd say that she tried to do it herself, not too successfully."

"How did you ever spot it?" Flavia asked.

"I've seen it before."

"But a lesbian with a child . . . Of course, that's possible."

At that moment a professional-looking man came in carrying a kit in each hand. He nodded a greeting, got to his knees beside the body, and slipped on a pair of surgeon's gloves.

In the few moments she had had to herself, Flavia had been thinking. "Can I talk?" she asked.

The criminalist looked up. "Don't mind me," he said. "Frank and I are old friends."

"I was puzzled by the way the bottom half of the pubic hair had been removed with the rest left intact. I know that some women shave, particularly in Muslim countries."

"They have to there," the criminalist contributed.

"Thank you. But I think I have it now. If she was a lesbian, then she might have done that as an aid to cunnilingus."

"Right," Frank said, "at least that's my opinion. Have you seen it before, George?"

"A few times." With a small pair of shears the criminalist snipped a tiny bit of hair off the victim's leg and placed it in a specially folded piece of paper. Then he looked up. "I know who you are," he said to Flavia. "I'm George Levinson."

"I'm sorry; I forgot to introduce you," Frank said.

"Greed, pure greed."

"Of course," Frank admitted. "Just to be generous, I'll let you explain to her what a three-way girl is."

"I know that," Flavia said. "And I saw her rectum. There's only one thing I can't understand. How could anyone possibly be attracted to this poor woman enough to want to have sex with her? After she's been used so many times, in so many ways, by others. The risk of disease if nothing else . . ."

The criminalist stopped his work for a moment. "You have no idea," he said, "what some people will do, or the chances they'll take, for sexual gratification. Or what forms that gratification can take. This is only a preliminary opinion, but this could very easily be a case of autoerotic suicide."

"The lieutenant thought so too," O'Farrell said. "God knows she didn't have much to lose, but she herself wouldn't think that way."

"Certainly not. I'm going to take the liver temperature. You might take the lady outside and tell her the camel story."

"I've already seen . . ." Flavia began and then realized how politely she had been invited to leave. When they were out of the wretched room, she turned to Frank. "The camel story," she prompted.

"At an isolated desert outpost of the French Foreign Legion there were no women. The enlisted men were totally out of luck, but the officers kept a camel for the purposes of relief.

"One day a new officer reported in and took up his duties. After a while he asked about women. He was told, 'We use the camel.' That thought repelled him, but finally his need became so great he got a step ladder and had sex with the camel.

"When he returned to the barracks he was asked how he had made out. He said that it had been awful. Better than nothing, but not by much. He then asked if all the other officers did the same thing.

"'Certainly not,' the commander told him. 'They get on the camel and ride it to the nearest whorehouse.'"

345

He watched her then to see her reaction. Her face did not change and he wondered for a moment if he had offended her. Then she had the good sense to laugh.

O'Farrell continued his lesson. "You saw that broken-down counter in there. Do you remember what was on top of it?"

"A piece of glass, that didn't fit."

"And on the glass?"

Flavia visualized it in her mind. "A little white powder, I think." As realization came she turned to face Frank. "Cocaine," she said.

"Very likely. Though if there was very much left, someone would have stolen it. Let me put you a little more in the picture. These poor girls who work this street, and others like it, have almost nothing. Often no regular place to stay, very little to wear, no personal possessions. They make good money, some of them, for a while, but it all goes for dope. Some use heroin, but more and more now it's cocaine. They don't care about anything else, just as long as they have enough to pay the candy man: the coke dealer."

Together they walked down the driveway between the motel buildings. The doors to many of the units were open, revealing empty interiors or an occasional piece of plywood waiting to be installed. For the first time since she had been responding to murder scenes, Flavia felt that she was being shown the whole picture: the social aspects that often bring murder about.

When they reached the street O'Farrell turned and walked her a little way to the east. "Up ahead you can see two more motels in this block. But don't ever pull in to spend the night. They're largely trick pads for the working girls. Some of them, like the one we just left, will rent a single room to four or five illegals from Mexico. It's rugged, but it's the best they can get."

"Fill me in on autoerotic suicide," Flavia asked.

Frank walked slowly, explaining things to her as though

she were a new recruit to the Bureau. "There are many different forms of sexual gratification, Flavia, from the normal ones to some that are very far out. Necrophilia, for example. One of them is an attempt to come to the very edge of dying, which is supposed to bring on, in some individuals, a massive sexual response. The usual method is by hanging."

"I read a paper on that," Flavia said, "but it was quite a while ago and at the time I wasn't really interested. Please go on now."

"A person, male or female, will rig up a method to hang themselves by slow strangulation. They always include a slip knot and a cord they can pull to release themselves. Then they put their neck in the noose and let themselves hang. At the last minute, just before they feel themselves going under, they pull the cord, release the slip knot, and save themselves. Except sometimes they wait too long, or the slip knot doesn't work. Some people do this successfully, time after time, but it's about as dangerous as anything they can attempt. Sooner or later most of them kill themselves."

Flavia suddenly raised her hands and clasped them together. "I've got it," she said. "The cloth padding around the neck. If someone wanted to strangle that poor girl, they wouldn't protect her neck that way: it would only make the job harder. But if the girl wanted to hang herself as you said, she would protect her throat, because she expected to live."

Frank turned around and started back. "If you need a training officer, I'll volunteer," he said. "I think someone wants to speak to you." He nodded toward a nondescript car that was pulled slowly up to the curb beside them. The passenger door opened and Dick Tracy got out. As Flavia looked inside, his partner, Frank Levitzky, raised a hand in greeting.

"We thought it might be a good idea just to let you know that we're here," Tracy said. "And we're not alone."

"Am I giving you a lot of trouble?" Flavia asked.

"It goes with the territory, Flavia, don't worry about it. But I do have a message for you."

"From Ralph?"

"Yes. He wanted us to tell you that Hellman's been spotted. He's reappeared from wherever he was. We think he bought the arson suspect story; that was a good idea you had. Ralph wanted you to know ahead of time that he'll probably show up for your class tomorrow."

39

For a moment that announcement created a knot in Flavia's stomach. She could not help it. Then she quietly composed herself and remembered that there were very capable people watching over her, people who were armed and experienced. She had learned quite a lot about the police since she had first walked into the Homicide Bureau, and that knowledge supported her now. She looked up to see the burly figure of Bert Larson, beard and all, approaching. As soon as he reached them he asked, "Is everything okay with you?"

"Fine," O'Farrell answered.

"I saw some types in a car pull up."

"They're part of Flavia's cover. We've got a blanket over her until we get this thing resolved."

They walked together back to the motel. "I hear that sociology is your field," Larson said.

"Yes," Flavia answered. "Right now I'm getting some valuable field experience."

Larson spoke to O'Farrell. "If you don't mind my asking, why the blanket for Flavia? Is she a source for you?"

"No, she's not," O'Farrell answered. "You know about the coat-hanger murders."

"Hell, yes—an awful thing."

"We have word she may be next on their hit list."

Larson reacted sharply to that. "If you can use some help on your task force, count me in. I can get the necessary approval."

"Thanks, Bert, that's appreciated," O'Farrell said as they turned back into the motel driveway. Then he added, "Why don't you fill Flavia in on the local populous."

Larson was glad to oblige. "Suppose you take a careful look at the people gathered around, in the space between the two buildings. Not a very good segment of humanity. There are eight or ten men there. They may look all right to you, but don't try to talk to any of them. I'm serious about that; I know them. Every one of them would as soon stab you as not if you said or did something they didn't like.

"The nine women are prostitutes; that's why they hang around here. That heavy-set one with the glasses is a dyke. She's especially dangerous."

"In what way?" Flavia asked.

"Physically dangerous. You may not know this, Flavia, but some of the most violent crimes are done by lesbians. The public might not believe that, but it's true."

The three of them stepped aside to allow the coroner's van to back out. "I think it's time for me to go too," Flavia said. "Should I speak to the lieutenant first?"

"If you want to," O'Farrell said. "Otherwise I'll pass the word for you. We'll all be here for some time yet."

"Thank you both, very much," Flavia said. "I've learned a lot today."

Bert Larson put a huge hand on her shoulder. "Just don't let it get to you," he said.

"I won't," she promised.

She got back into her car, fitted her seat belt, and locked the door. As she drove toward Los Angeles, the heavy rush-hour traffic was in full swing.

To give her mind something to do, she turned on the local news station. The announcer went through his cycle of major stories, Southern California news, the stock market report, and the baseball scores. The Angels had won; the Dodgers would not play until later. The weather prediction was for more of the same. There was no mention whatever of the death of a prostitute in El Monte. The station people probably knew about it, but not enough listeners would be interested for it to be put on the air.

When Flavia reached the apartment, Mott was not yet there. She let herself in with the key he had given her, checked the mail, and drew a hot tub. She wanted to wash herself, but even more she wanted to relax in the hot water and think.

She shed her clothes in the bedroom, and because she wanted to, she wrapped a towel around herself to go back into the bathroom. When the tub was ready she slid into the water and let its warmth permeate every part of her body.

She was acutely conscious that her own body was so like that of the unfortunate girl she had just seen sprawled naked on her side, every bit of her so starkly revealed, even her pathetic attempt to tattoo herself.

Not too long ago that girl had been someone's cherished little daughter. Or perhaps she had only been an unwanted nuisance, denied the wonderfully healing balm of love. Almost sick at heart for her, Flavia reached for the soap.

When her bath was over she put on fresh things and thought about dinner. She would have been glad to prepare something, but had no idea when Ralph would be coming home.

She sat down with a hairbrush in her hand to do some careful thinking. Her life had undergone so many drastic changes during the past few weeks, she was having trouble keeping up with herself. Until she had decided to do a book, and had asked for official help, she had been well started on a sound if not spectacular career. She had a good appointment at a highly respected university, one that would eventually lead to tenure if all went well.

She had not given much thought to marriage after she had had two severe disappointments, one in her native Spain and the other within the university community itself.

In Spain a marriage had been virtually arranged for her and the banns had been formally published. She would have been married long ago if the man who had been chosen for her had not taken her for a drive in his hundred-thousand-dollar sports car one evening along the Mediterranean coast. She had always visualized the coming of physical love into her life: somewhere in an elegant suite, her bridal gown carefully laid aside, she would receive her new and wonderful husband into her waiting arms. Instead he had forced himself on her, his breath hot on her neck, his demanding maleness ramming its way into her despite the fact that she was having the first day of of her period.

He had driven off, leaving her alone at her door, a disappointment and a frustration of his manhood. Fortunately it was her mother who had met her and in one glance understood. She had left Spain four days later and had never returned.

Some time later, when the scars had healed, a man almost too good to be true had appeared in her life. He was also an academic, quite a lot older than herself, but Catholic and wonderfully kind and gentle toward her. She had been increasingly interested until she discovered that he had an active lover who was another man.

That had answered her question as to why such an apparently good man had remained unmarried for so long. It had also been a severe traumatic shock that had sent her into an emotional tailspin. When she finally recovered her composure and regained most of her self-confidence, she found that she no longer relied on her Catholic faith and had lost any remaining desire to find a lasting relationship in marriage.

That had been it until she had unwittingly discovered something in Ralph Mott that had inspired her confidence. Without even thinking about it, she decided that if he wanted her, she would share his bed. It would not be for very long, almost everything mitigated against that, but it did give her a renewed belief that there were men in the world with whom it would be gratifying to have an intimate relationship.

Within a very short time he had by his quiet, considerate manner repaired and renewed many of her natural feminine instincts. In a way it astonished her, because the nature of his work hardly built up an image of him she could brag about to herself, or to anyone else. Back home in Spain policemen were not highly placed on the social scale. The fact that he was a lieutenant would carry no weight at all. As chief of police he might have been barely acceptable.

On the other hand, in simple plain terms, she thought he was a wonderful man. Not notably handsome, although he was most presentable, but as a friend and companion he was everything she could hope to find.

As she continued to brush her hair, she reaffirmed to herself that she was definitely not in love. If and when that level of attachment came, she would know it. But if he were to walk in on her at that moment, she would be very happy.

What she would do with her life when this was all over, she was not sure. Keep on teaching, of course, but not until Hellman and his partner were safely in prison would she be able to resume her normal work once again.

She thought of Hellman sitting in her class, a handsome, confident man, and asked herself with cruel directness if she wanted to see him go to the gas chamber. She thought of him as a person and came up with an emphatic no; that would be close to murder.

Then she thought of Mary Malone, still alive but with all hope of a normal life hopelessly ruined, and tears came to her eyes. The girl had been so totally innocent. Then she remembered the first body she had seen, visualized once again what he had done to that girl and how her life had been snatched away, and then she could no longer deny that she wanted him, and the other fiend like him, to be removed from society forever. At least they would have a merciful, pain-free death, and that was more than even the poor bulls in the corrida ever got.

She looked at her watch and wondered again what she should do about dinner. There was food in the refrigerator, she had seen to that, but she still had no idea when Ralph would be home. Things were not yet at a point where she would feel comfortable calling in to ask. She was still pondering the matter when the front door opened and he appeared carrying a large white paper sack. "Are you all right?" he asked.

She stood up to meet him. "I'm just fine," she answered. "I took a bath when I came home."

"I would too," Mott said. "I debated letting you go out there; I wasn't sure what you'd run into."

"Sergeant O'Farrell took me under his wing. He was a big help."

"I'll have to thank Frank for that. He's a solid citizen. I hope you like Chinese; I brought some home."

Actually she didn't at that moment, but there was no way she was going to tell him that. Nevertheless he read her out. "Or," he added, "we can put it in the refrigerator and go someplace."

A sudden thought came to her; she had no idea where from. "You haven't kissed me yet," she said, astonished at her own words.

He put the sack down and reached for her. "I've always wanted to pick you up," he said. "Do you mind if I do?"

"Go right ahead," she invited. "But don't carry me into the bedroom. That can come later."

Although she was not a small person, he lifted her with ease. He swung her gently from side to side, kissed her, then crossed the room and sat her down on the sofa. "That was nice," she admitted.

He sat next to her. "I have a confession," he said.

"You've decided to go back to your former wife."

"Hardly—she's remarried. No, it's something else. For reasons I'd rather not tell you at the moment, I wanted to be sure that you were away from this whole area this afternoon."

"You mean, you got rid of me?"

"Don't say that, you know better. Now don't ask me any more questions. What kind of wine would you like with dinner tonight?"

At the moment she thought of her rigidly moralistic parents and what they would think of her present cohabiting: something she had been taught was too wicked even to be contemplated. She knew then why she had been brushing her hair; she was enjoying the once-forbidden role she was playing. She had ventured far out from the path of proper decorum and had found that the forbidden meadows there were rich and green and the wildflowers bursting with their natural beauty.

She had played by the strict rules and look what had happened to her. Now she had by choice allowed herself to be captured by a man who had just held her in his arms as though she were his private possession. It was something very new in her life and the taste of it was sweet indeed.

"On second thought," she said, "perhaps dinner could wait just a little while."

By unspoken agreement Mott was always the first one up in the morning. He made use of the bathroom to shave, shower, and prepare himself for the day. Usually he managed to do it all in something around eight minutes.

355

After that it was clear for Flavia to take as much time as she liked.

On the following morning she did not appear as soon as he expected. When she was dressing in their bedroom, he made it a definite point to respect her privacy, so he left her strictly alone.

Since he was not too hungry anyway, he poured himself a bowl of corn flakes, added sugar and milk, and sat down to eat. He scanned the headlines in the paper, then turned to the sports section. He had progressed as far as the calendar section when Flavia came quietly into the room.

He hardly recognized her. Normally when she was going on campus she wore her hair up, not in a tight knot, but in a manner that did not invite familiarity. This morning she had contrived some bangs over her forehead that made a visible change in her appearance. Most of her hair was still up, but some of it had been allowed to escape around the back of her neck and down to her shoulders.

In some subtle way he could not begin to comprehend, she had used her cosmetics in a different manner. Her eyes, which were perhaps her best feature, seemed even larger and wider apart. The color on her cheeks was minutely higher. But despite the notable change, the means by which it had been accomplished remained all but invisible.

She had on an outfit he had never seen before; a one-piece combination rose-colored sweater and knit skirt with a small jacket to match. The sweater was cut high, almost up to her neck, while the skirt fitted smoothly around her hips. Without saying a word she came toward him, then turned and walked the other way.

It was obviously an expensive outfit, certainly designer created. It enhanced the clear smoothness of her complexion; the color was exactly right for her. But all this was secondary to the fact that it revealed her figure in a way that almost demanded, and certainly would get, immediate attention. As she walked away from him, the smooth movements of her buttocks were clearly visible.

There were no telltale lines to betray whatever undergarments she had on. When she turned back to face him once more, her beautifully shaped breasts were outlined with telling clarity.

As she stood there, saying nothing and just looking at him, it was all he could do to keep his hands off her. Normally such thoughts did not invade his mind that early in the morning, but he had never been in quite the same situation before.

"What do you think?" she asked.

"If you wear that outfit in the Homicide Bureau, the place will explode," he told her.

She lifted her head and pursed her lips a little. "I may do that," she said. "It happens to be the usual time for relaxed wear on campus; most of the women take advantage of it, undergraduate or faculty. It's something of a tradition. I've gone to quite a bit of trouble for Mr. Hellman's benefit. I hope it pays off."

"If it doesn't, he's dead," Mott said. But as he spoke an almost desperate fear gripped him: that in some way something might go wrong and Hellman *would* get his hands on her.

With that thought his whole body seemed to have turned to ice.

40

Flavia drove to the university quietly at only moderate speed, knowing that there were invisible people watching over her. Or so she had been assured. She parked on the usual faculty lot, carefully locked her car, and walked across the campus toward the social sciences building.

The day, she noted, was exceptional. The sky seemed very high with mare's tails of cirrocumulus painted across the otherwise pure blue. The air, for a welcome change, had a distinct freshness to it, one that hinted at the vast ocean that lay only a few miles westward. It was, as someone had once said, the curse of California: just one damn perfect day after another. Unfortunately people would not leave them alone. They robbed, they murdered, they raped, and they did every kind of heinous thing to destroy the gift they had been given. Sometimes they got away with it; when they were caught there was a hope-

358

lessly intricate legal process to be gone through; how far often depended on the defendant's ability to pay lawyers. If finally convicted and sentenced, no matter what the judge said from the bench the time given would be drastically reduced by policy and, usually, early parole. No one sentenced to ten years ever served anything approaching that time, and everyone concerned knew it. It had become a meaningless figure of speech.

"Dr. de la Torre!"

It was the same girl who had intercepted her the last time. As she came closer she paused for a moment. "Hey, wow!" she said.

"Wow what?" Flavia asked, pretending innocence.

"That outfit; it's sexy as hell."

"What do you think clothes are for?"

"I know, I sit in your class. But you're always so . . . conservative. Not that you don't look nice and everything, but you've been hiding yourself. If I had a body like yours, I'd join a nudist colony."

"It would be a mistake," Flavia said. "You probably wouldn't get anything like the attention you do now."

The girl fell in beside her. "Anyhow, Dr. de la Torre, we've all noticed how Frank Hellman keeps taking you apart; it's awfully damn obvious. I know he's been absent, but if he shows up today, you're going to have him climbing the walls." Suspicion lit her face for a moment. "You didn't do that on purpose, did you?"

Flavia looked at her a little coolly. "Mr. Hellman is one of my students. I have no interest whatever in cultivating his friendship. I don't step across the line that divides faculty from students, but if I did, he still isn't my type. As a matter of fact, I'm rather interested in someone else right now."

The girl snickered. "Have you seen the bumper sticker?" she asked. *"Be safe tonight—sleep with a cop."*

"He's much more than a cop," Flavia said.

"He'd have to be to get you. Especially the way you look right now. Ask him if he has a friend."

"Are you thinking about that bumper sticker?"

The girl reacted promptly. "Of course," she said.

When Flavia stood up to meet her first class, there were murmurs. She ignored them and delivered her lecture exactly as she always did and then opened the floor for questions. She answered several and then ended the session. The next one would be the one that counted: Hellman was one of the registered students.

As she walked toward the faculty club, she looked around her casually in what she hoped was her normal manner. As soon as she had done that, she wished she hadn't; she had not been able to detect the slightest sign that her guardian angels were anywhere about. Despite the crowds of students heading for the cafeterias and outdoor eating areas, she felt profoundly alone. She had gotten herself up in this outfit and now she would have to stick it out, no matter what anyone thought or said.

At the faculty club she ran into Dean Cargill who gave her a frank inspection. Then he came up to her and spoke softly. "If that doesn't do it, nothing will," he said.

"You know about it?"

"Yes."

"I'm supposed to be under protection," she confided, "but I can't detect anything at all."

"That's a nice jade piece you're wearing. I don't recall having seen it before."

"I like it," she responded, not sure whether the remark was an innocent compliment or a demonstration of knowledge. "It goes with this outfit, I think."

The dean looked at it again as it hung between her breasts. "I would certainly say so," he agreed, which left her in the dark as much as before.

She ate a scant lunch, not being in the mood for food. She kept her mind busy reviewing the lecture she would be giving in less than an hour's time. Once again she firmly resolved that she would conduct her class exactly as usual: anything at all apart from her appearance could tip Hellman off; she knew he was very sharp and would probably catch any deviation from the norm immediately. He would be a very difficult man to trap.

Since she was sitting alone, and no one appeared to be looking at her, she dropped her napkin and bent over to pick it up. "I'm scared," she said softly into the jade piece.

When she had finished she got up, paid her check, and quietly left the room. She glanced at her watch: fifteen minutes to class time. As she walked back toward her classroom, she felt like a member of the Light Brigade, except for the fact that she was supposedly under guard while the historic four hundred had had no chance at all and had known it.

It took her eight minutes to go back to the place where she earned her living teaching sociology. The room was as barren and impersonal as always; it had not been designed to accommodate unnecessary amenities. She went down to the front to lay out her lecture notes and discovered that a small sheet of ruled paper, one that could have been torn from a notebook, lay on top of her desk. Neatly printed on it were two words: DON'T BE.

A surge of new confidence ran through her. She had been told that the jade pendant could hear her and broadcast her words to her unseen watchers, but, like a computer operator dealing with a screenful of possibilities, miscellaneous calculations, and solutions, she wanted a hard copy. There it lay in front of her; proof that somewhere about her guardians actually did exist. "Thank you," she said in the empty room, and added, "I feel much better now."

The words were hardly spoken before the first of her afternoon-class students came in the door.

She sat at her desk until the whole group had gathered, then she called the roll.

"Gatewill."

"Here."

"Grimes."

"Here."

"Grunberg."

"Here."

"Hanks."

"Here."

"Hellman."

"Here." That same deadly mocking voice!

"Hull."

"Here."

She completed the list and closed her classbook. Then she stood up.

She could almost hear the reaction. It could have been something added to the subdued noise in the room, or something that had been taken away, she was only sure that a difference existed. She walked slowly to her accustomed position in front of her desk where she normally delivered her lectures, the air about her crackling as though a burst of Saint Elmo's fire was about to be let loose in the room. She put her hands behind her as she so often did and took a breath to begin. She looked about the room for a moment, glanced past Hellman without stopping, and started in on her subject matter.

"Having come this far," she began, "we all know what a compelling driving force human sexuality is. It's also present in animals when they're in heat, but it is doubtful if they fantasize as we do, recall past escapades or consciously plan new ones. Certainly they do not utilize artificial stimuli as we do; there is no animal equivalent of the nude females found in the popular men's magazines. There is no skunk of the month."

That produced a laugh: one she had intended to measure the attention and mood of her audience.

A hand went up and she nodded toward the female student who had a question.

"Dr. de la Torre, you know about the pageant of the masters in Laguna Beach."

"Of course."

"In re-creating some of the great paintings with living people, some of them pose nude. Do you consider that all right?"

"I can't see any possible objection," Flavia answered. "The pageant has been a major attraction for years and a very respected one."

"Would you personally be willing to take part?"

"If I lived there and they asked me, why not? Remember," she continued, "that the nude is not obscene and never has been, only what some people think of it. The stimulus that it provides, other than aesthetic, is totally artificial, something that has been created by superstition, fear, bigotry, and a whole host of other unwholesome attitudes of mind. It's an evil that we've created ourselves and the sooner we get rid of it the better."

She looked around the room once more and this time faced Hellman for a half-second. He was intently staring at the outlines of her breasts, the expression on his face more intent than she had ever seen. Resting her hands on the edge of the desk behind her she drew a deep breath to continue her lecture. Then she turned slightly to the side to walk casually across the room as she talked. She was aware then what a dead silence filled the room. Hopefully, the bait had been taken. Every movement she had made had been customary with her while lecturing; she was certain there was no giveaway there.

Fifteen minutes later, when the room was noticeably warmer, she turned her back for a moment, slipped out of her jacket, and walked to the blackboard where she picked up a piece of chalk. She began a diagram of human responses to certain stimuli and lectured from it for another ten minutes before the period was over. Not once by movement, by subject matter, or by tone of voice did she depart from the formal style she always used in delivering her lectures. She was intensely careful about that. When the bell finally rang, she was sure she had played her part well. She had half feared that Hellman might remain after class to ask an unnecessary question or two, but he went out with the others.

When the room had been cleared, she gathered up her materials as she always did and went to her car. She took a little time to arrange things, then spoke to the jade piece around her neck. "I'm going downtown. They're having an important sale of women's designer clothes."

That was enough. Presumably she would be followed wherever she went, but a little advance notice might be welcome. She drove to the huge department store and chose a lot that advertised validated parking.

Inside the store she rode up an escalator into the world of women's fashions and soon all but lost her identity in a gathering of female bodies searching the racks for things, feeling them, and holding them up in front of themselves before mirrors.

One woman, not pleased by what she saw, glanced at Flavia and said with bitterness in her voice, "God, I wish I looked like you do."

"Why don't you try light brown," Flavia answered. "I think it's your color."

Her suggestion produced an immediate reaction. "If I do find something, will you tell me what you think?"

Flavia smiled, recognizing the common symptom of someone who finds decisions difficult and likes to have them made for her. "Of course," she said.

"You're a movie or TV star, aren't you," the woman persisted.

On impulse Flavia did the kind thing. "No, just a housewife," she answered and then wondered if she had expressed a subconscious wish without knowing it. It was possible, but she had told a rare lie and even for a good cause that went against the grain of her being. She told herself that she *was* living with a man, so perhaps there was some justification. At least she had meant well and on that upbeat thought she dismissed it from her mind.

After some searching she found two possible choices that might suit her very well. She took them over her arm and headed for the dressing rooms. There she was fortunate, one was just being vacated and she was able to slip inside.

The store manager's secretary picked up the outside line and answered, "Mr. Goldman's office."

"I need to speak to him immediately," the voice on the line said. "This is a police matter and very urgent."

The secretary made a decision to put the call through. Normally she always referred outside callers to the proper department heads, but this was obviously not a routine call. She pressed the intercom button. "The police are calling," she reported. "They said that it's very urgent."

Goldman at once punched the button for the outside line and spoke his name. "What's the problem, officer?" he asked.

"Listen carefully. There are three bombs in your store. The first one will go off in fifteen minutes. You can't find it, so don't try. The second, in a different location, goes in half an hour. The last one is the biggest and can blow you to hell and gone."

Goldman was fast on the uptake. "What do you want?" he asked.

"An emergency public announcement from you that you'll hire only minorities until at least half of your staff is black. Do this in time and you may stop the second bomb. They're radio-controlled. The first one's already been triggered, just to let you know that we mean business." The line went dead.

Goldman lost not a second. He punched the direct line to Security. "We have a bomb threat, due to go in fifteen minutes. Evacuate the store, as fast as possible, all of it," he ordered. "Customers, staff, everyone. Don't hold up for anything. I'll call the police."

365

"Got it," the security chief said and began to punch his own buttons.

Throughout the store powerful gongs began to ring in a staccato pattern that every employee had been trained to recognize. Immediately doors to storerooms with rear exits were thrown wide open. Announcements of the immediate evacuation were made by all supervisory personnel and floor clerks, while cashiers swiftly locked their registers. Elevators were run to the top floors to pick up loads. Throughout the huge merchandising complex a PA system repeated the announcement. The word bomb was avoided, but the urgency was made clear.

Security personnel manned the tops of escalators that were all keyed to run downward. Freight elevators took on large loads from the upper floors and ran them down nonstop to the street level. Revolving doors were folded open to permit people to pass out unimpeded. Other security personnel began to run through the top floor making sure that it was totally vacated before going down to the next. One woman who had been standing in line at an adjustment counter refused to leave since it was her turn next. She was picked up by the arms over her vigorous protest and deposited on a down elevator. As soon as the top floor had been cleared, as far as could be determined, the security people, aided by other store personnel, used walkie-talkies to secure it, then rushed down the descending escalators to do the same on the next floor below.

In the women's better clothing section what had been an orderly crowd turned into a near riot. Women who still tried to reach for bargains were forcefully hustled away. Others quickly stuffed loose garments under their own clothing in the jam of people.

The section manager snatched open the fitting room door where Flavia was trying on a new, expensive outfit. Since she looked intelligent, the manager spoke quickly.

"This is an emergency evacuation," she said. "Never mind what you've got on; grab your own things and hurry."

Flavia responded immediately, still wearing the expensive dinner dress she had hoped would please Ralph. She came out into a mass of women who were being expertly herded through a wide stockroom door and toward a concrete staircase. Those who were obviously not ablebodied were quickly sorted out and loaded onto a freight elevator that closed its doors the moment it was full.

As soon as she reached the first floor Flavia was caught in a pressing jam, only able to move with the crowd that was flowing onto a loading dock. Police officers in uniform were directing the people toward the edge where ramps had been quickly rigged. With more space available, the jam lessened; Flavia turned to see which way to go. A black male hand grabbed the jade pendant around her neck and gave a sharp jerk, breaking it loose. From the back she saw the man take off and spring down from the ramp to the ground where a brief path was clear. Then he was gone.

Outside in the street all traffic had been stopped. Police cars, their roof lights revolving, were everywhere. A TV truck trying to get in was denied access. Because it was the only sensible thing she could do, Flavia went to her car that was parked a block away. Police were there too, gesturing traffic off the lot and forcing it to turn south down a side street. Obediently, she fell in line and did as she was directed.

For five blocks traffic was tightly controlled and kept moving. Then it was allowed to fan out, most of it toward the southbound ramps of the Harbor Freeway. For a moment or two she was undecided what was best. Turning back north invited disaster. Then she realized that she was only a few blocks from her own apartment. She took a deep breath and let it out in relief; her rent was paid, she had her key in her purse, and the phone was still connected. Once there she could call Ralph and tell him where she was.

She parked in her usual place and went inside, still wearing the dress she had been trying on and that would either have to be paid for or returned.

The air inside her small apartment was musty. She dropped her own outfit she had been carrying onto her sofa, put down her purse, and took a moment or two to compose herself.

She was standing there, in the middle of her little living room, when Frank Hellman came out of her bedroom. "Hello, sweetheart," he said.

41

Although he was only twenty-three years old, Isadore Lopez was already a complete professional; he was one of the very best car thieves in Southern California.

He knew the demand and the market for almost every kind of car of recent vintage and who would pay the most for each model. He knew how to unlock them in seconds and how to remove expensive stereo units in less than a minute if he happened to need one. But most of all he knew how to pick up cars without being seen, which streets to drive to get them undetected to the chop shops, and where the maker's secret numbers were hidden on the frames.

By careful study he had learned to reduce the risk of his work to a minimum. He had been stopped several times, but he had never been arrested. He always had a work order on the seat beside him authorizing him to take the car he was driving to a reputable dealer for repairs.

Sometimes he drove a tow truck with the AAA insignia prominently displayed on the side. He always had paperwork for that too, in case he was ever questioned.

Only once an extra-alert cop checked up on the Cadillac he was driving by calling the owner's telephone number shown on the work order. When the phone rang in the chop shop, "Mr. Shapiro" had confirmed the order and added that he had asked to have the car road-tested. The cop was satisfied and sent Isadore on his way. He would never be able to pick him out of a lineup later on; too many Mexicans looked alike and all wore the same kind of mustache.

The woman who left the Caddie on the street in Beverly Hills obviously wasn't the kind who worried about a few parking tickets; she was accustomed to having things her way. She took her purse and disappeared into a store where, Isadore knew, most customers stayed at least three-quarters of an hour, usually in an upstairs showroom.

He waited five minutes, then crossed the street and inspected the car casually; it was an attractive new Seville. While no one seemed to be paying him the least notice, he got out a piece of paper, pretended to check the license plate, and then used the key that had cost him three hundred dollars to unlock the car. Less than a minute later he drove it away from the curb, at risk for only a minute or two until he blended neatly into the traffic on Wilshire Boulevard.

He quickly turned down Robertson to break the continuity and made several more turns down streets that were almost never patrolled as he worked his way toward the Culver City area.

This time he had made his first great mistake. He had picked up a bait car and the hidden transmitter it carried betrayed his every move and turn. Overhead an unseen helicopter followed him easily while several surface units paralleled him like a group of destroyers around an aircraft carrier.

When he reached the chop shop, which had every appearance of being a legitimate auto body and repair facility, he pulled up outside and touched the horn in a short, coded signal. A metal roll-up door opened to admit him. He drove in with smooth professionalism: another job done; a thousand dollars earned for less then an hour's work. And when the car was finally sold, there would be a bonus; there were few others who could produce as well as he did.

In less than half a minute Metro Division cops were swarming into the place. Most of the mechanics, few of whom spoke English, sprawled on the floor as directed. The manager made a decision within seconds that he had no chance at that stage and allowed himself to be cuffed. He knew good lawyers and that was his next line of defense.

Riding with Metro on what was supposed to be a routine stakeout was Cadet Alice Okimoto who was due to graduate from the academy in three weeks. She had been with them before and she liked them; she only wished that they would stop calling her Fortune Cookie. She intended to be a police officer, dammit, and not somebody's Oriental doll.

When the sudden word was given that something was going down she alerted herself and was ready. As the cops poured into the chop shop, she found herself standing with nothing to do. Metro was damn efficient: the suspects were all either sprawled out on the deck or else were being systematically hooked up by efficient male teams. Her own temporary partner was on his hands and knees beside a suspect; as she approached him he waved her off.

She was already sworn, but she had not yet graduated, perhaps that was why. Determined to do something useful, she checked some of the other vehicles in the big shop. The only one not yet receiving attention was a solitary van, freshly painted, parked in a back corner.

She took out her notebook and wrote down the license

number. Then, since no one told her not to, she opened the side door of the van and checked inside.

The interior was very plush with a low divan-type seat running down one side. She had never seen one like it. When she checked it out the seat opened up and there was a space underneath that might have carried two surfboards. Or something else a lot more significant. With her flashlight she checked the carpeting, remembering a bulletin she had seen several times about a wanted van. According to the bulletin, any officer spotting a possible make was to call the task force directly at once at a given number.

Alice remembered the number; she had made it a point to memorize it. She found a phone on the wall, dropped in a quarter, and made the call.

In the task force room at the Hall of Justice a particular and fervent kind of hell was breaking loose. For the first time in living memory Ralph Mott had lost his cool; he was a man beside himself. But even under those circumstances he was not trying to find someone to blame. He was desperate for answers and his mind was totally focused in trying to find them, even if he had to pull them out of thin air.

"You lost her," he repeated into the land line telephone, just to make absolutely sure.

Dick Tracy didn't try to duck or mince words. "She had told us where she was going and we had people on hand. Miriam was in the area where she was shopping, keeping out of sight of course, when that damn bomb scare went down."

He stopped and took a moment or two to collect himself. "The store people obviously had contingency plans for something like this: they did a first-rate job of emergency evacuation. Busy as they were, when I told their Security we were covering a subject in a rose-colored knit outfit, they cooperated. We had people at all the likely exits where

Flavia might have gone out, but none of them spotted an attractive female dressed like that in the crowd."

"Who was covering her car?"

"You can chew my ass for this, Ralph, but we didn't have someone specifically on it. Two blocks north we had a surveillance unit continuously tuned to the bug on it. Since we knew exactly where it was, I thought that was enough."

Despite his near-desperate frame of mind, Ralph could not criticize that. It was standard technique, well executed. Before he could say so, Tracy heaped more ashes on himself. "When this whole thing went down, our tracking unit was caught on the wrong side of the jam and couldn't move either way. An L.A.P.D. lieutenant tried to help, but it was a physical impossibility to get the unit out of there in time. The whole scene was jammed with emergency vehicles, patrol cars, paramedics just in case, and hundreds of people pouring out of that store."

By making a determined effort, Mott got full control of himself once more. "All right," he said. "You're acting field lieutenant. Put a team outside my place to intercept Flavia the moment she shows. Also put a man inside to take any calls; he's to impersonate me if necessary. Get recording equipment on my home line as fast as you can."

"It's on the way now, Ralph, and Levitzky is already inside your apartment—just in case."

"Good! Ask L.A.P.D. to check out her own apartment; she might have gone there for something."

"They're doing that now. Another unit is checking her office at the college."

"One more thing," Mott said. "That was a rough experience she had. She could have stopped for a cup of coffee just to settle herself down. Get two teams on the job checking out likely places."

That was a desperation move and both men knew it. If Flavia had done that, she would have called in, but a check was still in order.

When Lieutenant Fitzgerald came in Mott pounced on him. "Are you free?" he asked.

Fitz shook his head. "I thought I'd better tell you," he said. "We've just had a call: an unknown white female described as thirty to thirty-five, attractive, shot and dumped in Cerritos. I'll call you the moment we've determined that it isn't Flavia."

Mott tried to swallow a sudden lump in his throat. "Thanks, Fitz," he said.

Sergeant Berkowitz was at his elbow. "I'll take over the phone if you'd like," he said. "I can alert all the L.A.P.D. stations and other jurisdictions."

Mott was grateful for the offer. "Keep the frequency open," he said. "I'm going to the store."

"Don't bust your ass getting there."

Normally sergeants, particularly those from other jurisdictions, didn't talk that way to lieutenants, but Mott knew what he meant and appreciated it. "If you can, pass the word to your people at the scene that I'm coming in."

Berkowitz flipped a hand in the air to indicate that everything was under control.

Despite the fact that there was still a considerable traffic jam in the central city area, Mott wormed his way through and parked his official car in a red curb zone close by the huge store.

His sheriff's ID got him through the police lines and inside the main entrance. His first step was to check with the bomb-squad people and their K-9 backup. A complete check of the store had not been completed, but no bomb had gone off after the fifteen-minute period had elapsed and the alarm was looking more and more like a hoax.

All of the senior store personnel likely to receive such a threat had been told exactly what to say. If the caller stated a specific demand, or imposed any time limits, the odds were increased that the call was genuine. But odds or no odds, the decision had been made that in the event of a threat, it would be treated as real and an evacuation

374

carried out, even though the cost would be high in pilfered merchandise, lost sales time, and the disruption of the whole facility.

It had been a hard decision, but the alternative was a risk that the store, for both business and moral reasons, was unwilling to take.

He located a harassed-looking executive on the main floor and asked directions to the women's designer clothing section. The executive glanced at his ID and then gave him the information. He ran up a back staircase rather than wait for an elevator and located the section manager without difficulty.

"I'm Lieutenant Mott of the Sheriff's Department," he said. "This is confidential, but we were maintaining close protection for one of our undercover people here just before the bomb threat. In the confusion we lost her. I know she came here in response to your sale. She was wearing a rose-colored knit outfit."

"I'm quite sure I didn't see her," the section manager said, "but I wasn't on the floor at that time."

"We had all the exits covered, but no one saw her go out," Mott continued. "I just want to ask one question: what if she happened to be trying something on when the order came to evacuate?"

"In a very short time situation we'd hustle her out of the dressing room no matter what she had on—assuming she was decently dressed, of course. If she had on a store dress, we wouldn't wait for her to change; she'd be told to evacuate as is and to bring her own garments with her."

"Could you ask your people about that? It's very important."

"As soon as I can, Lieutenant, but I'm the only one here right now. Only the supervisory personnel have been allowed back in the store until . . ." She was uncertain how to finish the sentence.

"But it is possible that our young woman was wearing something other than what she had on when she came in."

"Possible, certainly. We have quite a few dressing rooms and they're usually all busy when a sale is going on."

At that moment Mott's beeper went off. As he shut it down, the section manager pointed to a nearby phone. His heart pounding despite himself, Mott called in desperately hoping that it would be good news about Flavia.

The moment he got through, Sergeant Berkowitz gave him the word. "We haven't located her yet, but we have a suspect in custody. They're bringing him here."

"Who?" Mott almost shouted.

"A Willie Simpson: male Negro, twenty-five to thirty, five eleven, narrow build, moderate afro. On parole for two eleven; quite a rap sheet."

"Hold him there; I'll be right in."

"Damn right we'll hold him. Take your time." Berkowitz was not a man easily ruffled.

Eleven minutes later Mott had negotiated the traffic back to the Hall of Justice without too much regard for other cars, parked, and made his way to the task force room. The dejected-looking black that awaited him there sat hunched over in the manner of a man who has frequently been in police custody. As Mott entered the room, Berkowitz intercepted him. The L.A.P.D. sergeant opened his palm and displayed the jade-covered transmitter Flavia had been wearing.

"One of our units picked up the signal," he said. "They phoned for backup and collected Willie here. He's one of our frequent customers."

"Have you interrogated him?"

"We thought you might like to have that pleasure."

"Nothing else in the meantime?"

"No. A detective unit checked out Flavia's old apartment, but the manager had no idea whether or not anyone had been in or out. The rent had been paid and that was all that interested her."

"Did they check inside?"

"The manager had her orders—no one to be admitted

376

without a note from the tenant or a warrant. She did open the door, though, enough to let one of our people do a quick walk-through. No one was inside."

"Damn," Mott said. "That looked like a good bet. Did he check the closets?"

Berkowitz gave him a baleful look. "He reported that no one was inside," he repeated with deceptive mildness.

"Sorry, I'm not quite myself at the moment."

"Understood. Let's see what Willie can tell us."

Willie was taken to an interrogation room where he was planted in a hard chair. Across a table from him Berkowitz and Mott formed a formidable team.

Berkowitz held out the jade piece. "Do you know what this is?" he asked. He made the question an accusation; he was in no mood for the niceties.

Willie shrugged. Knowing that his position was hopeless, he tried for a deal. "I'll cop to taking it," he said. "And maybe I can help you, if you'll help me."

"How much can you help us?" Berkowitz demanded, making it put-up-or-shut-up time.

"I know who grabbed that jewelry case in the bus station last night."

"Not interested."

Willie ran his tongue over his thick lips. "Whadda you want?" he asked. "And how'd you find me?"

Berkowitz gave a good imitation of Count Dracula in a smiling mood. He dangled the jade piece before Willie's eyes. "This time, asshole, what you stole was a valuable piece of police property." He turned it over. "See the back? In there is a powerful transmitter. You grabbed it off a policewoman and now she's disappeared. That's how we tracked you, and why we lost her. It's your fault, Willie, and you're going to pay for it—all the way!"

Willie became visibly more agitated. "I didn't know about no policewoman," he said. "All I saw was this honky broad in the long white dress with this thing hanging on her. It was an easy grab and I took it. That's all. Ninety days, maybe."

"What kind of a dress?" Mott demanded.

"White, like I said. Kinda long. That's all I seen. I came up behind her and then I ran. That's all."

Mott got up. "Run him down to CJ and book him in. Grand theft will do until we get some more."

Berkowitz nodded silently. Like Mott, he knew there was nothing more to be gained from this witness. Willie would be in for a good stretch this time, unless they got the wrong judge, but that didn't greatly concern them at the moment.

To his personal humiliation, Mott found that tears were trying to force their way out of his eyes. He wiped the back of his left hand quickly across his face. As he returned to the task force room, a firm resolution was forming in his mind. One that could mean the end of his career and his employment in the only work he knew, but that was a minor consideration now.

The people who were in the room gathered around him, waiting for any work he had to give.

"We've got one thing," he said. "Flavia was last seen wearing a white dress. The credibility of that is pretty low, but she could have been changing in the store, trying something on, when the alarm went off."

He turned to a female investigator. "Get down to the store," he directed. "The sales people should be checking back in by now. Find out who cleared out the dressing rooms and if she remembers Flavia. You know what to ask."

The investigator gave a quick nod that she understood and hurried toward the door. She almost collided with a very big man, red-bearded, who was dressed in jeans and a work shirt. As she left the man came in. "Who's Mott?" he asked.

Ralph saw the police ID clipped to his shirt. "What can I do for you?" he asked.

"Bert Larson, Lieutenant, El Monte Police. I met Flavia

378

at a crime scene. We got the word she's missing. Since I know her, I came in to see if I could help."

Mott made a quick decision. "How far are you willing to stick your neck out?" he asked.

"Whatever it takes. That's why I'm here."

"Are you on orders?"

"All set; no problem."

Mott looked again at Larson and realized that this was just the kind of man he needed for what he had in mind.

He introduced Larson to the group and then forced himself to maintain at least the appearance of calm, despite the fact that he was close to boiling inside.

"It's been too long," he said. "Wherever she is, Flavia would have called in long before now—if she could. She'd know, or strongly suspect, that she'd lost her cover during the bomb scare. She hasn't come back to my place or shown up at her own apartment."

He let it hang there in the air while he took a fresh grip on his own nerves.

"We've got an APB out on Hellman," Sergeant Rogers said. "Also the Aero Bureau is covering the site they found in the San Gabriels, and as many others as possible."

Mott laid out what they already knew. "As of now, we've got to assume that Hellman has got her. God knows how he did it, but he has."

There was no dissenting voice.

At that point the phone rang.

Berkowitz swept it up. "Task Force, Berkowitz," he said.

He listened patiently for some thirty seconds, then he said, "Give me the license number."

The room was suddenly quiet; this could be a major break and everyone there knew it.

"Hang on," Berkowitz said. He called out a license number to the computer operator. "Run it *now*," he directed.

The operator punched keys and had an answer back from

Sacramento in seconds. "Stanley Witkowski, spell that please."

Mott heard her and his mind flashed back almost instantly to the report he had started to read—and hadn't finished.

The computer operator gave the address and the description of the vehicle.

Holding himself in tight check, because it had been his fault, Mott turned to Frank Salerno. "You and Carrillo checked out a Stan Witkowski?" he asked.

"You've got our report," Salerno answered.

"Did you check him for vehicle registrations?"

It hit Salerno like a blast of cold air. "No, we didn't. He had an old Honda parked outside; we took that to be it." As he spoke the words he knew already what was coming.

At that moment Mott showed what kind of a man he was. "It wasn't in your report; it should have been."

"Yes, sir."

"But I missed it too when I read it over, and that's an essential step in any investigation such as this one."

Gil Carrillo spoke up. "Does Witkowski own a van?" he asked.

In the dead stillness Mott answered. "He does. It's just been recovered and bloodstains are reported inside."

Frank Salerno jumped to his feet. *"Let's get the hell out of here!"*

Even knowing that every second counted, Mott remembered that he was still in command. He turned to Berkowitz. "I'm going after Witkowski myself. Have the van taped off and held for the lab people. You know what else to do. Take command while I'm gone. I need to borrow some speed loads."

"I'm coming with you," Larson said. "If I lay into him, he'll talk. I can get another job anytime."

"Get you asses in gear," Berkowitz said. "You'll have full backup and cover. I'll organize it."

Sergeant Pinelli jumped to her feet. "I know her too," she said. "You're not going to leave me out of this."

"This isn't going to be by the book," Mott snapped. "We're going to break that bastard as fast as we can. Any way at all."

"We're wasting time," Pinelli said.

As people surged toward the exit, Mott put up a hand to hold them back. "Salerno and Carrillo I want. The rest of you stay here to respond if you get any word at all."

That made good sense and was accepted. With the massive Bert Larson by his side, Mott rode down to the lobby and grabbed a car off the parking lot. Larson got in beside him, spoiling for action. Almost unnoticed, Sergeant Elsie Pinelli, who had put the wire on Flavia, jumped in the back. Salerno and Carrillo took another car.

Mott was speeding westward on the Santa Monica Freeway when he got a radio call from Fitzgerald. The body in Cerritos wasn't Flavia.

It was a thin straw, but he grasped at it; he had a desperate need for any ray of hope he could get.

42

For the first few seconds Flavia was frozen in shock and unable to help herself. Before she had time to come out of it, Hellman stepped next to her and took a firm grip on her upper arm. "I know you want to ask why I'm here," he said, "and how I got in. Never mind that; you're in danger and I'm here to help you."

She knew he was lying and that she would need her self-possession more than at any time in her life. She was terrified, and the knowledge of who and what Hellman was forced her to fight a rising sense of panic with all the mental power she had. She tried to speak, but nothing would form itself in her mind.

"Listen," Hellman said, biting off the words. "I'm older than your other students, you know that." He turned her forcefully toward the door. "If you don't know already, I've been in prison. I want to be very nice to you, but if you try to cross me, I can be very ugly."

She tried to pull away from him, but his fingers were like steel talons biting into her flesh.

"That isn't smart," he said and tightened his grip even more. "We don't have much time. We're going to walk out of here together before anyone else finds us. I've got a car outside."

Feverently Flavia hoped that in some way her cover people were still watching over her; it was the best chance she had. Then a knife blade was in front of her eyes. "You learn a lot in Soledad," Hellman said in a tight, hard voice. "So don't try to fight me. Get in the car and I'll explain."

The knife disappeared, then quickly she felt a tiny prick in her back. "I don't want to hurt you, so don't make me," Hellman warned.

Close to terror, but with her mind still working, Flavia knew that as of that moment she had no choice at all. She could scream, but if she did, who would help her? Who would go up against an armed man with a knife? If she tried that, it could be with the last breath in her body.

She thought to pick up her purse, then at once knew better: Ralph would be looking for her and it would give him an invaluable clue.

As though he were reading her mind, Hellman scooped it up and handed it to her. "Make one bad move," he said, "and I'll push this knife right through you and out your right tit. I know just where it is."

For a terrible, paralyzing moment, Flavia saw again the body of the girl who had been murdered and left in Big Tujunga Canyon. That helpless, tortured, naked thing had once been someone just like herself. Despite that horrible memory she remembered a basic principle in dealing with irrational people: don't aggravate them.

There was one thing that might help her to save herself. The other victims had all been young girls, some of them in their early teens. She had knowledge and skills far beyond their slender resources. As she stumbled down the stairs, the knife still pressing point first against her back, the few seconds of time allowed her to take a firm hold of herself and plan her counterattack.

She deliberately made a very hard choice, one many women might have rejected, but they had not seen what she had witnessed.

She turned her head partway toward Hellman and spoke over her shoulder in pretended anger. "You've got a helluva way of asking a girl for a date," she said.

Then, as well as she could, she walked down the steps from her second-floor apartment and looked at the nondescript car that Hellman had parked at the curb. With simulated poise she waited for him to open the door for her. When he did, she got in.

While Hellman walked around and slid behind the wheel, she made no attempt to get away. She had decided on her plan of action and whatever happened, she was going to stick to it. It was her best chance to escape the horrible fate of those other females who had been younger and less well trained than herself.

Hellman had her fasten her seat belt, then pulled the car away from the curb. "I'm sorry I was so rough with you," he said.

"You'd be better off now if you hadn't." She had chosen her role and was ready to play it to the limit, if it came to that. *Make a decision and stick to it*: she had learned that early in life and it had served her well.

A police car, running with its roof lights on, passed them going the other way. Flavia pretended to ignore it. If they had the description of Hellman's car, they would find it soon enough. And lying on the sofa of her apartment, where she had dropped it, was the shopping bag containing the outfit she had worn that morning.

"I've got this friend," Hellman said. "Her name's Mary Ellen. Her family's filthy rich and they've got a big house in the hills. But they aren't there now. I've got a key." His voice betrayed a fragment of uncertainty, as though he were planning aloud.

"I don't know about you," Flavia said, "but I'm not going to be any good, to myself or anyone else, unless I get something to eat pretty soon."

Hellman gave that very brief thought as he drove. "We can't go into a restaurant," he said in a voice that allowed no opposition. "You might try to pull something and that would be very bad for us both."

"How about some takeout?" she asked, trying hard not to betray the fact that she was playing for time. If her thinking was sound, every second could count in her favor.

"It's got to be a drive-in," Hellman said. "Someplace where we don't get out of the car."

Flavia waited a few seconds and then began her approach to the Stockholm Syndrome, the technique whereby captors are eventually made sympathetic to their victims. "I think now that you owe me an explanation," she said. She spoke the words carefully, without indignation, as though her mind were still open.

Hellman put his knife down, on the side away from her, while he lit a cigarette. "Do you think I'm good-looking?" he asked.

"Most women would think so," she answered.

"That isn't what I asked you."

"All right: you're good-looking."

"You had noticed that."

"Yes, just as I noticed how closely you inspected me every time the class met."

"You can't hate me for that."

"It's happened before."

"I'll bet it has. In case you don't know it, you're stacked like a brick shithouse, lady. That's why you're here now."

Flavia smoothed the skirt of the white dress she had on. "I know how things work," she said. "It's my field. No matter what the fundamentalists yell about morals, you could have all the women you want. Perhaps for the price of a couple of drinks, maybe not even that."

"What did they tell you about me?" He was still driving

385

north, staying off the main streets and making frequent stops as they were required. Clearly he wasn't risking being stopped for a traffic offense.

"Just what was on your registration card. Your name, class, and the subject you'd elected."

"I don't believe that," Hellman said. "You must have heard more than that."

"Why?"

"Because I'm an ex-con; that always comes out."

"Whether you believe it or not doesn't matter, but the fact is I didn't know it until you just told me." She had no compunction about lying to him; it was smooth and easy for her.

"You saw that I was older," he persisted.

"If I'd stopped to think about it, I would have presumed that you're a veteran. Maybe you are."

"No, I'm no veteran." He paused as if deciding how far to show his hand. "Maybe you think you can get away, jump out when we stop for a busy street. Forget it, you can't. I fixed your seat belt."

She tried it experimentally; when she pressed the release it remained firmly locked.

As if to make her feel worse, he stopped dutifully for a traffic light, then when it turned green he drove on through.

"When you're in the joint, you learn a lot of things," Hellman went on. "That seat-belt trick, for example. And you learn not to trust anyone, not even you, sweetheart."

Flavia knew she was expected to react to that; she did so carefully. "What did I ever do to you?" she asked.

"Nothing—not at first. Then you started living with that cop, so I knew which side you were on." He pulled into a Big Boy drive-in.

"You keep your mouth shut," he directed in a suddenly harder voice. "I'll do the ordering."

The girl who served them was cheerful, pert, and pretty. Hellman gave her a winning smile, but when she saw who was in the car with him, she let it wash over. She knew unbeatable competition, or so she thought, when she saw it.

Hellman put the large white bag she gave him on the back seat. "We'll eat when we get there," he said and pulled out into the traffic once more.

While that was going on, Flavia was carefully planning. She was playing the "going along" game, doing her best to be convincing. It could be a complete exercise in futility, but there was no other tack she could take with any hope at all of success.

Hellman was a monster, she knew that all too well. He could be playing with her cat-and-mouse style. But if she could convince him that it was all an adventure to her—slim as that hope was—it might stretch out the time enough for Ralph and his people to do something to help her.

She knew then that her guardians had lost her in the store evacuation; they would never have left her alone this long with Hellman. He had taken her against her will. That was kidnapping, a Federal offense that would cost him years more in prison if he were caught. He had to know the risk he was taking. She was locked in the car seat, unable to get out until he released her. And her jade piece had been stolen. There might be an APB out for his car, but she had seen only one police unit since her fear-filled ride had begun.

That left her with a terrible and bitter choice. If he demanded sex, she would have to agree and pretend a secret desire for him. If she didn't, he could force her with the threat of the cold steel death in his knife. Then he would probably kill her, taking out his frustrations by torturing her first. That awful prospect steeled her resolve.

The alternative was the Scheherezade Solution, to pretend with all the deception she could muster that she was having a wonderful time: to make it so great for him that he would want to have her again and again and would not kill the goose that was giving him glorious sex.

How revolting that would be, she froze out of her mind; if women in the past had been able to die for their faiths, tied to their stakes while the flames consumed them, she would be able to do what she had to do. Because he was going to succeed in possessing her either way, she would have to play her physical assets to the limit. It was a desperation gamble, she knew that, but it was the only one she had.

"When did you lose your virginity?" he asked her abruptly as he drove out.

"When I was raped at sixteen," Flavia answered. She was finding it easier to lie to him; whatever might work she would seize and use. "Did you phone that bomb scare to the store?"

"Of course. I knew they would be covering you, after you wore that sexy outfit. It was too goddamn obvious. So I screwed them up."

He remained silent after that as he drove on, giving her no clue as to what was running through his mind. Then he began to climb up into the foothills of the San Gabriels near Arcadia, where ordinary homes gave way to mansions. "We're almost there," he said at last. "I've got a friend of mine coming I want you to meet. I'm sure you'll enjoy his company as much as mine."

That swept away her last hope and left her shaking with fear.

43

As he sped westward toward
the ocean, Mott was obsessed by the desperate need to find
Flavia at the earliest possible moment. The only avenue
open to him was to make Witkowski talk and talk fast. If he
could do that without giving the suspect any grounds for
escaping the gas chamber he would, but nothing was going
to stand in his way.

To help regain his mental balance, he spoke to his
unexpected partner. "I'm almost certain that we've IDed
on the coat-hanger killers," he said, just to be sure that
Larson fully understood. "I think he'll know where his
partner is, the one who's probably got Flavia."

"How do you want to play it?"

"I want you to menace the hell out of him, but keep
hands off unless he tries to break away or becomes violent.
Then we'll do whatever's necessary to take him into
custody."

"That includes me," Elsie said unexpectedly from the back seat.

Larson turned partway around to look at her. "I heard about a female sergeant who responded to a four-fifteen bar last month in Carson; I think her name was Pinelli. When some big bastard went for her, she kicked him in the balls and threw him flat while she hooked him up."

"My godfather teaches judo," Pinelli said. "He's Japanese—fifth dan."

Larson turned back again, apparently satisfied.

Mott's mind was rigidly focused on the job at hand. "We interviewed Witkowski a few days ago," he said, "but we didn't check if he owned a van. Now we've got the van and apparently there's blood in it."

"So you want this Witkowski to spill his guts very fast, right?"

"Damn right."

"I'll see to it," Larson promised.

Mott continued to drive at close to pursuit speed until he almost whipped the car around a final corner and pulled up in front of the place where Witkowski lived. As he did so, he spotted an unmarked L.A.P.D. unit waiting in position. Two plainclothesmen immediately got out and introduced themselves. "More backups coming," the driver said.

"Good," Mott told him. "You can help us if you'll cover the exits. We may have to do some interrogation. The suspect is in his late twenties, five ten, poor build, probably badly dressed. Ex-con."

That was all the L.A.P.D. man had to hear. "I'll stay in front, my partner will cover the back."

The same youthful landlady opened the door. She took one look at Mott's face and said, "He's upstairs in his room." She knew what to expect and had no desire to get in the way.

Mott made surprisingly little noise as he took the stairs two at a time. Once in position he rapped gently on Witkowski's door to avoid alerting the man inside.

In a few moments the door swung open. Witkowski, wearing sneakers, blue jeans, and a torn T-shirt stared at him in startled surprise. "Whatta' you want now?" he asked.

"I have to talk to you."

"I'm busy right now and . . ."

Larson stepped forward. "You're making a mistake," he said.

Witkowski looked at the big man who towered over him and backed up. "I'm clean, I tell ya," he said. "Ask my parole officer."

"Fine, then invite us in."

Outside the two L.A.P.D. men closed in on the house. No matter what might go down, they were positioned to handle their part of the action.

With his mouth curled in distaste Witkowski half gestured with his arm, motioning Larson and Mott in. "When I got parole this last time, they told me to keep my nose clean and everything would be fine. Now all you guys do is hassle . . ."

Larson didn't let him finish. He pushed Witkowski into a chair and towered over him as Mott said, "You lied to me about knowing Frank Hellman."

"I said I knew him. Now unless you got a warrant, get out."

Larson bent over and thrust his huge bearded face inches from Witkowski's. "Don't get cute, mister," he warned. "If you want to save your ass, start talking."

When Witkowski appeared to hesitate, Mott set his voice at a stone-hard level. "We know all about you, Witkowski: about Hellman, your van, and all those young girls you murdered."

He paused a second or two, taking savage satisfaction as he watched a stricken look growing on Witkowski's face, a look that admitted to a terrible, paralyzing fear. At just the right moment he added another hammer blow. "And we've got the tape. All those girls screaming their lives out, *and your voice is on that tape!*"

Witkowski, who had been so sure he would never be caught, was ashen with terror. "You're lying," he said. "There isn't any tape."

"Any tape of what?"

"I want my lawyer."

Larson whipped into action. "Listen, asshole, you're had. You're looking right into the gas chamber where you're going to sit and gasp your life away. But you may not live that long." He flexed his huge hands and cracked his knuckles.

"You got no right . . ."

Mott produced his cuffs, letting Witkowski see them clearly. "You're under arrest," he said. "For kidnapping, mayhem, and multiple murder."

In one lightning-fast motion Witkowski bolted out of his chair and hurled himself through the door. As he jumped for the head of the stairs he saw a female deputy and thrust out an arm to slam her aside.

He made hard contact, but before he knew it his wrist was in an iron lock and he was being whirled through the air, completely disoriented. In one terrifying moment he saw the staircase below him, far below, then he was let go.

He crashed on his back, head downward. A sudden awful pain seized him and he couldn't move his legs to flee. Then Larson was on him, handcuffs bit into his wrists, and his entire world of secret horrors and terrible bloodlust collapsed around him and became his prison.

He lay perfectly still as Mott knelt beside him. "I'll give you one chance," he said, "but you've got to take it right now."

Witkowski was in such pain, and suddenly engulfing shock, his power of resistance was totally gone. He knew only one thing: an intense animal desire for self-preservation.

"Where's Hellman?" Mott demanded.

"I don't know." It was the truth. Witkowski forced out the words through his pain.

"Listen hard: he's got another girl. Only this time, it's *my lady*!"

Witkowski's eyes opened wide as the full horror of that hit him. The woman Frank had talked about: she was a cop's wife!

He clutched at the straw. "If I tell you . . ." he began and saw in Mott's face the end of his last hope. "I've got a phone number," he said.

The phone company made things maddeningly difficult. "I understand that this is a police emergency," the operator said, "but that is a highly restricted number. I don't have it and neither does my supervisor. You'll have to contact the business office and go through Security there."

Mott was barely civil as he hung up. He put in an immediate call to Homicide and asked who was available.

"Chuck Elliott's here," the barrel man told him. "Shall I put him on?"

"Please!"

The lieutenant was on the line in seconds. "What's up, Ralph?" he asked.

"I need help with the telephone company, urgently."

"I've got a contact. What's the problem?"

Mott told him and supplied the number. Elliott who was never ruffled by anything, promised to call back as quickly as possible. He was fully aware that seconds counted.

While that was taking place, Salerno was hit with an idea and acted on it. He fired up his car and with his partner beside him he headed south and then a few blocks east. He pulled up before a place listed on an intelligence work-sheet as Al's Sav-Mor Rentals. It stated that the owner had done hard time and maintained many criminal contacts. A footnote added that several other car-rental agencies with similar names in the area were reputable businesses.

At task force headquarters Sergeant Berkowitz was keeping very busy. He took a land line call from the female deputy who had gone to the department store. She reported that she had talked with a sales clerk who had checked out the changing booths when the order to evacuate had been given. She could not remember exactly, but she seemed to recall there had been a very attractive dark-haired girl in one of the booths. The customer had left immediately when she had been asked to evacuate. The clerk had no recollection of what she had been wearing.

Directly on top of that call he copied a broadcast on the special task force frequency: an L.A.P.D. patrol unit had found Flavia's car parked a short distance from her old apartment. Two L.A.P.D. detectives were en route to talk to the landlady and, if possible, to gain admission to the apartment. Berkowitz, whose efficiency was legendary, got a patch through to Mott and reported the new information.

Mott, who was pausing for breath, asked that the detectives check for any clothing lying about the apartment, or any evidence of a quick change Flavia might have made.

As soon as Berkowitz was through, Chuck Elliott took over the line. "I've got the location of that telephone number," he said.

Although it wasn't easy for him, Mott kept his cool. "Let's have it."

Elliott gave him the information. "It's a long way," he noted. "I can get a warrant and meet you there if it would help."

"Please," Mott said. "I need all the help I can get. And have the place covered as soon as you can."

"I did that while you were talking to Berkowitz. I'll bring some help in case we need it."

Mott paused and checked the scene once more. Witkowski, cuffed, was lying in the front hallway. Bert Larson was standing over him, just in case. The two plainclothes L.A.P.D. men were keeping the curious away. Sergeant

394

Pinelli stood awaiting further orders, a confident look on her face.

Since Pinelli had the rank, he gave her the job. "You know what to do," he said. "Send this asshole to CJ and have him booked in. Tell them who he is and have him put in high power. It's your bust, but use Bert for support."

"Gladly," Elsie said.

"Then take over the scene here. I think the landlady will cooperate, otherwise get a warrant. Do the premises top to bottom. You've got lots of L.A.P.D. backup."

"Leave it to me," Elsie said.

It took Mott almost an hour of concentrated, intense driving to get to the location in the La Canada area. As he approached the address, he recognized several cars that belonged to L.A.P.D. and the Sheriff's Department. That meant that the scene was well covered, front and back. He pulled up across a driveway and got out to find Elliott waiting for him. "Take it easy," Chuck said. "We've already been inside and the place is empty."

44

Sergeant Elsie Pinelli, who had been with the Department twelve years, had no hesitancy about taking over. When a marked L.A.P.D. unit pulled up outside to see if any additional help was needed, she welcomed the backup. When the two blue-uniformed officers came in, she asked, "Are you driving a cage-back?"

"Yes, ma'm," one of the men told her.

"I need transportation for a high-power direct to CJ," she said. "Our cars are all detective units."

"Glad to oblige. What've you got?"

"One of the coat-hanger killers." She didn't worry about the niceties of calling him a suspect.

"Outstanding!"

Bert Larson, his ID now clipped to his lumberjack shirt, came over. "The lieutenant asked me to help take him in," he said. "Any objections?"

"None at all," the L.A.P.D. man answered. "We like company."

"Then let's go."

As though it were a routine arrest, Witkowski was taken outside and put in the back of the patrol car equipped for carrying prisoners. From the rear seat there was no way of getting out: the windows did not open; the door handles worked only from the outside. Between the front and rear seats there was a strong steel grill with a fine mesh. Each time, before the car was taken out or after a prisoner was delivered, the rear cage section was searched for anything hidden or discarded by a previous occupant. Despite the street pat-downs that were restricted by law, many weapons had been recovered that way, and a steady flow of narcotics.

Larson got into the cage with the prisoner. Normally Witkowski would have been taken to the nearest station and booked, but this was a special case with sheriff's deputies involved. The officer who was driving started up, then radioed in that he was en route to Central Jail with a high-power prisoner. That would ensure a special reception, one that experience had shown to be essential.

Witkowski would not be mixed at any time with the general jail population. At the huge facility, particularly dangerous prisoners, or those accused of extreme offenses, were always kept in a special unit that was literally a very secure jail within a jail. Access to high power was tightly controlled, even for sworn officers.

Elsie turned toward the landlady. "Are you the owner here?" she asked.

"No, I'm the manager. How can I help you?"

Those were the words Elsie was glad to hear; if the woman had been antagonistic, things would have been much more difficult.

"I'd like your permission to search Witkowski's room," she said. "And any other parts of the house where he had access. We won't disturb your other tenants or go into their rooms."

"That's all right," the manager said. "Do I need to sign a paper or anything?"

"That won't be necessary. Thanks for your cooperation." The landlady wasn't quite through. "I'm so glad they left a woman in charge."

"That's because I'm a sergeant," Elsie said and then went back to business. The two L.A.P.D. detectives who had been first on the scene started working in Witkowski's room. Elsie called Berkowitz to bring him up to date, then with the landlady she toured the rest of the building.

Witkowski's room yielded up little of interest; he had been very careful. His considerable pile of skin magazines was gone through with professional thoroughness. "Here's a new one on me," one of the searchers said, and held up an issue called *Teen Ass*.

"There's a lot of rear-end books going around," his partner commented. "Any rough stuff yet?"

"Nothing that would stand up in court."

For more than an hour the calm, careful search went on. Some of the residents hung around hoping for something sensational, but nothing at all was taken from Witkowski's room.

The search then moved to the common areas where Witkowski had had access. It even included a dark, dusty attic where none of the residents were likely to go. It contained a profusion of junk, stacks of old magazines, and some broken furniture that might be taken down and fixed if the need became desperate.

One of the searchers gave his attention to an ancient wooden bed frame that stood in a far corner on four short legs. The pattern of dust on it appeared to have been slightly disturbed. He went over it with meticulous care, then he unscrewed the legs and checked the cavities where they fitted.

Inside one of them he found an enlarged hole just big

enough to hold a cassette tape. He removed the cassette very carefully so as not to destroy any prints on its surface and put it in an evidence bag. He had sweated through his shirt and the dust made him sneeze, but none of that mattered, because he was almost sure of what he had found.

The very fat man behind the counter of Al's Sav-Mor Rentals glanced at Salerno and Carrillo and made them for cops before they could say a word. "You need some help?" he asked.

Salerno nodded. "This one is heavy," he said.

"I thought they all were." The fat man saw Carrillo slip out the door, but he had expected that. He had been visited before and knew the routine.

Salerno went through the proper motions, expecting nothing. Later, if he had to testify in court, he would be able to state that he had followed the book to the letter. He produced a picture of Frank and passed it over. "Do you know this man?" he asked.

The moment he saw the photo the fat man knew it meant trouble. He rented his cars with "protection," but if he lied after he had been warned this was a heavy case it could be his own ass, and he had no intention of risking that.

"I'm not sure," he said.

Salerno knew that meant "yes," but he stuck to the official line. "Can you tell me if he rented a car here recently?" he asked.

The fat man moved his bulk with an effort, his huge belly an inert mass. He opened a box of dog-eared filing cards and pretended to look through. "What's his name?" he asked.

"Hellman. Frank Hellman." Salerno looked through the grimy window and saw his partner using his hand radio to run the license plates on some of the cars.

The fat man took his time, scrutinizing each card in pretended cooperation. Salerno didn't buy it, but despite

399

the mounting excitement he felt in the back of his neck, he didn't interfere: Gil Carrillo needed the time to check the cars.

The fat man pulled out a card. "It could be this guy," he said.

Salerno took the card. "Miguel Lopez," he read aloud.

"They don't always use their right names," the fat man said.

"But they have to show you their driver's license."

"Yeah, but they swap them around. None of our heaps are good enough for the pros to go after them."

Carrillo appeared in the doorway. "Bingo!" A white Plymouth with the wrong plates on it; they come back to a gray seventy-nine Buick."

Salerno reached for his cuffs.

"You'd better give me the rest of it," he said. "The charge is murder; you don't want to be an accessory to that."

"If I do, I'm in the clear."

"I'll report that you cooperated."

The fat man knew it was the best deal he could get. He had already guessed who Hellman might be and he wanted no part of it.

"You want a blue Nova," he said. He pulled a card and gave the license number.

Carrillo was on his radio in seconds.

From the Sheriff's Communication Center, a highly restricted facility atop a hill off Eastern Avenue in East Los Angeles, the word went out to all the law enforcement agencies in the Lost Angeles basin: begin at once and maintain an intensive search for a blue Nova—license given, but not verified. Even the FBI got the word; the priority code made it clear that all possible help was urgently requested. All available personnel, on duty or not, rolled from the L.A.P.D. and Sheriff's Stations, the California Highway Patrol, and all surrounding jurisdictions.

The task force put out a special broadcast advising of a

400

possible hostage situation involving a female in a long white dress. The request was to stop and check all blue Novas. A description of Hellman followed with the added notation "believed to be armed and extremely dangerous."

Thirteen seconds later the first blue Nova was stopped, on Ventura Boulevard in the San Fernando Valley. Officer Russ Long of the L.A.P.D. checked it out. The driver and only occupant was a sixty-six-year-old man who was clearly under the influence. Long made the bust and took him in.

Although she could not rightly blame herself, Flavia was outraged at having allowed Hellman to drive her halfway across the city without doing anything to prevent it. She had managed to stall a little with the meal device, but it had taken less than five minutes for the order he had given to be filled; the unopened bag was still on the rear seat.

Then she forced herself to accept the fact that there was nothing she could have done. The teenager in the drive-in might have helped, but there had been no way at all to alert her. A scream would not have helped: Hellman would simply have driven right out and silenced her quickly; she had no doubt he could do that very expertly. No, her best and only chance was to stick with her game plan and look for any kind of a break. But she could not help being desperately frightened.

Hellman turned into the circular driveway before an impressive mansion. "This is the place," he said. "Our little home away from home. All kinds of room to play around in and nobody coming for another two days."

He drove past the front entrance and then took the concrete driveway that led to the multicar garage in back. "Got to hide the car," he said. "It isn't mine, but I never take any chances—never! I learned that in prison too."

Flavia sensed that he was systematically trying to terrify her even more. That bit of knowledge helped her; his bravura was intended to cover up a weakness he had. He was not completely sure of himself.

"We'll go in the back," he told her. "Less chance of being seen. And don't worry about any servants; they only come in by day and they're gone too."

He stopped the car close to the back door where it was well out of sight of the street. Then he walked around to Flavia's side and opened the door. Pulling a flat tool from under the seat, he slid it into the lock of her seat belt and caught a wire he had fastened there. As soon as he pulled it back, the lock opened easily.

"Don't get out," he warned. "Try it and you're dead."

He turned to the house door, inserted a key, and opened it wide. He punched a code into a burglar alarm box and then gestured. "Come on in," he said. "This is our private love nest."

Flavia got out of the car and paused for a moment to toss her hair, hoping that someone might see her. But the whole area was surrounded by a high concrete-block wall that was shielded by a close row of tall plantings. She walked inside, swinging her hips a very little as she did so. She had fully accepted the fact that she would have to submit to Hellman's sexual demands, and do whatever she had to until Ralph came to find her. She did not doubt for a moment that he would; her objective now was to be alive and well when he did.

Hellman came in close behind her. He led the way into the kitchen, a large room that had both a walk-in refrigerator and a freezer. There was a large, metal-topped table for preparing food and a good-sized alcove that had been made into a breakfast area. He pointed. "Sit down there," he directed, "while I bring in our lunch. And don't move, unless you want to be put in the freezer."

"You're making a fool of yourself," Flavia said. It was a little risky, but it would build the image she was shaping for him and shake his confidence a little more at the same time.

He didn't answer her as he went out to get the bag from the drive-in. When he came back seconds later, she appeared to be waiting for him.

He put the bag on the table and sat down opposite her. He dug out two large burgers, two shakes, and a large order of fries. He pushed a burger and a shake toward her and set the fries between them. "Go ahead and eat," he said.

That was a totally unnecessary remark, further evidence that his self-confidence was not as great as he pretended it to be.

He took a large bite from his own burger; when his mouth was again empty he began to talk, obviously to build his image in her eyes. "This girl friend of mine who lives here, she can't get enough of it. A real nympho. Most of all she likes to be admired. Upstairs in the master bedroom where we're going, she loves to take all her clothes off and then parade around for me. She'll do it as long as I'll let her. She gets a big kick out of it. She told me once she wished there were fifty men there instead of just one."

"She can make that dream come true easily enough," Flavia said.

Hellman took another bite of his hamburger. "Do you remember Clara Bow?" he asked.

"I don't remember her; I've heard of her."

"Mary Ellen told me that once she was supposed to have taken on the whole USC football team."

Flavia shook her head. "It would hardly be fun to be number eighty-seven in that lineup," she said, and knew immediately that she had made a bad mistake.

Hellman picked it up instantly. "Of course not," he agreed. "It's going to be much more fun, just between you and me. Finish your lunch."

Not trusting herself to speak another word, Flavia ate silently, taking as much time as she dared. She had no idea how Ralph would find her, but the police authorities were enormously resourceful and they had the manpower. By

403

now the whole task force would be looking for her and probably every patrol unit in the Los Angeles basin.

Then, bitterly, she realized that she was rationalizing. There was no clue at all to tell them where she had gone; Hellman had told her that he wasn't driving his own car, and the one he had used was hidden where prowling units couldn't see it.

"You've had a tough day so far," Hellman said. "It's time for you to lie down on the bed upstairs and get some rest."

It was the moment of truth: she had to face up to the decision she had made, odious as it was. She thought again of the body in Big Tujunga Canyon and that dreadful memory helped her to find the strength she needed.

She raised her head proudly, as though she were facing the Inquisition in her own country. "I hope not alone," she said, hoping that those words would save her life.

Hellman sat very still and looked at her. "Are you trying to con me?" he asked.

"I told you I'd been raped," Flavia said. "When I was sixteen. He was my father's good friend and I didn't dare to tell what he had done to me. He was a revolting old man with rotten teeth and awful breath."

She paused in her invention, imagining what it might have been like if it had actually happened that way. "His penis was a horrible thing, and when he pushed it into my mouth . . ." She stopped and gave a convincing shudder.

"So he turned you off sex, right?"

That was the response she had hoped for, giving her the lead-in she needed.

"I had more sense than that," she said. "But I swore to myself that I would never have sex again with anyone that I didn't choose myself, no matter what the cost."

Hellman gave her a hard, distrustful look. "Do you expect me to believe you would have come here willingly?" he asked. His words were iced with hostility.

Flavia played her ace. "Why do you think I wore that

sexy outfit?" she asked. Then she added, truthfully, "It was for your benefit."

"Your cop friend isn't enough?"

"He's older. And he spends too much of his time with dead bodies."

She was almost afraid to breathe until she saw in his face that he had bought it. Suspicious as he was, she had presented him with a piece of hard evidence he couldn't deny.

"Let's go upstairs," he said. "I can phone my partner later on."

45

To Flavia it seemed as if an irresistible force was crashing down upon her: an immense, merciless mass that would bury her, body and soul, in a timeless pit. She knew what awaited her if she were to take the first step toward the staircase, but the time had come and the reality of her decision would have to be played out.

She focused her mind on the story of Scheherezade, the innocent young woman who had been seized for the sultan's pleasure. Like so many other virgins of her time, it had been her prescribed fate to be raped by him and then to await the headsman's ax in the morning. She had not been able to avoid the rape, but for a thousand and one nights she had forestalled her execution by her captivating storytelling, and at last had won her freedom.

To give in to what Hellman expected and would demand

of her would rob her of the last shred of her dignity. If she had to endure that in order to survive, she would. She remembered once again the image of the butchered girl in Big Tujuna Canyon. That reminded her with fresh intensity what Hellman was: a monster who delighted in torturing and killing his victims.

"Let's go," he said.

He was testing her then, forcing her to pretend that she wanted him to violate her. But if she could make him believe that she *did* desire him, that she reveled in his sexual skills, then he might spare her so that he could enjoy her again and again. But there could be no holding back; everything depended on how convincing a performance she could give.

As she walked from the kitchen Flavia forced a single idea to dominate her mind: she was an actress playing a role. She was about to create a character just as though she were doing it on the stage or for the benefit of a bank of cameras. She was no longer herself, she was a different person: a free-swinging, sexually liberated woman who would take all she could get wherever she could find it. And here was a handsome man anxious to demonstrate his prowess to her.

The mansion had an impressive staircase to the upper floor, one clearly designed to allow the residents to make a grand entrance coming down, whatever the occasion.

At a steady, moderate pace she climbed step by step, letting her hips swing a little from side to side as she did so. She was acutely aware of Hellman just behind her. He had studied the outlines of her body with relentless diligence in class; now unless she could find some means of escape she would be compelled to let him triumph and view every intimate part of her and discover that the reality was superior to his imagining. Alert for any move she could make, she reached the top, stopped, and looked over her shoulders—waiting for him to show her the way.

She had forced the terror out of her mind by concentrating totally on the performance she was giving. He had told her how good the girl who lived here was; she knew she would have to prove to him that she was far better. One strong asset was in her favor: she knew she had the equipment and the skill to pull it off.

The master bedroom was huge and lavish. The bed itself stood on a platform eight or ten inches above the floor, for no apparent reason other than display. The lighting was cunningly controlled to create an atmosphere of rest, almost of an exotic other world.

A deeply upholstered lounger stood out from one corner of the room. Hellman seated himself like a monarch about to preside over his court. "My little girl friend likes me to sit here while she strips for me. But I'm getting tired of her. Let's see what you can do."

Those shattering words, *"I'm getting tired of her,"* seized Flavia and stark terror came surging back. For a few seconds she was frozen, unable to bring her mind back to where it had been. Then, beside the bed, she saw a telephone and fresh hope leaped in her like a burst of flame. She would not be able to dial a number, he would never allow her to do that. Even if she could, she didn't know where she was, but she didn't have to.

911.

All she had to do was lift the phone and punch those three digits. That would light up a screen in the nearest police facility, one that would almost instantly display the number from which the call was coming, *and the address.*

If she got a chance to say anything at all, just the word "Help!" would be enough. Even if she didn't speak, the call would probably bring a response. She would have to wait for her opportunity, but the knowledge that she had that added chance lifted her spirits tremendously. Everything now depended on finding a way to make that quick, one-word call.

The birth of fresh hope thrust her back into her role. She walked over to a large, mirror-doored closet and looked inside.

"What're you after?" Hellman demanded.

"A robe of some kind."

"What do you want if for?"

She turned and faced him. "I like to look my best," she said. "The two ugliest things on earth are brassieres and garter belts."

He waved a dismissive hand. "Do it your way," he said. "Just do it."

She didn't reply to that. She opened one side of the closet, then the other in search of a robe. There were several, but none of them pleased her.

"Don't take too long," Hellman warned. "I don't have much patience."

She walked across the room into a sybaritic bathroom. It was principally black marble and mirrors with a Japanese *ofuro* bath and rich white carpeting to establish a contrast. She was about to take a huge bath towel off a rack when Hellman appeared in the doorway.

"Never mind all this shit," he said. "You can strip out of what you've got on. Mary Ellen does."

Flavia gave him an even look from under lowered lids. "Any way you'd like it," she said. "Then you'll know who's good."

"You want some music? The whole place is wired."

"I don't need any help."

"Then on with the show." He went back and plopped into the lounger, a sultan waiting for his slave to perform.

Flavia paused to take a tight grip on herself. Then projecting herself totally into her role, she stepped back into the room with an almost regal air. She paused and looked around, as if to reassure herself that the room was worthy of her. Then she crossed from one side to the other with consummate dignity, her chin high and proud. There she paused and slid open the zipper on the long white store dress she was still wearing.

She turned, faced her captor, and slipped the dress over her head with a smooth, easy motion that was charged with elegance.

The effect was exactly what she had desired. "You got her beat right now, sweetheart," Hellman said.

Her heart leaped at the words, because she knew she was succeeding. He had trapped her. Now, perhaps, she could trap him.

With a look of rich disdain, she walked once more across the room in her bra and panty hose, her poise immaculate. She could have been the highest-priced model in Paris parading in ermine, and Hellman knew it. His complexion was flushed and his body tense with eagerness.

When she had crossed the room to the opposite side she paused, faced him, and pivoted her body back and forth on her heels, a few degrees each way. Then she paused and stood perfectly still.

"You are goddamned sensational," he said. "You ever do this for your cop friend?"

"No," she answered coolly. "I didn't choose to."

Then at once his voice became harsh and demanding. "Get on with it."

She understood that perfectly: he was trying to maintain control and assert his authority. That told her that she was playing him the right way, convincing him that taking her by force would be the worst mistake he could possibly make.

She gave him a look of calm disdain: a risk, but an essential part of the role she was committed to playing. Once more she walked across the room until she stood before the mirrored closet door. Then, calmly and with no visible emotion, her back to him, she took off her brassiere.

She kept him waiting a few measured seconds before she

swung her body around and allowed him for the first time to see her breasts. Then slowly, and with the barest hint of a shoulder-swinging motion, she came toward him, letting him look his fill. All his longing for months was now being gratified, and he was savoring every bit of his triumph.

No one had had to tell her that she had an exceptional body. Her breasts were somewhat larger than the norm, but they stood straight out, her nipples tipping them perfectly. There was no hint of overweight or sagging: they were erect, poised, and perfectly formed. Her skin was flawless.

When she was six feet in front of him she stopped, giving him a full opportunity to appreciate her.

"My partner isn't going to believe this," he said. "I told him you were good, but I didn't know how goddamned good."

"When is he coming?" she asked.

"When I call him. But I'm not going to right away."

The landlady at Flavia's apartment did not appreciate another call from the police; she showed her scorn by telling them to go and get a warrant. She began to slam the door, but a foot blocked it as the detective in the doorway extracted a crisp legal document from his breast pocket and thrust it into her hands.

Less than three minutes later he radioed in that he and his partner had recovered Flavia's rose outfit from a shopping bag in her apartment. That supported the story that she was wearing a white dress. From the Com Center the fresh information was put out priority one to all units in the field.

The search for the blue Nova was kept up to the exclusion of almost everything else. Only the most urgent calls were put out; complaints about loud music and various other minor 415 offenses were ignored.

*   *   *

When she knew the time was just right, Flavia turned away from Hellman and walked with studied casualness to the furthest corner away from him. Half concealed by the bed, she kept her left side toward him as she rolled down her panty hose.

"Keep your shoes on," he called to her. "I like it better that way."

She glanced at a clock on the headboard: they had been in the house for almost an hour. Because they had to be searching for her, that extra hour might just be enough to buy her her life. She thought desperately hard, but could not find any way to escape the final indignity of allowing her captor to have sex with her. And his idea of sex would be almost sure to include more than the simple act of coupling.

That was the great barrier before her now, and it would take all the strength of character she possessed to overcome it. If she could tease him enough to force premature ejaculation, that could help a great deal.

Completely naked now, having ignored his request for shoes, she stretched her arms above her head and spread her fingers. She remembered how he had watched her hands in class; it was possible that he had a fetish about them. Then, with her hands casually at her sides she walked slowly toward him, watching his eyes. They were fixed on her vagina, drinking in the soft richness of her pubic hair.

"How do you like it?" she asked.

He did not answer, but continued to stare at her: at her pubis, at her breasts, and then with a curt motion he signaled her to turn around. Head high and proud she complied, remembering the Spanish painter who had seen her in a French-fold bathing suit and had told her that she had the most perfectly formed buttocks he had ever seen.

She had taken good care of her body because she knew it deserved it.

"I've seen a lot of naked women in my life," Hellman said. "It's a kind of hobby of mine. But nothing like what you've got."

It was all Flavia could do to control her breath and maintain the illusion she was enjoying the humiliation she was undergoing. His scrutiny of her body repelled her, but she could not afford to let it show. She had to maintain the attitude of a tempting package—one much too fine to be harmed in any way. If she failed, then everything was lost and she would have done this whole wretched thing in vain. Meanwhile every moment that passed gave her added hope that rescue was somehow, somewhere, coming nearer.

Hellman feasted his ego by keeping her standing there while he studied every minute detail of her wonderfully appealing body. It was all his now, to look at and savor as much as he liked. He knew, of course, that she was not doing it to please him; she would have fled on the instant if she had been able. She was doing it because he had captured her, broken down her arrogant pride, and taken command of her spirit. She was terrified of him, he knew that. Perhaps she knew about the others, more likely not, but it didn't matter.

He wished there was some way he could keep her, but the moment she was free she would talk—and she lived with a cop. If she thought she could con him into believing she was willing to become his girl friend, she was out of her mind. He was far too experienced to fall for that.

He smiled to himself, inwardly, as he remembered the frightened little twit who had tried to tempt him and Stan with her pitiful strip act. All she had had to show was a tiny pair of underdeveloped tits with barely formed nipples, a little swatch of thin pubic hair, and a skinny ass that wasn't worth a second look. When he had fucked her she had wept huge tears and had begged him never to tell

413

anyone, especially her mother. Because she was so thin and light he had taken her on his lap to do it. When he had penetrated her for the first time he had gotten a huge high out of watching her face as he had gone in deeper and deeper. Her blood had flowed liberally; he remembered how he had dipped his finger in it and had tasted it just to jolt her even more.

Later, when Stan was doing her, she had just lain there and let him go at it. The life had been all but out of her then; killing her had been an anticlimax. She had screamed all right, it was all on the tape, but the big kick he had expected hadn't come that time.

But it sure as hell would with this one. Because he had never had anything as rich and ripe as this in his life. And she was going to be for him alone: Stan hadn't done anything to get her, and she was too good for him anyway.

"Sweetheart," he said in his most appealing voice, "you're it. The greatest thing any man could ask for. So now we're going to have ourselves some sex. And as we do, I'll know whether you want to make it a regular thing between us."

"You should know that by now," Flavia said.

Hellman gave her a thin-lipped smile. "It's been great up to now, I'll give you that. And you sure know how to show your ass. But the payoff comes in bed. Give me the fuck I've been waiting too long to get from you and it'll be roses all the way. You can have your cop, just as long as I keep getting my share too."

"That's no problem," she said.

Hellman jumped to his feet. He took her by the arm, led her to the bed, and half tossed her onto the thick spread. Sitting on the edge he took off his own clothes and laid them on the floor. Before stretching out he took one more look around, just to be sure everything was as he wanted it to be. He checked every part of the room and didn't stop until he saw the telephone almost within his reach.

With a harsh little laugh he pulled out the module connector and tossed it under the bed. "Can't have you getting any ideas," he said. "That would spoil all the fun."

A violent reaction against her undeserved fate almost caused Flavia to lose control. Her frustration mounted to the breaking point, but she did not dare to let it show. This was her moment of truth; the matador was ready with the sword hidden under his cape, about to make a display of death to entertain the patrons.

She gathered every shred of courage she could command and said, "Let's see how good you are."

He took her savagely, penetrating her with heavy thrusts, grinning gleefully as he reveled in his conquest of her. Then very quickly he felt his climax coming, much too soon for his full enjoyment. But it was too late to stop. He had a sudden spurt of incalculable rapture and then it was over.

He lay back, sweating profusely. He had not realized he had been that close to the edge. In a way he had been cheated, but in a little while he would take her again and this time he would drag it out to the limit—just as soon as he recovered from the sudden exhaustion his orgasm had created.

He reached out an arm and gathered her to him. For the pure animal joy of it he rolled on top of her, then over, and on top of her again until they both fell off the edge of the bed onto the thickly carpeted floor.

He stayed on top of her, feeling her body pressed against his and breathing in her intense femininity. He shut his eyes for a moment, then opened them again to reassure himself that it was really Flavia. She smiled at him so bewitchingly for an instant he believed that he had been all wrong, that she *did* desire him and that he *could* have her whenever he liked, time and time again. He reached down to kiss her as the fingers of her right hand probed through his discarded clothing.

415

She raised her head a little to accept his kiss, her mouth partially open as if to invite him. As he raised himself to crush his lips against hers, with all her strength she drove his knife up to the hilt into the side of his abdomen.

46

Deputy Craig Myers had another two months to go riding with his training officer before he would be cut loose on his own. He had done creditably in the academy and had put in his time in Custody, now he was anxious for the day when he would be off probation and would be assigned his own car by the patrol sergeant. Meanwhile he was sensible enough to know that he was still learning a great deal about being a police officer.

When the emergency call for a maximum patrol effort had come in to the station, the sergeant had immediately rounded up every available man. There had been a few reserve patrol units on the lot, cars that were not scheduled to go out until the next shift. The sergeant assigned them out quickly, giving preference to his more experienced officers. The last car available went to Myers.

He listened intently to the short briefing. A blue Nova,

license number given, was urgently wanted. The driver had kidnapped a young woman who might or might not still be with him. He was reported to be armed and very dangerous. All blue Novas were to be stopped and the drivers IDed in case the plates had been changed or the information given was faulty. "In the event you spot the wanted vehicle, report in at once," the sergeant instructed. "Don't attempt a one-man felony stop. Follow the car and wait for backup." He then gave Hellman's name and description.

Within a few seconds he laid out the areas the added units were to cover. Myers, who was last on the list, was given part of the high-rent district. As he hurried out of the station toward his unit, Myers knew that for his first solo patrol he had drawn a hot one. His chances of finding the wanted blue Nova were minimal, he knew, but he was determined to put out his best possible effort.

He had a further incentive: it was his twenty-third birthday and he was about to ask the right girl the most important question of his life.

As soon as he reached his assigned area he began his patrol at a moderate pace, maintaining the right image of the Department, but not dawdling. There was very little traffic on the exclusive street, but that did not deter him in the least.

He had been driving for only a short while when he noticed that clipped to the material on the overhead sunshade there was a three-by-five card with the address of a house that would be vacant for a few days. In that robbery-prone neighborhood the patrol deputies had been asked to keep an eye out to be sure that it was undisturbed. Deputy Myers read the note and realized that the house was only a short distance ahead on the same street. He immediately decided to check it out as he went past.

Nothing at all happened until he reached the address; the four parked cars he had passed were all expensive makes and there had been no traffic whatever. The house in question had a circular driveway in front; Myers drove in and around to check the premises. When he discovered a continuing driveway that led to the rear he turned down it, enjoying the fact that he could go where others could not. If the neighbors saw the patrol unit on the property, so much the better.

There was a four-car garage in back, a generous parking area, and close to the house itself, a blue Nova. With a sudden sharp tingling in his spine he checked the number. Then, quickly, he grabbed for his microphone.

"Twenty-four Adam." In his excitement he forgot to add the station designator.

"Twenty-four Adam, go."

"I have the blue Nova." He had trouble keeping his excitement out of his voice as he read off the license number. He had hardly been out of the station fifteen minutes, but by incredible luck he had found the car that every patrol unit in the basin was urgently seeking.

There was mounting intensity in the dispatcher's voice. "Twenty-three Adam, give your exact ten twenty."

Deputy Myers read the address off the card and added, "I'm in back, near the garage. The Nova is here also."

"Twenty-three Adam, probable ten twenty-nine Frank David. Full support and backup coming. Good work!"

Craig Myers had already been told that the suspect was considered armed and very dangerous, also that he had taken a female hostage.

He knew that he should probably stay where he was until his backup arrived, but when he looked at the huge house and thought of what might be happening to the female hostage inside, he felt he had to take action. He got out of his unit, tried the back door, and found it unlocked.

There were only three possible ways he could legally go in: by invitation, with a warrant, or in exigent circumstances.

He sure as hell had exigent circumstances. He drew his weapon, pushed the door open, and entered in the proper manner, his gun held in front of him. The kitchen was empty.

"Sheriff's Department!" he called out, and in case anyone didn't understand that, he added, "Police officer!"

There was no answer.

He went through a short hallway into the main part of the house. Despite its many rooms, it seemed quiet and still. A quick look around convinced him that the main floor was empty. Still holding his gun ready for immediate use, he began to climb the stairs.

Halfway up he heard a noise.

He quickened his pace until he reached the top, then he paused and listened. He thought he heard someone, but he wasn't sure. Step by step he approached the source of the noise until he was looking into the master bedroom.

The sight he saw there froze him in his tracks. A naked female was lying motionless on the floor. Close to her there was a nude male half folded in fetal position, his hands clasped against his side. Blood was visible between his fingers.

Deputy Myers advanced into the room far enough to see that the male was apparently inert; the female was shaking with silent, possibly hysterical sobs. He immediately raised his radio and reported in.

"Twenty-three Adam, I am code nine on the second floor of my location. I have an adult male and a female, both nude. The male is bleeding from his side. Condition of the female not yet known. Request paramedics, female officer if available."

His last words were punctuated by oncoming flashing lights reflecting through the windows. He heard at least two cars burning rubber as they pulled up, others appeared to be coming from the opposite direction.

"Adam twenty-three, paramedics rolling. Stand by."

He knew what he had to do then: contain the scene. That had been pounded into him at the academy: maintain the status quo until a supervisor arrived, *unless urgent assistance was needed.*

At that moment the female moved and made an effort to get up. She appeared to be in shock. Myers had joined the Sheriff's Department because he wanted action; he was getting it now. Thrusting his gun into its holster, he helped her to her feet and guided her to where she could sit down. He was looking around for something to cover her with when two more deputies burst into the room, guns drawn.

Within seconds two additional deputies appeared and directly behind then the patrol sergeant.

The arrival of the supervisor took the load off Myers's back, but he still felt a heavy sense of responsibility. He was technically the handling deputy and the report would be his to write.

The sergeant took in the whole scene in one fast glance, then he motioned to the first team of deputies to check on the condition of Hellman. As he did so he stripped the spread off the bed and brought it over to cover Flavia. With Myers's help he tucked it around her, both for modesty and comfort. These essentials attended to, he turned to Myers and asked the perfect policeman's question, "What happened here?"

Myers gave a hurried account as a paramedic team came into the room carrying pieces of equipment. The deputy who had been checking on Hellman looked up. "Take care of the girl," he said. "This one's had it."

As one of the paramedics went to Flavia, his partner checked Hellman's condition. "He's gone," he said.

The sergeant turned to Myers. "Be sure to note the time the deceased was pronounced and by whom."

Myers flushed with sudden guilt. As the handling deputy it was his job to note down every incident. Several had already occurred and he had let them pass, completely forgetting the careful instructions he had received at the academy and in the field.

Stepping aside to give the paramedic with Flavia more

421

room in which to work, he pulled out his virgin notebook and dropped his pen in his haste to redeem himself. It seemed as if every pair of eyes in the room was on him as he briefly searched for it and then picked it up. It did not occur to him that he had had no opportunity to make notes until that moment.

Heading up the first page with the date, time, and weather conditions, he carefully printed in block letters his discovery of the Nova, and his report to the station. Remembering now what his training officer had so frequently stressed, he carefully put down his reason for entering the house, the fear that the female hostage might be in urgent need of help. That would prevent any defense attorney from claiming that he had had no legal right to come in.

Next he went to the first pair of backup deputies who had arrived and got their names. To that he added their time of arrival as closely as he could estimate it. He did the same for the second pair. The sergeant's name he already knew; he showed him arriving one minute after the first team had appeared. Then he got the paramedics' names and noted down which one had pronounced, and when. That brought him up to date.

He returned to where both paramedics were now looking after Flavia. "How is she?" he asked.

One of them answered him without stopping his work. "She may have been raped; that will have to be checked. Otherwise no visible physical harm so far. She's in mild shock; we're treating her for that."

Three more men in business suits came in. Myers went to them, notebook in hand. "Lieutenant Darrell Gordon, Homicide," one of them said. "What have we got?"

Once again in possession of himself, and carefully referring to his notebook, Myers gave him a concise and accurate rundown. Then he asked the other two deputies their names. He carefully checked the spellings as he printed out Sergeant John Laurie and Deputy Jack Fueglein, both from Homicide. That done he felt a little better. The pace in the room had definitely settled down. Hellman still lay where he had been found; his body had not been touched, pending the arrival of the coroner. Since he was out of public view, there was no need to cover him.

Lieutenant Gordon sent a deputy to stand by the Nova and see that no one touched it. Lengths of the familiar yellow tape had been stretched across the driveway entrances. A media truck had already appeared outside, bright lights shining on the front of the house. The uniformed deputies had left the room, only the paramedics and the homicide team remained. In that much more relaxed atmosphere Gordon knelt down beside the chair where Flavia was sitting, huddled in the bedspread the sergeant had provided. "Are you able to talk to me now?" he asked.

"Yes," Flavia answered. "Where's Ralph?"

"He'll be here shortly if he doesn't break his neck on the way. He's been driving a patrol unit, searching for you in the mountains. Now just tell me what happened."

Relief surged through Flavia, because she was back in the land of rational thought and action. She was thinking, trying to shape the words she would have to use, when Gordon came to her rescue.

"We know how you were kidnapped from your apartment; we found a witness. We got a make on the blue Nova a while ago. How did Hellman manage to keep you in the car while he drove here?"

Despite what she had been through and the way she knew she must look, Flavia kept as much composure as she could muster. "He had fixed the seat belt so I couldn't get out."

"I'm sorry, Flavia, I have to ask. Did he rape you?"

At that moment Ralph Mott burst into the room. That was all she needed and the last of her terror dropped away. He came to where she was with a warming smile on his face. She knew nothing about the mad driving he had done to reach her, about the way he had rushed the traffic lights and kept his radio open for every bit of fresh information he could get.

Instinctively he understood she didn't want him to make a spectacle of himself. She smiled at him and said, "I'm glad you're here."

He didn't need to tell her the enormous relief that had flooded through him when he had received the flash that she had been found, alive and apparently well. That communication passed between them without the need for words.

"There's one of those multijet showers in the bathroom," she said. "If you don't mind, I'd like to use it." She looked at Gordon. "Yes, I was raped. If you need medical evidence . . ."

Gordon shook his head. "Not in this case. But I'd recommend that you be looked at anyway. He could have infected you. I'd do that as soon as possible."

"I'll take care of it," Mott said.

Flavia, with Gordon's help, got to her feet; as she did so he wrapped the bedspread carefully around her body. "And could I have my clothes?" she asked.

Mott gathered them up and handed them to her as she entered the bathroom. As soon as the door was closed behind her, Gordon turned to Mott. "She a damn gutsy girl," he said.

"How did she manage it?"

"We haven't taken a statement from her yet; she really wasn't able to give one before you got here." That could be understood two ways and Gordon knew it. He had done it intentionally.

"Somehow," Gordon added, "she got hold of his knife and was able to . . ." He left it at that. "Gutsy girl," he repeated.

"She knew who he was," Mott supplied.

"Yes, I know. She must have been half out of her mind, but she made him pay."

"Thank God for that."

The deputy coroner came into the room. She was an attractive young woman who was probably not yet thirty, but she knew her job. She knelt beside the body and, as routine required, did a gun-shot-residue test on both of Hellman's hands.

The sound of a shower running came through the bathroom door. Gordon walked over and looked down once more at Hellman's nude body. "If he wasn't already dead, I think I'd have killed him myself," he said.

Mott knew that Gordon was too good a cop ever to do such a thing, but he wouldn't have blamed him if he had. "We were working on his partner," he said. "He wants a lawyer so we had to stop questioning him, but he's scared shitless."

"He's got reason to be."

"He'll cop, that we know. Especially now that Hellman's dead."

The paramedics had packed up and left. The homicide team was still gathering evidence. A photographer was busy recording everything. If he had been less than a lieutenant, Mott probably would not have been allowed to gather up Flavia's clothes for her. Crime scenes decayed rapidly, so everything possible had to be gotten the first time around.

Mott sat down, partly for comfort and partly to keep from letting his intense emotions show. From the first moment that he knew Flavia had been taken he had made a massive effort to keep himself under control. The fact that another young woman had been seized had been enough to outrage him; the added fact that it was Flavia had threatened to drive him over the brink. Gordon understood that perfectly and took care of all the details of scene-handling, which was his job anyway.

As the handling deputy Craig Myers remained on the scene. He had had time enough to remember what he had been taught about that responsibility and to realize that his baptism as a full-fledged field deputy had come sooner than he had expected. At the coroner's request he brought in the gurney and helped to spread out the large sheet of heavy plastic to receive the body. The homicide team lent a hand in wrapping it up and then adding the brown cover that concealed it from view.

What was left of Hellman was strapped on the gurney and wheeled out of the room. Only seconds after that Flavia came out of the bathroom. At that time and place her long white dress was almost incongruous. She had toweled her hair, which had lost much of its shape and form. She wore no make up and her face revealed starkly the ordeal she had been through.

She went to Mott and stood before him, seeming to ask if he would have her back. Without hesitation he took her in his arms and pressed her head against his shoulder.

"Her statement can wait," Gordon said. "I think we've all got the picture. Have her looked at and then take her home."

"I'll do that," Mott said. Then he asked Flavia, "Have you got all your things?"

She nodded her head silently against his shoulder.

He reached in his pocket and pulled out the jade piece with its broken chain. "Put this in your purse," he said. "And keep it there. We may not be all the way out of the woods yet."

47

Stan Witkowski had never been so utterly terrified in his life. He looked around constantly at his cell in high power as his mind searched frantically for any possibility of rescue. The wild joy, the surging orgasms he had experienced whenever he listened to the piercing screams of the girls as he twisted the wires around their necks: the memories of those soaring passions were now like monsters creeping from some unspeakable bog.

When he and Frank had started out they had known how to protect themselves against ever getting caught. They had looked forward to the wildest excitement, to exercising their ultimate power in defiance of the rules of society that they had both so detested. And how they hated the cops, and took revenge on them by giving them hundreds of hours of frustrating, useless work.

He had always held a secret in the back of his mind: if

427

something went terribly wrong, he would cop a plea. He would testify against Frank, blame the entire thing on him and plead that while he had been in prison Frank's perversion had so altered his mind that he had been unable to help himself.

They had had very little to fear in any event. The death penalty had been virtually stopped by the State Supreme Court. The maximum time for murder was something like seven years, but he would never have to do that. By turning state's evidence, he knew he would get off. A good lawyer would take care of everything.

But now, faced with stark reality, a whole series of horrible, suppressed images tortured his brain. For the first time he thought of the possibility that Frank might blame everything on him. It had been his van they had driven and the cops had told him that they had the tape. They couldn't possibly have found it, but how had they known about it? And his voice *was* on the tape.

Oh, God!

He shut his eyes and tried desperately to keep all thoughts and images of the gas chamber out of his mind. But the damning pictures he had once seen of it, and the steel chairs inside, kept coming back again and again until it was too much for him and shamelessly he began to cry.

Ralph Mott unlocked the door of the apartment and stepped aside to let Flavia go inside first. Neither of them spoke as she went directly into the bedroom.

When she reappeared she was wearing a pale yellow blouse and a midnight blue skirt that made a radical change from what she had had on. She had combed her hair and put on a little makeup, all that she actually needed. In appearance she was once again the very appealing girl who had become so much a part of Mott's life.

"I liked that dress very much when I picked it out," she said. "Now I don't think I can ever put it on again."

Mott walked over to her and put his arms around her once more. "I want to take you out for a civilized meal," he said. "I know you may not feel like it right now, but you need it and it will do you good."

"All right," she agreed.

She put on a light beige-colored coat and was ready. A half-hour later she was seated across from him in a pleasant restaurant where a single candle flickered in the middle of the table. "We'll start with a drink," he announced, and signaled to the cocktail waitress.

Before too long she began to feel better. The brief medical examination was over and she had been assured that she would be all right. The nurse had supplied her with a douche that had been as symbolic as it had been practical. Despite the intense terror she had known, it was all behind her now and the relaxing effect of her drink helped it to retreat further back in her mind. By some merciful mental process the awareness that she had recently killed a man did not invade her consciousness at all.

Although she was not especially a sports fan, Mott told her about a promising new infielder the Angels had acquired. Sensitive to her mood he dropped that topic and looked for something else to say until she laid her slender hand on top of his own. "Am I going to be in any trouble?" she asked.

He understood that she knew the answer, but she wanted reassurance. "There's no possibility of that. As far as the Department is concerned, you're a heroine."

"You see," she explained, "from the moment Hellman captured me—I guess that's the word—I stalled for time. I didn't know what you would be doing, but I knew how resourceful the Department is and I was sure that someone would find me. And that young deputy did."

"From what I hear, he handled himself very well," Mott said. "I'm going to write him an 'attaboy' for his file."

An attractive waitress was hovering in the background,

menus in her hand. Mott nodded to her and she came over.

"Good evening," she said. "My name is Ellen and I'll be serving you tonight."

Flavia smiled at her, the first smile she had been able to manage since her ordeal. She chose a Mexican dish that was on the menu; Mott opted for lamb chops.

When the waitress had gone, Flavia took Mott's hand once more. "Because I wanted to take as much time as I could, I exhibited myself to him," she said. "He'd been scrutinizing me so relentlessly, I knew he would fall for it. It was either that or else let him take me bodily much sooner than he did."

She paused and finished the last of her second drink. "I knew what would happen to me if I resisted him, and I knew that he wanted me to. So I played it the only way I could. I pretended that I didn't mind."

"And being a blatant egotist, he thought you really wanted to be intimate with him."

"Yes," she said. "I wanted to survive. The death-before-dishonor bit isn't part of my philosophy. And as far as his seeing my body is concerned, I'm well beyond the traditional taboos. Frankly, I think that some of them are ridiculous."

"Would you go to a nude beach?" Mott asked.

"Yes, if you took me. I'd rather not do it alone."

The waitress reappeared with generous bowls of salad. By mutual unspoken consent the topic was closed. The good food that came was what they both needed, and by the time the meal was over, Flavia was out from under the worst of her trauma.

When they were back in the apartment, Mott offered a suggestion. "If you'd be more comfortable, I'll be glad to sleep on the sofa tonight."

"No," Flavia answered. "One of the reasons I tried so hard to survive was to be able to come back here, just as we were. I'll feel better to have you with me. Only . . ."

"Of course not," Mott interrupted her.

When they were in bed together, he held her very tenderly until she fell asleep. Then, his own mind unable to control its restlessness, he lay next to her, keeping a silent watch, until his beeper went off a little after four in the morning.

When he called in, the barrel man told him that he had been paged by mistake. There was a homicide, but Ken Chausse would handle it. There was a message, however. The captain would like to see him and Flavia in the morning. No time was specified; they could come in whenever they liked.

In the morning Mott got up, shaved, showered, and dressed while Flavia was still asleep. She had been closer to total exhaustion than either of them had realized. He was eating a bowl of raisin bran and scanning the morning headlines when she appeared in an apricot-colored robe and sat down, holding her head in her hands. "Did it all happen?" she asked.

"Yes, but that part's all over now."

"He told me about his partner."

"He's in custody, and he'll never walk the streets again."

"I need some hot coffee."

"It's all made and ready for you." He gestured toward the coffee maker he had bought shortly after she had moved in.

After she sat down with her cup, he told her about their appointment with the captain.

"It won't take me long to get ready," she said. "I should meet with a class this morning, but I think the dean will excuse me."

"If he's read the morning paper he will," Mott told her. "I just wish they hadn't run your picture."

"Why?"

"I'll explain later."

Captain Grimm received them in his office in the quiet manner that was his trademark. His secretary provided coffee without being asked and then closed the door behind her as she left.

"You're quite a famous young lady this morning," the captain began. "Billy Hinkle and his people have been busy covering the bases."

"I don't like to cause trouble," Flavia said. "Also I don't care for notoriety."

"In this business there are times when you can't help it, Flavia."

He paused to take a little of his own coffee. "I asked you to come in because I realize fully what you've been through. I suspect you've had all the homicide scenes you'll want for a while."

He had given her the opening, now he waited for her reaction.

She looked at him very calmly. "If you thought I was that weak-kneed," she said, "why did you take me on in the first place?"

Grimm could have answered her, but he didn't. "How is your book coming along?" he asked instead.

"I was looking for a pivot point," Flavia answered. "Something that would bring the sociological aspects into a clear, sharp focus. I floundered over that a little until I responded to a one eighty-seven out on the desert. The attractive mother of two young sons was raped and beaten to death with a hammer."

She spoke the words dispassionately as if by doing so she could alleviate some of the horror of their meaning.

"There I saw in reality so many different things: racial tension, the effect of savage brutality, the reactions of children, the husband of the victim, the neighbors, the mother of the suspects, the investigators, the legal complications—almost a whole society contained in that one incident. That's a bad word, because for the people involved it was a catastrophe."

The captain considered that for a few moments and drank some more coffee. "Do you want to go on?" he asked.

432

"Yes," she answered.

Grimm changed the subject. "Do you remember the time you spotted a suspect because he committed most of his crimes while it was raining?"

"Very well."

"That solved a homicide for us. So you earned this." He took a small box off his desk and handed it to her. She knew what it contained before she opened it. "Captain, will you put it on for me?" she asked.

"There's a small price for that service."

"I'll pay it, gladly."

Captain Grimm came from behind his desk, took the 187 pin, and fastened it to her blouse. "Welcome to the team," he said.

In exactly the proper manner she kissed him. "I trust that's not beneath your dignity," she said.

"You're welcome to test it out anytime. Now, Flavia, one warning. Whenever we had a big, sensational case, a few egomaniacs try to force their way into the spotlight by copycatting."

"I'm well aware of that, Captain. I teach sociology, you remember, and that's a well-known phenomenon. I'm willing to risk it. About my book: I'm learning more and more each time I go out. Until it's finished, I don't want to stop what I've been doing."

"All right, we'll keep your name up at the barrel and keep calling you."

"Thank you."

When they had left the captain's office, Mott stopped in the hallway. "I've got to go back to work," he said.

"And I've got to see the dean."

"I'll have someone drive you to your car."

"That will help. Can I truly wear this pin?"

"You'd better, at least around here."

The door to the Homicide Bureau opened and one of the detectives on watch came out. "I heard you were here," he said. "We've got one, under a freeway bridge down toward Long Beach. Can you take it?"

"Yes," Mott answered. "I want someone to drive Flavia to her car."

"No, problem."

As he went into the Bureau, through the ancient double doors, Flavia came next to him and plucked at his sleeve. "This one might be interesting," she said. "Are you trying to get rid of me?"

Mott stopped, turned to her, and spoke without realizing what he was saying. His speech came automatically from somewhere deep in his subconsciousness: "No. Not now. Not ever."

Moisture showed in Flavia's eyes. "Do you mean that?" she asked.

Mott knew at that moment that he fervently did.

"Yes," he said simply. "This is a helluva place to say it, but I'm not very good at these things."

"I'm glad for that," she said. "I don't want to go to my car, Ralph. I'll call the dean, then I want to go with you."

He looked at the 187 pin she had so fairly earned.

"Let's go," he said. "I'll take you to some place nice later on and we'll talk some more. About a lot of things."

"I'll be listening to every word," Flavia said.